Gone Too Far

"An intriguing, fast-paced combination of police procedural and thriller."

—*Kirkus Reviews*

"Those who like a lot of family drama in their police procedurals will be satisfied."

—*Publishers Weekly*

Trust No One

"*Trust No One* is Debra Webb at her finest. Political intrigue and dark family secrets will keep readers feverishly turning pages to uncover all the twists in this stunning thriller."

—Melinda Leigh, #1 *Wall Street Journal* bestselling author of *Cross Her Heart*

"A wild, twisting crime thriller filled with secrets, betrayals, and complex characters that will keep you up until you reach the last darkly satisfying page. A five-star beginning to Debra Webb's explosive series!"

—Allison Brennan, *New York Times* bestselling author

"Debra Webb once again delivers with *Trust No One*, a twisty and gritty page-turning procedural with a cast of complex characters and a compelling cop heroine in Detective Kerri Devlin. I look forward to seeing more of Detectives Devlin and Falco."

—Loreth Anne White, *Washington Post* bestselling author of *In the Deep*

"*Trust No One* is a gritty and exciting ride. Webb skillfully weaves together a mystery filled with twists and turns. I was riveted as each layer of the past peeled away, revealing dark secrets. An intriguing cast of complicated characters, led by the compelling Detective Kerri Devlin, had me holding my breath until the last page."

—Brianna Labuskes, *Washington Post* bestselling author of *Girls of Glass*

"Debra Webb's name says it all."

—Karen Rose, *New York Times* bestselling author

ALL
THE
LITTLE
TRUTHS

OTHER TITLES BY DEBRA WEBB

ALL
THE
LITTLE
TRUTHS

DEBRA
WEBB

THOMAS & MERCER

Published by Thomas & Mercer, Seattle

www.apub.com

Amazon, the Amazon logo, and Thomas & Mercer are trademarks of Amazon.com, Inc., or its affiliates.

ISBN-13: 9781662508844 (paperback)
ISBN-13: 9781662508837 (digital)

Cover design by Shasti O'Leary Soudant
Cover images: © Mark Fearon / ArcAngel, © Arletta Cwalina / ArcAngel

Printed in the United States of America

Shout-out to the amazing Maureen Downey, who kindly agreed to lend me her name for use in this novel! This book is dedicated to YOU and all the other readers who have taken this wonderful ride with me. Here's to many, many more stories to keep you up all night!

Three things cannot be long hidden: the sun,
the moon, and the truth.
—Buddha

1

The Murder

Thirteen Years Ago

Friday, October 6

Nashville Zoo at Grassmere
Elysian Fields Road, Nashville, 8:30 p.m.

The zoo was closed.

No one was supposed to be here. Her mother would be furious that she hadn't been honest about her plans. This was her mother's number one rule: always tell the truth. Never lie to her.

But this time the rules could not stop Lucy Cagle. Not for any reason. Her mother wasn't the only one who could uncover the facts in the deepest, darkest places they were buried. She wasn't the only one allowed to ignore the rules when necessary. How many times had she heard her mother say that some things were worth the sacrifice?

Lucy had decided she would use her senior thesis to prove the apple never fell too far from the tree. Like mother, like daughter, and all that.

Her mother wanted Lucy to be a doctor like her father, and he was a great doctor. His work was important, admired . . . noteworthy. But Lucy wasn't interested in a medical career. She wanted to be an investigative reporter, like her famous mother. She wanted to be fearless and groundbreaking.

Tonight was her big chance.

Lucy shivered. It was oddly cool for an evening so early in October. She should have brought a sweater or a sweatshirt to pull over her blouse. She'd worn this low scooped neckline for him. It was impossible not to notice the way he stared at her chest every time they were together. He was like twenty-three; he should have gotten over such adolescent fixations by now. Lucky for her, he hadn't.

Tonight was the night. He had promised to tell her all his secrets. She had led him on with the possibility that she would be his girlfriend. At first, he'd been reluctant. He'd pointed out several times that guys like him didn't get girls like her. And she'd said all the right things. Innocently touched him in all the right places and pretended to be totally obsessed with him. How many times had she heard her mother say getting the job done wasn't always easy or pretty?

If she were honest with herself, she would have to say this had been kind of easy. He was really handsome. Nicer than she had expected, and he made her feel things too.

Lucy rubbed at her arms. She had to stay focused. She had him on the edge now—the point of no return. He wanted her to know him . . . all of him, including the family secrets he feared would put her off. They had spent so much time making out . . . had almost gone too far a couple of times. He couldn't be in the same place with her without going crazy, he insisted. She wasn't exactly unaffected. Which was why she'd had to insist on many of their rendezvous being in public places like that car wash. Even then, it hadn't been easy to ignore those unexpected feelings.

Sacrifice, she repeated silently. *This was worth the sacrifice.*

Lucy glanced around, suddenly angry that he wasn't here already. He had told her he would be behind the giraffe house at eight. For half an hour she had been standing out here in the dark. He never made her wait like this.

She snatched her cell from her shoulder bag and was ready to call him and tell him off when she spotted headlights in the distance. She held her breath and watched as the lights bobbed, turning from Elysian Fields Road onto the narrow street that led into the zoo employee entrance.

Finally.

She shoved her phone back into her bag and stayed in the shadow of the trees, waited for him to park. The firm smack when his car door closed made her jump. No sound or light had warned her when the door opened, so she hadn't noticed that he'd gotten out. Why hadn't she noticed before that his interior light didn't work? Weird. She shook off the creepy sensation.

Lucy took a deep breath and squared her shoulders.

"Are you hiding?" he called out, sounding a little amused and something else . . . anxious, maybe.

Annoyance puckered her brow. Why would he ask such a silly question? Her car was parked not a dozen feet from where he'd parked his own. She rolled her eyes. Maybe he was as nervous as she was. Just because he was older didn't make him immune to uncertainty.

Lucy suddenly wished she was immune. None of this had been as easy as her mother made it look. And, giving him a break, she supposed that spilling the family secrets wasn't exactly a cakewalk either.

Another deep breath. Showtime. Lucy adopted a pout and stepped forward, away from the shadow of the trees. "You're late," she accused with just enough irritation, she hoped, to have him second-guessing himself.

He moved toward her with that sexy swagger of his. As he drew closer, she noted the grin. Despite her best efforts, she smiled, then gave herself a mental kick. This was serious. Not a game. This was bigger than some high school romantic adventure with an older guy. She had to remember that above all else.

"I'm here now," he said, finally stopping so close that she could feel his breath on her face.

Steeling herself against an all-too-human reaction, she challenged, "Are you ready to do what you promised?"

As if to underscore her demand, a cold wind kicked up, sending a fresh wave of shivers along her skin. He had insisted that before they took their relationship any further, he wanted to be totally honest with her. He wanted to tell her all his secrets. She'd already told him all hers, she'd assured him, making him feel guilty for keeping his own. But she hadn't told anything even close to the truth. He had no idea who she really was.

The tiniest flicker of regret flared inside her.

Stop. Remember the bigger picture.

His grin widened, and her heart thumped harder. She really, really hadn't meant to like him so much. He would get into serious trouble for all that he'd told her already.

How did her mother do it?

"Come on. Let's get out of here." He put his arm around her and ushered her toward his car.

They usually met somewhere like this and then went out in his car. She had been too afraid of running into some of her friends and her car being recognized. He could never know that she was the daughter of Louise Scott, the hottest investigative reporter in the Southeast. She glanced up at him, studied his profile in the moonlight as they walked through the darkness. He trusted her.

How would he feel when he learned the truth? The knots in her belly tightened.

He paused at the passenger side door and opened it. Lucy stood in the V made by the open door and waited for him to go around to the driver's side. When he opened his door, she bit her bottom lip, then smiled. He smiled back at her. This was it. Tonight, she would get the whole story on his family. All the secrets that had stayed hidden for decades. Nothing else mattered.

Her mother was going to be stunned. Maybe even speechless.

She settled into the passenger seat and closed the car door. He slid behind the steering wheel and did the same. For one long moment before starting the engine, he simply stared at her. Her skin prickled with anticipation. Or was that fear?

This is it, girl. Stay cool.

Rather than start the engine, he reached toward her. "I'm sorry, Lucy."

Before his murmured words were fully out of his mouth, something closed around her neck . . . tightened until she couldn't scream . . . couldn't breathe.

Heart thundering, she clutched at the thing . . . choking her . . . frantically dug at her skin to get her fingers beneath the thin wire . . .

Help! What should have been a scream was nothing more than a squeak of pathetic sound.

He stared at her . . . his eyes full of something like . . . regret. His mouth was moving with the words he spoke, but she couldn't understand. Her ears were filled with the sound of her blood roaring . . . her heart pounding.

Help! Help! But the words couldn't get free.

His door opened, and he got out.

Help!

She kicked. Twisted her body. Dug her fingers deeper . . . blood oozed between them, down her throat.

Her car door opened . . . hands grabbed at her body, but the noose grew tighter and tighter . . . her legs flailed helplessly, and then her fingers slid away from her throat. The hope that he would rescue her died.

Her vision faded to darkness, and she thought of her mother and her father. How sad they would be. She should have listened to all their warnings.

2

Now

Monday, December 4

The Finnegan Firm
Tenth Avenue, Nashville, 2:30 p.m.

Finley O'Sullivan watched from the corner of her eye as Nita Borelli, the firm's receptionist—office manager and drill sergeant, really—hung a holiday wreath on the open door of Finley's office. The woman had been decorating for Christmas since Thanksgiving.

Finley blinked, refocused on the case report on her laptop screen.

Nita scooted around behind Finley's chair and placed a mini tree with glittering red balls on the credenza.

Ignore.

Finley had no interest in holidays.

She didn't care that others—like Nita—did; she just didn't. Not anymore. For her, holidays no longer carried the luster they once had.

He's been dead for almost eighteen months . . . time to fully immerse back into the land of the living, Finley.

She kicked the voice out of her head. Like moving on was so easy. She loved her work. For that matter, she was back to actually liking her life . . . but not all things could be embraced at once. Not all the little pieces of a shattered existence fell back into place at the same time.

Finley stretched her back, then her neck. She had stopped caring about much after her husband's murder. Her own injuries from that night had taken months to heal. As if that horrifying event hadn't been devastating enough, she'd suffered a very public crash and burn in her position as an assistant district attorney in the Davidson County DA's office. Her downfall had been the most talked-about news around town for days and days. No biggie, right? Particularly since she'd decided ending it all would be the best route to go anyway. Why hang around and deal with all the damage?

Except she hadn't been able to check out without first getting the guys who had killed her husband and ruined her life. The police certainly hadn't managed the feat. Really, who could let something like that go? Definitely not Finley O'Sullivan.

"This looks good here, don't you think?"

Finley shook off the thoughts and stared at the sparkling angel Nita had perched on the table between the two chairs facing Finley's desk.

"Sure." She flashed a fake smile at the lady. "I think that'll do it in here. It's a small office. Don't want to overwhelm clients."

Nita lifted an eyebrow and shot Finley a look that was oddly daring or maybe ferocious. "I have covered for you in various ways and on numerous occasions since Jack brought you on board last January, have I not?"

Wow. That was not the response Finley had anticipated. She forced a more realistic smile and nodded. "You have. Several times."

Who knew the woman would get so bent out of shape over a few decorations?

"Which means you owe me," Nita pointed out.

"I do," Finley confessed, smile fading as she recognized where the older woman was going with this.

"I like Christmas," Nita said. "I like decorating for Christmas. It's important to me. This"—she gestured to the decorations she had added—"is how you repay me. You let me do what I want, okay?"

Finley nodded, deciding this particular holiday was some sort of trigger for Nita. "Absolutely."

"Good." She executed an about-face and exited the office.

Finley stared at the angel. As long as Nita didn't show up at Finley's house with a box of decorations, she could get through the holiday season with whatever the woman opted to do around here.

Maybe it was time to get over her minor aversion to celebrating anyway. Truth was, if there had ever been a time to celebrate, it was now. Seventeen months and a couple of weeks after *that* night, and Finley was okay. Really okay. She'd learned all the little truths about the man she'd married and the reason he'd been murdered. She'd forgiven him—Derrick, the husband she had loved with all her heart—and she'd forgiven herself for her part in what had happened to him—to them both. And, to some degree, she had moved on.

Work was great. Her personal life was getting there. She and her mother, the Judge, were making an effort to have a more normal relationship. She and Matt were a couple now. A smile tugged at her lips. Matthew Quinn had been her best friend since they were little kids. He had seen her through everything, from her rebellion against pink at age ten to surviving the brutal invasion that had taken her husband's life. Matt had been there for her while she struggled to heal from her own physical injuries and then while she fought to find the truth and to see that justice was done. She wasn't sure either of them had anticipated their relationship moving to this level, but so far, so good.

Told you he was in love with you.

Finley savored the memory of her husband's voice before setting the remembered words aside. Derrick had told her this on more than one occasion. Apparently, he had been right. Maybe he had also known that she had always been a little bit in love with Matt too.

Matt was a big part of the reason she had been able to move on with her life at all.

She liked where things were going now. Liked her life.

A rap on her door drew Finley's attention there. Jack gave her a nod. "Got a new client. You want to join us in my office?"

Jack Finnegan, her godfather, owned this law firm. He was one of the top criminal defense attorneys—if not *the* top—in the Southeast. New clients called and burst through the doors every day. Every. Single. Day. Most of whom Jack passed off to other firms he trusted. He only took on a few cases each month. After all, he was only one man, and he certainly didn't need the money. The few cases he accepted were ones, he had explained to Finley, that felt right. Clients who needed his special brand of lawyering. To stand in her doorway and say they had a new client, as if the event was a rarity rather than an everyday occurrence, meant only one thing.

"What kind of favor do you owe this one?" Finley asked as she rose from her chair. She grabbed her suit jacket and tugged it on.

Jack stepped into her office and closed the door behind himself. He made a face she knew well—one that said he was about to tell her a story that wasn't entirely complete or at least not the whole truth. Knowing the complete story would not be in her—meaning his—best interest, of course, so he would only pass along the truly relevant parts.

"Actually, it's his father I owe a debt of gratitude."

"Aha," Finley said with a nod. She reached for a notepad and pen. "Just how bad is this guy?"

While Jack Finnegan was the very best in his chosen field, Finley had a pretty damned good record herself—on the opposite side of the aisle. She'd worked her entire career until shortly after Derrick's murder to put away the defendants who had the misfortune of ending up in a courtroom with her. Jack, on the other hand, did all in his power to keep that from happening—which was also why he was so selective about his clients. As often as not, they weren't exactly innocent or even particularly good, but they also weren't always *directly* guilty of the charge levied. Sort of like guilty once removed.

Finley wasn't complaining. After her crash and burn in the courtroom, she'd been on probation with the bar. Not that she'd cared about her career. At that point, she'd wanted to die more than she had wanted anything else. But Jack wasn't standing for it. He had picked her up from the very bottom and forced her to come to work for him as an investigator. *Forced* might be the wrong choice of words. He'd made her an offer she couldn't refuse. He didn't give a damn, he'd claimed, whether she cared about living or not; he just wanted her to try for her mother's sake. He had promised Finley that if she couldn't find her way back, he'd personally put her out of her misery.

Nearly a year later and she was still here, and ending things was only a bad memory.

"Twenty-eight years ago," Jack said as he leaned against the closed door, "I found myself between a rock and a hard place on a certain case. Raymond Johnson did me a tremendous favor. His son Ray needs me now."

Johnson. The name sounded vaguely familiar and not in a good way. "What kind of favor?"

Jack waved a hand. "We don't need to go there. Suffice to say I feel compelled to do this. His father is an old man. He's dying. Terminal cancer." He pressed his lips together, then said, "I really do *have* to do this, Fin."

"Okay. So what's the situation with this client?" She propped a hip on her desk and waited.

"You probably remember Lucy Cagle's murder."

Wow, now there was a major blast from the past. "Sure. She was a senior over at Harpeth Hall." Harpeth Hall was one of Nashville's elite private preparatory schools for girls. Lots of celebrities had attended the school. "They never found her killer, right?"

Finley remembered the way the story had swarmed through the prestigious schools in the area. Though Lucy had lived in Franklin, not so far from Finley's Belle Meade home, Finley had been a year older, and they had attended different schools. The high-profile murder had been horrifying to all other teens at the time, at least for a little while. Like all else during those challenging years, the awful event had dwindled into the background of the roller-coaster ride of angst and exhilaration. Finley hadn't kept up with the case during her university years, and by the time she had graduated from law school and started at the DA's office, the case had been long cold. She did have some recollection of a ten-year anniversary documentary about the case a few years back but nothing else. For a resurrection—what, thirteen years after the event?—there must be new evidence.

Jack shook his head. "In all this time, Metro never even had a real suspect. But last week there was a potential break." He gestured to his shoulder. "One of those little strappy bags you girls liked to carry back in high school was found at a construction site."

Finley's instincts stirred. "They've connected the bag to Lucy Cagle?"

"They have. Had her driver's license inside."

"How is this find connected to the new client?"

"The construction site was an old warehouse the Johnson family has owned for fifty years. It's been empty for the past two decades, and the son—our client—finally sold it. There will be new condos there—as soon as this mess is straightened out."

Finley's first thought was that any client with half a brain would surely have removed incriminating evidence before selling the property, had he been aware it existed. This was possibly a good sign as regards his innocence.

"Let's see what this Mr. Johnson has to say," Finley suggested, standing once more.

Jack nodded and turned to the door, but hesitated. "You know, it's okay to announce your intentions anytime you like. I really am good with your decision. In fact, if you will recall, it was almost my idea."

Finley's old boss, Davidson County district attorney Arthur Briggs, was up for reelection next year. And Jack was right. He was part of the reason she was leaning toward a possible run against Briggs. Though Finley wasn't so sure she was as good with this new career path as she'd first thought, thus the reluctance to officially announce the intent. At this point, when she considered the idea, she found it difficult to draw in a decent breath.

"I have plenty of time. The sooner I announce I'm running, the more time Briggs will have to render me miserable with his attempts at making me look bad."

District Attorney Briggs was basically worthless at his job. Successfully prosecuting the bad guys might not happen if not for the ADAs on his staff. Briggs was more interested in making himself look good than in seeing that justice was served. People in Davidson County were not happy with him, but he would do all in his power to see that Finley and anyone else who ran against him looked worse.

The truth and the trouble were, there was plenty of fodder that could be misconstrued where she was concerned.

"You'll kick his butt," Jack assured her as he opened the door.

She would certainly try. Maybe. If she didn't change her mind.

Jack's office was just two doors down from her own. The offices weren't laid out in any sort of traditional manner. After Jack's own fall from grace five or so years ago—he'd lost his twenty-five-year battle with alcohol—he had resurrected his career using this old church. He insisted he'd thought it was a fitting new beginning. And it had worked out, that was for sure. His former office had been in one of Nashville's premiere buildings downtown, with a slew of other high-profile attorneys, where he had been a senior partner. There had been a whole host of assistants and other clerical personnel as well as paralegals. In retrospect, maybe all that pressure was part of the reason Jack had fallen off the wagon.

In any event, his career's resurrection had taken an entirely different route. Low-profile office, fewer clients. He did the work he loved and let the rest go on to attorneys with different aspirations.

For a while, Finley had thought that was what she was doing working with Jack. But then she'd realized if she didn't step up to make change, change might never happen. Hence, the potential run for Davidson County DA.

Jack waited for Finley to enter his office before him. He was old fashioned that way. No matter that he looked a bit like a rogue with his ponytail and his vintage suits. Finley had decided long ago that Jack liked putting people at ease by coming off as soft and maybe not so sharp. But that was far from accurate. The man was as fierce as they came in a courtroom and possessed a damned-brilliant, razor-sharp mind.

Ray Johnson stood as Finley entered the room. He appeared to be in his mid- to late forties. Blond hair that was going gray fast, which likely explained why he wore it short. Pale skin, freckles. Nice suit, but the silver wasn't a good color for him, even if it did provide a sense of cool reserve, which she doubted he possessed. This she based on the tattoos peeking above the collar of his shirt, the hard lines of his face, and the stone-cold gaze from those deep-blue eyes.

Not a friendly-looking guy for sure.

"Mr. Johnson." She extended her hand.

"A pleasure to meet you, ma'am." His grasp was firm. Hands callused. This close, it was obvious the man worked out, probably lifted weights. "Call me Ray. Mr. Johnson is my pop."

"Ray," she said with an acknowledging nod.

Finley counted three rings on his right hand, two on his left. She'd also spotted another tattoo when his cuff slid back as he reached for her hand. Nothing against tattoos or jewelry, but if they ended up in court, Finley would ensure that he ditched the extra rings and wore a dark-blue suit that would flatter his coloring. There was makeup for the tattoos, considering some folks saw the markings as negative, particularly in the defendant of a criminal case.

The three of them took their seats, and Jack kicked off the meeting with "Ray, why don't you walk us through what's happened since the discovery of the handbag at the construction site?"

Johnson gave a succinct nod, held Finley's gaze without looking away, as if she'd been the one to make the suggestion. "My pop received a phone call from one of the cops on the scene. A guy he knew from way back. That was on Wednesday of last week, but we didn't get the official visit from the detective on the case until Friday." He relaxed deeper into his chair. "Frankly, I wasn't that worried about it until the call I got this morning."

So, a cop the father knew had tipped them off, and Johnson hadn't been worried that evidence from a thirteen-year-old murder had been found on his property. Seemed strange that he hadn't been at least a little concerned.

"Why weren't you worried?" Finley asked, more curious than anything.

He glanced away now. She'd called his bluff. He was worried. Who wouldn't be? There was no statute of limitations on murder. His pretense was likely related to wanting to come off as innocent of any possible connection to the find. Or maybe he wanted to prove how unimportant all this was in the grand scheme of his life.

He did give off a bit of an arrogant vibe.

"First, no one in my family, including me, even knew Lucy Cagle." He lifted his chin defiantly. "Obviously we saw the news back then, and what happened to her was a damned shame. But it had nothing to do with us. Second, the warehouse sat empty for two decades. We were always running the homeless out of there. Anyone could have left the purse on the premises." He stared directly at Finley then. "I damned sure would have moved it if I had hidden it there."

Yeah. She figured as much. So far, stupid didn't appear to be one of his unflattering assets. This was something else most folks recognized about Finley right off the bat—she could be on the skeptical side. Hazard of her past career. Trust was something people had to earn, at least from her. She didn't blindly go in believing all she was told.

"The police obviously understand that to be the case," she pointed out in an effort to lower his tension. The fact that he hadn't been arrested implied as much.

Johnson nodded. "I think so, but they're still looking at me closer than I'd like."

"Meaning?" Finley prompted.

He glanced at Jack, then settled his gaze on hers once more. "The detective called this morning. He found no prints on the bag, except the girl's—the one who got murdered. But he says there were a couple of cigarette butts found near the purse. He wants me to agree to a DNA test to rule me out, considering I smoke." He patted his chest where a pack of cigarettes was ensconced in a breast pocket. "Have for thirty years."

Not exactly a point to brag about, in Finley's opinion.

"This could be a problem," Jack indicated.

Finley did not agree. In fact, she felt quite the opposite—assuming their client had nothing to hide. "If you weren't involved in the victim's murder, why not allow the detective to rule you out? It's a common practice that could basically end any further issues for you."

Johnson looked from Jack to Finley, hesitated long enough to release a big breath, then spilled the reason for holding back. "My DNA could potentially link me to other crimes from my younger years. I'd just as soon not go there."

Well, that was certainly an acceptable answer, even if it wasn't one an attorney wanted to hear from a client. *Jack, Jack, Jack.* How had he managed to accumulate all these not-so-upstanding friends?

Because on some level, he was broken, just like Finley. There were some fractures that never healed, no matter how much time passed and no matter how you moved on. They were just there . . . marring the person you wanted to rise above. But those fractures, those dim little scars . . . wouldn't go away quietly.

She shifted her attention to Jack and waited for him to spell it out for this guy.

"I won't sugarcoat the situation," Jack said. "This is a problem."

Johnson gave a nod. "This is why we need your firm. My pop says you're the best defense attorney on the planet," he said to Jack. Then he turned to Finley. "I've heard things about you, Ms. O'Sullivan. The cops can't prove I killed that girl, but I can't prove I didn't, which only leaves one choice: find out who did kill her. You can do that . . . I know you can."

Finding the truth was sort of Finley's specialty. She did so often, even when their clients would prefer she didn't. As for her reputation, most cops didn't like her. Didn't want her involved in a case. Because, ultimately, finding the truth was not necessarily about simply finding the evidence. Motive, means, and opportunity were not always the perfect storm for closing a case. Cops didn't like it when Finley interfered with their tried-and-true methods. She complicated things, forced the assigned detectives to work harder to wrap up the case. Johnson had opted not to mention this part in his little speech about his faith in her, but she suspected he was well aware.

"Is that what you want, Ray?" she asked point blank. "You want me to find the truth?"

The hesitation was ever so slight . . . just the tiniest hint but enough for Finley to comprehend that whether he admitted it or not, he had some reservations about the idea. What he wanted, she understood perfectly, was for this to go away. Sooner rather than later.

"Yes," he insisted. "It's the only way I can be saved from a murder charge for a crime I didn't commit. You know how Metro is. Closing a high-profile cold case would be a big deal for any detective."

Whether it was true or not, his answer was the one Finley had wanted to hear.

"Who's the detective on the case?" She had made more than her share of enemies at Metro. The detective in charge of the case could make her job far more difficult.

"Eric Houser," Johnson said. "You know him?"

Relief washed through Finley. She knew Houser well. More importantly, she could trust him. Like her, finding the truth was more important to him than merely finding a way to close the case. He was one of the few at Metro who still liked her.

"Houser and I are on good terms," she said. "He's an excellent detective, and he's thorough. If you have nothing to hide related to the Lucy Cagle murder, you have nothing to worry about with Houser."

Johnson grunted a "yeah right" sound. "If he's so good, maybe he can find my brother."

Finley frowned, in part because Johnson skipped right over her assurance about Houser but mainly because she had no idea what he meant by the comment. "Your brother?"

"Ian," Jack explained. "Ray's younger brother disappeared around that same time, only a few days after the murder, in fact."

Interesting and most assuredly not in a good way in relation to their client's situation.

"Was there ever any suspicion that his disappearance was connected to Lucy's murder?" Finley asked Johnson.

"The cops talked to the old man, but to my knowledge, no actual connection was ever found." Johnson made a face and turned his hands up. "Ian was just lazy and wanted out, I think. When he vanished, I told the old man he should just let him go. The little shit wasn't worth the trouble of looking for him."

Sounded like there had been no love lost between the brothers.

"I'll need everything you have on the search for your brother," Finley told him. "Any PIs you've hired to search for him. A complete statement on when exactly and why—if you know—he disappeared. The names of his closest friends. I'm assuming, since the police learned of his disappearance, that your father filed a missing person report."

"Monday, October ninth, is the last time anyone saw Ian," Johnson said. "And yeah, the old man filed a report. Since Ian was twenty-three at the time, I don't think the cops did much about it other than to look into whether he knew the Cagle girl or not." Johnson lifted one shoulder in a halfhearted gesture. "We hired a PI, too, but we got nothing from him either."

"Still, I'll need his name."

The missing brother was a good potential lead, no matter that a connection to Lucy Cagle had not been established thirteen years ago.

Maybe Houser was looking at the wrong brother.

3

Finley sat in her Subaru for a while after parking in her driveway. The house was one of the bungalows built in the middle of the last century. Small. Practical. When her late husband purchased the house, it had been pretty much a wreck. Still was to some degree. Jack and Matt had helped her paint the interior and redo the bathroom, which had needed an update badly. Then, over the summer, Finley's dad and Jack had painted the exterior a crisp, clean white. Even with the aging greenish-gray roof, it looked considerably improved. Thanks to the newly added foundation support, the small front porch no longer leaned to one side. Really, it hardly looked like the same place.

In late October she and Matt had decided to take their relationship to the next level, and he'd moved in with her. Determined to help out with renovations, he had insisted on launching a landscape overhaul. After all, he'd said, autumn was the perfect time for planting new shrubs. Finley had let him. Who was she to come between a man and his shovel and lawn mower. The landscape looked better than ever before. A nice row of shrubs marched along the fence line around the property. More shrubs hugged the foundation. Matt had pointed out all the ones that would bloom next year and provided the expected colors.

Finley had no issue with all the new stuff as long as she wasn't expected to water it or care for it in any way. Experience had proved that she would kill a fake plant.

Derrick would have approved of the upgrades. Like Matt, her late husband had been keen on home improvement. Finley only cared that the roof no longer leaked and all the plumbing and electrical functioned properly.

Judge Ruth O'Sullivan, Finley's mother, still thought it was ridiculous that Finley wanted to stay here after all that had happened. This was where her husband had been murdered. Where she had sustained horrifying injuries. The *Murder House*, the media had dubbed it at the time. Not that the media bothered to honor all crime scenes with special names, but Finley had been a high-profile ADA who was married to the victim and whose mother happened to be a prestigious judge, which added up to higher ratings.

But this wasn't the murder house anymore. It was home, at least for now. Finley had learned over the past year that though this part of the neighborhood was sort of a low-end one, it was up and coming and, more importantly, the neighbors were priceless. She glanced in her rearview mirror at the house directly across the street. The lady who lived in that house had probably saved Finley's life back in September by taking out a would-be killer with her gardening shovel. This same neighbor had likely saved her the year before as well. Helen Roberts had called 911 the night Derrick was murdered. The speedy response no doubt contributed to Finley's survival.

Why would she be in a rush to move?

Finley climbed out of the Subaru. As she closed the door, she glanced across the street. Roberts was usually milling about in her yard or walking her little dog at this hour of the evening. Not tonight. Maybe she had already done both in deference to the earlier sunsets this time of year. Decembers in Nashville weren't usually terribly cold, but the days were far shorter for sure.

Mulling over the array of delivery options for dinner in the area, she headed toward her porch. Last time it had been Chinese. Maybe Mexican tonight. Or pizza. She should text Matt and see what he was in the mood for, since he wasn't home yet. Like her, work sometimes kept him late into the evening. His new position in the governor's office had proved a bit less of a time suck than his previous work as liaison between the mayor, the chief of police, and the DA's office. The real measure of his new job was that Matt was happy. He loved his work. Each day seemed to bring some new kind of excitement to his role in the state political arena.

His happiness was all that mattered to Finley. She smiled as she dug in her bag for her keys. Truth was, she, too, was happier than she had expected to ever be again. A lot had come together over the past few months.

Her cell vibrated with an incoming text, and she tugged it from her bag along with the keys. Hopefully it was Detective Houser. She'd left him a voice mail earlier that afternoon. The sooner she could talk to him, the sooner she would have a clearer understanding of what was going on with the Lucy Cagle case.

Not Houser. *Matt.*

Be home in an hour or so.

Her smile widened, and she responded with a thumbs-up.

A high-pitched bark—more a piercing yap—had a frown tugging at Finley's brow. The backyard, maybe? She dropped her cell back into her bag. Keys clutched in her hand, she skirted the porch and walked around to the backyard. She didn't have a dog. She had a cat. Well, it was sort of hers. It had shown up earlier in the summer and decided to stay—at least so far.

She squinted into the darkness, spotted a little white fuzzy dog. The animal's front paws rested against the trunk of the one decent-size tree on the property, and he yapped wildly at something in the branches above him.

Was that the neighbor's dog? Her face scrunched in confusion. Helen Roberts had a little white fur ball that looked somewhat like this one. A Pomeranian, Matt had called it. Strange. Roberts never allowed her dog outside her fenced yard without a leash.

"Hey, doggy." Finley had no idea what his—or her—name was.

A yowl from above had her glancing up. Cat sat on a limb, staring down at them. So, this was why the dog was back here barking. Apparently, he'd chased the cat around the house and up into the tree.

"Not very neighborly of you," she pointed out as she walked closer to the dog and crouched down to his level. Perched on one of the lower branches, her cat stared down at the nuisance below. Finley checked the dog's collar. The neighbor's address was on the collar but no name for the dog.

There was something in his fur. She squinted to see better. Dirt or mulch? What in the world . . . ?

Then she spotted the bush he'd been digging around. He'd dug past the mulch and into the rich black bagged dirt Matt had added to each shrub he'd planted. He would not be happy about this intrusion.

Finley scowled at the animal. "Does your owner know you're here?"

The dog stared at her, cocked his head in a way that said "What do you think?"

"Let's get you home." Wincing in expectation of being nipped, she reached for the dog. To her surprise he jumped into her arms. "Maybe you're ready to go home."

Finley stood, the dog in her arms. She glanced up at the cat. "I assume you can get yourself down."

The cat looked away, as if the very idea that he might not be able to deal with this tree situation was ludicrous.

Finley walked around the end of the house and across the street. The neighbor's gate was open. Concern needled at her. In all the time she'd lived on this street, she had never known Roberts to leave her gate open this way. Most likely she didn't want any of the neighbors' pets getting to her flower beds, and she certainly didn't want her dog wandering off.

After closing the gate behind herself, Finley put the dog down, dusted off her jacket, and headed for the porch. When the dog started yapping again and darted around the corner of the house, heading for the backyard, she decided to follow. Maybe Roberts was working in her yard and hadn't noticed the dog wandering off. Not likely, Finley decided, since she would surely have heard him barking. The woman watched that dog the way a new mother watched her child.

Thankfully, well-placed exterior lights prevented the yard from being totally dark. A step around the rear corner, and Finley spotted the trouble. Helen Roberts lay facedown in one of her many flower beds.

Oh hell. Finley's pulse kicked into overdrive as she darted across the yard. She knelt next to the elderly woman. "Mrs. Roberts, are you okay?"

Her skin felt warm. Eyes closed. Finley chewed her lower lip. No response to word or touch. She placed two fingers against the older woman's neck to find the carotid pulse. A little slow and certainly faint, but it was there. Relief rushed through Finley. She took a breath to calm the rapid beating in her own chest.

Afraid to move Roberts but certain she needed her face turned in such a way she could potentially breathe easier, Finley gently shifted her head so that her face was not planted in the mulch like one of her prized rosebushes.

"Mrs. Roberts, can you hear me?" Finley surveyed her body. Saw no blood or other indication of trouble. This was good, right?

"I'm calling for help," she said as she tapped the necessary numbers into her cell.

When the dispatcher assured Finley that help was on the way, she sat down in the grass and held her neighbor's hand. After a thorough sniffing of his owner and Finley, the fuzzy dog collapsed onto the ground next to her as well.

"She'll be okay," Finley found herself saying to the animal.

She hoped so anyway.

Vanderbilt Medical Center
Medical Center Drive, Nashville, 8:50 p.m.

Finley had been waiting what felt like forever but was really only an hour and a half or so. She was tired. She had freed her hair from the stretchy band that held it in a ponytail and massaged her scalp to relieve some of the stress there. She was so ready for a shower and to crash on her sofa with Matt. She had sent him an update about the neighbor. He was home already, promised to have dinner waiting for her.

A smile tugged at her lips. For a year she had barely remembered to eat. Rarely kept food in the house. To have dinner prepared and waiting was fairly new territory. She liked it. Was grateful for Matt in so many ways.

She glanced at the time on her cell once more. The minutes seemed to drag by.

The paramedics had prepared Finley for what Roberts would need at the hospital. Identification. List of medications. Et cetera. When the ambulance had left with Roberts, who had regained some semblance of consciousness, Finley had taken the dog inside, fed him in case Roberts hadn't, and refilled his water bowl. She'd grabbed the woman's handbag, checked to ensure her wallet containing her ID and medical card were inside, and plucked the house key from its place on the table by the door. Before leaving she had checked for prescription medications and found none. Finley was very grateful for the heads-up from the paramedics, which prevented her from arriving at the hospital only to have to return to the house for the needed items.

Since her arrival there had been nothing to do but sit here in the waiting room and, well, wait. So she had occupied herself with continuing her perusal of the World Wide Web regarding the new case. Lucy Cagle's murder had happened in October, thirteen years ago. She had just turned eighteen. She was an honor student bound for premed at Vanderbilt University. Her middle school and early high school years were filled with extensive travel and distinguished academic awards. All this had been included in the many newspaper articles about the victim. The links related to the tenth-anniversary documentary had been particularly helpful in Finley's online search. But it was her mother, Louise Cagle, a.k.a. Louise Scott, who fascinated Finley on a totally different level. Her work in investigative journalism was unparalleled. The cases she'd dug into were gritty, grisly murders and horrifying missing persons.

Lucy's father had been a doctor, which may have been her reason for choosing the medical path. A prestigious heart surgeon, no less. Sadly not even a month after Lucy's murder, and on Halloween no less, he had died, ironically, of a heart attack. Finley supposed even a top cardiologist couldn't save himself if his ticker decided the stress was just too much. Grief was a massive stressor.

As for Ray Johnson and his family, theirs was a whole other story. The old man had been suspected of all manner of criminal activities, from prostitution and drugs to human trafficking and murder. Nothing ever stuck, and the rumors had dropped off over the past decade since the son had taken over. Still, not exactly nice people. The rumors and unsubstantiated allegations made her wonder about Johnson's fear of DNA connecting him to old crimes.

"Roberts family."

The announcement snapped Finley from her musings. She shot to her feet and moved toward the man in the scrubs who'd spoken. Tall, slim, salt-and-pepper hair, thick-lensed glasses. The doctor, she hoped.

"I'm Finley O'Sullivan," she explained. "Mrs. Roberts's neighbor."

"Dr. Rick Herron, cardiac surgeon. I was called in to evaluate the patient." He frowned, glanced at the chart he held and then studied Finley via those thick lenses. "Does Mrs. Roberts have any family?"

Finley shook her head. "Not to my knowledge. I've lived across the street from her for more than a year, and there's no one that I know of." Finley abruptly remembered her neighbor having mentioned a husband. "She said her husband had passed away. Other than that, I've never noticed her even having visitors."

Herron took a big breath, let it go. "Mrs. Roberts has a very serious heart condition. There are indications of several other mild heart attacks. She's going to need open-heart surgery, and that surgery won't wait. Unfortunately, at this stage, the risks are elevated. If she'd come in a year or more ago, it would have been far easier."

Worry twisted tighter inside Finley. "Can you do it now? I mean, without a family member to give consent?"

"She's awake. Groggy, but awake. She has agreed to the surgery, but I feel like any family she has should be made aware of the seriousness of the situation. Since you aren't aware of any family, perhaps you can speak with her and see if there's anyone. When the nurse asked, she didn't respond."

That was Mrs. Roberts. She had her own way. "I'll talk to her."

He nodded. "Good. I'll have her nurse take you back. Try not to tax her, though. She doesn't need any added stress. We have the surgery scheduled for tomorrow morning. It would be good to have any family she has here for the surgery. Just in case."

Nothing he said sounded good as far as odds went, in Finley's opinion.

"I'll see what I can do," Finley promised.

"Until then, we'll keep her medicated and comfortable. Follow me," he said as he turned back to the double doors that led into the bowels of the ER.

As soon as Herron introduced Finley to the nurse assigned to Roberts, one Hazel McCarthy, they quickly moved on to Roberts's room. On the way, Nurse McCarthy explained that Roberts was awaiting transfer to the cardiac intensive care floor.

McCarthy paused outside the door. "Let me know if you need anything."

"I will. Thank you."

When the nurse had headed back to her station, Finley opened the door and stepped inside. Helen Roberts lay on the bed, her face even more pale than usual. Her thin body too still. All manner of tubes and wires snaked from machines to her body or vice versa. She looked old and helpless . . . alone.

Regret knotted in Finley's belly. No one should be alone at a time like this.

She stepped to the bedside. "Mrs. Roberts."

The older woman's eyes fluttered open. She stared up at Finley, looking like a frail and vulnerable version of the person Finley knew her to be. The one who had fearlessly wielded a shovel against a hired assassin.

"You gave me quite a scare," Finley said when her neighbor didn't speak. "Your little dog alerted me that something was wrong, and I found you in your backyard."

"I need to go home."

The rusty words were scarcely audible. Roberts stirred as if she might try to get out of the bed. Finley put a hand on her shoulder. "You need to save your strength. They're doing surgery in the morning. Do you understand the situation, Mrs. Roberts? Your condition is very serious, and surgery to hopefully alleviate the trouble has been scheduled for tomorrow morning."

Roberts drew in a weary breath. "It's bad."

Finley managed a reassuring smile. "But you're in good hands. They'll get you fixed up, and then you can go home."

Roberts gave a listless nod, as if she comprehended that Finley's words were possibly wishful thinking.

"Is there anyone I should call? A sister or brother? Cousin? Son or daughter?"

Roberts licked her dry, cracked lips. "No one."

Damn. Finley had been afraid of that. "A friend or pastor?"

This was the South, after all; most everyone had church family. Well, everyone except Finley. Church hadn't been on her calendar since she was a kid. Law school and life had crowded it out.

Roberts gave a faint shake of her head. "No one."

"All right, then," Finley said quickly as if it was no big deal. She certainly didn't want the woman to feel even worse about being alone. "Tell me what I can do to help. I'll take care of your dog, of course. Water any flowers or plants that you say I should. Take in your mail. Anything else?"

Roberts clutched at Finley's arm with surprising strength and pulled at her. Finley leaned closer. Roberts studied her for a long moment. "Whatever you do," she said, her words broken, barely a whisper, "don't let him out. No . . . no matter how much he begs."

Finley patted her neighbor's hand, the one clutched around her arm. "You have my word. I will not let him out under any circumstances."

Roberts held tightly to Finley until her eyes closed and she lost her battle with the drugs no doubt dragging her back into unconsciousness. She needed all the rest she could get before tomorrow's surgery.

Finley watched her sleep for a bit before leaving the room. She checked in with Nurse McCarthy, ensured she had Finley's cell number and then left the hospital.

The reality of being so ill with no one to be at her bedside or to see after her was difficult to watch. There were times over the past eighteen months when Finley had wanted to push everyone away . . . had wanted to be completely alone. But now she comprehended the mistake in that thinking. Being alone wasn't all that it was cracked up to be. As much as she would like to proclaim that she needed no one . . . it wasn't true. She was immensely thankful for Matt and Jack and her family—even the Judge. Not that the two of them were ever going to have a traditional mother-daughter relationship, but they had a relationship. One they could both live with for now. Would it evolve as time went on? Maybe. At least it was a beginning, and it made Finley's dad immensely happy. This was the thing about life. No matter how much Finley had wanted to pretend she hadn't needed anyone after Derrick's murder, it was a lie. Being alone like that—hurt and overwhelmed—was never a good thing.

Once in her car, she sent Matt a text to say she was headed home.

As she drove she thought of her neighbor's insistence that she not let the dog out. Finley was confident she had meant without a leash. Roberts had taken him for walks daily. Finley could let him out in the yard as long as she ensured the gate stayed closed. No way was she going to be the one who let something happen to the woman's dog. Finley suspected that might just push her over the edge if she somehow managed to hang on through tomorrow's surgery.

Roberts had no family, no friends or church support system, which explained why the dog meant so much to her. The animal was her family. All Finley had to do was ensure the fuzzy thing stayed safe until Roberts was home again. Should be easy enough.

Famous last words.

4

Matt opened the front door with a glass of her favorite red wine already in hand.

Finley tossed the well-worn messenger bag she used as a carryall onto the sofa and reached for the glass. "Thank you." She drank long and deep, standing right there in the threshold.

When she finally came up for air, he ushered her inside far enough to close the door. The scent of spicy tomato sauce filled her lungs. "What is that amazing smell?"

"Your favorite marinara."

She smiled, suddenly starving. "You are the best."

She had blown through lunch in a meeting with a team of local powerhouses who hoped she would run for DA. Though the meeting was held in a private room at a posh restaurant, Finley hadn't managed more than a couple of bites of salad. The Judge had latched on to Finley's mention of potentially going up against Briggs. She desperately wanted Finley to reach for the brass ring the way she had.

Obviously, Finley's former ambition hadn't taken a permanent leave, since the idea of this career move appealed to her on some level she hadn't yet fully analyzed or embraced. *If* she tossed her hat into the ring for Davidson County DA, there were hoops to jump through. Funding was one of those essential elements. The group her mother had thrown together was an enviable one for certain. Notable attorneys; a federal public defender and a couple of former prosecutors; a past, much-loved mayor of Nashville; and two major-corporation CEOs. Not a list to scoff at, for sure.

But Finley wasn't ready to make any promises to or deals with powerful people.

"Let's eat," Matt said, taking her hand and drawing her from the thoughts and toward the kitchen. "And you can tell me all about your new client."

"I hope you ate already." Finley hated the idea of Matt waiting until this hour just so he could eat with her.

"I only got home at nine." He shrugged. "The timing actually worked out for us to have dinner together."

Like he would have eaten without her. He was far too much of a gentleman.

The table was set. The bottle of wine he'd opened stood waiting for Finley. Steam rose from the marinara sauce ensconced on a bed of pasta. Colorful salads sat in bowls. All of it looked amazing.

Cat lounged on a stack of boxes standing next to the back door. His tail whipped as he cast Finley an uninterested glance. The boxes held Derrick's clothes. Finley intended to put them in the garage with a host of other items headed for donation. The back door was as far as she'd gotten with them. Generally, Matt would have taken care of the heavy lifting without her even having to mention it, but he wouldn't move any of Derrick's things unless she specifically asked him to. It was a respect thing. Finley loved him all the more for it.

"You shouldn't have gone to all this trouble," she insisted as the scent of herbs and spices had her sinking into the chair he'd pulled back.

"I have a hidden agenda."

"Wait." Finley held up a hand, then reached for the wine and refilled her glass. She indulged in a long swallow, sighed, then said, "Okay, go ahead."

He laughed. "It isn't that bad," he assured her. "In fact, it's good. But first, we eat."

Matt sat at the other end of the small rickety table. He portioned the marinara and pasta onto a plate and passed it along to her. Then did the same with another plate for himself. For a while they ate. She munched on her salad and overindulged in the pasta. By the time she placed her fork on the empty plate, she was stuffed.

Matt poured her more wine, then set the bottle aside. "I understand you met with the committee the Judge put together."

Finley rolled her eyes. "You mean the band of serious donors she assembled."

Matt sipped his wine. Usually he was a beer man, but there were just some dishes that cried wine, he would say. "How do you feel about the support they offered?"

Finley pondered the question. "I feel like I'm not ready to commit to anyone as to what my platform will be."

Matt's smile was restrained, no matter that his lips twitched with the need to let it slide across his face. "Did you say as much?"

"Mostly I just listened."

He knew her too well to believe for a second that she would go for the promises and the backroom deals. No way. That said, she comprehended that it took money to run a successful campaign. Why couldn't she just tell the folks about herself and what she wanted and be done with it? The answer was easy and wholly frustrating. Because her opponent would spend millions proving she was the worst person on the planet and that no one could do the job as well as him.

"When you officially make your announcement," Matt said, his gaze steady on hers, "the governor will announce his support."

Her jaw dropped. She snapped it shut. "Are you serious?"

"Why wouldn't he give you his support?"

"Because I'm a bit of a has-been. I crashed and burned publicly. Not to mention I've done some veering over the line when it came to finding the truth about what happened to Derrick." She wanted to be excited. She really did. The governor's support was a big deal, and she had no doubt that Matt was primarily responsible for it. But she had to be realistic. She came with a considerable load of baggage. Every scrap of which Briggs would dig up and use against her.

Matt knew the things she had done. Gunshots echoed in her brain as a blaring reminder. She had been present at the killing of two of the three men responsible for her husband's death. She blinked at the memories. Ignored the memory of blood spatter on her face. But she hadn't killed anyone. Was she guilty in some way of how their deaths came about? Maybe.

Did she have regrets?

Not a single one.

Those bastards had deserved exactly what they got. Carson Dempsey, the pharma king ultimately responsible for Derrick's murder, would get what he deserved as well. His trial was coming up in a few months. He was on house arrest with his passport seized and his accounts frozen until then. His wife had left him, and all his friends had turned their backs on him.

The idea made Finley incredibly happy.

"Fin"—Matt reached across the small table and placed his hand on hers—"you are an amazing person. An incredible attorney. But above all else, you have this way of seeing and understanding people. And you care about justice. About the truth. Few who rise to a position of considerable power have that." He shrugged. "Maybe they did once, but it's long gone by the time they reach that pinnacle. I know you. You won't let that sense of right go. You will be exactly who you are, no matter how high and how far you go."

She did not deserve this man. She studied his handsome face, the trusting eyes she knew as well as her own. Every line and angle of his face was etched in her memory. Matthew Quinn was a very, very good man . . . friend and now lover.

"You have to stop doing this, Matt." She squeezed his fingers.

"Doing what?" That handsome face rearranged into confusion.

"Being so damned perfect and doing way too much for me."

He laughed. "I am far from perfect."

Not true, but she let it go. He would never accept such a compliment.

They cleared the table and did the dishes. She washed and Matt dried. He had reorganized the few cabinets so things would fit in a more user-friendly way. Her method of kitchen organization was nonexistent because she never bothered to cook when it was just her in the house.

"So, come on. Tell me about this new—sketchy according to Nita—client."

Finley laughed. Couldn't help herself. "Is there anything that woman doesn't tell you?"

Matt grinned as he propped himself against the counter. "Not much. She likes me."

Finley leaned next to him. His arms went around her and pulled her closer. "Nita's not the only one. Everybody likes you."

He was the one who should be running for DA. Matt would win on his smile and charm alone. The fact that he was a stellar attorney would be icing on the cake.

"You are too sweet." He kissed her on the temple.

She relaxed, could stay like this all night. "You remember the Lucy Cagle murder?"

His brow furrowed. "I do. Damn, that was a while back."

"Yeah. I was a freshman at Vandy, and you were a sophomore." She smiled, remembering the long hours they'd spent pretending to study when they were actually dissecting the dynamics and politics of university life. Even then they were like attorneys brainstorming.

"Feels like a long time ago." His voice sounded distant. He was remembering too.

"No kidding." She sighed. "Raymond Johnson Senior—our client's father—used to be big into construction, then he downsized into the real estate sales side of things. His son and namesake, Ray, took over for him about twelve years ago."

"The father made several fortunes with suspect backing," Matt noted, no doubt recalling details from criminal cases where Johnson had been a suspect but never charged. "The son only had to step into his shoes and maintain the status quo to keep the money rolling in."

"That's the one. Anyway, one of the warehouses he recently sold to a developer has become a crime scene. They found Lucy's handbag. Allegedly, it has been there all this time. The case has been reopened based on the find, and since there were a couple of cigarette butts in the vicinity, they want Ray to agree to a DNA test. Purportedly the test is to rule him out as a suspect, considering the warehouse belonged to his family at the time of the murder and until its sale."

"Can they extract DNA from cigarette butts thirteen years old?" Matt swiped at her cheek. "Marinara."

She grinned. "Thanks. It's been done successfully. No reason to believe it couldn't be done in this situation."

Matt gave a nod. "All right, then, if he's innocent, what's the problem?"

"Good question," Finley agreed. "Ray doesn't want to give a DNA sample. He insists he's innocent in the Cagle case, but the results would possibly connect him to other criminal cases."

Matt laughed, a quick burst that perfectly summed up her feelings on the matter as well. "That could definitely be problematic."

"The thing that I can't figure out," Finley said, thinking about the research into both the Cagle and the Johnson families she'd done before leaving the office and then while waiting in the hospital, "is the victim's mother—Louise. Remember she used the byline Louise Scott?"

"Oh yeah, big-time investigative journalist. Is she still alive?"

"Don't know. Her husband died suddenly only a few weeks after the daughter. Not even a month after his death and with the case having gone nowhere, the mother just fell off the face of the earth. I found zero about her after mid-November that year. I thought I would knock on some doors tomorrow. See what I can find out from former colleagues, neighbors. That kind of thing."

"Who's the detective on the case?"

"That's the upside. It's Eric Houser."

"The two of you work well together," Matt pointed out.

"We do." Finley liked Houser. He was one of the good guys. "I'm hoping to review the official case file ASAP, and maybe I'll find something more there. For now, I'm in gather mode."

"Johnson is lucky to have you and Jack on the case."

"He may not feel that way by the time I'm finished," she confessed.

"True." Matt chuckled. "Hey, I stopped by my house today and picked up a few Christmas decorations. I thought it might be nice to get into the spirit."

Apparently, Nita wasn't the only one feeling the season. Finley flashed him a smile she hoped would pass for the real thing. "Sounds good."

"When Nita called, she warned me you probably didn't have any decorations."

Oh, she was going to get Nita Borelli one of these days. "She's right. I had some at one time, but I think I tossed out all that stuff." Because she had lost interest in holidays. Because she had thought she would never have reason to celebrate anything ever again.

"You always had a tree at the condo."

He was right. She had gone all out for Christmases. The Woodmont condo had been her first real home after law school. She'd even had a few friends over for small holiday gatherings each year. But then she had met Derrick, moved here, and before she knew it, her life had blown up.

"Having one last year didn't feel right," she confessed.

"Of course it didn't, and if you don't want to have one this year, I understand."

The man was too thoughtful for his own good.

"This year is a new beginning," she said, making the decision then and there. Dr. Mengesha, her therapist, would be proud. "We should have a tree."

The spark of eagerness she saw in Matt's eyes was reason enough to go the distance for Christmas if it made him happy.

"We could take a ride out to that Christmas tree farm next week and get a real one."

"Sounds like a date."

There were a lot of decisions she needed to make going forward. Like selling her condo on Woodmont. Maybe soon, before the market dropped off. She couldn't see herself there anymore. Actually, for the past couple of months, she had been waffling on where she saw herself in the future.

She glanced up at Matt. Wherever she was, she wanted to be with him.

The thought of her neighbor's dog abruptly intruded. "I should walk over and check on the dog. Maybe turn on a few lights."

Matt shook his head. "You shower. I'll take care of the dog and the lights."

Always the gentleman.

Just one more thing she loved about him. As strong and self-reliant as Finley was, she appreciated a thoughtful man all the same.

"Thanks. The key's in my bag. I fed him earlier, so you should only need to check the water and let him out, I guess. But watch him closely, Mrs. Roberts seemed worried about him getting out of the yard."

"Will do." He kissed her forehead. "What's the dog's name?"

She followed him into the living room. "I have no idea. I didn't think to ask, and it's not on his tag or collar. I'll ask when I talk to Mrs. Roberts again."

Matt hesitated at the door while she fished out the key. "We do need to know his name. Otherwise we'll end up calling him Dog."

Finley grinned, placed the key in his hand. "You mean, like I call the cat *Cat?*"

"We have to name that cat." A grin teased his lips. "All pets should have names."

"Guess so," Finley admitted. Until recently she'd figured the cat would just wander off one day and not come back. The idea that he would become a permanent fixture in her life hadn't occurred to her. "Let's call him Lucky, since he was lucky I fed him instead of shooing him away when he started hanging around."

"Lucky it is." Matt opened the door but paused before leaving. "Like me for realizing the only woman I would ever want had been right beside me all along."

Oh yeah. Finley was incredibly grateful for this man.

5

Tuesday, December 5

Maureen Downey, the newspaper's managing editor for the past twenty-five years, had agreed to meet with Finley. Whether she wanted to help or hoped for a scoop was yet to be seen.

Finley waited in Downey's private lobby on the top floor of the shiny glass building once called Palmer Plaza. The *Tennessean* had moved to this location a few years back. It was one of the few newspapers that remained available in newsstands and via delivery to doorsteps. The *Tennessean* was still the go-to source for folks in the Nashville area.

The assistant finally looked up and smiled. "Ms. Downey can see you now." She gestured to the double doors on the other side of the lobby. "Go right on in, Ms. O'Sullivan."

Finley stood. "Thank you."

She crossed the small lobby and entered the private domain beyond. Unlike the waiting area, which lacked windows, the office showcased a spectacular view of the city. In the middle of that panoramic view was a wide desk seemingly sculpted from glass and stone. The woman in charge stood behind it. She gave a nod, and the door behind Finley closed. She hadn't realized the assistant had followed her.

"Ms. O'Sullivan." Downey smiled as she skirted her desk. "Very nice to meet you."

Finley met her in the middle of the room and grasped her outstretched hand. "The pleasure is mine, Ms. Downey."

Downey was tall and trim. Even close up, she looked younger than Finley had expected for someone with more than forty years in a tough business. Blonde hair that just touched her shoulders and an attractive face that featured the fine lines created by time and a full life.

"Please, join me." Downey moved to the group of comfortable chairs that took advantage of the glorious view. "Can I get you anything? Water? Coffee?"

"No thank you." Finley took one of the chairs facing her host.

Downey crossed her legs and stretched her arms along the back of the wide white leather chair she'd chosen. She appeared relaxed, comfortable in her own skin. "You want to know about Lou—that's what we called her," she said, kicking off the conversation. "One of my all-time favorite people. We were dear friends for many years. I adored her. She helped me through the most difficult time in my life—the death of my husband. I can't imagine how I would have gotten through it without her."

When she said no more, Finley explained, "I'm hoping to find her, actually. Metro PD is reopening her daughter's murder case, and I would very much like to speak with Ms. Cagle."

Downey nodded, her expression shifting to one slightly more guarded. "I see. Evidently Metro is keeping this very quiet, because I had not heard."

With the kinds of sources this woman had no doubt cultivated over the decades, Finley didn't see how that was possible, but she opted not to say as much. Then again, Houser was particularly careful with the release of information.

"This is the very early stages. An exploration of options, actually."

Finley felt confident Houser would be meeting with this woman soon enough. He had sent Finley a text this morning and asked if they could catch up at lunch. His morning was wall-to-wall meetings she suspected were related to the Cagle case. Finley hadn't mentioned her appointment with Downey when she responded. She and Houser were friends, but this was work. This was about her client.

"I will tell you," Downey said before drawing in a deep breath, "I have not heard from Lou since a few weeks after her husband's funeral—around Thanksgiving, I believe. When Lucy was murdered"—she closed her eyes for a moment—"it was a terrible, terrible time. Lou and I both had daughters the same age. Our only children. We were both nearing forty before we jumped into the parenthood game." She smiled. "And then our girls gave us so much joy we regretted having waited so long." She gave a nod. "You may have heard, my Jessica is running for a state senate seat next year."

"Congratulations." Finley produced the expected smile. She'd noticed a headline in the *Tennessean* about the candidates for that seat but hadn't skimmed the article. "I'm sure you're very proud."

"I am. After law school and several years in private practice, Jessica felt she wanted to do more for the community." Her eyebrows raised. "I'm hearing rumors you're having similar thoughts. That your intention is to give Briggs a run for his money next year."

Finley's lips strained to keep a smile in place. "I'm considering the possibility."

"Can I quote you on that?"

For two beats Finley didn't respond, and then the hesitation was gone. The uncertainty vanished. "Of course."

Downey smiled. "Excellent."

Back to business. "Did Ms. Cagle move away?" Finley could see how Cagle would want to leave the life that had been so shattered. After her husband's murder, Finley had waffled between wanting to disappear completely and wanting to do all in her power to get the people responsible. The latter had won out in the end.

"I wish I knew. I can't tell you how I've missed my friend. Wherever she is, she has abandoned everything and everyone who was a part of her life. She had a brother who has since passed. He stopped hearing from her the same time the rest of us did. Her parents died before Lucy was born. Her in-laws, who lived down in Florida until they passed; close friends here; no one heard from her again after her husband's funeral. Her house was abandoned. I was so worried about her, and for years I felt certain she would eventually come back to us. So much so I kept the outdoor maintenance up and paid the taxes on the property for her. God knows it's the least I could do. The paper is still making money on Lou's work, and she had made investments in the paper's stock eons ago. But I suppose at some point I'll have to make other arrangements."

"Because she never came back," Finley pointed out.

Downey pressed her lips together for a somber moment before responding. "She did not. And if anyone knew how to disappear without leaving a trace, it was Lou. She was as good as any detective. Better than some."

"Was?" Finley asked. "Do you think she's dead?"

Downey's expression shifted to surprise as if the thought had not occurred to her. "I hope not. I have no reason to believe she's dead, but the truth is I have no idea. I prefer to think of her as living somewhere writing her memoirs. I suppose the past tense is subconscious. An admission I don't want to consciously own."

Finley believed her. "Do you feel she grew disillusioned with the police when her daughter's killer couldn't be found? The loss of her only child and then the death of her husband may have been the last straw."

"I'm convinced that was the case," Downey agreed. "The police kept coming up empty handed. Lou even hired a private investigator, and he discovered nothing useful either."

Finley wasn't surprised Cagle had sought out private resources. With the kind of assets available to the family, of course they'd hired a PI. "Do you recall the private investigator's name?"

"Not offhand, but I'm sure I can find the information. If you'll leave a card, I'll see that the name is found and passed along."

Finley removed a card from her bag and placed it on the table between them. "Lucy was headed for medical school, like her father. Was there any talk of perhaps disgruntled family members after the death of a patient? Maybe her murder was related to a patient her father had lost."

Downey shook her head. "Nothing that I'm aware of. If Lou thought her husband's work had anything to do with Lucy's murder, she never mentioned it, and I'm confident she would have. As I say, we were close."

"What about her work? Was Lou investigating a particular story at the time? Maybe something that put her and her family in the line of fire?"

"Yes, always. Lou was a high-profile personality. Actually, she had just been offered a prime-time slot for her own television show." Downey smiled. "I remember she was torn about the offer. She insisted on tabling the talks until she finished the story she was developing at the time. Then Lucy was murdered. But, as I said, the police found nothing that connected Lucy's murder to her mother's work or anything else."

"Was her work in progress ever published?" According to what Finley had found online, nothing had been published from Louise Scott after Lucy's death.

"It was not. She never turned in another project."

"Do you know what she was investigating?"

"I do. We always discussed her ideas. You may not recall," Downey ventured, "but there were a number of young women, children really, who were going missing every year. This was not new even then. Tennessee, like all other states, had and still has its share. But Lou had a few leads about a human trafficking ring in the Nashville area. Those leads she didn't share with me, since they were unconfirmed. She felt strongly about confirming all her leads before putting them on the table, so to speak. I think the concept of the story she was building was very close to her heart, since many of the victims across the nation were our daughters' ages and younger. She wanted to stamp out anyone involved in that ugly business—particularly in our hometown. She realized she couldn't stop the problem worldwide, but there was something she could do here, at home. We both expected the story to be a big one."

"Do you have her notes? Working papers? Anything that might help me see where she was going with the story? Who she had interviewed?"

Downey studied Finley for a long moment. "Isn't this the kind of question the police will ask?"

"I would hope so," Finley agreed. She chose not to say more. Less was always best.

"I looked you up," Downey said, her expression moving toward skepticism. "You work for Jack Finnegan. This makes me believe you have a client who's already involved somehow in the reopening of this case. Are you trying to find Lucy's killer, or are you trying to keep Lucy's potential killer out of trouble?"

Fair question. "I'm trying to find the truth," Finley said. "Jack's job is to defend his clients. My job is to find the facts . . . either way."

Downey considered her response for a time. "The answer is no. I do not have Lou's working notes. Whatever she had, she took with her when she disappeared."

Downey glanced at her Apple Watch. "Excuse me, I need to respond to this." After a few taps, she glanced up once more. "Do you have any other questions?"

"Just a couple more," Finley assured her. "Was Lucy seeing anyone? A boyfriend maybe?"

Downey shook her head. "No one anyone knew about, anyway. Certainly Lou was convinced there was no one, or she would have pushed the investigation in that direction." Downey glanced at her watch once more.

Finley recognized this was her cue. "I believe that's all for now. Thank you, Ms. Downey, for seeing me."

They stood, and Downey followed her to the door. Finley wondered if there was more she had to say but wasn't sure she could trust Finley with whatever it was.

At the door, Finley hesitated. "Were Lucy and her mother close?" Downey appeared taken aback by the question. "Yes. Very close."

Finley had read the articles published about Lucy's murder. Her body had been found on a deserted side street in a not-so-great part of town at the time. Not exactly the sort of place a young girl from a prestigious family would frequent after dark. "Is it possible Lucy had a friend her mother didn't know about? Someone who ultimately took her life?"

The Johnson family had a long history of skirting the edges of the law. Ian Johnson had gone missing shortly after her death. It was a lead worth following up on.

"I'm certain the answer is no. Lucy was an excellent student and a bright and kind young woman of means with very high standards. She would not have wanted that sort of friend. The police interviewed her closest friends at school, Gwyneth Larson—now Garrison—and Natalie Williams. If either of them was able to provide a name, I'm not aware of it, and I firmly believe Lou would have told me."

For a woman who had made her life's work keeping the public informed of the news, Downey's answer to that particular question seemed a bit naive. Intelligence and privilege were hardly foolproof safeguards against mistakes, especially during the teen years. The names of the friends she had mentioned had been a part of the original investigation. Both teenagers, at the time, had spoken to the police as well as reporters about their relationships with Lucy. Much of the information about the investigation had been used in the tenth-anniversary documentary. But there was one name Finley abruptly realized had not been mentioned in any of her research. One that Downey had not mentioned even now.

"Still," Finley countered, "*if* Lucy had a secret friend, how could her mother have been confident she would know? The girls at school might not have been completely forthcoming. Lying is more often than not a part of the teen years. Loyalties are tested, and the parents are frequently on the losing end."

"Because my daughter would have told us after . . . what happened," Downey said, obviously flustered. "Jessica would never lie to me."

Jessica had not been named in a single article or commentary about Lucy's death. Her mother would have seen to that. From the moment Downey mentioned having a daughter the same age as Lucy, Finley had instinctively known that the daughters would have been friends. They grew up with moms who were dear friends—who worked together. If the two girls hadn't been friends, there would have been a compelling reason. Either way, Finley had needed confirmation.

Finley shrugged. "Your daughter may not have known," she countered. "Just because—"

"You're wrong." Downey's posture stiffened. "Jessica would have known. She and Lucy were best friends. Closer than any of the others."

And there was the answer Finley had really wanted.

Had she asked about Lucy's friends, Downey would have given Finley what she wanted her to know—the names of the two girls she'd first mentioned. Certainly, she wouldn't have put her own daughter in the line of fire.

"Thank you," Finley said before exiting the woman's office.

Finley thanked the assistant and headed for the elevator. She imagined Downey would be on her cell, calling her daughter at that very moment, warning her not to talk to Finley if she showed up.

Funny how in a murder investigation everyone wanted the truth so badly—unless it somehow hit too close to home.

Mel's
McGavock Pike, Nashville, Noon

Mel's was an East Nashville European-style café and wine bar created from a restored 1930s craftsman bungalow. Inside was reminiscent of a French bistro, with bar seating as well as a small dining room. Eric Houser knew the owner and had ensured he and Finley were given the proverbial corner table. Finley ordered a white wine and the house ricotta-and-local-blueberry tartine. Houser had gone for the braised lamb torta. Since he was on duty, he chose sparkling water.

After her meeting with Maureen Downey, Finley had intended to track down her daughter, Jessica, but there hadn't been time before her lunch with Houser. With his busy schedule, she might not have another opportunity in the next twenty-four hours to talk with him face to face. Passing up the opportunity wouldn't be smart. In murder cases, timing could turn out to be everything.

"Have you spoken to the detective who was in charge of the case thirteen years ago?" she asked after their drinks were brought to the table.

Houser glanced at Finley's stemmed goblet, then studied his water glass as if he wished it were something else. "Daniel Blake died a couple of years ago, but I've been reviewing his notes. I'm happy to fill you in on anything you'd like to know as long as the offer goes both ways." He lifted his gaze to hers and smiled. "I'm sure that's why you called."

Finley made a face, feeling deservedly guilty. "I know, I know. I haven't talked to you in a while, and then I call and it's about a case." She turned up her hands. "I'm seriously out of practice with the *friends* thing. I'll try to do better."

She really should be ashamed of herself. Houser had taken a serious beating and a bullet because of her. He'd almost died. She owed him. He was one of the few who had gone above and beyond for her.

His smile widened to a grin. "It's okay. I get it. We're all busy. And you've got this new man in your life."

"Matt is not new," she countered, unable to prevent her own grin. "We've known each other forever. Been best friends for as long as I can remember."

"But you're more than friends now," Houser pointed out.

Finley sensed a touch of jealousy. Was that even possible? Did Houser have a thing for her? He was single. Handsome. Very good at his job. Surely not . . . but maybe. If so, she hadn't noticed before. Or maybe she was overreacting to his comment. She'd spent so long being excessively protective of her personal life, she still found it difficult to speak so freely about it—even with a friend. A friend who was a lot like her. He came from a family of medical professionals, but he'd decided being a doctor wasn't for him. He'd dropped out of premed and joined the Nashville Metro Police Department. He was a rebel. A true friend. One she didn't want to lose for any reason.

She pushed the idea away. "We are."

Houser gave a nod. "Good. You should move on with your life. You punished yourself long enough."

Okay, so maybe she had gotten that wrong. Good. She liked Houser. "Thanks. I'm getting used to the idea of not being miserable. It feels good."

"I'm glad. Really glad."

There was a moment of silence, of knowing. It felt comfortable.

"So hit me with your questions," he said as he raised his glass for a drink.

Finley shifted into full investigative mode. "Is there a complete list of Lucy's friends in the notes? I'm looking for anyone close to her, particularly anyone she seemed to be involved with on a romantic level at the time." She had the names she'd read about online—the same ones Downey had confirmed, save her daughter, of course. But there could be others in the official case file that she had not seen as of yet.

"A couple of close friends from school. No one that really stood out as a bestie. No boyfriends—that her parents knew about anyway."

No bestie. Hmm. "It would be really helpful to see the case file," Finley ventured.

His grin resurfaced. "Sent it to your email before driving over here. I sent you a copy of everything I'm allowed to send."

Finley dug her phone from her messenger bag and checked her email. There it was, just like he said. She opened the email and perused the attached PDF. Several names were listed but not Jessica Downey's. So, Finley had been right. Jessica was being protected. The *why* was the question. Why wouldn't Downey and Cagle want the police to know Jessica's name? If she had information that might help find the bastard who killed Lucy, why not tell someone? There was the chance, of course, she had known nothing, so exposing her to the investigation was unnecessary. Still, naming her would have been the right thing to do.

"Anything you weren't expecting there?"

Finley would share her thoughts on Jessica Downey with Houser, just not yet.

"Not at all. Thank you for sharing."

He nodded. "You have anything to share with me yet? Like why your client refuses to submit to a DNA test?"

"I think he's just worried that there will be a mistake and then he'll end up attached to another case somewhere down the line." The waiter appeared with their food, giving her a moment's reprieve.

As soon as the guy had bid them a bon appétit and disappeared, Houser stared expectantly at her.

"You know some people are paranoid like that," she went on. The truth was, sometimes it paid to be. "With all the strange things occurring with DNA sites, I can see his hesitation." It was true. Maybe not in the case of her client, but . . . there it was.

He grunted a sound that might have been agreement but not quite.

"You realize that warehouse was empty for a very long time," she reminded him. "Anyone could have put that purse there."

His eyes narrowed, searched hers. "You like this guy?"

"Johnson?" she asked, feigning uncertainty at his query. This was a question she preferred not to answer. Her personal thoughts could shine a bad light on a client. That was never a good thing, and Houser was well aware of this.

He leaned forward ever so slightly. "If you don't know his history, take my word, he's a piece of work."

"His father has a shady sort of reputation," Finley agreed. "I've heard his name over the years—rarely in a good way. Since Jack took him on as a client, I've done some research. There are all sorts of rumors. Drugs. Guns. I even read one report that suggested he used to hire assassins to take out his competition. But none of it seems to have been substantiated. You have anything that says otherwise?"

"He was never charged with anything," Houser admitted. "The sons, either, but that doesn't mean they're innocent."

"Agreed," Finley said. "So, what do you know about the younger son, Ian? I haven't really found much on him." Approaching the subject of Ian was touchy. Since he'd disappeared around the same time as Lucy Cagle's murder, there was risk involved with even mentioning his name. His name would already be in the file, since Johnson had mentioned his father being questioned about the younger son once the missing person report was filed. Finley would dig deeper into what Houser had sent her when she had a few minutes.

"He disappeared just days after Lucy's murder. But he wasn't listed as missing until a week later."

So far the facts lined up. Always a good thing.

"According to the report," Houser went on, "there was some confusion about the timing. The father said he disappeared that same weekend. The brother said it was a few days later. There was no reason at the time to suspect a connection, although considering how high profile the

Cagle case was, I'm not surprised his disappearance was checked out. Everything that happened during that time frame was checked out."

No question. Finley had been too caught up in her freshman year at Vandy to be aware of the deeper details. Now, however, as a former assistant district attorney, she was well aware that in a case like the Cagle murder, every rock was turned over.

"But, as you can imagine," Houser continued, "there wasn't a lot of follow-up on a guy that age deciding to leave town without telling his family, particularly considering the family. Ian may have simply wanted to separate himself from the others. That was the thinking at the time, based on the notes in the case file. But, in light of this new discovery, it puts a whole new spin on the missing son."

"The family offered no explanation of why he disappeared at the time?" Finley asked.

Johnson had said basically the same thing as what Houser found in the file. But was he regurgitating the conclusion of the detective on the case? Or had the family had reason to believe this was true at the time? Finley would like to hear anything either man, the older brother or the father, had to say thirteen years ago. The statements made from a thirteen-year distance were often far different from the thoughts at the time of the event.

Not that it would make much difference, she supposed. Unless she could find someone able to connect Ian Johnson to Lucy Cagle before her murder, the only connection would be, as Houser said, the newly found handbag and a few cigarette butts, and that was anemic at best.

"Basically nothing we could confirm," Houser said. "The detective who took the report said Ray mentioned something about his brother wanting to do his own thing. The father, however, repeatedly suggested that one of his competitors in the business may have taken his son. The detective considered both possibilities, but nothing was found either way. Lucy's friends from school, Garrison and Williams, couldn't confirm that Lucy had a man in her life, but they both believed she was secretly seeing someone. But they had no idea who it was. Nothing they said could push Ian Johnson or anyone else into the suspect category."

"And that was the end of it?" Finley prodded. It seemed wrong to have let it go so easily, but hindsight was almost always twenty-twenty.

"That was essentially the extent of the investigation into Ian Johnson's disappearance, yes. If someone took him out, his body was never found. He hasn't resurfaced, which makes me think he's dead. When I spoke to Ray—before he hired your firm—he claimed he and his father never heard from Ian again, but who can trust anything those two say."

"He's probably under some building that sprang up during the time frame he disappeared," Finley suggested. It was the way things were done in the older Johnson's day. If his enemies were responsible, that would likely have been the way of it.

Houser's eyes narrowed again. "In my opinion, this new evidence suggests that Ian did know Lucy. If that's the case, he may have been involved on some level with her murder. His brother may have eliminated him to keep the trouble away from the family."

There were crime families who would go that far. Finley was aware it happened, but this was a fishing expedition—for her and for Houser. The more she could learn, the broader her grasp on the situation. As for the other way around, she had an obligation to protect her client.

"Would the father have allowed one son to kill the other?" Finley countered. "Unless you found something in the family history to suggest as much, I'm not buying it." At least not yet.

The last time she and Houser had worked together, sort of, they had a common goal—get Carson Dempsey. This time they were on opposite sides of the case. This time would be different.

Mostly.

"Raymond Johnson Senior is basically a mob boss," Houser said, glancing around to ensure none of the other patrons were paying attention. "He's a bad man, Finley. So is his son Ray. Don't be fooled by the stories they concoct to make you believe otherwise."

She smiled. "You think I could be fooled that easily?"

Houser picked at his food. "No."

He didn't sound so sure. She started to repeat the question but decided to move on. "What about friends of Ian's? I assume he had friends and they were interviewed."

"Three friends. Troy Clinton, Skyler Wright, and Aaron Cost. Cost died in a car crash a couple years back. Thirteen years ago, all three claimed Johnson was not involved with Lucy Cagle. All three insisted they didn't know her."

Of course they did. They were Ian's friends. "All right, then, since I haven't read the case file yet and you obviously have, why don't you tell me more of the details about Lucy's murder and what you feel has changed—beyond the obvious—with this new evidence."

He pushed his plate away as if he'd lost his appetite. "Thirteen years ago," he began, "Lucy's body was found in her car on the side of Coventry Drive near the zoo at Grassmere. It was as if she'd just pulled over and fallen asleep slumped over the steering wheel. Except she was dead."

Again, he glanced around before going on. "The medical examiner's report listed the cause of death as ligature strangulation. The suspected weapon was a garrote, a wire thin enough to slice through the skin. The wire was nowhere to be found in the car, and blood evidence—or the lack thereof—suggested she had been murdered somewhere else and then placed in her car and abandoned on the dark street."

Finley was familiar with the area where her car had been discovered. At the time, it had been wooded on both sides with no streetlights nearby. No witnesses had ever come forward. Obviously, the killer had gone to great lengths to ensure nothing was left behind. No prints and not a single speck of evidence. The car had been utterly spotless.

"I'm assuming," Finley offered, "you and the previous detective, Blake, believe the killer was either a pro or smart. Or maybe he watched a lot of *CSI* and got lucky that no one came along to catch him."

"That was mostly the thinking at the time." Houser glanced at his food once more, but then looked away. "Except I don't think it was luck. I think it was because the killer or the cleanup guy—maybe both—were pros. Your new client is a pro, Fin. A very bad guy." His attention shifted to his water glass, but he didn't bother to pick it up.

Okay, there was something going on. "What's the deal, Houser? Why all the warnings, as if I don't recognize a bad guy when I meet one?"

His gaze swung up to hers. "Can I help it if I worry about you?"

Wait. Wait. Wait. She and Houser had been friends for a while. He'd had her back when it counted. But this was more than the Johnson family's level of evil and Lucy Cagle's tragic murder. Finley's senses prickled with anticipation or something on that order. She braced. "What's going on?"

"I received some intel from a reliable source this morning." He looked her straight in the eye. "Totally unrelated to the Cagle investigation."

Even though she suspected that would be the case, a trickle of something icy slid through her veins. "Okay."

"Carson Dempsey has reached out to a source—a dark contact." He hesitated. "We don't know the details, but what we do know is that it was about *you.*"

"Why is that news?" She refused to show uneasiness of any sort.

Finley was responsible for the man's son being sent to prison, where he was quickly murdered by those who wanted one kind of revenge or the other against his father. She was the reason Dempsey himself was going to trial for numerous crimes. Clearly, he wanted revenge. Killing her husband wasn't enough.

"Just listen," Houser countered. "I need you to watch your back, Finley. Tell your family—tell Jack and Matt—that we have concerns about his intentions."

She held up her hands. She was not going to cower like a scared animal for Carson Dempsey ever again. "Okay, I'll tell them. But just so you know, I haven't spotted anyone following me or watching me, and I haven't stopped keeping an eye out for trouble. I'm not sure I ever will. What I will not do is live in fear of that bastard for the rest of my life. Not happening."

Dempsey's thugs had followed her for months. They had watched her.

Now they were all dead.

"Just don't let your guard down, Fin," he urged her.

"Don't worry," she assured him. "I can take care of myself."

"I would have said the same," he argued.

And yet while he was attempting to help Finley bring down Dempsey, Houser had ended up beaten and shot in a low-end motel room with a dead potential key witness. It was a flat-out miracle he had survived.

"Got it." She reached for her wine to drown the images that went with the memories.

"Be extra careful," he said quietly. "That's all I'm asking."

She nodded, took a big breath. "I will. Believe it or not, I actually have a lot to live for these days. I'm not dancing on the edge anymore."

She wasn't. Mostly.

He smiled. "I'm glad to hear it." The worry lines on his face melted into a smile. "What's the deal with the rumor I'm hearing about a run for DA?"

"I haven't *officially* announced, but I'm leaning more and more in that direction."

His smile widened to a grin. "Men like Dempsey won't stand a chance."

She could hope. That was her goal. To stop bastards like him.

"You were one of the people who got me thinking about it," she reminded him.

He gave an acknowledging nod. "I'm glad I played a small part. Maybe in return you'll have me come work for you when you win."

"Deal."

They talked awhile longer about the Lucy Cagle case and the lack of useful information. It was clear to Finley that Houser was being careful about what he shared. She supposed she understood. The girl's murderer had gotten away with what he'd done for a very long time. If Ray Johnson was the one, it was time he paid the fiddler for the dance. If it was his younger brother, then he had to pay as well—assuming he hadn't settled up already.

As they left the café, Finley sensed there was something more on Houser's mind.

She paused next to her Subaru. "Just spit it out," she ordered. "I can tell there's something else you're not telling me."

When he still hesitated, she gave him a look that said "spill it."

"There's this one report in the file." He tucked his sunglasses into place. "It may have been nothing."

"We're talking about the Cagle murder case?"

"Yeah." He took a breath, seeming to need to buy time. "It's a statement from a man who worked in social services. Evidently there was some vague connection to Lucy and her family, but like I said, I guess it turned out to be nothing."

Her instincts stirred. Two nothings added up to something. He should stop beating around the bush and give her that something. A name would be helpful. Social services could mean some sort of abuse or other family issue. She couldn't see the trouble being from the Cagles, or it would have been all over the news. It was possible it was the family of one of Lucy's friends.

"It must be something, or you wouldn't bring it up," she argued.

He cleared his throat. "Yeah. Okay. Barton O'Sullivan."

"What?" Finley drew back slightly. Her father knew the Cagle family? She supposed that was possible . . . but in his capacity as a social services director? How did she not know this? Then again, why would she know it? She and Jack had only just taken the case yesterday, and she hadn't spoken to her father since.

"I wasn't sure telling you—"

Before Houser could finish, Finley interrupted, "Are you saying there was some sort of complaint filed and my father did the investigation in his capacity as a social services director?"

"At first," Houser explained, "Blake thought maybe there had been some sort of incident that your father had investigated. But that turned out to be wrong. It wasn't work related."

Finley digested this information. "It's conceivable," she said with some measure of reluctance, "my parents were acquainted with the family on a social level."

She could see the possibility. The Cagles were a high-profile family. Her parents were as well. It was probable that they'd run in at least some of the same social circles. It wasn't unusual that she hadn't known Lucy personally. Finley's parents had friends and acquaints whose children she hadn't known back then. The idea wasn't a stretch at all. Yet, in this context, saying so felt wrong somehow. Maybe it was the way Houser was tiptoeing around it.

Houser looked away. "I think it might be better"—he reluctantly met her gaze once more—"if you asked your father about the details."

The vague uncertainty she'd felt going down this road suddenly morphed into sheer dread. "You're saying something else entirely."

Not possible. *No. No. No.* Finley knew her father. He was a good guy . . . a man above reproach. He would not . . . *could not* be involved in some way with any aspect of this case that was not on the up-and-up.

Impossible.

Houser stared at the ground. "Finley"—his gaze shifted nervously to hers—"I'm saying that your father may have been involved with—"

"No way." She shook her head. "No way in this world was my dad involved with Louise Cagle. He would never do that. Never."

Houser rubbed a hand across his jaw. "Not with Louise," he said quietly, too damned quietly. "With Lucy."

6

Willie, the house manager, had said Mr. Bart would be home by two.

But he wasn't. The lady kept apologizing to Finley as if it were her fault Barton O'Sullivan hadn't arrived at the time he had stated when he left the house. Finley told the exasperated woman it wasn't a problem. No, she didn't want Willie to call him. Finley wanted to surprise her father with an impromptu visit. No, she didn't want coffee or tea or a soft drink.

She just needed to talk to him . . . to clear up this misunderstanding.

Eventually Willie had gone on about her business. The woman had worked for Finley's parents for as long as she could remember. She had done the grocery shopping before home delivery became a thing. She saw that housekeeping stayed on their toes, and she handled the laundry and the dropping off and picking up of the dry cleaning. Basically, she *managed* the household. She was even more of a perfectionist than the Judge. She'd given Finley a dressing down more than once about leaving her stuff lying around all over the house.

This is why you have your own room, young lady. Not everyone is so fortunate.

As for housekeeping, it sounded like a whole department, but it was really only a trio of ladies who came in once a week to do the cleaning of this massive place. They also showed up to prepare for special occasions. The Judge certainly wasn't home long enough to do the cleaning or the shopping. But she did cook. Well, mostly her husband did. Finley's dad was a hell of a cook.

From her seat on the third step of the front staircase, she surveyed the grand entry hall. It was almost as big as her whole house. Her mother wouldn't be able to clean this place alone if she worked on it all week.

Who needed a house this large?

Finley dismissed the thought. She had decided to stop disparaging her mother for needing to keep up with the Joneses. Her massive home in such a prestigious neighborhood was part of who she was. Call it privilege, call it whatever. She had inherited well and could spend her own money in whatever manner she chose. It wasn't like she stole it from someone else or allowed others to provide for her.

Finley's father couldn't care less about the big house and the grand address. He was a good and kind man who went out of his way to help others. Case in point, the lifetime of service to the community.

Houser had to be wrong. Her father would never, ever do such a thing.

As if her renewed worry had summoned him, the front door opened, and her father walked in. Carrying a slim briefcase tucked under his arm, he spotted Finley as he closed the door.

"Finley." A smile slid across his face. "What a nice surprise." But then he considered that his one and only daughter didn't just show up unannounced unless there was a problem, and his smile shifted into a frown. "What're you doing here in the middle of the afternoon? Is everything all right?"

She pushed to her feet and crossed the shiny marble floor to hug him. Worry flooded her as he hugged her back. She felt sick at even the notion Houser had put in her head. The thought of asking this question . . . of opening that can of worms was nearly more than she could bear. She loved her father. They had a close and wonderful relationship. She did not want *this* to change the way they were. If Houser was wrong—and he had to be—the idea that she would even ask this question would alter things somehow for her father, damage the strong bond of trust between them.

Did she really have to do this? If she didn't, Houser would, and he might drag her father in to his office. Yes, she had to do this.

"Hey." He drew back. "What's going on? You okay?"

She nodded. "It's this case I'm working on."

He frowned, then grinned. "I tell you what, let's do like we did when you were fifteen. Have chocolate milkshakes and talk about it. Ice cream fixes everything."

She forced a smile, no matter that inside she was aching. "Sounds good."

Finley followed him to his office, where he left his briefcase, then they strolled to the kitchen. She told him about finding her neighbor facedown in her backyard and about her surgery—which Finley should be hearing news of soon.

"Good grief," he said, frowning. "I hope she's going to be all right."

"Me too," Finley agreed. "So how's work going?" she asked as he poked around in the massive fridge.

Her father had retired from a lifetime of dedication to social services. Actually, he'd retired a little earlier than he'd planned so he could help her through rehab after *that* night—the night Derrick was murdered and she was raped and beaten nearly to death. Her father was the one who took care of her. But then after she was back on her feet, he had grown bored, so he'd accepted a position on the Belle Meade planning commission. Mostly he worked from home, but she supposed it made him feel as if he were continuing to do his part for the community.

Finley imagined that with a wife who stayed in the limelight all the time, it was difficult for her father to ever feel he'd done enough. But would that make him step so far across a line?

No. No way.

As he scooped chocolate ice cream into the blender, he talked about the new businesses vying for growth options in the area. New estate-home developments. Even the plan for a new elementary school.

Finley tried to listen, but the words just jumbled in her brain.

When he'd poured the milkshakes into tall glasses and inserted straws, he grinned. "And here we are."

He placed one in front of her and the other on the counter as he settled onto the stool next to her. He took a long sip from the straw. "Hmm. I haven't lost my touch." He looked to her for confirmation.

Finley drew a long swallow and made a satisfied sound. "Delicious as always."

"What's going on, Fin? You seem worried. Everything okay with Matt?"

She laughed. "You can do better than that, Dad. You know everything is perfect with Matt because Matt is Matt."

He laughed. "You're right. Silly of me to ask."

Matt was the smartest and nicest guy in the universe. He was always good.

Deep breath. Just do it. "Jack and I have a new client."

Bart's eyebrows went up in question as he sucked on his milkshake.

They always had a new client, he was likely thinking. Why the big announcement?

"Is Jack okay?" he asked when he'd swallowed.

"Jack is great." Finley fiddled with her straw, decided it was best to just rip off the Band-Aid without further ado. "Our new client is Ray Johnson."

Her father's expression shifted. Seemed to close. He pushed the milkshake aside, having apparently lost his appetite. "Jack is representing him? What's he done?"

Finley nodded. The conversation instantly and abruptly felt awkward, and she hadn't even gotten to the uncomfortable part yet. "You remember Lucy Cagle? The girl who was murdered when I was a freshman at Vandy? Her mother was that big deal . . ."

Her thought trailed off at the look on her father's face. He stared at her in something like shock or despair. The weight of the shift derailed her thought process. Had her heart sinking.

Finley blinked. Cleared her throat. "Lucy was that big shot investigative reporter's daughter."

"I know who she was."

His voice sounded hollow, an echo coming from far, far away. His face remained closed. He didn't want to talk about this. Suddenly she didn't want to either.

But she had to . . . she could not unhear what Houser had said. Could not unsee the look on her father's face at this very moment. She had to confirm this entire scenario was wrong. She would not breathe deeply again—her heart would not beat properly again—until she heard the words from her father.

"Did you know her? Lucy, I mean."

Her father stared at his half-finished milkshake. "Of course, I knew her. She was at the top of every news feed for months. It was a tragedy. A terrible time for the whole city. All of Nashville adored her mother, and Lucy was taken from her in the most brutal way. It's not the sort of thing you forget."

The chocolate suddenly tasted bitter in Finley's mouth. She tried to swallow, but somehow her throat could not complete the action. "How did you know her?"

His gaze collided with hers, a hint of anger there now. "What do you mean?"

Finley mustered her courage and said what had to be said. "You were close to Lucy somehow. I can tell by your reaction to my questions." When he only stared at her, she went on. "There's a report in the case file about you."

He shook his head in that exaggerated way that suggested he wanted to wail. "Now that . . . that was a mistake." He drew in an uneven breath. "Louise hired a private investigator when the police failed to move quickly enough to find Lucy's killer. This . . . this PI discovered that Lucy and I had talked on a number of occasions. It was completely innocent."

Finley struggled to keep her voice steady as she forced the necessary words from her mouth. "What did you talk about?"

"We . . . we . . . talked about . . . different things."

The shock of denial quaked through Finley. This was not possible. This was her father. There had to be a mistake. A misinterpretation . . .

But his face and manner said otherwise. Every tell was there. The abrupt glances away. The stumbling over words . . . the shifting in his seat. The closing in on himself as if to protect the secret part he wanted no one else to see.

A stone sat squarely in her throat, choking her. Her heart felt as if a big hand had reached into her chest and squeezed the life out of it.

"What different things?" Her own voice sounded foreign to her ears. *No. No. No.*

"She—Lucy—was doing her senior thesis on missing children, and she . . . she interviewed me." He scrubbed a hand over his face. "We talked about the issue many times. I pulled together statistics and so forth for her. But it wasn't enough. She wanted to understand how parents coped and the steps they took to try and find their children. She was . . . was *consumed* with her research."

A deep sadness had fallen over his face. Slumped his shoulders. Talking about Lucy seemed to pain him deeply.

Finley looked away. Couldn't bear to see what he was hiding, but it was there . . . written all over him.

"I tried to tell her she was going too far . . ." His voice was low now, barely audible. "She wouldn't stop. She was like you, driven . . . determined. I should have realized sooner, and maybe I could have done more to stop her momentum into trouble."

Finley couldn't continue just sitting there. She slid off the stool and paced the floor. "In what way was she going too far?" she demanded, her words sharp.

He looked at her. Blinked. "The investigation . . . her investigation. She wanted to be like her mother. She wanted to do a big exposé on missing children in Nashville to prove she had the chops. To get her mother's attention."

Finley stalled, stared at her father. "She was headed to medical school."

He sighed, the sound so weary. "She didn't want to go to medical school. She wanted to be an investigative journalist. Her mother pressed her toward the other." He pushed his milkshake away. "Maybe out of fear. You may or may not know Louise was almost killed during a couple of her biggest investigations. I suppose she wanted something safer, something less risky for her only child. This was why Lucy wouldn't tell her mother about her thesis. She knew her mother would put a stop to it."

Finley slumped back onto her stool. "You were helping her with this secret investigation."

He nodded. "As much as I could. I only knew the statistics, particularly of the children in the system who disappeared. Obviously, there was only so much I could tell her, but some parents agreed to speak with her. Frankly, it was a risk to even go that far, but I sensed she might actually have a chance at saying something people would listen to . . . something meaningful in a way to which anyone and everyone could relate. But I was wrong. I should have gone to her mother and told her what Lucy was doing. Maybe then . . ." He shook his head. "Maybe she would be alive today."

The rush of relief sucked everything out of her. Finley was an idiot. Not for one second should she have allowed herself to believe her father would have done such a vile thing. The idea of him being involved with another woman—particularly one barely above the legal age of majority—was ludicrous, and she had known it. Damn Houser for making her doubt this man for one second.

"So," she ventured, relieved but still in need of details, "the PI discovered you were helping Lucy, and this led to the police looking at you with suspicion?" That part still didn't make complete sense.

Another big breath evacuated from her father's chest. "I'm going to tell you this, and then that's all I'm saying on the subject."

Her face scrunched in confusion. "Why?"

"Because"—he looked at her with his father face, the one he rarely used, the one that said he was the boss and she had gone too far—"I do not wish to discuss the subject with you or anyone else."

Houser was off on his idea of what her father's involvement with Lucy Cagle implied, but he was right about one thing: there was something more here. Something more than Finley was going to hear even from her father—the man who seldom ever in her entire life said no to her.

"Okay." She nodded. "Tell me what you *want* to tell me."

"Louise Cagle had no idea her daughter was working on this missing-children exposé. When she came to me after Lucy's murder, I didn't want to tell her the things Lucy had said about her desire not to go to medical school. I didn't want to cause Louise more pain. Her daughter was dead, none of it was relevant anymore." He shook his head sadly. "I suppose this made me look as if I was hiding something. I've never been very good at lying."

Finley felt weak with another rush of relief. This was true.

"Poor Louise was so frantic to find whoever had hurt her daughter that she saw what she wanted to see." His face pinched with regret. "That I was lying. When things escalated, I had no choice but to tell her everything. I will always regret having to do that." A deep sadness settled on his face. "Sometimes there are things better left unsaid when those things will change nothing or will add nothing good or relevant to the narrative."

Finley got what he was saying. "Thank you for telling me."

His face shifted to one of worry. "Fin, don't trust anything this Johnson fellow says. He and his father are very bad people."

She scoffed. "Don't worry. I stopped trusting Ray Johnson the moment he opened his mouth. Maybe even before."

Her father smiled sadly. "I should have known you would see through him."

"Who was the PI?" She was still waiting for info from Downey on the private investigator. Maybe her father could point her in the right direction.

"Jerry . . ." He squinted with the effort to recall. "Bauer. Jerry Bauer. He has an office downtown, if he hasn't retired."

"I'll talk to him. See if he came up with anything on Lucy's case." Finley hugged her dad. "Sorry for putting you through this. I'm sure it was painful."

He hugged her tight. Drew back and looked her in the eye. "Just promise me you'll watch your step with the Johnsons."

She patted his chest. "I always do."

Finley thought of something else her father might be able to help her with. "Did Lucy ever talk about a boyfriend? She was a senior in high school. Surely there was a guy in her life."

Her father's expression closed again. He shook his head. "Not that I can recall."

Had he not looked away. Had he not visibly tensed beneath her touch, Finley might have believed he was telling her the truth.

But he wasn't.

Her father was lying.

7

Almost two hours later Finley was still reeling to some degree after the conversation with her father. Though she had pretty much convinced herself there would be a logical and acceptable answer to his avoidance of her final question, she wouldn't be able to rest easy until she knew the why and how of it. For the moment, she had to set it aside and move on.

There was a considerable amount she still didn't know about Lucy Cagle and her famous mother. Until she had a good handle on those two women, it would be difficult to fully interpret the events surrounding Cagle's murder and how—if at all—Ray or Ian Johnson played into it. She'd spent a good deal of the past two hours looking into Louise Cagle. Where she grew up, went to college, and so forth. Louise's maiden name had been Peters. She'd grown up in Knoxville. Unfortunately, as if Louise had vanished into thin air, all information ended thirteen years ago. Hopefully the PI would have something more.

Finley stared up at the thirty-one stories of stone, steel, and glass that was the Fifth Third Center of downtown Nashville. The skyscraper was called the Center Stage for downtown, even though it had lost its standing as the tallest building years ago. Connecting the arts and business district with a range of tenants from legal and financial to health care and hotels—not to mention a few popular restaurants—it remained a much-desired location. Obviously Bauer Investigations was not your typical middle-of-the-road PI shop. She shouldn't have expected less, considering the client thirteen years ago had been Louise Cagle. Cagle would have wanted only the best for finding her daughter's killer. A quick Google search and a few calls to sources had confirmed the conclusion. Jerry Bauer was top of the heap.

Inside, the sprawling stone-and-marble lobby was accented with classic wood details. Not shabby at all. Clients and employees hurried across the space, several with cell phones attached to ears and others hastily checking their watches to ensure they weren't late. Finley scanned the directory and then headed for the bank of lavish elevators. Inside, she selected the number and readied for the ascent to the eighteenth floor.

Once the doors opened again, she stepped off the car and walked along the corridor until she found the suite marked as Bauer Investigations. No doubt he had clicked a few keys to find out who she was. Anyone who kept up with the Dempsey case would certainly know the name Finley O'Sullivan.

She entered the suite, stepping into a small lobby complete with a few upholstered chairs, a table adorned with fresh flowers, and a neat stack of brochures about the firm. The reception desk was unattended. She glanced around and, with nothing else to do, opted to take a seat. She smoothed a hand over her black trouser legs and adjusted the matching jacket. A nondescript black suit was her go-to work ward robe. Easy to accessorize and always in fashion. Ponytails and little or no makeup kept her life simple. Over the past year, she'd cultivated a great appreciation for simplicity.

Half a minute later, an older man appeared. The photo he used on his website was at least a decade old. Still, he cut quite an imposing figure.

"Ms. O'Sullivan." He walked toward her, extended his hand. "I'm Jerry Bauer."

Finley stood, gave his hand a shake. "Thank you for making time in your schedule for me."

He smiled. "I always have time for the Judge's daughter."

He did know who she was. Maybe good since he seemed to be a friend of her mother's. Maybe bad since he would know she worked for Jack.

And that her father had been on his investigative radar thirteen years ago.

"Join me in my office," he offered.

She followed him into the corridor beyond the lobby and through the only open door. He indicated the chairs that fronted his desk while he skirted around to the other side.

"What brings you to see me, Ms. O'Sullivan?"

"Finley," she suggested as she settled into one of the leather chairs. He lowered into his own.

The office was fairly large, with an inspiring downtown view. Comfortable seating. Sophisticated, uncluttered decor. Like the man, she decided. He wore a stylish, high-end suit, a crisp white shirt with a couple of buttons open at the throat. Thick white hair worn in a trendy slicked-back style. Classically handsome face. Tall. Wide shoulders. Lean build. He looked strong, capable. The perfect draw for clients. Frankly, he should update his professional photo. He looked far more distinguished now.

"Finley," he acknowledged with a nod.

"Metro PD is reopening the Lucy Cagle case."

He nodded. "I heard."

Of course he had. "They've found new evidence they feel will provide the break they failed to discover thirteen years ago."

His clasped hands rested on his desk; his expression and bearing gave away nothing of his feelings on the matter. "It's a shame it took so long."

"It is." She nodded her agreement. "Only a few weeks after the murder, Lucy's mother hired you to look into the case," Finley went on. "I hoped you could provide any insights you discovered during your investigation."

"You know," he leaned deeper into his chair, dropped his hands to the arms. "I'm quite fond of Ruth. She's a good judge and a fine person. We don't always see eye to eye on cases and politics, but she has earned my respect. These days I generally leave my office by four, but since you are her daughter, I stuck around to make time for you."

Finley recognized a new tension in him and braced for evasive tactics. His words warned that he'd already decided how he intended to approach her questions. "I do appreciate your time."

Jerry Bauer wasn't just well respected; he was considered the best of the best in Tennessee. He might be nearing seventy, but one would never know it based on his appearance or his status in the business. His time was valuable.

He flashed another smile, and the tension she'd sensed slipped away. "As you mentioned, Louise hired me after Lucy's murder, the very day after her husband passed, in fact. His sudden death devastated her all over again, and she needed someone to help. No matter how many friends one has—or even family—it's easy to feel alone during a time like that."

No question. Finley had been there. She relaxed, decided he had opted to talk to her rather than to give her some reason he could not. The only question now was how much of what he knew he would tell her.

"I'm not sure if you know this or if it matters with regards to what you're looking for, but Louise treasured her family. Lucy was her only child, and she adored her. When Louise began her career, she made the decision to use her husband's first name—Scott—as her surname rather than using Cagle. She hoped this would provide a layer of protection for her personal life. For the most part, I believe it did. Those who took the time, obviously, figured out she was Louise Cagle, but for most of her audience she was just Louise—or Lou, as some called her—Scott."

"Except you can't protect someone who won't let you," Finley suggested. "Lucy had ideas of her own about what she wanted to do with her life."

He cocked his head ever so slightly. "You've been talking to your father."

"I have." She reminded herself to breathe. Any personal aspect to a case, especially when it hit this close to home, was disturbing on some level. One would think she would be accustomed by now to having her personal life dragged into cases. Evidently that particular discomfort never got easier.

"I gave Bart a hard time back then. I regretted it to some degree later, but it was necessary. Louise was desperate to find the truth about what happened to her daughter—as any parent would be. He knew things he felt were better left untold, and I had a problem with that. We worked it out in the end. He and Louise came to a sort of compromise they could both live with, as I recall."

"How did you feel about your discoveries related to Lucy and my father?" She preferred that Bauer provide his version of what happened thirteen years ago. Giving away too much of what she knew would only hold him back.

"It wasn't about how I felt," he countered. "I can tell you how Louise felt. She very much wanted Lucy to go into medicine, like her father." He gave his head a little shake. "But Lucy had other ideas. She was a very bright young woman and quite ambitious as well. More than anything, she admired her mother. She adored her father, mind you, but she saw in her mother what the fans saw—a sort of magic that charmed them. The magic, of course, was nothing more than hard work and incredible tenacity." He paused for a moment, seeming lost in thought. "Along with a good deal of brilliance. Lucy was enthralled with her mother's work. Certainly, more than she would have dared to let on. You know how teenagers can be."

"A teenager being inspired by a parent has never been cool," Finley agreed.

So far, so good. His story lined up with her father's. She waited for him to go on, hoping for more corroboration.

"She overheard Louise discussing how she intended to dig into the possibility of human trafficking in Nashville," Bauer continued. "Thirteen years ago, no one would have thought that such a thing existed in our town, but they would have been wrong. Lucy covertly used her mother's notes to do some digging of her own. She also chose a route her mother had not yet considered, and that's where your father came in. The idea that children in the foster care system might be lower on the police's radar, thus making them more vulnerable. Turns out she heard about a student at another school who'd gone missing two years before. She did some research and discovered this young girl disappeared from her foster parents' home and wasn't even reported missing for more than a week. This was why she sought out your father. Bart was helping her with that scenario. The idea made the story she sought more her own, she told him."

"Did she find a particular lead or a source that may have put her in a precarious situation?"

Finley knew that place well. Sources, leads, evidence: those were all things that could be dangerous to the inexperienced when burrowing into the evil that men could do. Some people would do anything to keep their secrets buried.

For a long moment, Finley wondered if Bauer intended to answer her question. His hesitation, she decided, wasn't about her. It was about something else . . . something he wasn't prepared to share, she suspected.

"What did your father tell you?"

And there it was. At least part of the thing that held him back.

"He preferred not to talk about those aspects of his interactions with Lucy."

Bauer nodded. "I see." He studied her for a moment. "Tell me, Finley, in what capacity are you here? News travels quickly in certain circles. I'm aware your firm is representing Junior—my not-so-kind nickname for Ray Johnson. He's not one of my favorite people, but that's irrelevant. What is relevant to me is if you believe what I know might help you support your client's claim of innocence?"

It was that way, was it?

She paused a moment, chose her words carefully. "The firm's client has not been charged with any crime as of yet. We can't be sure that he will be. If he is, Jack will do all in his power to defend him to the best of his ability. My goal, Mr. Bauer, is to find the facts—whatever they are. If you can help me toward that end, I would greatly appreciate it."

His eyes narrowed. "You were an excellent prosecutor. I've been intrigued by the cases you've taken on with Jack Finnegan. You're smart, and you're persistent."

Her patience thinned, but she didn't want to put the man off. "Thank you for the compliment, but I didn't come here looking for accolades. I came to a highly recommended source for help in finding the truth. My hope is that you can help me with that. Did you find any connection between Lucy Cagle and the Johnson family?"

Bauer took a half minute, every second of which he studied her closely. Finally, he said, "If I knew who murdered Lucy Cagle, that person would be in prison today. What I did and still do suspect is that someone like the Johnson family was likely involved. The final pieces of Lucy's research into a human trafficking ring no doubt led her to local organized crime. I have no idea what she discovered since any records or notes she kept were not found, but I firmly believe what she learned is the reason she's dead."

Did her father know this as well? Finley blinked away the thought.

When Bauer said no more, Finley asked, "You've uncovered nothing else? No useful connection? Not in all these years?"

His head moved slowly from side to side. "Nothing." He drew a long breath. "If I may, I'd like to offer you some advice."

"Advice is always welcome," she prompted.

"Ray and his father like playing the good old boy role. A little rough around the edges but all soft in the middle. People view them differently for that reason. In fact, I'll bet when you first met your new client, you immediately labeled him a bully, a thug. Maybe not as bright as the average businessman. Cocky without the intellectual capacity to be properly arrogant."

She pursed her lips to prevent a smile. "Pretty much."

"You would feel the same if you met his father, Raymond Senior."

"You're suggesting this is not the case." Finley saw where he was going.

"It is not the case at all. Ray Johnson is very smart. Perhaps not brilliant but smart enough to have helped his father run what is, without question, even if without evidence, an organized crime family for most of his life. From who builds what to who sells what in this city, that family has been involved on some level for at least two generations. Believe me when I say, Ray wants you to see him as a not-quite-so-smart bully. He wants you to believe he isn't capable of a complex plot. But he is. I am one hundred percent certain of that, if nothing else. Whether he or his family was involved in Lucy's murder, I can't say. Certainly I can't prove it one way or the other. Chances are, even if you find some little something that has been overlooked, you won't be able to prove it either."

Finley chewed on his opinion for a bit. "Not even with this new evidence?"

He chuckled. "They find her handbag after all this time along with a cigarette butt or two? Gimme a break. Who's to say the butts were actually with the handbag? Maybe someone planted one or both there?

Or they were simply there. After all, the warehouse was in the family for decades. No doubt Ray or his old man burned a few smokes on the property. Anyone could have tucked the handbag there after Lucy's murder. To be blunt, if the police don't have more than that, they are wasting everyone's time."

Finley agreed. This was a man with finely tuned reasoning after decades of work in the field of investigation, as well as many sources, including at least one in Metro.

"If the killer—whoever he was—stowed the handbag there all those years ago," she suggested, hoping to tap into that wealth of experience, "why leave it—especially if it could connect him to the murder—when the property sold? He had to know it might be found. Why not go back for it?"

Bauer allowed a grin. "Good point. Let's look at this a different way, shall we? Who's to say the killer is still around or even alive. Or maybe Ray found it and left it there for the new owner to find."

Now he'd lost her. "Why would he do that?"

"To have a little fun with the cops who are always trying to bust his balls? To provide a reason for hiring Jack Finnegan—and *you.*"

Finley turned her hands up. "I can't think of a single reason he would want to hire my firm, much less me. Can you?"

"This is the trouble I see," Bauer countered. "Whoever did this had a strong motive for going with the flow on this big new find or for making it happen—whatever the case might be. Either way, you and Jack should be concerned as to what exactly the endgame is. Who is using you? Metro—in an effort to finally learn the truth? Or Johnson, to prompt something he wants to happen?"

Finley allowed his insightful words to sink in. "You've given me something to think about," she admitted. "What are your thoughts on the younger brother, Ian? He disappeared right after Lucy's murder."

Again, Bauer took a moment before answering her question, maybe gathering his thoughts. Maybe figuring out what part of the truth he would give her.

"Ian was babied by the old man. His favorite, some would say. He got away with not being as good at being bad as his brother. I'm guessing that got him killed." He flared his hands in question. "The timing was likely a coincidence, since I couldn't find a connection between Lucy and Ian. Or maybe Ian's killer took advantage of Lucy's murder to make it appear the boy's disappearance was connected. Trust me when I say no one, and I mean no one, would have wanted to face old man Johnson's rage. If someone—a competitor or former ally—took Ian out of play, that person would have gone to great lengths to avoid being caught."

Finley figured this was as much as Bauer intended to share, so she moved on to the other mystery in this case. "Where did Louise Cagle end up? She seems to have disappeared after her husband's death. I would very much like to speak with her if possible. I'm certain she would be interested in this turn of events. Has she contacted you?"

Bauer leaned forward, braced his forearms on his desk once more. "When Metro continued to come up empty handed and I was unable to do much better, and considering her husband's sudden death, I'm guessing she couldn't take it anymore. She vanished. I haven't heard from her since. Phones were cut off. Her house was closed up. It still sits there today, just as she left it. I honestly have no idea what became of her."

"I find it wrong somehow," Finley argued, "that such a beloved icon of the community would just throw away everything . . . stop looking for her daughter's killer and disappear. I tried a search of Louise before she was famous and came up with nothing helpful. Her family was from the Knoxville area, but since her family has all passed away, I wasn't sure if there was anyone else I might be able to track down."

A faint smile touched his lips. "I did the same thing thirteen years ago. Louise had one brother. He hadn't heard from her the last time I spoke with him."

"When was that?" Didn't actually matter, since the man was dead, but Finley was curious.

"Several years ago, I believe. Before they released that anniversary special about Lucy's murder." His smile faded. "To my knowledge, there's no one left."

"With all her sources," Finley pushed, "it's possible Louise has a friend in Metro who knows what became of her. Maybe someone who helped her disappear."

"It's possible, but I have quite a few myself, and they all know I would like to find Louise. I'm sure I would have heard if anyone in Metro was in touch with her."

His certainty was almost too solid—as if he'd gone to great lengths to be prepared for her questions. Or maybe he really had wanted to find Louise and wasn't able to. Sometimes admitting one's own limitations was the hard part.

Finley stood. "Thank you for making time for me on short notice. I hope you'll let me know if you learn anything new."

He rose from his chair and stretched out his hand. "I hope you'll do the same."

Finley gave his hand a shake. "Count on it."

Bauer escorted her to the elevators and watched until the doors had closed with her inside, maybe to ensure she actually left. His answers, for the most part, had felt on the up-and-up, to a point, but there was some little something that didn't sit right with her.

The elevator opened into the expansive main lobby, and she wandered back to the entrance. More troubling than what Bauer wasn't telling her was what her father wasn't telling her. Were the two hiding the same thing? She no longer worried that there had been some untoward relationship between her father and Lucy Cagle. Actually, she had known that was impossible from the beginning. But, like Bauer, there was some piece of this puzzle that he was holding back.

But why hold anything back after all this time?

The air was brisk as she stepped onto the sidewalk. Since she hadn't bothered with a coat today, she was thankful for the tee she'd worn under her blouse. The sun had dropped behind the high-rises that crowded in on downtown, and all the streetlamps and stringed lights had come to life. She walked toward the intersection to catch the traffic light. She'd parked in the garage the next block over.

As she waited for the signal to change, she noticed a car stopped on the other side of the street in the eastbound lane. The traffic light on that side was green; the car should have been moving. She glanced toward the vehicle that seemed to hover on the street, prepared to but not progressing. The driver's window powered down, and a man sporting a hoodie and sunglasses, even as full-on dark descended, turned toward her.

A car whizzed past him, then another, but he sat completely still. Even when a horn blared, he didn't move. He just sat staring at Finley.

Suddenly he smiled, powered his window back up and drove away.

The signal changed, and pedestrians moved past her. One bumped her shoulder.

Finley didn't move. *Couldn't* move.

She hadn't recognized the face. Wouldn't have with or without the sunglasses, she suspected.

The three thugs Carson Dempsey had hired were all dead.

This was someone new . . . someone who had definitely been watching her.

In her bag her cell vibrated, but she remained frozen . . . unable to properly react.

This man . . . this new watcher . . . she didn't have to wonder if Dempsey had sent him. He had. She was certain. There was no one else who would be so interested.

He still wanted to get to her.

Only this time everything was different. She had taken his son. She had destroyed him. He had no one left and certainly nothing to lose. This time she understood with absolute certainty that he didn't just want to watch her . . . he wanted her dead.

Vanderbilt Medical Center
Medical Center Drive, Nashville, 5:40 p.m.

The call had been from the hospital. Helen Roberts had survived her surgery, and Dr. Herron wanted to speak to her representative.

Finley was it for now.

"She came through the surgery surprisingly well," Herron explained. "But she's not out of the woods yet. The pain meds will keep her sedated to a degree for a while. Don't be surprised if she sleeps a lot. We'll keep a close eye on her. I doubt she'll be released for a number of days, considering her overall condition. We need to watch the situation for a time to ensure she regains her strength."

"Thank you," Finley said. "Is it possible for me to see her?"

"You can, of course, but she may not be responsive. Tomorrow she should be more so." He gestured to his right. "She's in room five oh four."

Finley thanked him again before he walked away. They'd met at the nurse's station on the cardiac intensive care floor. She walked the short distance to Mrs. Roberts's room. Pushing through the door slowly just in case there was someone on the other side, Finley surveyed the room.

No nurse or anyone else, just the sound of the machines monitoring the patient. She pushed the door closed and walked toward the single bed that stood in the middle of the small space. The light was dimmed, but even so, her neighbor's face stood out, pale white, in the near darkness. She looked small and frail, far older than Finley suspected she actually was.

Funny how this little old woman could have been so strong with such a serious underlying heart condition. She'd seemed tough, confident, judgmental, and nosy. Finley shook her head. She'd turned out to be a damned good neighbor.

Considering the surgeon was surprised at how well she'd come through the surgery, maybe she was stronger than even Finley had realized.

For a while, Finley stood by her bed. She wasn't really sure why. Roberts slept quietly. The only sounds were the machines. No one else came into the room. Finley glanced around, wondering if she should leave. Her gaze stalled on the bedside table. There were no flowers. How sad it was to reach this age and have no one to send flowers. Finley could get very upset with her mother at times, but she would never want her to be alone at a time like this. Her dad either.

She wouldn't want to be alone at a time like this.

The last was the hardest part. The climb back up from not caring if she lived or died had been harder than she'd anticipated.

But here she was.

From what Finley had witnessed the past year and a half, her neighbor was strong like that. She would make it through this.

Eventually, Finley decided to go home. Matt would be there by now, and she didn't want to be so late again.

She stroked the sleeping woman's hand—the one without all the tubes stuck into it. "Don't worry, Mrs. Roberts. I'm taking care of the dog. I'll check on your houseplants and water whatever needs it when I get home. Just focus on healing, and I'll be back tomorrow."

No response, not even a twitch. If she could hear, at least Finley had said the right things. Hopefully.

She left the hospital, watching the people and cars around her closely as she crossed to where she'd parked. Her cell shimmied in her pocket, but she ignored it until she was locked in the car. She started the engine, allowed the call to go to the speaker system.

It was Jack.

"Hey," she said as she eased out of the slot.

"Just catching up with you, kid," her boss said. "I'm headed to the Drake."

When Jack Finnegan had been a partner in a prominent law firm, he'd owned a gorgeous town house in a prestigious Nashville neighborhood. Now he operated his exclusive, as he liked to call it, firm from a former church, and he had made a home by renovating two rooms at the Drake—an iconic has-been motel.

His methods and lifestyle these days were certainly different from before. Unique, Matt would say. As long as he stayed sober, Finley didn't care where he lived or how he operated.

"I'm leaving the hospital after checking on my neighbor. Headed home." She should give him an update on what she'd learned today. "I spoke with Houser and with Jerry Bauer, a PI Louise Cagle hired to look into her daughter's murder."

"Did you learn anything we might need if this thing catches fire?"

Finley hesitated for only a moment. Jack was her godfather. He adored her and her family. Had secretly been in love with her mother for most of his adult life, which was just another part of his fall off the wagon half a decade ago, but he'd dealt with that. He and Finley's dad were friends—more than friends, really. Jack loved Bart like a brother, and the feeling was mutual.

Taking a deep breath, she plunged into the story of what she'd learned about her father's involvement with Lucy Cagle.

"I'm glad it turned out to be nothing, kiddo," he said, his relief almost palpable.

She opted not to mention that she wasn't completely convinced it was nothing, but she sure as hell hoped that proved to be the case.

One thing was certain, and Finley said as much. "I'm getting the impression the Johnsons are far more than just low-level developers."

"Yeah, they're not exactly altar boys, which is why we will focus only on the Cagle case." Jack heaved a sigh. "I know how you feel about guys like Johnson, Fin, but I couldn't say no. We okay on this one?"

She appreciated his concern, but she'd learned long ago that as an attorney, sometimes you just had to do the job whether you liked the client or not. "We're good."

"Glad to hear it. What's your overall take so far?"

"So far," she pondered the question, "I don't think the police have one damned thing that actually ties Ray to the Cagle case." Finley considered something Bauer had said. "You know, we talked before about the idea of why someone would have left evidence of murder lying around on his property. I mean, if our client is guilty, why leave proof lying around, particularly when he was ready to sell the property?" She made the turn for Shelby Avenue.

"Makes no sense," Jack agreed.

"Unless," she tossed out, "someone put it there when it was time for the warehouse work to begin. Maybe that someone wanted this evidence to be found."

"You mean an enemy of our client? Otherwise I'm not seeing the logic in that scenario. Where you going with this, kid?"

"Not an enemy, and you're right, there is no logic. *Unless*," she countered, "the goal was to prove something to the police using *you*." And me, she didn't add.

The silence on the other end of the line told her he was weighing the possibility.

Finley pulled into her driveway. "Is there something you need to tell me, Jack?"

"I don't think this is about me," he argued. "Look, I'm home, so I'll catch you in the morning. Night."

"Night."

Finley shut off the engine and dropped her head against the seat. Apparently, her father wasn't the only one hiding something. Made her feel less guilty about not mentioning her potential new follower to Jack. But still, how were they supposed to move forward with this case if no one wanted to be completely truthful?

Damn it, Jack. What the hell did you do?

O'Sullivan Residence
Shelby Avenue, Nashville, 11:30 p.m.

Finley couldn't sleep.

Matt had fallen asleep a minute or so after closing his eyes. He always did.

She did not. *Ever.*

Tonight, she lay in bed facing him. He was on his back, his left arm thrown over his head, resting on the pillow. She studied his profile. He had the perfect profile. Classic cheekbone structure. Strong jaw. Perfect aquiline nose. She smiled, barely resisted the urge to reach out and trace those handsome features. Gorgeous blond hair and amazing blue eyes. Derrick's face had been more rugged but equally handsome. Her heart squeezed at the memory of him.

Sometimes, when she thought about it, lying in bed with Matt felt strange, considering this was the bed she had shared with Derrick and the fact that she loved them both.

Matt, she had loved her whole life. He was like part of her. Derrick was the unexpected. The total opposite of Matt. She had fallen in love with Derrick over the course of a few weeks. The journey had been fast and reckless. Exciting and forbidden. Fiercely hot and out of control.

Matt, on the other hand, was reliable and charming. Their journey had started when they were toddlers. They'd been best friends for as long as she could remember. They'd always had each other's backs. As kids they had promised each other that if they didn't find anyone else, they would get married and have a kid just to make their parents happy.

How she loved this man. She stared at him. Tamped down the need to wake him and tell him about the man in the car who had been watching her. But she didn't see the point. Right after that she'd gotten the call from the hospital about Helen Roberts. By the time she'd gotten home, taken care of the dog, and watered the plants, she'd convinced herself that she had likely imagined the trouble.

The man may have been some guy trying to flirt with her.

Now there was a stretch. But it wasn't completely out of the realm of possibility.

Maybe he'd been looking at someone else. She hadn't taken the time to glance around to see. Houser's words about Dempsey had been echoing in the back of her brain. So she'd just walked straight to where she'd parked, climbed into her Subaru and gotten the hell out of there.

But now, lying here in the dark in the same house where three bastards hired by Carson Dempsey had invaded and murdered her husband and left her damaged and broken, she had second thoughts.

She could not allow Matt to be hurt again. He'd been run off the road, crashed his car and suffered serious injuries the last time one of Dempsey's thugs went after him. Houser had said Dempsey had reached out to a *dark* source—about her. If he was up to something, she had to make sure no one she cared about was in the line of fire again.

She nestled closer to Matt, hugged his arm and pressed her face against his bare chest. She had only recently started rebuilding her personal life. She would not allow anyone to touch it. Not again.

This time she wasn't waiting around for Dempsey's thug to make a move. If he came around again, she would move first.

8

After the Murder

Thirteen Years Ago

Monday, November 20

Bauer Investigations
Church Street, Nashville, 10:00 a.m.

Louise sat in the chair facing Jerry Bauer's desk. He scanned his notes, flipped through the pages.

There were things she should say. Questions she should ask. But her brain refused to send the proper messages to her lips.

She had buried her precious daughter just over a month ago. As if fate was determined to finish her off, she had buried her dear husband a mere seventeen days ago.

How was she supposed to go on?

Air filled her lungs unexpectedly. She wished it would stop. The idea that her body would continue to support her living was an utter betrayal.

Louise wanted to die.

However fierce the desire, she was too much of a coward to take her life.

How very sad was that?

She had lost her precious, beautiful Lucy. She closed her eyes, unable to even think her name without suffering the agony that crushed all the way to her bones. The horror was unsurvivable, and yet here she sat, still breathing.

It was no wonder Scott had suffered a massive heart attack. She'd tried CPR. But he was gone. Like her, he hadn't wanted to stay in this life any longer. She prayed each night that an aneurysm or a heart attack would take her. But her damned heart continued to beat . . . continued to pound out the perfect rhythm for survival.

It should have been her who died.

Her fingers tightened on the chair arms to prevent fisting and then pounding against her chest. She suspected Jerry wouldn't know what to do if she fell apart in his office. The world expected certain things of the indomitable Lou Scott.

Only someone who had lost what she had would understand.

However strong a person was, there were some things they simply could not overcome.

Louise would not overcome this. She had no desire to. If she was brutally honest with herself, the only reason she accepted the idea of continuing to breathe was for the sole purpose of finding the person who had murdered her sweet Lucy.

She summoned her strength and asked, "Have you found anything at all?"

She should have said this a bit less sharply. After all, it was nearly Thanksgiving. Jerry had intended to take the whole week off but had come into his office today because she could not bear to wait another minute to speak with him. He had taken time away from his family to assuage her desperation.

Jerry stopped reviewing his notes and settled his gaze on hers. "I have great admiration for you and your work, Lou." He took a breath. "That said, I don't want to promise you something I cannot deliver."

This was such bullshit. "I don't need you to impress me," she snapped. "What I need is for you to find something I've missed. I'm compromised." She blinked back the burn of tears, damn it. "My emotions have betrayed me, causing me to be unreliable. I need details from someone unaffected. You have a stellar reputation, Jerry. Do not let me down."

Jesus Christ, he'd been on the case now for three weeks. Surely he had found something.

He braced his elbows on his desk and rested his chin on the tops of his hands for a moment as he considered her words. He nodded then. "Were you aware your daughter was working on a secret project?"

Louise frowned. "What sort of secret project?"

"I interviewed a number of her fellow students from Harpeth and learned they were assigned a senior thesis as a major part of their semester grade. Had Lucy spoken to you about this project?"

Louise's frown deepened as she tried to recall her most recent conversations with her precious daughter. "I don't recall her mentioning a thesis, but that wouldn't be unusual. Lucy is—" Louise moistened her lips. "Was an excellent student. She rarely asked her father or me for any help with assignments. So, I doubt she would have mentioned it."

He scrubbed a hand over his jaw as if hesitant to go on with whatever it was he had to say. "Her theme or subject for her thesis was the missing. As in missing persons, younger ones more precisely."

Uncertainty pricked at Louise. "I'm—was working on a story about the people who go missing in our own city. But she and I didn't speak of it. Lucy was a very busy young woman. She didn't have time to pay much attention to what I was doing."

"There's someone I think you should speak with."

He said this with such a veil of mystery, Louise wanted to reach across the desk and shake him. Could the man not just say whatever it was he'd discovered and be done with it?

"What does that mean?" she demanded.

"I found that Lucy had been talking with . . ." He hesitated for three beats. "With a man who works in social services."

"Are you suggesting she was involved in some way with this man?"

Jerry shook his head. "Not in an inappropriate way," he hastily assured her. "I was concerned about that, as well, when I first learned about him. But that wasn't the nature of their relationship, as far as I have discerned."

Relationship? Oh good God. "Who is he? Give me a name, and I will speak with him."

"Barton O'Sullivan. He's the director of social services in Davidson County."

Louise straightened, confusion and shock rushing through her veins. "Judge Ruth O'Sullivan's husband?"

Jerry nodded. "Yes. He insists he was helping Lucy with research."

Something inside Louise shifted. A strange sense of calm fell over her. "You leave Mr. O'Sullivan to me. Do you have anything else for me?"

"Not yet, but I will continue to dig for answers."

Louise stood, suddenly feeling steadier than she had in weeks. "Thank you. Let me know when you have anything else."

She exited the office.

Finally, a reason to want to keep breathing.

Whatever Barton O'Sullivan had done or been to her daughter, Louise would know the whole of it.

Even if it ruined them both.

9

Now

Wednesday, December 6

Warehouse Crime Scene
East Trinity Lane, Nashville, 9:30 a.m.

The warehouse was smaller than Finley had expected. She parked in the paved lot to wait for Houser. The building was an old one for sure. Two stories. Crumbling brick with big metal-framed windows, plenty of missing and broken panes. Situated in East Nashville within a mile of major thoroughfares like Ellington Parkway, Dickerson Road, and Interstate 65. Zoned for mixed-use retail space.

This was where Lucy Cagle's handbag had been found.

The idea that Lucy may have come here for some reason the night she died was as viable a scenario as any other. There had been no cameras in the area. No witnesses ever came forward from this neighborhood or any other. The image of her waiting in her car as Finley waited now flickered in Finley's mind. If Lucy had known Ian Johnson, they could have met here. The warehouse had been empty then as well.

But for that scenario to have legs, she needed to find a solid connection between Lucy and Ian. His disappearance around the time of her murder was not enough without some sort of proof they even knew each other.

Finley surveyed the structure. The demolition work had been stopped. A bulldozer and an excavator sat abandoned a few yards away. Part of the wall on the west side had been demoed. Bricks and other rubble lay in a pile. Yellow crime scene tape draped around the perimeter, giving the site a foreboding feel.

This sudden discovery of evidence all these years after the murder sparked a number of questions for Finley. Most of those questions were related to location. Lucy's body had been found more than a dozen miles away on Coventry Drive. Assuming she had not come to the warehouse for some reason, why bring her handbag all the way over here? Had the killer kept it as a souvenir? Tucked it away for safekeeping and then forgotten it? This building had been empty for decades. Had he lived or worked nearby? Used the old warehouse as his private storage area? Lived here, as so many squatters reportedly had? If the latter were the case, why hadn't the police found anything else?

Then again, maybe they had and just weren't sharing yet. There were rules about sharing in every investigation. Houser had no obligation to immediately share new finds, but she had hoped he would do so a little more quickly than usual since they were friends.

If the situation were reversed, would she?

Probably not.

Enough said.

Houser's shiny silver sedan rolled up next to her dusty Subaru. How did the man keep his car so clean?

Finley got out and tucked her fob and cell into her back pockets, leaving her bag in the car. She tapped the door handle to lock it up before strolling to the front of Houser's vehicle.

"Sorry I'm late," he offered as he emerged. Houser wore his trademark suit. Dark trousers that fit snuggly as was fashionable for men his age. Same with the jacket. The charcoal color looked good on him.

Beneath the jacket he wore a sweater over a collared shirt. All of which was perfectly coordinated, as if he'd come to a fashion shoot rather than a possible crime scene.

"No worries." She glanced around. "There are a lot of houses and businesses around here. Was this place secure?" She flashed him a doubtful look. "Seems to me like anyone could have walked in and left that handbag." She gestured to the exterior of the warehouse. "I don't see any security cameras. But I do see lots of broken windows, making for easy access points."

He made a distasteful face. "You sound like a defense attorney."

Finley laughed. "Just pointing out the holes in your theory."

He tucked his hands into his trouser pockets. "So you're already convinced your client is innocent?"

"You're already convinced he's guilty?" she tossed back at him.

He lifted his shoulders, let them fall. "I don't know. Maybe I just want him to be guilty."

"Because he's not a good Catholic boy?"

His eyes narrowed and his brow lined with frustration or maybe impatience. "Why would I care about his religious status?"

She shrugged. "I don't know. I just remember googling you back when we first met, and there was some mention of you being Catholic. Maybe it was the photos from your older brother's wedding." Houser had been accompanied by a blonde female, but Finley hadn't found a photo in the lot that showed the woman's face. Honestly, she had no clue why she had even mentioned it. Maybe the jealousy ping she'd felt yesterday had her wondering why he wasn't married himself.

None of her business. Clearly her brain was not operating on all cylinders this morning. More coffee. She'd had one cup before getting caught up in a second review of the case file Houser had sent her yesterday, and then she'd lost track of time.

"We going in or what?" He jerked his head toward the warehouse. Obviously, she'd struck a nerve. "Just waiting for you to lead the way."

As she followed him to the entrance, she wondered if maybe it was the mention of weddings rather than religion that had hit a nerve.

Houser removed the tape that sealed the door and marked the warehouse as a crime scene. He unlocked the door and opened it, then gestured for her to go inside. All the windows, even the ones grimy from years of neglect, prevented the interior from being very dark. A good thing since the electrical supply would have been disconnected before demo started. The partially demoed wall on the west end also allowed extra light to filter in. Most of the missing brick had fallen from the second floor. Someone had added support on that side of the building to prevent the upper floor from falling down since the building was now a crime scene. Orange construction fencing had been installed to keep out the curious. Like that would actually work.

Unlike most newer warehouses, the floor was wood. The kind found in old gymnasiums. The floor was remarkably clean in spite of the current circumstances. Apparently, someone had kept the place swept out. She supposed the cleanup was necessary when the place went on the market. There were no shelves or leftover boxes or containers. The space was empty. This also made sense, she supposed, considering the sale. But why leave the purse and the cigarette butts behind?

"The purse was found in a janitor's closet." Houser headed toward the rear of the ground floor.

Finley followed. The closet was located beneath the staircase leading to the next floor. It was smaller than she had expected. Enough room for mops and brooms and the large sink that hung on the wall but not much more. A narrow door next to the sink stood open. The space beyond it was lined with shelves for storage.

"The purse was found on the top shelf."

"May I?" Finley indicated the small closet.

"Sure." He said nothing more. Just looked away, busying himself with surveying the space he had no doubt thoroughly inspected already.

Houser was apparently still miffed. Who knew the man was so sensitive about religion or wedding photos? Maybe he'd been engaged to the blonde and they'd broken up. Or maybe he'd left the church and didn't like talking about it. In her experience working with Houser, this was the first time she had found him to be so sensitive.

She stepped inside the tight space. The top shelf was above her head. "Who found the purse?"

"One of the construction team members."

"In here," she asked, "on that top shelf?" Sounded sketchy to Finley.

"The guy said he always goes through the buildings about to be demoed. Claims you find all sorts of things. Money, jewelry. His boss backed him up."

Okay. Finley could see that. "That explains how he found the purse, but what about the cigarette butts?"

"Down there." Houser pointed to the floor beneath the lowest shelf.

"Someone stood around in this little closet . . ." She turned all the way around. Four feet by six, maybe. "Long enough to smoke a cigarette or two?"

"Maybe smoking wasn't allowed, and he hid in here."

In a damned broom closet that anyone could have accessed?

"Come on, Houser," she argued. "This evidence is sounding thinner all the time. If you don't have prints or blood or something on the purse, I can't see how you expect to go the distance with this inquiry into Johnson."

Finley knew exactly how the DA would see it, and it would not be to Metro's advantage.

"We're doing all the necessary testing. We'll have the results back on the cigarette butts tomorrow. If your guy had nothing to do with Lucy Cagle's murder, he should be only too happy for us to rule him out."

He held up a hand when Finley would have reminded him of Johnson's reasons. "Yeah, I know his story, but I'm not so sure I believe him."

Finley made a noncommittal face. "I'll talk to him again, but no promises." She looked Houser straight in the eye. "Seriously, the handbag and the cigarette butts could have ended up here at different times. Anyone could have smoked a cigarette right here without having a clue that handbag was on the top shelf. This is a reach, Houser, and you know it."

"Maybe." He looked away. "Maybe not."

There was no question in her mind that Metro was pushing this in hopes of finally getting the goods on a Johnson. It was far too thin otherwise. Unless, as she'd already considered, there was something more Houser hadn't shared as of yet. Finley let the idea go for the moment. "I'd like to see the evidence."

"I can maybe arrange that. We'll have to do it at the lab since it's still there."

"I appreciate it." She shook her head. "But I'll say it again, Houser, unless you found some sort of evidence on or inside the handbag itself that connects it to Johnson, you're going to have a hell of a time selling this to Briggs. It would have been too easy for anyone to put that purse here at any point over the past thirteen years."

"I get that too." He exhaled a big breath, clearly weary of the discussion.

"What's the deal?" Finley watched his face closely for tells. "You got a personal beef with Johnson?" This whole thing felt completely un-Houser-like.

He considered her for long enough to have her wondering if he intended to answer one way or the other. Finally he said, "People who make their way in this life by cheating and hurting other people just rub me the wrong way. You should do more research. See who the Johnson family really is. You might not like what you find."

"I already know I won't," she confessed. She didn't like the vibe Ray Johnson exuded. But that wasn't the issue here. The question was whether he was guilty of murder. "But it's not my job to like him. My job is to find the truth."

Houser made a sound of disbelief and shook his head. "You're the only member of a criminal defense team I've ever met who wanted to know the truth about a client."

"You'd think more cops would like me." She walked out of the cramped closet, took a breath.

"If it helps," Houser said, joining her, "I like you." He chuckled. "I mean, better than I like most lawyers."

A few months ago, she would have told him she wasn't a lawyer anymore. But her probation had been lifted. She could practice law again if she chose. She was more pleased about the decision than she'd anticipated. Maybe deep down she really, really was excited about the run for DA. Admitting that her former ambition was back kind of felt premature, but maybe it had returned.

"Speaking of which," he went on, "I saw a mention of you on the local stories page in the *Tennessean* this morning."

"About me?" She put a hand to her chest in anticipation of having to protect her vital parts from some unknown attack. This couldn't be good.

"Maureen Downey says you're running for Davidson County district attorney." He grinned. "I hope it's true that you're finally making the official announcement."

She had known that off the cuff response would come back to haunt her. Not quite so quickly, but there it was. "I have not made the *official* announcement per se, but I did agree that she could quote me on the possibility."

"Guess you have now."

Apparently so. She would be hearing about that from the Judge and her father . . . not to mention Jack.

"You'll let me know when I can see the purse," she reminded Houser, shifting the subject back to the case.

"Sure. But I'm curious how you think it will help with your client."

"Maybe it won't. But the things a woman carries in her purse say something about who she is, where she's going at any given time. You'd be surprised what you can learn from a tube of lip gloss."

He visibly relaxed the slightest bit. "Then I'll be sure to get you in. I could use a reading on what Lucy was up to at the time of her murder."

"Her cell phone was never found." Finley glanced around. "I'm surprised it wasn't with her purse."

"There was nothing else belonging to her in this building."

Finley surveyed the floor. "What about in the crawl space? Since the structure isn't on a slab, there could be some space under there."

Houser nodded. "It sits about two feet off the ground in the back and maybe ten inches in front. There's nothing down there, trust me. We had guys under there as well."

"Good to know you're being thorough."

"Anything else you want to see?" He spread his arms apart to indicate the building at large.

"I'm here, I might as well go upstairs."

Houser led the way. "There's no attic. The ceiling up here is vaulted."

"What's your lieutenant saying about this case?"

"He thinks we won't have enough to charge Johnson or anyone else." He walked to the center of the enormous space, looked around as if he hadn't been here before. "Like me, he wishes."

Finley scrutinized the dingy, cracked plaster walls that may have once been white. The wood floor was a duplicate of the one downstairs. Up here, instead of plaster on the ceiling, there was more wood. The structure would have made nice condos. Too bad it was being demolished rather than renovated.

Her gaze landed on Houser once more. "Since you've repeatedly reminded me how bad the Johnson family is, tell me what I need to know beyond what I might find on the net or in another review of your case file. Save me the trouble of digging deeper into the family history."

He walked toward her, his face serious, set in stone. "The old man, Raymond Senior, took his father's real estate holdings and created a nice-size development empire. He bought up property dirt cheap, then hung on to it until the value in the area went through the roof. He had that kind of patience. There have been rumors of rent gouging. The storage and transport of everything from stolen goods to drugs and guns. Even people."

Finley held up her hands. "But none of the rumors were ever substantiated."

Houser looked away. Took a breath. "True, but here's a perfect example of how they've gotten away with their dirty deeds all these years. About fifteen years ago one of his low-rent motels was connected to prostitution, but the whole thing ended up being put on the manager. The dumbass copped to charges and insisted the Johnsons knew nothing of his extracurricular activities. The manager's wife and kids got a nice house in a nice neighborhood and a new SUV, while dumbass got a few years in jail. They're all living happily ever after now with the ex-con running another motel for the Johnson family. I can give you half a dozen more examples very similar to that one."

"The Johnsons are organized crime." This wasn't new to Finley. She'd found the rumors and suggestions. Bauer, Jack, and her own father had confirmed as much. The PI, Bauer, had mentioned that Louise Cagle had been working the human trafficking angle in the area. If Lucy knew this, and Bauer believed she had, she would have been going after that angle as well. Had she found it in Ian Johnson or his family, or both?

The idea only reinforced Finley's feelings about their new client, and none were good.

"They are," Houser agreed. "But they don't play by the usual rules. The old man made his own rules as he went along. He's not the richest organized crime boss in the area, but he's the old guard. No one messes with him, because he's ruthless. There are rumors of torture and murder when it came to the competition."

"But now he's dying," Finley pointed out.

"He's dying, and the wolves smell blood in the air."

Finley got it. "They're all wondering if Ray is up to the job of taking over for real or if there's a chance someone can take him out."

"Exactly. If Ray had something to do with Lucy's murder, we may be running out of time to prove it and see that he pays the price."

"On the other hand," she countered, "if a competitor wants Ray out of the way, what better means than to see that he's charged with murder by stashing evidence at one of his properties."

"I'm telling you," Houser argued, "this family is involved."

Finley studied him a moment. "What's your connection to Lucy Cagle?"

He blinked, blanked his face. "I don't know what you mean."

She decided then and there that his earlier prickliness hadn't been about religion or weddings. It was about this case.

"This is a flimsy case, to say the least," she said straight up. "We both know it. But you're pressing like you've got this one nailed. There has to be more evidence than you've told me about or a compelling personal connection. Trust me," she reminded him, "no one is more familiar with the combination of personal and murder than me."

He stared at her for a bit before he spoke. "She was my girlfriend."

Finley's instincts were on point. She bit back the first response that rushed to the tip of her tongue—like the fact that he could have told her this. If she waited a few minutes, maybe it wouldn't come out like an accusation. "I've been hoping to find details like this. Hard to do when there's no family left and any social media she had is long gone."

Houser stared at the floor, hands on hips. "It was a long time ago. She was seventeen, I was nineteen. She had bigger plans, and I thought we were meant to be together forever."

Oh hell. "She was the blonde with you at your brother's wedding."

He nodded. "It was immature of me. I thought I had my life all figured out and she was part of it." A big breath blasted out of him. "I was wrong."

"I'm assuming you weren't still together when she was murdered?"

He shook his head, laughed softly. "You know, most kids at that age are totally focused on social life and sex and anything but the future. That wasn't the case with us. The future was all we talked about. Except, she had a different plan from mine." He gave a nod. "In the end, she moved on, and I was a little slower on the uptake."

Now a missing piece about her detective friend fell into place. "Was Lucy part of the reason you decided on law enforcement rather than medicine like the rest of your family?"

"Yeah." He gave a sad smile. "I could never get past the idea that her murder was unsolved. I wanted to be the detective who prevented cases like Lucy's from going cold. When this piece of evidence appeared out of the blue, I felt like I had the chance I'd been waiting for to find her killer."

"I take it your lieutenant doesn't know about your relationship with Lucy."

"No. He does not, and I would like to keep it that way."

Finley held up her hands. "He won't hear it from me." She was the last person to judge anyone about personal involvement.

"Thanks."

"Okay." She took a breath. "We can't be standing around here like this if we want to solve Lucy's murder."

His eyes told her just how grateful he was that she understood. "I'll get an appointment with the lab for us to view the evidence."

"Great. Be prepared to tell me all about Lucy—no exceptions."

"I will be happy to tell you all I know."

Now if only her new client would do the same.

10

Johnson Development Group
Hillsboro Circle, Nashville, 10:30 a.m.

Finley parked in the small lot that fronted Ray Johnson's office. The building was an older one tucked in among dozens of other offices and various retail spaces where Hillsboro Circle met Hillsboro Drive. She spotted the black BMW he drove parked in the narrow alley next to the building. He was here. Good. She preferred surprise visits, so she hadn't called.

More than a cold call on Johnson, she desperately wished she could talk to Lucy's mother. But no one seemed to know what had become of her.

Finley finished off the coffee she'd grabbed at a drive-through and tucked the empty cup into the holder on the console. According to what she knew about Louise Cagle's movements after her daughter's murder, she had hired Bauer Investigations in early November thirteen years ago. Nearly a month of waiting for the police to come up with something and the sudden loss of her husband had been all she could tolerate. If Bauer had been any more successful, there was no record of it, and he hadn't admitted as much.

Louise "Lou" Cagle/Scott had gone into seclusion or left this world less than a month after hiring the PI. Why then? Why not give the respected private investigator more time? Why not continue prodding the police? Finley needed to understand why Cagle had made that decision, and so far no one seemed to know the answer.

It was often said that disappearing completely was impossible with all the tracing ability available today. But like Maureen Downey had pointed out, if anyone knew how, it was Louise.

Finley reached for her bag, but her cell vibrating on the console caused her to grab it instead. Maybe it was finally a return call from Jessica, Maureen Downey's daughter. She checked the screen. No such luck.

Matt.

She accepted the call, looking forward to hearing his voice and at the same time worrying that something had happened. "Hey."

"Hey," he said back, his calm, deep voice making her smile. "Your name is trending around here."

Finley rolled her eyes. "Great."

"Did you really tell Maureen Downey you were running?"

The humor in his tone told her he was teasing. Sadly, he wasn't far off the mark. "I didn't say it exactly, but I may have alluded to the possibility in a moment of weakness. What can I say? I wanted information from her, and I felt compelled to give her something."

"Ah, even the slightest hint can come back to bite you when uttered aloud with a career reporter in the room."

"I guess I just don't have your prowess when it comes to the press. You'll have to teach me."

"I can do that."

Even this—a simple phone call from Matt—made her ridiculously happy these days.

A woman, young, sharply dressed and bearing a black briefcase, exited the Johnson offices. Not anyone Finley recognized. A client, maybe. One of his real estate agents, possibly.

"I should go. I'm at Ray Johnson's office for an impromptu visit."

"Give him hell, Fin. Make him tell you all his secrets."

Her smile tugged wider. "Don't worry. I plan to."

"See you later."

"For sure." She ended the call and tucked her phone into her bag. It had been a while since she'd wanted to go home this early in the day. Most of the time, work consumed her, and she only went home when there was nothing more she could do. But these days she couldn't wait to get home . . . to Matt. It felt good to actually feel a full range of emotions again.

Derrick immediately flashed in her mind. Not since she lost him had she felt anything even remotely like this. Though she still missed him, she knew deep in her soul that he would want her to move on.

Finley emerged from her Subaru and slung her bag on her shoulder. The sky was a clear blue. No humidity. Crisp air. She drew in a deep breath. She'd forgotten how much she liked this time of year. Feeling another smile stretch across her face, she headed for the entrance of their new client's place of business. Actually, he owned an array of properties, but this was the one where he conducted his affairs. At least the part that fell within the boundaries of the law.

A bell overhead jingled as she pushed through the door. The lobby was average in size, vintage black-and-white tile on the floor. Wood paneling on the walls. A couple of windows sporting blinds. Formed plastic chairs that looked less than comfortable. A wooden desk from last century sat next to the cased opening leading to the suite of offices beyond the lobby. At that desk sat a young woman, redhead, lots of makeup, and with way too much cleavage on display. A living, breathing cliché.

The woman's gaze skimmed Finley from head to toe, taking in her navy trousers and jacket, conservative pale-blue blouse buttoned to just below her throat and accompanied by a dark-blue sweater vest. Navy was Finley's other go-to color.

The redhead smiled. "Good morning. Welcome to the Johnson Development Group. How may I help you this morning?"

"Good morning." Finley stepped closer to the desk. "I'm Finley O'Sullivan. I'm here to see Mr. Johnson."

The woman—Sylvia, according to the nameplate on her desk—glanced at her desk calendar, the paper kind. "Is he expecting you?"

"No," Finley confessed. "I was in the neighborhood and thought we could catch up."

Sylvia blinked. "I'll check with him to see if he has some time available for you." She rose from her chair and walked into the corridor. Her turquoise dress fit like a glove and showed off a very nice, very taut figure.

Finley sighed. She really needed to start working out again.

Maybe one day.

Sylvia returned to the lobby. "Ray said you should come on into his office." She indicated the corridor. "The door at the end of the hall."

"Thank you."

Finley started in that direction, and the door at the end of the corridor opened. Ray Johnson smiled broadly at her. "Why, good morning, Ms. O'Sullivan."

"Good morning."

Since he remained near the door, she was forced to sidle past him to get into his office. No doubt this was one of his "I'm in charge" tactics. Either that or he was a perv who wanted her body to brush his.

Finley suspected it might be both.

"To what do I owe this pleasure?" he asked as he strode across his office.

The room had probably once been two offices, but he'd made one large space out of the two. Beige carpet. More wood paneling and no windows. Apparently, he didn't want to risk anyone peeking in at him or having an unnecessary access point. Only a man with something to hide was that paranoid.

"I wanted to go over a few things with you," Finley said as she waited for him to round his desk.

He gave her a nod. "All right, then. Have a seat."

She settled into the one chair in front of his desk. Placed her bag on the floor at her feet. He dropped into his chair and braced his forearms on his desk. Ready to do battle.

"I'm all yours," he said with a wicked grin.

"Tell me about some of your ongoing projects."

Confusion flashed on his face before he was able to banish it. "Let's see." His brow lined in thought as he surveyed a whiteboard mounted on the wall to the right of his desk. "If you'll have a gander at my board, you can see we're working with a partner developer on a new restaurant on McKennie Avenue next to the Wash—that former car wash turned eatery. Then we have a small mixed-use development over on the north side of the city. Several smaller office spaces scattered all over Nashville and Brentwood." His attention settled fully back on her then. "Of course, we have more of those older warehouses we're hoping to offload to other developers."

"Impressive." Finley reached into her bag and retrieved her notepad and a pen. "I'd like you to walk me through a few things."

"As I said, I'm all yours." He leaned back in his chair.

"On the day of Lucy Cagle's murder," she began, "take me through your schedule to the best of your memory."

He stared at her for a long moment, then nodded. "At the time I wasn't aware it was a particularly important day, so my memory may not be perfect. But after Ian disappeared and the police started asking questions, I made it a point to go back and look at my calendar."

Finley waited, pen ready, for him to go on.

"Pop and I were here, at the office, that morning." He glanced around the room. "This was his office back then." He pointed to the wall of framed photos and certificates. "Those are some of the bigger deals he made over the years. A few of the awards from the city and the Chamber of Commerce he received. He did a lot of good for this city in his time."

"How's he doing?" Finley asked. He was dying. The more appropriate question would have been "Is he comfortable," but his son might not appreciate the pointed query.

"As best as can be expected, I guess. The doc says he's got maybe another couple of months at best. As long as we can keep him out of pain until then, we'll be doing all we can for him."

"I'm sure he appreciates that you're here for him."

A nod, then, "He's still grieving losing Ian." Anger flared on his face. "I don't get how the bastard could do that to him. Just disappear and never come back."

"Do you think his decision to disappear was related to one or more of your business deals?"

He exhaled a big breath. "It's possible. Pop made some backroom deals with some very bad people back in the day. I've tried to separate from that kind of business over the past few years. They say we can shed our past like a snake sheds its skin, but it's not as easy as it sounds. Trust me."

"So the day Lucy was murdered, you began your day here in the office."

"I did. We had a conference call with a couple of builders. Went over upcoming jobs that were scheduled for completion. It was a Friday, so we generally made it a light workday."

"Did you hear from Ian that day?"

"When I went home that evening, he was getting ready for a date. Pop was pissed at him for not showing up at the office. My wife—at the time—and I left about seven to go to dinner. The two of them, Pop and Ian, were having a big-ass fight in the living room." He shrugged. "Wasn't unusual, so my wife and I didn't think much of it."

"Where did you go to dinner?"

"Jimmy Kelly's Steakhouse." He grinned. "The best steak in Music City."

Finley knew the place. Who didn't? It was a Nashville icon.

"Our waiter—that's what Shelia and I called him—is still there. Teddy Withers. I always thought he had a thing for my wife, but turns out he prefers men. I guess that's why I like him so much. I can take the women I date there for dinner and never worry about the waiter."

Finley lifted an eyebrow at him. "Is there a story that goes with that fear?" Paranoia, really, but she doubted he would have appreciated her analysis.

He made a face, laughed. "Yeah. I took my girlfriend—the one before my wife, ex-wife—to Skull's Rainbow Room, and she went to the bathroom in the middle of the meal, and when she stayed gone too long, I went to check on her. She was in the damned ladies' room getting it on with our waiter." He shook his head and muttered "Damn bitch."

"You were in the office most of the day," Finley said, moving on. "Then went home and took your then wife to dinner. What time did you go home?"

"We were home by eleven. We had dinner at Jimmy Kelly's and then drinks at the Corner Bar on Elliston and Twenty-Second."

"How were things when you arrived back home?"

"The house was quiet, and we presumed everyone was either out or in bed. We went to bed and . . . well . . ." He smirked. "You know."

Yeah.

"But you can't confirm your father or your brother were home."

"I cannot."

"The three of you, four counting your then wife, lived in the house. The same house you and your father live in now."

"That's right. My daughter was there, too, she was just a toddler then. It was the homeplace. My grandfather built the house for more than one generation to share. The way it used to be."

Finley would throw herself off a bridge if she had to share a house with the Judge.

"You have children?" She knew the answer already but liked hearing her interviewee's version of the answer.

"Two daughters, one in high school, one in middle school. They live with my ex."

"Going back to the day after Lucy was murdered, when did you see Ian or your father next?"

"At breakfast. We have breakfast together—or we did—every morning."

"How did Ian seem?"

"Weird. Off." He made a noncommittal face. "Not himself. Hung over, maybe."

"What about your father?"

"He was his usual grumpy self. Pop has never been a morning person, though he has been up by six every day of his life. Anyone who sleeps beyond that hour is plain lazy, in his opinion. He used to kick me and Ian out of bed at six oh one if we weren't up."

Sounded like a total asshole. Finley kept that to herself.

"Ian never mentioned anything about Lucy or that night?"

"Nope. He just acted strange after that." Raymond's forehead puckered. "But I'll tell you like I told the cops back then, as far as I know, he never even knew her. None of us did. To our knowledge, she was just another rich girl who got herself murdered."

Finley chose to ignore his insensitive conclusion about Lucy. "You said Ian was acting strange. How do you mean?"

"Too quiet. Withdrawn. Combative. I thought it was drugs. But I got one of those home drug tests and made him take it, and nothing showed up. He never acted the same after that. Three days later he was gone. Pop and I searched far and wide for him and never found him. He was just gone."

He wasn't the only one who disappeared after that case. Lucy's mother seemed to have vanished without a trace as well. Coincidence? Maybe.

"But you're certain he never said anything. Never gave any indication that he knew Lucy. Her murder was on the news. You didn't notice a particular reaction during any of that?"

"I can't say that I did. I was busy doing my work and his. Trying to keep him out of trouble with Pop."

"After he disappeared, did you find anything in his room that suggested he knew Lucy or that he had other concerns that might have prompted his disappearing act?"

He shook his head. "Nothing. After he'd been gone for a while, we tore his room apart. Found nothing. We even hired a PI, and he got nothing. Not a single lead. Ian just vanished . . . like into thin air."

Except he didn't. Dead or alive, he was somewhere.

"Did you find the name of that PI for me?"

He snapped his fingers. "Damn it. I forgot to look into that." He pressed a hand to his chest. "I swear I will get the information to you."

Mildly annoyed but moving on, Finley asked, "Do you believe your brother—who was, according to your earlier statement, twenty-three at the time—would have been capable of cold-blooded murder?"

"Maybe. I can't say for sure. You know, I think he saw me as the enemy since I was always following Pop's rules and doing the work. He didn't share a lot with me. Frankly, we weren't that close."

"What about friends? Did he have friends he shared his personal thoughts with?"

She'd asked him to prepare a list. So far, he hadn't done much of what she'd asked. Just further proof he wasn't really concerned about where this investigation was going. To her knowledge she didn't owe the IRS anything beyond what she'd paid already. That said, if she received a letter indicating she did, she would damned well do all necessary to prove she didn't. His lack of concern was overplayed, to say the least.

Ray tugged open the center drawer of his desk. "I did remember to make a list to give to you." He pulled out a notepad and tore a page free, passed it across his desk. "Those are the three guys that Ian hung with. The one guy—Aaron—he died. But back then—after Ian went missing—they told us nothing. Maybe now they might share more. Not with me, God knows I've tried over the years. But maybe with you."

Finley glanced at the names on the list. The same ones Houser had mentioned. Addresses, workplaces and phone numbers were included. She tucked it into her bag. "I'll see what I can do."

"I hear you and that cop were at the warehouse this morning."

The memory of the man she'd seen watching her last evening pinged her senses. "Do you have someone following me, Mr. Johnson?"

"Ray," he reminded her. "And no, I do not. One of the neighboring businesses saw people there. The cop's car he recognized. Yours he didn't, but I knew it was yours when he described it." He stared at her a moment. "What's your take on this evidence they found?"

"Flimsy at best." She saw no reason not to tell him how she felt. He was the client, after all.

He chuckled. "Yeah. Definitely flimsy."

She stood. "If you recall anything else from the time frame surrounding Lucy's death, let me know."

"Be careful out there," he said when she started to turn away.

She paused, locked her gaze with his and held it for a bit. "I can take care of myself, Ray."

He grinned. "Yeah, I heard about you. But still, be careful. There's some twisted MF'ers out there."

He was right about that.

Most likely he was one of them.

Rollins and Downey, Attorneys at Law
Lea Avenue, Nashville, 11:40 a.m.

Finley decided she wasn't waiting for Jessica Downey to return her call.

The firm's receptionist had attempted to put Finley off, but she had stood her ground. She wasn't leaving until she spoke with Downey. A friend at the DMV had provided the information on the car Downey drove, and that car was in the parking lot. Unless she had left with someone else, the woman was here.

The building that housed the small firm was more or less basic. Plain. Not the place one would expect to find a graduate of Harpeth, but then the real story was in the work, and Jessica Downey did good work. Lots of pro bono and lots of causes that others didn't so easily want to take up. But certainly excellent credentials for seeking political office.

Jessica Downey appeared in the small lobby. "Ms. O'Sullivan, you may follow me to my office."

About time. Finley pushed to her feet and followed the other woman. Like her mother, Jessica was tall and slim. Her blonde hair was longer. Also, like her mother, she dressed impeccably. Sleek sweater dress in a creamy white with matching boots. She was only a year younger than Finley, but they hadn't attended the same school or university, so they didn't know each other beyond their legal reputations.

Downey gestured to a chair and resumed her seat behind her desk. "How can I help you?"

Finley took the seat and studied the other woman for a moment. "I'm sure your mother told you I would be calling."

"She also told me I shouldn't waste my time speaking with you."

Finley appreciated a straightforward response. "Well, not to worry, I'll be brief. Your mother said you and Lucy were best friends."

"We were until she was too busy with other people to have time for me."

There was an unexpected answer. "When did this happen?"

"Early September." Jessica lifted her chin defiantly. "After the tragedy, my parents decided that it would be in my best interest if they didn't mention my and Lucy's relationship or our recent breakup. When my mother spoke to Lucy's mother about the situation, she understood. Louise knew I would never hurt Lucy or conceal information about her that could have helped the investigation. They both felt that having the police treat me like a suspect would have been too much."

"Who were these other people who kept Lucy so busy?" Finley asked, going directly to the important details.

Downey tucked her hair behind her ears. "I have no idea. I can only tell you that she broke every date we planned. Never returned my calls. It was like she was obsessed with someone new. One of our other friends thought maybe she had a new boyfriend. I really don't know. I only know that she ghosted me before ghosting was a thing."

"Who were her other close friends?" It never hurt to get a second or third opinion.

"Gwyneth Larson—Garrison now. Also, there's Natalie Williams."

Finley nodded. "How long were the two of you best friends?"

"Since before we were toddlers. Our parents were friends and colleagues, so we spent a lot of time together." She blinked rapidly, then stared out the window into the lackluster view of a parking garage. "Maybe we grew tired of each other or outgrew each other." She shifted her gaze back to Finley. "Lucy was a wonderful young woman, but she was driven. I was—still am—but not like Lucy. She was very much like Louise. She would have done anything to accomplish her goal. I suppose I weighed her down with my reticence."

The stark emotion that had stolen onto Jessica's face underscored the painful truth in her words.

"I appreciate your honesty," Finley said. "I'm certain that no matter your differences, you want to see her killer brought to justice."

"Of course." She cleared the emotion away. "But the way I hear it, your firm is representing the wrong side."

"I'm looking for the truth," Finley assured her. "I intend to find it."

"I hope you do find it, really I do."

Finley decided one more push was in order. "You don't recall anything that might help with the investigation into her murder? A name she may have mentioned. Something she did that was not normal for her."

For a beat, then two, Jessica didn't respond. Finally, she said, "I followed her once. When she blew me off. She met with an older man." She glanced away, cleared her throat. "Someone around our parents' ages."

The idea that she was likely talking about Finley's father made her ill.

"After she died, I was sick that I hadn't told anyone about what I saw. Finally, I broke down and told my mother. But she told me not to worry. The man I had seen was helping Lucy with a project. He wasn't the one who hurt her."

Shaking inside despite her best efforts, Finley retrieved a business card and passed it to the other woman. "I hope you'll call me if you think of anything else that might be useful in my search for the facts."

Jessica studied the card, then nodded. "I will."

Finley thanked her and left the office. She managed to keep her emotions to herself until she was in her car and driving away. Then she screamed.

Maureen Downey had known about Finley's father, and she hadn't said a word.

Was there one damned person in all this that she could really trust? Apparently not.

11

Bart O'Sullivan had chosen this particular diner because the music was loud and it was off the beaten path. More importantly, they weren't likely to run into anyone who recognized either of them.

Bart scanned the tables in the country-style diner. He spotted Maureen and headed in her direction. Menus and sweating water glasses waited on the table.

"Good to see you." He pulled out a chair and sat down. It wasn't actually good. He was well aware this was about Finley and the investigation. God almighty, to have lived through this nightmare once was bad enough.

"I wish I could say the same," Maureen snapped as she waved down a waitress, "You eating?"

Bart shook his head. "No thanks. I'll just have the water."

He couldn't possibly eat. Not if his life depended upon it. He waited patiently while she ordered a Cobb salad with dressing on the side. When the waitress had gone, Maureen settled her attention on him once more. "Your daughter came to see me."

He restrained his irritation. Being unkind wouldn't help anyone. "I wondered about your source, since you published that tidbit about her potential run for DA."

He struggled not to allow his frustration to show. He was confident Finley had not been ready to make her consideration public. But that was Maureen's way. She liked getting ahead of the crowd. Her ambition was the reason she remained managing editor of a paper like the *Tennessean* after all these years.

"She asked about Lucy."

The idea made him sick to his stomach. "Her firm is representing Ray Johnson."

"I know."

The resignation in her eyes matched the worry and defeat warring in Bart's gut. How had this been set in motion again after all these years? It was supposed to be over. How the hell had it happened?

"What did you tell her?" Maureen asked.

He forced away the worry gnawing at him. "I told her the truth." He reached for his water. "Most of it anyway. Lucy wanted a big story. She came to me for help." He gulped down a third of the glass in hope it would slow the swelling in his throat. The emotion rising high enough to choke him from the inside out.

"This is Bauer's fault," she grumbled. She glanced around as if she feared the man would appear out of the crowd gathering in the popular diner.

The waitress arrived with Maureen's salad. The waitress smiled and asked Bart if he was sure he didn't want anything, and once more he declined. How could he eat with this business hanging over his head? How could *she*? For heaven's sake, it was a disaster.

"He was only doing his job." Bart focused on controlling his runaway heart rate. He had to be calm. Had to behave as he always did; otherwise, Finley would recognize there was something wrong. He knew his daughter. She would see through him in an instant. Dear God, what would he do then?

"Bauer's one job was to find Lucy's killer." Maureen stabbed her fork into the salad. "He failed. If he had done his job . . . we wouldn't be in this situation."

Bart clenched his jaw. He swallowed the thickening lump climbing up his throat. Drew in a tight breath. "But we are . . . in this situation." He closed his eyes and fought to evict the demons clawing at his thoughts.

"I wish Lou were here," Maureen said, emotion making her voice unsteady. "But I don't blame her for what she did. How was she supposed to resume her life after it was all gone? Even her work couldn't balance it out."

"If I had lost my daughter—my only child—and then my wife . . . ," he said, his voice sounding distant, disconnected. He rallied his composure before he lost complete control. "Nothing could possibly balance out that loss."

Maureen nodded. She placed her fork next to her salad as if she'd lost her appetite. "I don't know what I would do if something happened to my Jessica."

"Therein lies my rub," he said with something that sounded and felt far too much like defeat. "My daughter is representing that scumbag, and I am terrified that it will all blow up and she'll be hurt. I can only hope for her sake and by some miracle she won't be successful."

"She's never failed before," Maureen argued. "What are the odds she will this time?" She closed her eyes a moment, shook her head. "How did this happen? Of all the law firms in Nashville, why did the bastard have to choose Jack Finnegan?"

"Anyone who's smart wants Jack," Bart confessed, sick to death of the worry throttling through him. "He's the best."

"As long as he's sober," Maureen amended.

"He's sober." Bart braced his elbows on the table and clasped his hands. Rather than pray, which would do no good whatsoever, he pressed his fists to his lips. When he could speak, he said what he knew to be a fact. "And you're right. Finley will not stop until she finds the truth, and then—"

"No," Maureen argued. "We have to find a way to make sure that doesn't happen."

He turned his hands up, aghast. "How do you propose we do that?"

"Every good newswoman knows how to turn most any situation around."

What on God's earth was she suggesting? He waited for her to go on. His anxiety far too out of control now to attempt a response.

"When you want to cover something up or keep it under wraps, you create a diversion. You ensure the players don't have time to focus on the things you want to stay hidden, so you give them someplace else to focus. You direct the narrative."

Bart was afraid to ask what she had in mind, but he recognized it was necessary. "Meaning?"

"I'm going to fuel the speculation I started about your daughter running against Briggs—she admitted as much, so I feel well within my right to move on it. I know Briggs, and he'll have no choice but to react. The fire will catch fast, believe me. Finley won't have as much time to devote to the Johnson case. She'll be too busy trying to control the flames."

Bart laughed, no matter that inside he wanted to cry. "You have no idea with whom you're dealing. Nothing—do you hear me, Maureen?— nothing will stop her."

Maureen stared at him for a long time without saying a word. What was there to say? The loud music and hustle and bustle of people faded into the background.

"Then," she finally said, "what you're telling me is that we're fucked."

He nodded. "Without question."

12

Stratton Residence
Sigler Street, Nashville, 12:50 p.m.

The former Mrs. Ray Johnson, Shelia Stratton, lived in a high-end urban condo on Maverick Row just steps from the Gulch and Music Row. She drove a top-of-the-line Mercedes and, judging by the outfit she wore, shopped at only the finest boutiques in the city. A sleek jumpsuit, white, silk perhaps, that draped her toned, tanned body like it had been made just for her.

Was everyone working out except Finley?

"Well, now," Stratton said before blowing out a plume of cigarette smoke. "That really was a long time ago." She tapped out the cigarette in a nearby ashtray, ran her red-nailed fingers through her long blonde tresses. "You know, I was a stripper when Ray and I met." She smoothed a hand over the silk draping her thigh. "I still could be if I wanted to."

"I'm sure you could." Finley smiled. "So, Ray mentioned that you went to dinner," she prompted. She couldn't believe Ray hadn't called and coached the woman. Or maybe he had, and Shelia was just trying to play it cool and act as if he hadn't.

"Oh yes." She smiled. "I remember now. We had dinner at Jimmy Kelly's." She pursed her lips in thought. "We may have gone for drinks after. We usually did, but I can't say where. I just can't remember." She grinned sheepishly. "I generally had too much to drink. But I don't do that anymore." She gestured to the Bible lying on the coffee table in front of the white leather sofa in which she reclined. "I found Jesus, and my life has completely changed. That's why I don't do the shows anymore. And the girls, of course. I have the girls to consider."

Finley nodded. "That's wonderful."

Shelia held out her left hand and showed off a massive diamond ring. "In fact, I found myself a preacher man."

This preacher must make a lot of money. Finley banished the thought and asked, "When's the wedding?"

"Not until June. We're waiting for school to be out. Then the girls will be with their father for the summer, and I'm honeymooning in Paris!" She stared at her ring.

"Were you close to Ian?" Finley prodded, drawing her back to the moment.

Shelia stared at Finley then. The lady wore some serious eye makeup. She batted those heavily mascaraed lashes as if Finley had said the words aloud. "Not really." She made a cutesy face. "He was way more handsome than Ray but too young for me. Besides, he wasn't really into the business, and I needed a man with a plan. No deadbeats for me."

Of course.

"Do you remember the Lucy Cagle murder case?" So far, the woman had been no help at all. But she had confirmed her husband's alibi. Sort of.

"Oh." She pressed a hand to her throat. "It was just awful. Truly awful. And she was so sweet."

Tension fired through Finley. "You knew Lucy Cagle?"

"I did—well . . ." She made another of those cutesy faces. "I didn't really *know* her. She was the tour guide when I visited Harpeth. I wanted to get my little Rayelynn signed up early. She was already showing off her genius at just two years old." She waved a hand and rolled her eyes.

"Rayna hadn't been born yet. Anyway Lucy was just the sweetest thing. So helpful. She did some babysitting for me a few times."

Finley steadied herself after that jolt. "Really?"

"Don't tell Ray. He didn't like me leaving our little girl with anyone else. But she came over to the house . . ." Shelia inclined her head and thought for a moment. "Three or four times that September." She frowned. "Before she was murdered. Poor thing."

"She probably met Ian when she was there," Finley suggested.

Stratton looked as if she'd just swallowed a bug. Her hand was back at her throat. A pallor slid over her face. "I don't think so. Ian would likely have been at work. There was never anyone at home except Rayelynn when Lucy was there."

"Your little girl must have loved her," Finley said with a bright smile, in hopes of allaying the woman's sudden uncertainty.

"Oh she did," Stratton agreed. "She adored Lucy." Worry worked its way onto her face. "I hope you won't mention this to Ray. He would be furious. Talking about Lucy is forbidden. You being his lawyer, I'm sure you understand. Besides, I had a little side gig going at the time, and he doesn't need to know about that."

"Side gig?" Finley's eyebrows arched upward.

Shelia blushed. "A secret friend."

Finley figured as much. "There's no need for me to mention our conversation to Ray. Did Ray ever leave sensitive documents in his home office?"

Shelia waved her off. "You don't need to worry about that. No one was allowed in Ray's home office. Never. I made sure Lucy knew that. He would go crazy if anyone did. Even when the kids were older, they were never allowed near that door."

All of which meant Lucy had unfettered access to Ray Johnson's home office at least three or four times before her murder.

How had no one else found this connection to the Johnson family?

Cagle Residence
Murfreesboro Road, Franklin, 2:00 p.m.

Finley had caught Downey as she returned to her office after a lunch meeting. She had hesitated at first but in the end caved and provided Finley with the keys to the Cagle house so she could have a look around. Finley didn't quite get the hesitation. Downey claimed to want to help with solving Cagle's murder. Why waver?

Maybe she felt protective of the things the family had left behind.

Either way, Finley was here now. She pulled into the driveway and climbed out of her Subaru. Murfreesboro Road was a busy one, though traffic was fairly light at the moment. That would change soon. The property, Finley scanned the yard with its enormous trees and the brick house, was on the national register of historical places. It was a multi-million-dollar estate, but not the kind like in the neighborhood where Finley had grown up. This wasn't new high end; this was top of the line from the long-ago past.

She liked the idea of it.

She started toward the keypad that would open the gate, and a dark sedan braked to a stop on the road, drawing her attention there. She stilled, stared at the vehicle. Same as the one she'd seen when she'd left Jerry Bauer's office at the Fifth Third Center. The driver's window powered down, and the same face with the sunglasses and the hoodie stared at her . . . smiled.

Rage roared through Finley, and before she could stop herself, she was striding for the road. Foolishly she didn't even look as she stepped onto the pavement, moving toward him.

"You looking for me?" she demanded.

His smile widened, and he floored the accelerator, rocketing away with her barely a yard from him.

"Bastard!" She stared at the license plate. *TEN* . . .

A horn blared.

Finley's attention jerked toward the sound.

A car coming from the other direction came to a squealing halt and waited for her to move out of the middle of the road.

She flinched. Damn. She held up a hand, looked in the other direction to ensure there was nothing coming from that way before crossing back to the Cagle driveway. By the time she reached her Subaru, she was shaking.

Deep breath.

Damn it. She hadn't gotten the full license plate information. But she had almost gotten herself run over. She kicked the rear tire of her Subaru. Pissed beyond measure, she yanked open the driver's side door and grabbed her bag. She clawed out her cell and put through a call to Houser.

"Afternoon, Finley."

"I need a meeting with Dempsey."

The silence on the other end of the line amplified how unexpected her request was. Not to mention how unlikely such a request was to be approved. She'd made the call and the demand on emotion, not logic. And by God, she'd meant it.

"Why do you need a meeting with him?"

At least he didn't say she was nuts or tell her up front that her request was impossible and completely ridiculous.

"He has someone following me again."

Another extended silence, then, "Are you certain?"

His question sent her into a pissed-off zone she rarely allowed herself to enter. "Really? You're asking me if I'm certain this new shadow is like the three pieces of shit who followed me for months—after beating and raping me? I think I would know, Houser. Besides, you said yourself Dempsey had reached out to someone."

"Okay, okay." He heaved a big breath. "Did you get his license plate number?"

"No. The car that almost ran me over distracted me, and the bastard got away."

"Damn it, Finley. You have to be more careful."

She took a slow, deep breath, then another. "Can you get me in to talk to him?"

"I can try. Give me some time, and I'll do all I can."

Her pulse slowed to a more normal rate. "Thanks. Call me when you get it worked out."

"Hey, before you go, is Johnson still refusing the DNA comparison?"

"You'll need to ask Jack that question," she dodged. "But I'm guessing you can figure it out without going to the extra trouble. Thanks, Houser."

Finley ended the call. She entered the code to open the gate, then climbed back into her car and drove up to the Cagle house. The gate closed automatically behind her. She sure as hell didn't want that guy following her onto the property if he decided to cruise by again.

She got out and walked around for a few minutes to cool down. This was not Houser's fault, and if he could get this meeting, he would be doing her a huge favor. She'd have to keep that in mind and reciprocate.

Deep breath. Time to focus.

She put Dempsey out of her head and focused on the house. It was brick. Old brick, like at least a hundred years old. She surveyed the landscape. Several acres, well treed and heavily planted with shrubs. Downey had someone taking care of the property as far as the lawn maintenance. That same person occasionally checked inside to ensure there had been no leaks or issues. The alarm system was active, so she'd given Finley the code.

Faded wicker rockers sat on the long, narrow porch. Finley paused at the front door and readied to tuck the key into the lock. The plaque announcing the home was a historically significant one confirmed her thoughts about the brick. The place was 153 years old, to be exact. She wondered if Cagle or her husband had inherited the property.

Inside, Finley entered the code for the alarm and then surveyed the entry hall, which was just that, a hall with a staircase to one side. Though it was plenty large enough, it wasn't like the grand foyers of modern mansions. High ceilings. Original wood floors. Very nice. Near the door was a bench with coat hooks above it. A thin layer of dust covered the table that stood beneath an antique oil painting of a barn scene on the long wall leading deeper into the house.

A parlor on her left held the expected furniture, sofa, chairs, tables as well as a baby grand piano that seemed to gleam despite the layer of dust. She wondered who in the family had played it or if maybe the piano had been for show. A conversation piece to amuse guests. A marble-clad fireplace. A towering shelving unit lined with books—most looked to be first editions or collectibles—filled an entire wall adjacent to the fireplace. Finley walked around the room, checked in table drawers. The only painting on the wall was the one of the family—Louise, Lucy, and Scott—hanging over the fireplace. Finley guessed that Lucy had been ten or twelve at the time of the sitting.

She trekked through the rooms like a beagle on the scent of its prey. The usual family room was next. She checked the drawers and shelves. Fanned through books and magazines. Looked under any piece of furniture that didn't sit flat on the floor.

The dining room was spectacular in a vintage sort of way. A large chandelier hung from the inordinately high ceiling. She searched the buffet and china cabinet and found nothing but dishware. Spanning the backside of the structure was yet another family room with a towering stone fireplace and vaulted ceiling that led into the kitchen. This part wasn't original to the house, but both rooms were well done.

These final two downstairs rooms took some time for her to explore. She opened every cupboard. Checked every drawer. Didn't leave out the appliances or the pantry. Most of what one would expect to be stored in a pantry was gone. No food at all, not even canned or dry goods.

For the best, she supposed, considering no one had lived in this house for nearly thirteen years.

She moved up the stairs and to the bedrooms. There were five, each with its own bathroom. Three of the five were like hotel rooms, nicely decorated but with empty closets and drawers. Guest rooms. The owner's suite was exactly as Louise Cagle had left it, or at least it appeared that way. Husband's and wife's clothes in the closet. Intimates and other personal items in the drawers. Finley took some time to carefully go through everything. She was purposely saving Lucy's room for last.

Finley was surprised there was nothing in Louise's room from her work. No notepads. Sticky notes. No books she or her husband might have been reading. There were framed photos, but not a whole lot of mementos otherwise. Finley looked through the jewelry box as well. Lots of high-dollar items in there.

Slowly, she turned around, taking in the room as a whole. There hadn't been a home office downstairs. Not one up here either, so far. Where did the high-profile reporter do her homework?

With no ready answer at the moment, she moved on to Lucy's room. The space was the typical teenage girl's bedroom. Pink walls, white canopy bed. Fluffy, lacy bedding that had once been white but now was a little off-white. Stuffed animals were piled on her bed. Popular celebrities from the latter part of the first decade of the new millennium dotted the walls in posters. Lots of books on the shelves. Mostly fiction. If she'd had a laptop, it was gone. Finley checked drawers, under and inside pillows, animals, and even the mattress but found no journal or diary. No notes or photos.

As with the other rooms, she checked inside, behind, and under every single piece of furniture. Then she moved on to the walk-in closet. Finley smiled as she perused the space. The girl had a lot of footwear. She checked inside all the shoes and boots. Then moved on to the clothing, and there was plenty of it too. Nothing in the many, many coat and jacket pockets. Nothing in the dozens of purses.

Half an hour later, she had found nothing in or under anything. Lastly, she checked the bathroom. She picked through all the cosmetics and hair products, even peeked into the toilet tank as she had all the others. Nothing.

With nowhere else to look, Finley closed the door to Lucy's room as she had all the other bedrooms. She walked along the hall in both directions to ensure she hadn't missed a door. Nope.

No home office. Strange.

Finley moved down the stairs and wandered through the first floor again, just to be certain she hadn't overlooked a space. She had to be missing something somewhere. She exited the house via the back door and had a look around.

Large back porch and outdoor kitchen. Lots of seating areas with faded, dry-rotting cushions. Beyond the house was a massive detached garage that was obviously not original. She would check there before she left. An enormous pool with a discolored and faded cover surrounded by iron tables and chairs that sported a little rust here and there. All flanked the wide porch.

Then her gaze landed on another, smaller structure. It was built from the same brick as the house and looked original to the grounds.

"Bingo."

Finley headed in that direction. French doors fronted the small building. She wasn't so sure they were original, but they were old. She checked the handle. Locked. She dug out the key ring Downey had given her and went through the keys until she found the one that fit.

Inside, Finley smiled. A brick fireplace stood in the middle of the maybe fourteen-by-twenty single room. Floors were the same wood as the ones in the house. The wood ceiling soared upward with crossbeams.

The front of the space, nearest the french doors, was set up like a small parlor with a love seat–size sofa and chair. A metal-and-glass table. Framed photos of Louise Scott accepting her many awards lined the brick walls.

Beyond the fireplace was the second half of the space. This was what she had been looking for. A desk and chair. Anticipation fired in Finley's veins. No laptop or other computer, but there were notes and notepads, a sticky note dispenser. All the things one would expect in a working office. A bookcase lined with research volumes. And a sizable bulletin-style board covered the majority of the rear wall. Lining the board were printed images, newspaper clippings, and notes—pages torn from a notepad and sticky notes—from side to side and top to bottom.

Finley's pulse skipped into a faster rhythm as she moved closer.

All of it was about Lucy's murder.

Across the middle of the board was a timeline starting the week before Lucy was murdered and ending on Thanksgiving, just over a month and a half later. But it was the beginning that snagged Finley's full attention. *Follower spotted.* Had someone been following Lucy? Why wasn't this in the case file Houser had emailed her? Why hadn't Downey known? Or Finley's father?

Finley took out her cell phone and photographed all the notes and images. She moved from side to side, top to bottom, until she ensured she had them all. Then she started back at the beginning. She read every article, every note. Someone, presumably Louise, had kept close tabs on the detectives involved in the investigation. She had done in-depth research on persons of interest, but none included a member of the Johnson family.

Two of the five people she had been investigating were male students who attended school with Lucy. Those Finley recalled from the articles in the tenth-anniversary special. Both were cleared by the police. Two others were her friends, Garrison and Williams, from school, sans

Jessica Downey—both of whom had been interviewed for the anniversary special. But it was the fifth photo that sent a twisted array of emotions swirling inside her.

Eric Houser.

He was far younger, nineteen or twenty years old, but it was him. She would know those eyes . . . the jawline and his lips anywhere.

"What the hell are you not telling me, Houser?"

Simply being her former boyfriend wouldn't have landed him on that board. There had to be more.

Finley moved to the desk. She opened drawers, picked through the contents. She found the usual. Office tools, extra notepads. She fanned through each. Pens. Pencils. Paper clips. Business cards. Finley picked up the stack and shuffled through them. The cards were from other reporters, lawyers, detectives. A collection of the sort of people an investigative reporter would need to know for research and source purposes.

The final card gave her pause . . . *Jack Finnegan.*

Finley stared at the card. "What the hell, Jack?"

Thirteen years ago Jack would have still been practicing law at the Finnegan, Cooper and Baker firm. The hottest, most widely acclaimed law firm in Nashville at the time. It was possible Louise Cagle had talked to Jack for research purposes on a particular case she was investigating. Could have been twenty years ago. Twenty-five, for that matter.

But why hadn't he told Finley about knowing Louise Cagle beyond her public persona?

First her father, then Houser and now Jack? Finley placed the cards back where she found them. This was getting old, and she liked it less and less. She trusted her father and Jack. Trusted Houser. Why would they let her down like this? Particularly in a murder case where Jack's newest client was a person of interest?

"We will be talking about this, Jack."

Finley finished her search of the home office space and walked out. She locked the door and headed toward the detached garage.

Why hadn't Downey told her about all those notes? She'd said she didn't have any of Louise's working notes. Finley supposed Downey had meant her working notes as far as what she did for the paper. Still, the idea that she would fail to mention this mother lode made no sense.

Nothing about this case made sense.

Who were all these people covering for?

13

Jack was at his desk going over a case file when Finley arrived. She wouldn't have been able to sneak up on him like this except that Nita wasn't at her desk, which was highly unusual. It was possible she had an appointment or some errand to run. It was just strange to walk in and not see her. The only time that happened was if Finley showed up before 6:00 a.m., which was like almost never.

The reading glasses Jack wore were the only thing that gave away anything about his age. He still wore that long ponytail he'd had since college. There were plenty of silver strands threaded through his blond hair, but they were barely noticeable. It was his blue eyes that got to the ladies, though. He had great eyes.

Most importantly, he was brilliant, and Finley felt grateful to have him as a part of her family. Growing up she'd called him Uncle Jack. Now that they worked together, it was just Jack.

If she moved on with her career plans, she would miss seeing this guy every day.

Sensing her presence, he glanced up. Smiled. Nice smile too. "Hey, kid, you ready to call it a day?"

There was just one little thing about Jack that bugged the hell out of her. Sometimes he lied. Most of the time his little lies were about his drinking. But he'd been sober for over five years now. Still, occasionally, like now, a tiny little untruth popped up in the course of things.

She entered his office and settled in the chair in front of his desk. "We have to talk about a couple of things."

"Uh-oh." He closed the file in his hand. "This sounds ominous."

She held up the keys to the Cagle property. Downey had told her to keep the keys for as long as she needed them. "Maureen Downey has been taking care of the Cagle house all this time. She felt she owed Louise that much, and there were apparently some residual earnings from Louise Scott specials that sold to other papers or networks. Plus, she had invested in the paper, so there's that."

"Did you find anything?" He removed his reading glasses and placed them on the file. "Or was everything packed up?"

"The whole house is just as the Cagles left it." Finley hesitated. "Except for the kitchen. All the food products were removed. Trash. That sort of thing. Otherwise, their clothes—it's all there."

His eyebrows reared up as he leaned back in his chair. "Weird. But interesting."

"I went through the entire house. Did a thorough sweep." She had checked out the detached garage as well before she left. Nothing out of the ordinary there. All three of the family vehicles had been parked inside. Looking over Lucy's car had sent an icy streak rushing through Finley's blood.

Who had Lucy gone to meet that night?

That person was the key to everything.

"I didn't find anything. At first, I was confused because I didn't find a home office in the house. For someone like Louise Scott, that seemed unlikely. But then I found her office in a smaller building behind the house. The husband had one too. I found his in the finished upstairs over the garage. He had a man cave complete with a very large pool table up there. The family vehicles were on the main level—including Lucy's car. There was also a good-size safe room—the kind for tornadoes, only bigger than any that I've seen before. It was open, so I checked it out too. Nothing there but the typical survival stuff."

"I'm sure the residence was gone over thoroughly by the police after the murder."

"No doubt. I didn't really expect to find anything, but oversights happen." She nodded slowly. "Oddly, I did find something in Louise's office that I didn't expect."

"A map to where she's been hiding all these years?" He grinned.

"Funny." Finley told herself to relax, but she'd been humming with frustration since leaving the property. "No, I found her case board on Lucy's murder. Complete with an extensive timeline and endless articles, notes, and images of people."

His eyebrows shot up in interest then. "I hope you photographed everything."

"I did. Honestly, I was surprised Downey didn't mention it to me. It's been so long maybe she forgot about it. Though I don't see how. Then again, Ray Johnson didn't seem to know or had forgotten that evidence from a murder had been tucked away in one of his warehouses."

"Until we have no other choice, we're assuming he didn't know it was there," Jack reminded her.

"Anyway," Finley went on, rather than debating the point, "the only thing new I found on the case board was a reference to a *follower* the week before Lucy's murder, but there was no additional clarification."

"Did we miss that somehow, between your research and what Houser gave you?"

"No. This was the first suggestion Lucy had a follower." She took a breath. Couldn't put the rest off any longer. "As I was going through Louise's desk, I found a stack of business cards. One of them was yours from your days with your former partners."

He made a surprised face. "Really?"

Then he made a mistake. He picked up his glasses and settled them back into place and fiddled with the file he'd laid aside when she arrived.

"What aren't you telling me, Jack?"

He looked over his glasses at her. "She may have gotten one of my cards at the firm. All the partners had cards handy in the lobby."

"But she didn't have a card from any of the others," Finley pointed out. "Only from you."

He removed his glasses once more. Tossed them aside. "All right, already. She came to me just before Halloween that year. She felt the police weren't doing all they could. I warned her she was expecting too much. They can only find what's left for them to find. If there's no evidence, no clues, they can't make them up. They just have to keep looking."

Finley felt certain Jack had been a bit more diplomatic, but she got the picture. "How did she take it?"

"How do you think? It wasn't what she wanted to hear, but it was the truth."

Sadly, it was. Finley wanted to be relieved by Jack's answer, but it was too soon. There was more. Unquestionably.

"Why did she come to you and not one of the other partners?"

He shot her a look. "You have to ask?"

Yeah, yeah. He was the best attorney in town. That, too, was true.

"Did you give her any other advice?"

"I suggested she find a good private investigator. They can do things the police cannot. She said she'd been thinking about it. She had a good many sources and had, to that point, been relying on them. After nearly a month of finding basically nothing, she was desperate, as you can imagine."

Finley waited a few seconds, then, "Tell me the part you haven't shared so far."

His cheeks puffed with a big breath. "We had a thing for a while back in the day. Before she married Scott Cagle. It was . . ." He shook his head. "It was nothing more than two very busy, very ambitious people filling a need. Neither of us had time for a relationship, so we had sex. She met Scott, and that was the end of it."

As much as she hated to admit it, Finley grasped the scenario all too well.

Though she got what he was saying and personally didn't have a problem with it, that was not the biggest issue with what her boss had just shared. "You're not concerned that your relationship with her all those years ago makes for a bit of a conflict of interest with your new client?"

He gave his head a quick shake. "I am not. Are you?"

Finley thought about it for a few seconds. "I can go either way."

Jack rolled his eyes. "You don't think I can separate my past feelings from a current situation?"

"Maybe." Now for the other revelation. "Here's another news flash. Ray's ex, Shelia Stratton, knew Lucy. Had her over to the house—the Johnson house—to babysit the kid a few times."

Jack's face fell. "Are you freaking kidding me?"

"Nope. I interviewed her today to confirm his alibi, and she mentioned how sweet Lucy was. It went from there."

"Why would—no offense—a rich kid like Lucy need to babysit anyone's kid?"

"'To get access to the home office of her project target."

Jack swore. "This could be a problem."

"Most definitely." Finley stood. "Houser is getting me in to view the evidence. Hopefully by tomorrow. I'll ask him about this alleged follower, and at some point, I'll probably go back to the house and have a second look."

"You planning to tell him what the ex-wife said?"

"Depends on where this all goes. But it feels significant."

Jack exhaled a big breath. "Damned significant, but not something we have to disclose just yet."

"True."

Jack's forehead creased into a deeper frown. "What's this I'm hearing about you requesting a face-to-face with Dempsey?"

So Houser had outed her. Damn him. "I've noticed a guy." She shrugged. Blinked at the remembered sound of a horn blaring as she had stalked toward the dark sedan just a couple of hours ago.

"Explain," Jack ordered, using his "don't even think about leaving anything out" voice.

Her gut tied into a dozen or so knots. "Like before. Following me. Watching me."

"Have you seen him more than once?"

She looked straight at her boss, her godfather, a man she loved, and did what she had to do. She lied. "Once. Outside the Fifth Third Center after I met with Jerry Bauer."

"You're sure this was related to Dempsey."

"I am. Reasonably so anyway." Houser said Dempsey had reached out to a connection. It had to be him. Houser had probably already spilled this to Jack as well. Still, Finley searched Jack's eyes for a long moment. "Is there someone else you're concerned might have a hired thug following me?"

He made a face as if he was considering how to answer, which meant he didn't want to tell her but had no choice. This was a dance they did often.

Jack finally shrugged. "I wouldn't put it past the old man to have someone watching you."

"Call him," Finley said. She had specifically questioned Ray Johnson about this. Damn it. "Ask him."

Jack didn't hesitate. He made the call. Turned out old man Johnson wanted to see them both. In person.

Johnson Residence
Wilson Pike, Brentwood, 5:15 p.m.

The house wasn't as grand as many of those belonging to the city's old money families, but it was very nice and quite stately looking. Neatly landscaped. Wide, welcoming driveway. Finley had followed Jack there in her Subaru, since she needed to go by the hospital after this to see her neighbor. Matt had called; he wouldn't be home before seven or so, which worked out well with her schedule. If he got there first, he would feed and walk the dog. Check the water bowl and take Roberts's mail in the house. If Finley was still at the hospital, he would text her with an update and a photo she could show Roberts. Seeing her dog might make her day.

Ray Johnson met them at the door. He looked Finley up and down. "You didn't get enough of me this morning?"

She smiled rather than tell him that she'd had enough of him before they even met. "Your father asked to see us."

He gave a nod. "Follow me."

They entered through the double front doors into a spacious-for-its-day foyer. Nice wood floors. Crisp white walls. The decorating was sparse, but it was well done. Minimalist with class, she decided. Not what she'd expected from this family. But then she hadn't met the old man, and the mother had died more than two decades ago. She doubted Ray's ex had a hand in the sedate decor.

The dining room and kitchen were recently updated, clean and sleek. There had to be a housekeeper. Ray Johnson wouldn't know a broom from a mop.

They passed the home office on the way to the staircase that was in the back of the house rather than the front. Ray's office, she assumed—the one to which Lucy would have had access. No lock that Finley could readily see.

The stairs were tucked away in the kitchen–family room area. Again, Ray led the way to the second floor. Jack followed behind Finley. The father's bedroom was the first at the top of the stairs.

The smell of death assaulted her senses the instant they entered the room. A nurse ducked out once they had gathered around the hospital-type bed. An IV line ran from a bag on a pole to his right arm. A couple of medical machines stood next to the bed. A water pitcher and prescription bottles sat on the bedside table next to his unencumbered arm.

Raymond Johnson Senior and his son could have been twins if not for the heavy wrinkles and a completely gray, quickly receding hairline. The older man's skin was paper thin, with equally thin and feeble muscle beneath.

He was the image of death when cancer was called to mind. Not a good way to go.

"Pop, this is Finley O'Sullivan, and you already know Jack."

Mr. Johnson nodded while he eyed Finley far more keenly than she would have thought him capable. Maybe his vision was failing too.

"She any good at what she does?" He turned to Jack with the question.

"There's no one better," Jack said.

Finley thought that might be a bit of a reach.

Johnson looked to his son. "Leave us. I want to speak privately with our guests."

"Whatever makes you happy, Pop."

Ray executed an about-face and walked out, closing the door behind himself.

Finley wouldn't have expected him to take a dismissal so well.

"How're you feeling, Raymond?" Jack asked.

"I'm dying," Johnson tossed back. "I feel like I'm overdue."

"I'm sorry to hear that."

Johnson laughed. "You and maybe one other person." He shifted his attention to Finley. "You know about my other boy, Ian?"

"Yes. Ray told me."

"You think you can figure out what happened to him?" He exhaled a rattling breath. "I'm dying. I'd like to know. Maybe see him, if he's still alive."

"I can try," Finley said. "His trail is thirteen years cold. It won't be easy."

"You find him or whatever happened to him," Johnson said, "and I will donate ten million dollars to that campaign of yours."

A tight laugh burst out of Finley. Talk about an unexpected shock. "Sir, I'm not looking for donations. I haven't even officially—"

"That's not the way I hear it."

"I appreciate the offer," Finley said, "but I'm reasonably sure that would be a conflict of interest, under the circumstances."

Johnson shrugged. "We can discuss all that when you find him."

Finley smiled and left it at that.

"I worry Ray might have run him off," the elder Johnson went on. "He never wanted a little brother. He was nine before we had Ian. He'd been the only child all that time, so he didn't take the new arrival well."

A thought occurred to Finley. "I'll make a deal with you, Mr. Johnson," she said.

His expression perked up in anticipation.

"You tell me everything you know about what happened to Lucy Cagle, and I will find out everything there is to be found about your younger son."

His eyes narrowed. "What makes you think I know one thing about that girl?"

"You don't need me to spell it out for you. There's a reason the handbag belonging to Lucy Cagle ended up in one of your warehouses. These things don't happen without a reason. And I have my doubts as to whether they would happen on your property without your knowledge."

Something like anger sparked in his eyes. "You work for me, Miss Sass Mouth. Keep that in mind when you speak to me."

"I don't work for you, Mr. Johnson. I work for Jack." Finley enjoyed saying as much, maybe more than she should have. But he'd started it. "If you want my help, you will keep that in mind as we move forward. Assuming we do."

The stare-off lasted a full five seconds; then he burst out laughing. "Damn, Jack, she's got your spunk for sure." The laughter died instantly. "Find out about my son," he said, "and I'll make sure you get everything you need."

Finley didn't care for the hint of malice she heard behind his words.

"Raymond," Jack said, "I have a concern that may or may not involve you or Ray."

Johnson turned to him. "If he's giving you trouble, I can fix that."

Jack shook his head. "It's not trouble just yet, and we aren't sure where it's coming from, but someone has been following Finley. Dark sedan. Guy wearing a dark hoodie and sunglasses."

Johnson turned back to Finley. "Is there some reason I should have someone following you?"

"If you feel the need to have someone following me," she countered, "you should fire our firm right now. Trust is everything, Mr. Johnson."

The old man considered her ultimatum, then said, "I have no one following you. Ray!" He shouted only the once for his son before he came into the room.

Finley imagined Ray had been standing outside the door with his ear pressed there.

"What's up?" He looked from Finley to Jack before resting his gaze on his father.

"Do you have someone following Ms. O'Sullivan?"

Ray chuckled. "I told her already that I do not." He turned to Finley. "If we decide to hire someone to follow her, I'd like to volunteer for the job."

Finley rolled her eyes. She described the guy and the car to their client.

"We do not," he repeated, "have anyone following you. I can make that happen if you feel you need some extra security."

Finley held up a hand. "I can handle this myself, but thank you for the offer. I was only curious if the surveillance was coming from your camp."

"You have my word, Finley," the younger Johnson said, his face dead serious, "we are not watching you or following you. Your reputation precedes you. We know you'll get the job done."

Finley could live with that . . . for now.

"Let us know," Jack said, "if anything new comes up, and remember"—he looked to the son—"do not speak to anyone about this case. If anyone from Metro wants to talk to you, you make sure I am with you when that happens."

"Yes, sir."

The old man glanced repeatedly at Finley while he and Jack chatted a minute or two more. He didn't trust her. She figured he didn't trust anyone. If he didn't, that made them even, because she damned sure did not trust him or his son.

Ray escorted them to the door but hesitated before opening it. "Shelia mentioned that you'd visited her," he said to Finley.

"I confirmed your alibi," she returned.

"The thing you need to know about my wife," he went on, "she sometimes suffers from these moments of grandeur where she thinks she knows something or someone she doesn't. Don't trust everything she says. You have my word she won't say the wrong thing again to anyone."

Finley hoped his assurance didn't mean he'd threatened his ex-wife—or worse. "Good to know."

Outside, she and Jack walked quietly to their vehicles. A glance back at the house told her Ray had gone back inside, but he was likely watching.

"He's hiding something," she said to Jack. "Something that will turn this case upside down."

Jack glanced at the house. "I've got a bad feeling you're right."

Finley thought of her father and Downey . . . they were both hiding something relevant as well. Where the hell were all these secrets going? Somewhere along the course of this investigation, they would collide. Worse, who would be left standing when it was done?

"Be careful out there, kid."

"You too."

They shared a quick hug and went their separate ways.

Her cell vibrated, and she reached into her pocket as she navigated the evening traffic.

Houser.

"Hey."

"Hey yourself," he said. "If you have a few minutes and can meet me at the lab, you can see that evidence now."

She grinned, executed a little air punch of victory. "I'm on my way. Thanks."

"Just keep it on the down-low, would you? I can't be doing this for every attorney who gets involved with one of my cases."

"Sure. Of course. I understand." He was doing her a huge favor. She got it.

"You do know I'm only doing this for you because you're going to be the next DA and I want to be on your good side."

She laughed. "Don't hold your breath. See you in twenty."

Finley ended the call and headed for the lab. A new rush of anticipation had her pulse keeping time with her driving speed. Both were a little over the limit.

14

The lab was closed, but Houser's sedan sat in the lot as promised. Finley parked next to him. When she emerged from her Subaru, he was waiting for her on the sidewalk leading to the entrance.

"I take it we're going in after hours to prevent any questions."

He shrugged. "Let's just say I have a friend."

"Friends are good," Finley acknowledged.

Houser started walking, and Finley did the same.

"He's meeting us at the employees' entrance."

Where the sidewalk and the main entrance intersected, they headed left and skirted the front corner of the building. Once around back, she spotted a single car in the smaller rear parking area. Houser's friend, she imagined.

On the way here, she had called Matt to say she might be around eight getting home, and he'd reminded her they were scheduled to have dinner with the Judge and her father at eight. Finley had forgotten. She always did. No matter. Now that Matt had reminded her, she didn't have a lot of time for easing into the questions she wanted to ask Houser about the Cagle house. Going straight to the more sensitive queries was rarely the best route, but sometimes there was no help for it.

"Have you been to the Cagle home since the case was reopened?"

He sent her a questioning sideways glance. "I'm sure someone else lives there by now."

"Nope. Maureen Downey, Cagle's former employer and the managing editor at the *Tennessean*, has been taking care of it all this time. When Cagle disappeared, she stepped in and kept the taxes paid and the necessary maintenance done. The place has been sitting there just as the family left it all these years."

He stopped. She did the same. "Have you been to the house?" he asked, an urgency in his eyes.

"I was there this afternoon. I still have the keys."

"Okay." He seemed to consider her answer but said nothing, then suddenly started to walk again.

So that was not the reaction she had expected.

Just before they reached the employee entrance, she added, "Cagle kept a home office there. She turned it into a sort of murder room, complete with a case board and lots and lots of notes and photos."

Houser hesitated again. His friend waiting on the other side of the door gave Finley a little wave. She waved back.

"And," Houser prompted, his expression oddly devoid of tells.

Ah, he wanted her to spell it out, did he? She could do that.

"First off, there was a timeline that began the week before Lucy was murdered. The one notation mentioned a *follower*. Was there anything in the case file—maybe the part you couldn't share—about a follower?"

Obviously, there were some things the cops on a case didn't share until they had no choice, but this was Houser—her friend. She had hoped he wouldn't do that with the sorts of details left hanging after the case went cold. How could she find the truth if relevant information was not revealed? She already had way too many others keeping little truths from her.

He shook his head. "No mention of a follower. Not from any of the people interviewed. Not from the mother or father. Are you sure the notation was about someone following Lucy?"

She tilted her head and considered the question. "I can't be sure, of course, but that's the way it looked based on the way the notes on other aspects were laid out."

"Then Louise Cagle knew something we didn't. Anything else?"

Finley looked him in the eye. "There was a photo of you—back then. Cagle considered you a person of interest. Any idea why?"

Finley didn't like accusing this man of anything. He'd been a good friend to her . . . taken a bullet for her . . . but she needed the whole story. If this was the only way to get it, then so be it.

Houser glanced at his waiting friend before locking his gaze with Finley's once more. "I suppose because Lucy and I dated for a while. I told you that."

Finley tamped down her frustration. "Fine." She gestured to the door. "We going in or what?"

Houser signaled to his friend, and the guy opened the door. Finley stepped inside and thrust out her hand. "Finley O'Sullivan."

The younger man in the white lab coat gave her hand a quick, hearty shake. "Evidence tech Brett Taylor. I've heard all about you, Ms. O'Sullivan."

"Finley," she said.

He grinned. "You're a legend around here, Finley."

Finley bit her lips together to hold back her own grin. It wasn't often she heard compliments like that from anyone related in any capacity to Metro.

Houser chuckled. "Don't go giving her the big head, Brett."

Taylor's face reddened. "Sorry. I get carried away."

"Ignore him," Finley said to the guy. "He gets grumpy when I trump him." She glanced at Houser. "And I just did."

Taylor laughed. "Follow me, Finley, I'll let you peek at that purse." They headed along the corridor. "You can't touch anything," he explained, "but you can look, and if you need to see a different side of anything, I can touch it."

"Got it," she said, flashing him her best smile.

He blushed and hurried a little faster toward their destination.

Finley had been here before, but it never ceased to amaze her just how large the lab was. More than eighty thousand square feet spread over two floors. State of the art. Serious tax dollars had gone into this place.

Taylor led them to the Evidence Receiving Unit. "Since the evidence has already been processed, we've stored it back in a vault. Tomorrow we'll be moving it to the Property and Evidence Section, where it will wait for its day in court, so to speak."

Finley was fully aware of the steps. The preservation and protection of evidence was paramount to any case. She was extremely lucky to be getting an advance in-person look in her capacity as the firm's investigator. Generally, her team would have to be happy with photos.

She and Houser waited in a small room outside the vault while Taylor retrieved the evidence. The room had a couple of stools that stood next to a stainless steel table. A light/magnifier combination had been mounted to the table for closer inspection of the evidence.

"I hadn't seen Lucy in a while when she was murdered," he said quietly. "Her mother talked to me, of course. Evidently, I was the last boyfriend she knew about. If Lucy was with anyone after me—on any kind of steady basis, I mean—she didn't share this with her mother."

Finley couldn't see a savvy investigative reporter listing Houser on her case board if he hadn't been in the picture for a while. Didn't make a lot of sense. Then again, there hadn't been a picture of Finley's father. Maybe Cagle hadn't known about him when she created the case board. But why not add him later?

It was also possible that Cagle had been unraveling by that point. To lose so much in such a short period of time was not easy to come back from. Maybe she'd lost her edge too. Finley knew that place too well. There were times when you only saw what you needed to see.

"I would like a walk-through of the house," Houser said, interrupting her intense thoughts. "Hey."

She shifted her attention to him, lifted her eyebrows in question.

"I'm doing you a huge favor and taking a big risk letting you see this evidence in person. I need you to do this for me."

This made her chuckle. "Kind of a 'you show me yours and I show you mine' thing?"

Exasperation claimed his face. "Yes."

She might be enjoying this a little too much at this point. "We can go to the house tomorrow. I have dinner with the Judge tonight."

He visibly relaxed. "Thanks."

She shook her head. "I was never going to hold out on you, Houser."

He smiled, did one of those half shrugs. "I may have known that."

Yeah right. She'd had him worried.

Taylor appeared with the evidence. He placed the container on the table, efficiently removed his gloves and tugged on a new pair, then placed a sterilized tray next to the container. Taking extra care, he removed the purse and the cigarette butts from the container. Each item had been tucked into a clear evidence bag.

Finley's heart beat faster. The idea that this handbag was the last personal item Lucy touched got to her. It always did. No one's life should be taken from them. This—the girl's small Louis Vuitton multicolored handbag—had been important to her. A status symbol that was likely more about the fashion of the day than how much it cost. Lucy had this small bag with her when she encountered the man who murdered her. If there was anything on or in this bag that helped identify her killer, they needed to find it.

When Taylor had placed all the items from the container onto the tray, Finley was surprised to see more than the slim wallet that matched the handbag, Lucy's driver's license, and a tube of lip gloss. There was a car wash receipt dated three days before the murder.

She looked at Houser. "You didn't mention the car wash receipt."

"The car wash is out of business now. Torn down to make room for a strip mall."

"Who owned it?" She knew before he answered, and the fact that he'd held out on her made her more annoyed than it should have. This seemed to be the way of her relationships with the men in her life—except for Matt.

She took a mental step back and reminded herself that Houser was a cop; she was part of the defense team for a potential suspect. Of course he held out on her to some degree. Just because they were friends didn't change the rules of the game. She should have expected there would be something.

"I'll just wait over here," Taylor said as he backed away from the table. "Let me know if you need me."

"Johnson Development built it," Houser explained with audible reluctance, "along with two others. This is the only one that has been torn down—ironically not even a week after the murder. A strip mall quickly popped up in its place."

Now she was just straight-up angry. She had no illusions her client was an innocent victim in this, but the possibility that Johnson had torn down a car wash just because Lucy patronized it once was taking a hell of a leap, in her opinion. "Are you suggesting more evidence was hidden there? Obviously, there wasn't a body buried under the concrete."

"All the car washes had cameras. It kept the employees in line and protected the owner from customers saying any damage to their vehicle happened at the car wash." Houser held up both hands when she would have interrupted. "Tear it down and you get to remove the cameras without drawing the wrong attention."

Finley's jaw dropped, and her anger dissipated as quickly as it had come. So maybe he had a valid point. "Okay." She was the one flashing her palms in surrender now. "Thanks for the heads-up."

"But you're wrong," Houser went on. "Lucy's body was found, yes, but there is one body we haven't found." At her expectant look, he said, "Ian Johnson's."

Well, hell. He made another damned good point.

Finley decided not to comment or to mention her interview with Ray Johnson's ex just yet. After all, Johnson had said his ex wouldn't be repeating her story. Instead Finley studied the items on display once more. The purse was monogrammed with the designer's distinctive initials. Fairly new at the time the victim carried it. The lip gloss was a brand Finley remembered being popular in those days.

Her frustration flared again, this time at their damned client. Johnson was keeping things from her. No real surprise there, but for him to keep something this blatant—considering he had to have known Houser would likely note the timing of the teardown—made her furious. When high-profile cases like this one were reopened, the new detective always searched for the little things previous detectives had overlooked. Like changes in property ownership or major renovations. The car wash receipt alone wasn't proof of anything, but it placed Lucy on Johnson property. Add her presence to the subsequent teardown, and a red flag went up. Putting her frustration aside for the moment, she moved on to the cigarette butts. The distinctive green lettering on the butts signified a once-popular menthol brand.

"Do you have DNA back on the cigarette butts?" An idea was taking shape, and she wasn't sure she should make the suggestion to Houser—the enemy, basically. She thought of the car wash and how cocky Ray Johnson was, and she decided just maybe she would go for it.

"DNA came back this afternoon," he confirmed. "All we need is Johnson's to rule him out."

She rolled her eyes. "Give it a rest. We both know you don't want to rule him out."

"We also," Houser pointed out, "both want the same thing—the truth."

She couldn't deny this, but she also had an obligation to protect her client as long as he wasn't a threat to anyone else.

A plan formed in Finley's mind. She loved it when inspiration struck so quickly. "I need to make a call."

Houser nodded to Taylor. "Thanks, man. We'll get out of your way now."

Finley waved to her new fan and decided it would be smart to remember his name.

Houser escorted Finley from the room, retracing their steps to the employee entrance. They said nothing as they moved through the quiet building. When they'd exited into the dark evening, he said, "Make your call." He jerked his head toward the picnic tables under a group of trees. "I'll wait over there."

Finley waited until he'd settled at one of the tables, his feet on the bench. She turned her back on him and walked to the corner of the building as she put through a call to Jack. He answered on the second ring.

"Hey, kid, what's up?"

"So I just had a look at the evidence," she said without preamble.

"Anything interesting?"

"There was a stub from a car wash."

Jack grunted. "Okay."

She explained the car wash connection to the Johnsons and the subsequent teardown. "We need to know why he closed and tore down that particular one when he did."

"I'll pay him another visit first thing in the morning. This is the sort of thing best done in person."

"Agreed." After a moment's consideration, she said, "The DNA is back on the cigarette butts. I actually don't believe it's relevant. Think about it, the purse is found on the top shelf in a mop closet. Also found are a couple of cigarette butts—not on the top shelf. Way in the back under the bottom shelf. Come on. It's been thirteen years. Who was doing the sweeping in that warehouse?"

"It was shut down before the murder and has been all this time," Jack pointed out. "So maybe no one—at least not efficiently anyway—has been keeping the place cleaned up."

She supposed he was right about that, but the place had looked pretty damned clean to her—the signs of demo aside. "I'm thinking that even if there's a DNA match, proving the butts connect to the handbag beyond a shadow of a doubt would be basically impossible. With that in mind, I believe if we really want to put this to rest, we have Ray's DNA done at our favorite private lab, then we have our lab compare the results. If it's not a match, we can negotiate terms with Houser to ensure the results are not run through the system."

The idea was a bit of a stretch, but she was reasonably sure she could pull it off with Houser. The end result would tell them if Metro had any other real evidence in this case against their client. Certainly, without the DNA match he would have to fork over whatever else they were keeping on the down-low for now—assuming that was the case.

Not to mention she would be a lot happier about representing Johnson if she knew he was innocent, although the cigarette butts alone were not going to prove that one way or the other, in her opinion. Particularly in light of what she'd learned from the ex about Lucy babysitting in their home. The woman wasn't stupid. She had *accidentally* shared that information with Finley for a reason. And then she'd let Johnson know she'd done it. A bid for a boost in child support or alimony, Finley suspected. On the other hand, when you got right down to it, with the old man dying and Ian long out of the picture, Ray Johnson was the only person standing in the way of Stratton's children inheriting the business and the money. She could want her ex out of the way.

Sounded like motive to Finley.

"I'll talk to him," Jack said. "If he agrees, I'll get it done ASAP."

"If the DNA doesn't match, then Ray's off the hook with Metro for now."

She had a feeling he and his father were both guilty of many things. But judging the two was not her job.

"Anything else?" Jack asked, drawing her back to the conversation.

Finley glanced at Houser and considered that she was already running late, but she had to know. There was a very good chance this investigation was going to get ugly. "Just one thing, for my own peace of mind. I need to know what kind of favor Johnson did for you, Jack."

The silence that followed set her further on edge. The truth was, maybe it didn't matter, but Finley had a feeling it might. Either way, she needed to know.

"Twenty years ago," he said wearily, "I made a mistake. I took on a client—a woman—and I stupidly got personally involved. Turned out her old man wasn't as ready for the divorce as she had thought. He came after me. Blew up my car. Hell, it's a miracle no one was injured. When I found out he worked for Raymond Johnson, I went to him and asked for his help. He told the guy if he wanted to keep his job, he should back off. If I had my guess, he likely suggested if the guy wanted to keep breathing as well. Either way, the old man probably saved my life."

"Jesus Christ, Jack," she muttered. "We're representing this piece of shit because you couldn't keep your—"

"Hey, hey," he interrupted. "We all make mistakes. I may have made more than my share during certain periods of my life, but I did my best."

The point was one she couldn't argue.

"You need to find someone, Jack, and make it real." She said this knowing that the only woman he had ever really loved was her mother. But her mother was taken. "You deserve someone who makes you happy."

He grunted. "Have a nice evening, kid. I'll go see Ray and the old man in the morning."

"Don't push him about the car wash," she said on second thought. "Just get him to go along with the test, and let me know what he says. We can hit him with the car wash once we get the DNA hurdle behind us."

Finley ended the call and strode over to where Houser waited.

"I may be able to work this DNA thing out," she announced, "if our conditions are acceptable."

His expression shifted to one of cautious optimism. "What, pray tell, are your conditions?"

"If Johnson agrees to the test, we'll have it done at a private lab of our choosing. You provide your results, and our lab will make the comparison. If there's no match, you let it go."

"And if he is our guy?"

Finley smiled. "He won't be." The smile eased into a frown as she considered how to approach the next issue. "When Ray Johnson's wife at the time was interviewed, she insisted she'd never met Lucy or even heard of her." Finley had read this in the case file Houser had sent.

He nodded. "That's right."

Finley held his gaze for a moment before continuing. "Talk to her again. Tell her you know she lied, and offer her a deal."

His eyes narrowed. "Are you trying to tell me something, Finley?"

"All I'm saying is that she isn't his wife anymore. If you think about it, she has way more reason for wanting to tell the whole truth now than she did thirteen years ago." Finley waved goodbye and walked quickly to her Subaru.

One thing she had learned since graduating from law school was that when something was overly obvious, it was rarely what it appeared to be.

The flimsy evidence Metro had against their client was over-the-top obvious.

The truth, Finley suspected, lay in the reason for the evidence appearing out of the blue after all these years.

The trouble was in finding the person behind that reason.

But there were other things, like the ex-wife's supposed slip. Houser needed to take that ball and run with it. Maybe it would end up being a pointless play; maybe it would end up a winner.

The ex-wife may have put the evidence in the warehouse. The question then became how and why she had access to Lucy's purse.

Women had killed for far less than fear their sugar daddy was about to be brought down by someone determined to get the story. Since the ex no longer needed Ray Johnson around to get what she wanted, maybe she had decided to get him out of the way.

Just one more potential suspect in a case that should have been solved more than a decade ago.

15

Vanderbilt Medical Center
Medical Center Drive, Nashville, 7:30 p.m.

Helen Roberts was awake.

Finley smiled as she walked into the room. "You're looking better."

Roberts only stared at her as Finley came up to the side of her bed. She searched Finley's face as if looking for some trouble or bad news.

When none came, the older woman said, "Did they teach you to lie like that in law school?"

Now there was the Helen Roberts Finley knew and appreciated. "Among other things."

Roberts was no fool. She recognized she looked like hell. Maybe her heart issue was the reason she seemed so much older than she actually was. Finley had thought she was in her midseventies. As it turned out, according to her hospital paperwork, she was only sixty-nine. Bad genes? Hard work? Hard life? Who knew?

Roberts had pleasant eyes. Her hair was gray and usually twisted into a bun of sorts, but since coming here it hung past her shoulders in a knotty mass.

"Don't get any ideas about combing my hair," she said, following Finley's gaze. "They can cut it off."

Finley didn't bother mentioning that untangling hair was not one of her finer attributes. She'd hated it when her mother had done it to her as a kid. She made sure hers stayed in a clip or ponytail to avoid the problem.

"I brought you a pic of the dog." She tapped the screen of her cell and displayed the photo Matt had sent. "I forgot to ask his name."

Again, Roberts watched Finley closely for a few beats before answering the question. "Spot." She studied the screen, her face softening the slightest bit.

"Oh. Okay," Finley acknowledged. The name was weird because the dog had no spots, but whatever. "We're keeping your mail on the kitchen table. And don't worry, we make sure the gate is closed, and we watch closely whenever we take Spot into the yard to do his business."

"I appreciate that."

Finley produced a smile that quickly drooped. Damn it. She'd forgotten to have flowers sent to the room. No one should be in the hospital and not have flowers. Worse, she knew her neighbor loved flowers. The gift shop downstairs would be closed by now.

"I checked with the nurse," Finley mentioned when Roberts said no more, "and it looks like you may have to stay until the end of next week. You okay with that?"

Disappointment flickered in the woman's eyes. "I guess I have no choice."

"Well, I'm having dinner with my parents tonight, so I should get going. I'll be back tomorrow evening. Call me if you need anything. I put my card by your phone." She nodded to the handset lying on the table next to the bed. "The nurses have my number as well."

Roberts blinked but remained silent.

"Bye." Finley turned away and headed for the door. What a strange woman.

"Finley."

She paused and turned back to her neighbor.

"You needn't waste your time coming here to see me. Just take care of my dog. Keep my house secure, and that will be enough."

Finley ignored the dismissal. This woman might be stubborn, but Finley was equally so. "Good night. See you tomorrow."

O'Sullivan Residence
Jackson Boulevard, Belle Meade, 9:30 p.m.

The Judge hadn't even appeared annoyed that it was eight thirty before Finley and Matt arrived or that Finley was wearing the same clothes she'd worn to work rather than dressed for a special evening at her parents' home.

Matt, on the other hand, looked impeccable with a navy suit jacket and light-blue polo that matched his eyes. The jeans were washed soft and fit him as if they'd been tailor made for him. He looked amazing. Always did. Ever thoughtful, he had been waiting to drive her here as soon as Finley arrived home.

The dinner, like everything the Judge did, was spectacular. Pork tenderloin with rice and asparagus. The wine was paired perfectly, which made Finley really happy. Matt refilled her glass as if she'd said the words aloud. She smiled at him. He always took care of her. When she'd been in the hospital and then in rehab after the night her husband was murdered, he had come to see her every evening without fail. Her father told her that even before Finley regained consciousness, Matt was there reading to her, talking to her.

How had she gotten so lucky to have a man like Matt for a friend? For her everything? She smiled. Maybe she was like their cat, lucky.

"Are you keeping the governor in line?" Bart asked. "I hear he's a stickler for details."

"That he is," Matt agreed. "It's a very good thing I am as well, which makes it easy to keep up."

"He walks the straight and narrow," the Judge confirmed. "We're fortunate to have a man like him in office."

The Judge glanced in Finley's direction, and she immediately shifted the narrative before the DA's race came up. "Did you know Louise Cagle?" Finley asked. "Jack and I are involved in the reopening of her daughter's homicide case."

The horror that claimed her father's face had Finley regretting she'd brought up the subject. "I thought you," Finley went on, directing her comment to the Judge, "may have known her from one of your committees."

Ruth O'Sullivan was involved in all sorts of charity organizations. More importantly, her support was never about a photo op. The Judge gave her all.

Ruth sipped her wine before she spoke. "I didn't know her beyond her reputation. Like me, she was a very busy woman with a family. She did interview me once. Three or four years, I think, before her daughter was murdered. I'd just accepted my judgeship a few months before the interview. Louise was very smart, very sharp."

"Detective Eric Houser is conducting the investigation since new evidence was found," Finley explained.

Ruth nodded. "I heard something about the case. Jack is representing Ray Johnson."

"He is."

Ruth savored another sip of wine. "Even the worst of thugs are entitled to adequate representation."

The comment, though true on one level, hit a nerve, because Jack was the very best. *Adequate* was not even in the ballpark of words that described his legal prowess. Finley drew in a breath and kept her mouth shut. She was working extra hard to get along with her mom . . . to be more patient and less sensitive to her occasional cutting remarks that were rarely intended the way Finley chose to take them. She felt confident both Matt and her father were holding their breath.

"I suspect he would fit neatly into the category of thug," Finley agreed. "However, at the moment I'm leaning toward someone else as Lucy's killer."

The Judge made an "aha" face. "The missing brother, I presume. I recall his disappearance came up during the investigation, but no connection between him and Lucy was found." She turned to her husband. "What was the younger brother's name?"

Bart shook his head, his face pale, maybe even a little sweaty. "I'm afraid I don't remember."

"Ian," Finley supplied. "The second child who came along well after the first and caused a split in whatever *daddy* had to pass along." These were the details tugging at Finley. More so now that new connections— however vague—to Lucy had come to light. The car wash receipt; the idea that the ex-wife knew Lucy. Couple those with Lucy's handbag being found in the warehouse, and in Finley's opinion, coincidence was on its way out the window. Which was exactly why Metro had homed in on Ray Johnson. That said, their evidence was still flimsy at best.

"You think the older brother," Matt said to Finley, "Ray, had a grudge against his younger brother."

"Maybe. He may have been the one to tell him to split after the murder. The tragedy worked great for him. Positioned him to inherit everything and ended any need to compete for *daddy's* attention."

"But you believe," her father said, his gaze on hers, a flicker of worry there, "the Johnson family was involved in her murder."

"It's the only lead for now. I don't think Houser will get to trial with the evidence he has shown so far. He'll need something more to make that happen. Basically, I think this whole exercise is a fishing expedition that may or may not produce the hoped-for results."

"But," her father repeated, "is that what you believe?"

Finley tried to read the worry, or whatever it was, in his voice and eyes. "I'm leaning that way, yes. It's only the lack of solid evidence that keeps me from being certain."

Bart turned his focus back to his food.

"Sounds like Metro is fighting an uphill battle," the Judge noted, drawing Finley's attention. "Johnson is lucky to have an attorney of Jack's caliber on his side." She smiled. "He may, however, regret having you digging around."

Finley gave her a nod. And there it was. Proof that Finley had taken the Judge's earlier comment the wrong way. It would take time to get beyond that automatic response. "We'll see. I've barely started my investigation."

"You know Finley," Matt pointed out with a grin. "She won't stop until she finds all the little pieces."

He knew her well.

Matt made a face then, checked his smart watch. He looked to Finley. "According to a contact of mine at our local ABC station, we should turn on the news."

They all relocated to the family room, where Bart powered on the television and selected the channel. The Judge and Matt stood a few feet from the large television screen as a reporter, Jason Bentley, spoke from an office Finley recognized instantly. The office of Davidson County District Attorney Briggs—her former boss.

While the reporter waxed on about the esteemed DA, Finley sidled over to her father and whispered, "You okay?"

He blinked at her, frowned. "Of course. Why do you ask?"

"I thought maybe the subject of my new case might have made you uncomfortable."

"Certainly not." He worked up a fake smile. "You and I talked all that out already."

His immediate shift of attention to the television and the nervous twitch near his eye said otherwise.

She wrapped her arm around his. "Love you, Dad."

He peered down at her. His smile was real this time. "Love you, too, sweetie. I just need you to be careful. This client of Jack's and his family are not good people."

She leaned her head against his shoulder. "I'll be careful."

This seemed to satisfy him for the moment.

Bentley's questions related to next year's election drew Finley's interest back to the television. He deliberately tossed out a number of negative points that kept popping up in the news. Briggs had been accused repeatedly of being too soft on crime. Most recently his travel budget had been attacked after a disgruntled former assistant spilled about him using travel funds for personal vacations. All of which Briggs strongly refuted.

It was when Bentley moved on to who might be able to unseat him that Finley saw her name scroll across the screen.

She went cold, then hot. Every muscle in her body tensed.

"The rumors are growing that former assistant district attorney Finley O'Sullivan will be running against you next year."

Briggs smiled in that condescending way of his. "As you probably know," he said from behind his too large, too ornate desk, "I brought Finley O'Sullivan onboard. She was a brilliant young attorney at the time. I had high hopes for her."

"A perfect record of wins," Bentley pointed out. "Her record stands unbeaten."

Briggs shook his head. "What happened to Ms. O'Sullivan was a true tragedy. After her husband's murder, she was not the same. She fell apart. You likely know this as well."

"It was the headline at the time," Bentley agreed. "But she's pulled herself back up. She's handling some very high-profile cases with Jack Finnegan's law firm. She still appears to be a force to be reckoned with."

"She is very talented," Briggs agreed, "as I said. But there are underlying issues, baggage that comes with the tragedy she suffered."

"She single-handedly brought down Carson Dempsey," Bentley reminded the DA.

"I like this guy," Matt said.

"He's good," Finley's father agreed.

"Wait for it," the Judge said. "I've seen him in action before. He always does a setup before jerking the rug."

Finley steeled herself and waited through a number of other nice comments about her work as compared to that of Briggs. But then the tone of the exchange took a different direction.

"You believe Finley O'Sullivan is unstable," Bentley suggested.

"She has been in therapy for a long while now," Briggs said. "There were several unsettling episodes that occurred during her battle to prove Carson Dempsey was responsible for her husband's murder. Being the district attorney and representing the people of this county involves a good deal more than just taking down the bad guys. We have rules. The letter of the law. If you break those rules and the law, there is no place for you in a position of power."

A blast of rage rushed through Finley. She turned to her parents. "I think it's time for me to call it a night." She shifted her attention to Matt then. "You ready?"

"Whenever you are."

Finley hugged her parents and thanked them for the lovely dinner; then she was out of there.

Mainly because she refused to explode in front of witnesses. Except for Matt.

They were driving away before she dared to speak.

"Briggs is the scum of the earth."

"Definitely," Matt confirmed as he made a turn. "A total snake."

"He wanted to give me a taste of what's coming." She saw right through the son of a bitch. He wanted her to see that the race would be personal, ruthless, painful.

Matt braked for a red traffic light. "I know you can't possibly be scared."

Finley's head swiveled in his direction. "Hell no."

"That's what I thought," Matt said, hitting the accelerator as the light changed to green. "You have walked over hot coals . . . over glass.

You"—he glanced in her direction—"have been to hell and back twice over and survived. Let Briggs throw out all those accusations in an effort to make you look bad. He will not win."

Finley considered the things Briggs had said. All of it was true. At least he wasn't lying about her, but that would likely come in time. Would people understand that she'd done what she had to do? Would they see that Dempsey had left her no choice? Briggs would present her bloodied history in a way that twisted her actions toward the negative. She would have to work hard to deflect his perverse criticisms.

Was it worth the fight?

Her life would no doubt be turned upside down again. People would be watching closely to see if she might crack this time. It was possible that the tension could cause friction between her and Matt.

So, Finley asked herself once more, would it be worth the fight?

Hell yes.

16

After the Murder

Thirteen Years Ago

Tuesday, November 21

Tennessee Department of Human Services
French Landing Drive, Nashville, 2:00 p.m.

Barton O'Sullivan stared, unseeing, at the reports. He could not concentrate.

Louise Cagle's husband had died. A sudden heart attack, and the man was a heart surgeon. But who wouldn't have a heart attack after what happened. Dear God, what else was the poor woman supposed to suffer? She was alone now. Devastated. With the death of her husband, she had lost everything.

What was he saying? Losing a child was unbearable in and of itself.

Bart gritted his teeth. He could not feel this guilt. He couldn't. He simply could not. What happened to Lucy was not his fault. She was dead; nothing he did or didn't do now would make a difference.

Except to her grieving mother.

He closed his eyes, pressed his fingertips there. He couldn't change what had already happened. He could not undo any of it. It was done. That poor girl was dead.

A light rap at his door, and Bart struggled to pull himself together. His secretary would have messages for him. She'd taken a late lunch. He had work to do. He had to focus.

"Come on in."

He straightened and drew in a deep breath. *Move on. Don't look back.*

The door opened, but it wasn't his secretary.

It was *her* . . . Louise Cagle.

His heart stuttered to a near stop. He shot to his feet as if a spring had been released.

"Hello." He forced his lips into what he hoped passed for a smile. "I'm sorry, did we have an appointment?"

She closed the door behind herself and walked right up to his desk, her face set in stony determination. "I want to know how you were involved with my daughter?"

"I . . ." Fear strapped a stranglehold on his throat. "I'm not sure what you mean. I didn't—"

"Yes, you did," she snarled. "I hired a good private investigator, and he found evidence of your meetings with my daughter."

She glared at him with such ferocity that he had to force himself not to stumble back. "I knew your daughter," he confessed. "She came here to my office for research on her thesis paper."

"You expect me to believe that story?" She shook her head. "If my daughter needed research sources, I could have given her an endless supply."

He moistened his lips, struggled to slow the organ now floundering in his chest. "She . . ." He swallowed the lump swelling in his throat. "She didn't want you to know the subject of her paper."

This statement gave the poor woman pause. The weakness, the defeat, the devastation she felt showed through her anger. "What on earth are you talking about?"

"She wanted to surprise you with an in-depth story that would rise to the level of the work you do." He managed a half smile that trembled on his lips. "She was so in awe of you. She wanted to show you she could do it too."

"Why?" Louise shook her head. "This makes no sense. My Lucy was headed to medical school."

This was a part he didn't really want to share, but he wasn't sure he had a choice.

"Lucy wasn't interested in medical school."

Louise launched into a tirade.

Bart held up his hands and waited for her to quiet. "She didn't want to tell you for just this reason. You and her father had her future all mapped out for her, but Lucy had other ideas."

Louise's face fell. The stark new flash of devastation in her eyes knifed into his chest. God almighty, he did not want to be the cause of more pain.

"She admired you so," he hastened to add. "She wanted to be just like you."

Louise shook her head. "Why should I believe you?" Fury tightened her features once more. "I haven't turned your name over to the police yet, but they will figure out she came to see you all too regularly. If you're not telling me the whole truth, you will regret it. I know who your wife is. I can cause both of you a great deal of trouble."

Good Lord. If Ruth learned about this, he would never hear the end of it.

More importantly, he could not become a person of interest in this case. He could not tell anyone all that he knew. Not to help this poor, sad woman. Not to keep his wife from learning about his involvement.

Not for anything in the world.

"You tell me," Louise said, snapping him back to the here and now, "what I want to know, and I assure you that your name will never come up in the investigation."

How could she offer a promise like that?

Every part of him started to shake. "How can you make such a statement?"

If she knew what he knew . . . she would go straight to the police, and then—

She pressed closer to his desk, her gaze fierce and fixed on his. "You have a daughter close to the same age as my Lucy."

He nodded. His throat thickened to the point he could no longer breathe. Why did she think he couldn't give her the answers she wanted? How could she know? The ache of defeat tore through him.

"You have a wife you love and admire."

"I . . . I do. Yes." Dear God, how could he explain that his daughter and wife were his world . . . he had to protect them?

"If you were in my shoes and someone had taken those things from you," she pushed on, "what would you do?"

"I . . . can't." The weight of the burden he carried caused a moan to burst from him. "I . . . I just can't."

Her eyes widened. Sweet Jesus, he had already said too much.

"I will not go to the police," she pleaded. "You have my word. I have other ways of taking care of whatever needs to be done. *No one will ever know I spoke to you.*"

His gaze locked with hers. "What do you mean?"

"Trust me, please," she begged. "Just trust me. Not once in my career have I ever betrayed a source. I will not betray you. Not to anyone."

The air filled his starving lungs. Did he dare? What if she got herself killed based on what he told her? He couldn't bear to be the reason . . .

"Tell me," she urged. "Please tell me what you know. I can see that you know something—something you want to tell me. Something important about my daughter. Please . . . I just want peace. I'll never have that until I know."

God forgive him, but he couldn't do this. He could not watch this misery and keep this awful, awful secret any longer.

He had to tell her . . . to *help* her.

17

Now

Thursday, December 7

Vintage Autohaus
Mcmillin Street, Nashville, 8:30 a.m.

It was a new day, and Finley was moving on to the next stop on her list. Friends of the missing Ian Johnson. The best part about reinterviewing potential witnesses thirteen years later was seeing just how much their statements changed. People changed. Grew more mature—hopefully. Memories dimmed or sharpened. Perspectives shifted. Regrets echoed. It was always interesting to see the differences. Then, her job was to determine which—if any—of those changes made a difference.

The first name on the list of Ian's friends was Troy Clinton. Clinton had started a small auto shop after high school and now operated the biggest mechanic shop for vintage and foreign cars in Nashville. Lined up along the lot awaiting his skilled touch were high-end Mercedes, BMWs, Land Rovers, and even a Rolls-Royce, among others.

Finley closed the door of her Subaru and started toward the office entrance. The shop, too, was vintage. A small office with a full glass front and a line of six bays for servicing vehicles. A good-size fenced lot attached to the office end of the building safeguarded the cars awaiting service. County records showed Clinton had bought the property from the Johnson Development Group. Finley wondered what kind of discount he'd been given and for what reason.

Finley pushed through the entrance door, setting the attached bell to jingling. A young man who looked to be in his early twenties glanced up from the glossy hot rod magazine he'd been flipping through.

He smiled. "Morning, ma'am. Can I help you?"

The name tag sewed onto his khaki shirt said Trey. He looked enough like Troy to be his younger brother, which she suspected he was. Southern people liked naming offspring after themselves or something similar. She would bet money the two had a father named Trent or Trace. Finley was a perfect example. The *Fin* in Finley was from *Finnegan*. She'd been named after her godfather. Her middle name, Bishop, she shared with her mother. It was her maternal grandmother's maiden name.

"Trey, I'm looking for Troy Clinton. Is he here today?"

He gave her a nod. "That's my brother. Hold on and I'll go get him."

Trey disappeared through a side door that was also glass and led to the extended area where the work happened. He hustled down the line of bays holding cars currently being repaired or serviced. From outside, the bays looked to be separate spaces, but they were actually one long rectangle. The young man stopped at a Porsche and spoke to the man with his head poked under the hood—which was actually at the back of the vehicle instead of the front.

The man leaning over the engine raised up and glanced in her direction. Finley figured he was Troy. He wiped his hands on a shop cloth and followed Trey back to the office. Once through the door, Trey resumed his skimming of the magazine with all the fancy cars and the half-naked chicks while Troy tucked the shop cloth into his back pocket and smiled—one exactly like Trey's.

"Morning, ma'am. How can I help you?"

"Mr. Clinton, I'm investigator Finley O'Sullivan, and I'm looking into the murder of Lucy Cagle. Do you have some time to answer a few questions? Ray Johnson gave me your name."

Clinton did that hitch with his head. A kind of upward nod of acknowledgment. "Sure. Ray mentioned you'd be calling on me." He gestured to a door on the other side of the room. "Why don't we step outside?"

He crossed to the door and opened it but waited for Finley to exit first. The door led to a covered patio area, complete with picnic tables, within the fenced lot. A break area, she supposed. Beyond the patio were the vehicles waiting for service.

Troy leaned a hip against one of the tables. "So, they found something on her case after all this time?"

"They did."

He nodded. "About time."

"Did you know Lucy?"

He shook his head. "Only what I saw on the news."

"You were friends with Ian Johnson."

"I was." He laughed. "We were tight. Me, him, Skyler Wright, and Aaron Cost. Aaron died in a car crash year before last."

"Have the three of you kept in touch?"

"Pretty much. I mean, we run into each other from time to time, but we all have wives and families, so not like we used to. Skyler and I lost touch with Aaron's family after he died."

"Leaving behind a young family is never easy," she said.

"No, ma'am." He stared at the ground, as if considering his old friend and those he left behind.

He appeared at ease answering her questions. Johnson had given him a heads-up, so it was entirely possible he'd also provided guidelines for the correct answers. Particularly if her assessment of the real estate deal they'd made for this property proved accurate. Finley would know soon enough if Clinton owed a debt of gratitude to his old friend's big brother.

"Looking back to when you were friends with Ian," Finley said as she settled onto one of the picnic benches, "would you say he was a good guy?"

Troy glanced across the lot of cars before meeting her gaze once more. "Look, I don't like talking bad about people, but the Johnsons, they're not exactly good people, if you know what I mean."

Finley gave a nod of agreement. "I know what you mean."

"But Ian was not like the others. He was a good guy. He cared about people. He was a bit of a nerd. He liked reading and gardening." Troy laughed. "We all considered him kind of weird that way. But I guess it made sense, 'cause back when he was a really little kid, he spent most of his time in the garden with his mom. Ray sure didn't want anything to do with him. His mom was especially protective of him, but she died when Ian was like ten, and excuse my French, shit got real after that."

"How do you mean?" A line of tension slid through Finley.

"The old man wanted to toughen Ian up. Make a real Johnson out of him. So he knocked him around some." Troy laughed a dry sound. "Hell, Ray even tried to drown him in the bathtub once."

Her tension shifted to outrage. "Ian told you this."

"He did." Troy's expression turned uncertain. "You're not going to tell Ray everything I say, are you? I don't want any trouble with him."

"I'm not going to tell Ray anything you say." She forced her muscles to relax in hopes of preventing an outward display of her reaction to his words. The idea of someone picking on a child had always been a sore spot for her.

"Okay, so Ian always said Ray hated him." He scrubbed at his jaw. "I don't know if he did or not, but I can tell you he didn't like having a little brother. In my opinion, Ray preferred being the only son. When Ian disappeared, I figured Ray had run him off. Told him he'd kill him or something if he didn't stay gone."

"Were you aware of Ian's involvement with Lucy Cagle?" Finley watched her subject carefully as she made the statement.

His face blanked. He blinked. "What do you mean?"

"Ray said they were dating." This was a total fabrication, but Troy couldn't possibly know that. What she needed was his natural, spontaneous reaction to the idea. If Lucy Cagle and Ian Johnson were connected in any way, this was the most likely scenario. If Troy Clinton had been told not to talk about Lucy, this was the best way to suggest that directive had changed.

A halfhearted shrug lifted the guy's shoulders. "I don't know if I'd call it dating. They met up a couple of times. He thought she was pretty and sweet." Troy rolled his eyes. "Ian was into sweet. The rest of us wanted the wild ones. The ones who would . . . well, you know. Not Ian. That rich girl was more his style."

Adrenaline fired through Finley's veins. And voilà. Proof Lucy had a connection to Ian Johnson. Finley needed more. Every ounce of restraint she possessed was required to remain seated. She wanted to grab the guy and shake more information out of him. He was larger than her and stronger, no doubt. Not to mention his alliance assuredly lay with the Johnsons, if for no other reason than sheer survival. No matter, she wanted—*needed*—to somehow prod him to tell her every damned thing he knew!

"Do you think Ray would have killed Lucy in an effort to control Ian?"

Troy's expression shifted to one of wariness. "I ain't calling no one a killer. The Johnsons have been good to me. They treated me right when I bought this place. Ray's even sent business my way."

Too pushy. Too pointed. Finley scrolled it down a notch. Clinton had read her anticipation too well. "I'm only asking if you think Ray would have gone to great extremes to either control or push away Ian. He let me know he wasn't happy with the relationship."

More lies. But sometimes it took a carefully framed deception to get the truth.

Troy considered her question for a moment. "If Ray was going to kill anyone, it would have been Ian. But to tell you the truth, I don't think Ray would kill anyone. He's kind of a blowhard, if you know what I mean. He likes pushing people around and puffing out his chest, but the follow-through doesn't live up to the preview. Personally, I think he hoped to run Ian off with those tactics."

Possibly. Finley chose a simpler question next. "Did Ian talk to you about Lucy?"

"Not much. It all happened really quick. They met completely by accident. She had a flat tire, and Ian helped her out. They exchanged phone numbers and met up a few times. I think he really liked her."

"Did you speak with him after her murder?"

Troy moved his head side to side. "Ian like went into seclusion. He didn't answer his phone. Didn't go out. I even went to his house. I knew he was there because his car was there, and he wouldn't come to the door. He wouldn't talk to any of us. I never saw him again after that. And then Ray said he was gone."

"When was the last time you saw him?"

He thought about that for a while. "The day she was killed, I think. I ran into him at Sonic. We talked for a bit. Ate burgers and fries." His expression shifted to one of surprise. "You know, now that I think about it, he said something . . ." His forehead furrowed in concentration. "Something about getting away from it all. But I didn't think anything of it at the time. Later, I figured he had either made good on it or Ray had finally succeeded in running him off."

Finley's pulse was tripping at this point. "Did he mention anything about seeing Lucy that day? Maybe he mentioned plans with her."

Troy shook his head. "I even asked him about her. You know, if they were getting serious or whatever, and he closed down. I figured she told him she couldn't see him anymore. I mean, let's face it, they weren't exactly from the same kind of families. The relationship was never going to work."

"Did he seem angry when you asked about her?"

Troy appeared to think about the question before answering. "Not angry, no. In a hurry to get away from the question. I got the impression he didn't want to talk about her that day."

"One last question," she said. "Why did you tell the police a different story thirteen years ago?"

The man stared at the ground for a moment before meeting her gaze. "Because I was afraid of what Ray and his daddy would do if I told the truth. It was a little crazy around that time, and we were all worried about getting pulled into the investigation." He shrugged. "It's guys like us who get nailed when rich white girls get murdered."

Finley struggled with the urge to demand more answers . . . to rant at this guy for keeping the truth from the investigation thirteen years ago. *Stay cool.*

"Thank you." Finley withdrew a card from her bag and handed it to him. "If you think of anything else that might help us solve this mystery, I would appreciate a call."

He tucked her card in his shirt pocket. "No problem." A pained expression scrunched his face. "Just make sure you don't tell Ray all the stuff I said about him. I mean, I'm not afraid of him anymore or nothing like that, but he can make problems with my business."

"Not a word," she promised. "This conversation was about helping me determine what happened to Ian, and nothing else."

They walked back through the office. At the door to the front parking area where she'd left her Subaru, he said, "Ian is—was, whatever—a good guy. I don't think he would have hurt Lucy or anyone else."

Finley thanked him and headed to interview number two. She preferred doing these sorts of interviews cold in hopes of getting truer responses. More often than not, it worked.

The interview with Skyler Wright went basically the same way as Clinton's. He seemed surprised to be visited by Finley, giving her the impression that Troy and Ray had not given him a heads-up. He, too, claimed Ian had a thing for Lucy, though he couldn't say for how long or how serious the relationship was. Wright also insisted that fear of getting into trouble had kept him from coming forward thirteen years ago. As with Troy, she read no deceit in his voice or mannerisms. If either had been lying, they were damned good at it.

After interviewing the two people who were supposed to be closest to Ian, the consensus was the same: Ian Johnson was a good guy. He wouldn't hurt anyone.

Ray Johnson was a bad guy who wanted rid of his little brother.

Most important of all: Lucy Cagle and Ian Johnson had been involved.

Funny how it seemed someone really wanted the world to know that now—after all these years. When the stars all aligned that perfectly, Finley always worried.

She had a feeling the other shoe was about to drop.

Cagle Residence
Murfreesboro Road, Franklin, 10:30 a.m.

Houser was waiting at the gate when Finley arrived. She entered the code, and the two of them drove down the driveway and parked near the house. This was her way of showing her appreciation for that visit to the lab. Truth was, she would have done it anyway. Houser was one of those people whose good side she wanted to stay on.

The opportunity to witness his reactions to Cagle's office and murder board was a fringe benefit.

"It's hard to believe this place has been sitting here for thirteen years," he commented as Finley got out of her car.

"I guess Louise just couldn't deal with handling the closure. Then she disappeared. There wasn't anyone else, so the responsibility would have fallen to some attorney, if the family had one." Really, Finley got it. The idea, at the time, had likely felt overwhelming. The more time that passed, the easier it became to just leave everything as it was.

Houser surveyed the place. Shook his head. "I had no idea it was standing here empty."

"Only empty of people," Finley pointed out. "All the things that belonged to the Cagles—even the most private stuff—is still there, just like they left it."

"That's bizarre."

Finley nodded. "Like a museum no one visits."

She had been guilty of keeping her house that way for a very long time as well. Derrick's clothes had remained in the closet. Every little thing had stayed in place—even the Fourth of July decorations they'd put up just before Derrick was murdered. It had taken more than a year for her to move on. She could see how Maureen Downey simply hadn't been able to deal with what was left behind.

"You mind if we walk through the whole house?"

Finley pushed aside the painful thoughts. "Not at all. I have some time before my noon meeting."

She unlocked the front door and showed him around the first level. Like her, he was surprised at the lack of clutter and said as much. Again, Finley noted how tastefully done the home was. Upstairs she did a little more looking in Louise's and Lucy's rooms. Not that she expected to find anything she'd missed, but it kept her busy while Houser wandered around.

When he was satisfied he'd seen everything he needed to in the house, they moved on to the garage. Finley saved the best, Louise's home office, for last. They both spent some time going over Lucy's car, which had been returned to the family once the lab had completed its forensic work. Then did the same with Louise's and her husband Scott's.

"The last time anyone saw Louise Cagle," Houser said, "was when she left her office on Thursday, November twenty-third. The security guard remembers wishing her a happy Thanksgiving. The detectives searched her office thoroughly, went through every piece of paper and found nothing that gave any indication whatsoever of where she'd gone or why she'd abruptly left. The same was said about the house. They came, they looked, they found nothing."

Being here, seeing all the family's things, pained him. The hurt was palpable in his voice. He really had lived with this hanging over his head all this time. Finley hoped whatever answers they found would give him closure. No one appreciated the importance of closure more than she did.

"Come on." Finley headed for the walk-through door that led from the garage into the backyard. "I'll show you the really interesting part."

He followed her to the small brick building that may or may not have been original to the property. It seemed to have been built from the same brick, but whatever its original purpose, Louise Cagle had turned it into the perfect escape for her work at home. Why had she left all the work she'd done on Lucy's case behind as well? Had she gone off somewhere and just ended her life?

As sad as that idea was, it was the only one that really made any sort of sense.

Inside, Houser took his time looking around. As he moved into the back section of the one-room structure, he gave a long, low whistle.

Finley asked, "There was no mention of this, no photos, nothing in the case file?"

He shook his head. "Nothing. I can only assume she started the board a week or so after Lucy's murder. The police would have already been here and gone." He pointed to the annotation about a follower. "I wish we had more on that."

"Me too." Finley watched as he surveyed the board from one end to the other. He paused on the photo of his much younger self.

"Damn. That's unnerving."

"Why do you suppose she put your photo on the board?"

He stared at the floor a moment before meeting her gaze. "I wasn't happy when Lucy moved on. I called a few times. Showed up at her door and spoke angrily to her." He shoved his hands into his trouser pockets. "No one is more ashamed about that than me. I was young. Stupid."

Full of hormones, Finley thought.

"She was smart to question you," Finley said. "Any investigator worth his or her salt would have done the same."

"She believed me," he said, his eyes telling Finley he desperately wanted her to believe him too. "That's why she didn't give my name to the detectives on the case."

A logical explanation. "Okay. She believed you."

"It's important to me," he said, an urgency in his voice, "that you believe me."

"I believe that you had nothing to do with Lucy's murder," she allowed. "I believe you want to solve her case because you feel a personal obligation to her. I believe you will get this done."

He nodded. "Thank you. I want to find the truth more than you can know."

She was familiar with that place too. More than she would like to be. "I interviewed two of Ian Johnson's friends from thirteen years ago."

He looked surprised. "Wright and Clinton?"

"You talked to them?" Finley doubted they had gotten the same responses.

"They're on my list, but they've avoided me so far. They were both interviewed—along with another guy, Aaron something—after Ian was reported missing. Cagle was pushing Metro, and they were trying to connect the dots to anything and everything. At that time, all three claimed not to know Lucy. They insisted Ian didn't know her either."

Finley lifted her eyebrows. "You will find it interesting that both Clinton and Wright were more than happy to talk today about Ian's infatuation with Lucy. You should follow up with them. See if they give you the same story they gave me."

"Which was," Houser prompted.

"Ray basically bullied his little brother. Made it obvious in word and deed that he didn't want him around. Both Clinton and Wright insisted that Ian wouldn't hurt a fly. Both seemed to think Ian and Lucy were involved on some level right up to her murder."

Houser turned back to the case board. "I wonder why Louise didn't personally question any of Ian's friends. Or any member of the Johnson family for that matter. If Metro questioned his abrupt disappearance after Lucy's murder, why wouldn't she follow up? She was too good at digging into cases and had far too many resources to miss something like that."

"Then again," Finley countered, "we figured it out because someone wanted us to." She thought of what Bauer had said. "The handbag and other items were found, and those things led us to the Johnsons, and suddenly all these unexpected pieces start falling into place."

Houser's eyes narrowed. "You think someone planted them to lead us there."

"The PI, Bauer, sure seems to think so." She walked closer to the case board. "Makes sense, if you think about it. All this time there has been nothing, and suddenly we're being spoon-fed this connection to the Johnsons."

"I don't like it," Houser confessed. "But you're right, it makes a sort of twisted sense."

"Ray Johnson gave me the names of Ian's friends, and they told me a story that fit the narrative except for the answers I prompted with a narrative of my own. His ex-wife did the same. He had to know I'd be questioning her." She met Houser's gaze. "Did you talk to her yet?"

"Like Ian's friends, she's avoiding me."

Funny, Finley mused. It was almost as if Ray Johnson wanted her to know this version of the truth. But no one else. She had a bad feeling where that might be going.

"Fin?"

She blinked. "Sorry, I was thinking . . ."

"Do you think any of this is leading us to the actual truth?"

Did she? "Who knows? But truth or fiction, it all leads to the same place—the Johnsons. The old man is dying. Ray is poised to inherit everything—as long as Ian doesn't reappear and demand his share. Or unless he ends up out of the picture and the ex-wife and kids get everything."

Houser nodded, his face grim. "I can see where you're going, but I need more than conjecture to make a case related to Ian or Ray's ex-wife or some business competitor. Fact is, I'm hanging on by the skin of my teeth with Lucy's case. Any minute now I may be ordered to stop wasting resources if I don't come up with something."

Finley considered the case board and all it contained, as well as what it didn't. "It all just stops without finding any definitive answers. Why simply fade away before finding the truth? Why didn't Louise hang on? And where the hell did she go?"

These were the big questions in Finley's mind. It was also the part that made the least sense.

"Maybe she couldn't get past the new loss when her husband died. It pushed her over the edge."

Possibly. Cagle had disappeared just over three weeks after his death. "But there's a difference between losing a spouse and losing a child," Finley contrasted for the sake of argument. "There's also a difference between a natural death and a murder. I don't get why she let the murder of her only child go without a more extended fight—no matter that her husband had a heart attack and died. It doesn't fit with what we know about her."

"Maybe she let it all go," Houser suggested. "She may have gone somewhere private and checked out."

Also a possibility. Finley had certainly considered that route several times. She searched the images and notes on the board again. *Why did you stop looking?*

"I had a phone conversation with your father."

Finley snapped back to attention. "You did?" She imagined that went over like a lead balloon. Her father—for whatever reasons he wasn't sharing—was extremely sensitive about this case.

"He explained about the research Lucy was doing and how he was helping her."

Deep inside a defense mechanism kicked into gear. Finley couldn't have missed the doubt in Houser's voice if she had tried. As certain as she was that her father wasn't telling her everything, she was one hundred percent certain he had nothing to do with Lucy's death.

"He said," Houser went on, "he didn't really know her mother beyond her public image."

Now Finley was just pissed off. "Do you have reason to *not* believe what he said?"

The hands that had been deep in his pockets now withdrew and braced on his hips as he glanced away from her and at the floor. "I can't say that I didn't believe him, but I noticed something yesterday that gave me pause."

Finley went dead still, not even breathing. "I'm listening."

Houser met her gaze with unmistakable reluctance. "I decided on an impromptu face-to-face visit with your father just before lunch yesterday." He shrugged. "You know how it is."

She knew exactly how it was. To speak in person was far more telling than a phone interview. To do so cold was even better. Houser thought her father was lying, and he wanted to confirm as much with a face-to-face meet.

"But when I turned onto his street for the visit, I spotted him driving away from the house."

"You followed him." Finley couldn't keep the outrage out of her tone. She clamped down on her emotions, forced herself to hear him out.

Houser nodded. "I don't know, it was just a hunch. A sudden itch I felt compelled to scratch."

"Where did he go?" Finley's throat felt dry. Her heart rate had started to steadily climb.

"To the Five Points Diner over on Woodland."

"Okay." Finley braced for the rest. Whatever he had to say, he wasn't looking forward to the punch line or he wouldn't be dragging it out so.

"He met Maureen Downey there."

Finley frowned even as a trickle of relief had her breathing again. "I have no idea why he would meet with her. I wasn't aware he knew her, personally or otherwise."

"Well, that's not the troubling part."

So, it got worse. Shit. "Don't keep me in suspense."

"After they left the diner, your father drove to Ray Johnson's office. He went inside but came right back out. Since Johnson's car wasn't around, I'm assuming he wasn't in."

Uncertainty and no small amount of fear chased Finley's outrage away. Why the hell would her father visit Ray Johnson?

"You have any ideas on why he would lunch with Downey and then try to see Johnson?" Houser asked.

"I do not," she stated, her words brittle, "but rest assured I will find out."

"Thanks," he said, "for giving me a heads-up on what you learned from Ian's friends and Ray's ex-wife. And for telling me about the house and showing me around."

It was a struggle, but Finley somehow set worries about her father aside for a moment. "You can thank me by getting me that meeting with Dempsey."

"I'm working on it."

Barely able to hold herself back from rushing out of the house and to her car, Finley checked the time. "I should get going."

"Me too. I have a one o'clock with the chief."

Finley readied the alarm system and locked the door. As calmly as possible, she waved to Houser as he drove away.

Worry twisted in her gut like barbed wire. What the hell was her father doing?

18

Since Finley couldn't reach her father—a good thing, considering she needed to cool down before confronting him—she moved on to the next item on her list: interviewing Lucy Cagle's other two known friends. If their statements changed to the degree Ian's friends' had, Finley was going to start to wonder about the detective who led the original investigation.

Gwyneth Garrison was a counselor at her and Lucy's alma mater. Garrison had agreed to meet Finley at the school's Alumnae Relations building. There was an empty office, she'd said, since the coordinator position had not been refilled. She suggested they would have more privacy there.

Finley suspected the woman primarily preferred to keep the meeting away from any place where she might be seen during their appointment. Finley had no issue with that.

She had attended an elite private school as well, but this one took prestige to a whole new level. All girls, and totally focused on grooming young women to reach their maximum potential. Many celebrities had attended the prominent school. Reese Witherspoon, for one. Who

Debra Webb

wouldn't want to attend this school—as long as parents had somewhere in the neighborhood of forty thousand a year to contribute.

Louise Cagle had graduated from Harpeth Hall, and she'd intended for her only child to do the same. Lucy had almost made it. With honors, no less.

Gwyneth Garrison had been one of Lucy's closest friends, according to the case file. This information was confirmed by both Maureen and Jessica Downey. The other close friend, Natalie Williams, had not yet returned Finley's call.

Since she was employed by the school, Garrison could not have avoided Finley if she wanted to, though she had tried. She hadn't answered her home phone or her cell, but she was unable to evade a call to the school when it was transferred directly to her office and the aforementioned celebrity alum's name was used.

"How do you know Reese?" Gwyneth asked as they settled into the plush chairs that made up a conversation corner in the large office.

"Our parents belong to the same country club." This was true . . . once. Finley had no idea if it was still true.

She forced a tight smile. "I'm glad you weren't simply using her name to reach me. I would have called you back when I had time."

Finley held up her hands. "Absolutely not." This wasn't entirely true, of course, but neither was the other woman's statement.

"So, how can I help you, Ms. O'Sullivan?"

"The Lucy Cagle homicide case has been reopened, and I'm plowing through all those thirteen-year-old details."

Garrison nodded slowly. "I see." She took a breath. "Lucy and I were friends. Good friends, I would say. Like all the girls in our class, we were very competitive. As I told the detectives after her murder, Lucy was working on her senior thesis. She would not tell me what it was about." She shrugged, shook her head. "I suppose I didn't deserve her trust when it came to schoolwork. I had stolen her ideas a couple of

188

times. I'm not proud of it, but there it is. I'm sure you read where her mother told the detectives as much."

There had been no mention in any of the statements Finley had seen, but she appreciated the woman's honesty, however it came about, and said as much.

"Did Lucy have a crush, a special guy or girl in her life?" What eighteen-year-old didn't? And yet the info in that area of the victim's life was sparse.

"No girl crushes for sure," Gwyneth said. "She dated a guy pretty steadily over the summer before senior year. Eric something." She made an "aha" face. "Houser. He's a police detective now."

"Why did she and Eric break up?"

"I think because things got too serious . . . too heavy. She really wanted to focus on her education." Gwyneth rolled her eyes. "Unlike the rest of us."

Garrison was married with three kids. She had gone straight from college to marriage and motherhood, not taking on a career until her kids were in school—private school, of course.

"Around the time of the murder, was she seeing anyone at all?" Finley pressed.

"She mentioned a guy a couple of times. She never told me his name, but she kind of went all gooey and sweet when she mentioned him. I asked her, but she would never talk about specifics. I'm sorry. I really don't know any more than that. Lucy was a wonderful person. A good student, a caring friend. My goodness, she was always volunteering to help others. And I'm not just saying that because she's dead. You can ask anyone from our class. They will all tell you the same—Lucy is the last person we expected to meet with a tragic ending. She was as close to an angel as you'd find."

"No trouble with anyone, ever?" Finley didn't doubt Lucy had been all the things everyone said, but even the best human messed up sometimes. Said the wrong thing. Made a mistake. Something.

"Never." She shook her head. "In fact, I recall when one of the custodians was ill. He'd lost his wife. My goodness, Mr. Brewer has been here as long as I can remember. He must be the oldest working custodian in Tennessee." Garrison made a face as if remembering something, then shook it off. "Anyway, Lucy set up a chain of helpers to take dinner to him at home each evening. To help out with anything he needed, like laundry. It was incredible. She made sure he was taken care of for a whole month. It was December of our junior year. She even made sure that she and the other girls, including me, who had joined in to help went to see him on Christmas Day, bearing gifts. Mr. Brewer had no children or other family, so he would have been alone otherwise."

Finley jotted down his name on her notepad. "Do you have his home address? Phone number?"

"I can get that information for you." She made a quick call to the administrative office. When she'd passed along the information, she offered, "Would you like me to introduce you to Mr. Brewer? I have a few more minutes before my next appointment."

"That would be great."

They left the office and exited the small building. At least small compared to all the other grand structures on the campus. The walk to the visual-arts building took only a few minutes. Garrison chatted the entire distance, pointing out the different buildings and other important features as if she were giving a campus tour. Finley suspected she hoped to prevent additional questions about Lucy. Most people were uncomfortable when it came to murder investigations. Who wouldn't be?

Whatever Garrison's reason, Finley did not pick up on any tells suggesting the woman was hiding information or lying. Her discomfort was not unusual, particularly considering the admitted competitiveness between her and the victim. Guilt was not always deserved but often a burden to carry nonetheless.

Finley thought about Johnson's ex-wife's statement and decided to get Garrison's take on it. "Do you recall during senior year Lucy having taken on any babysitting jobs?"

Garrison stopped at a door marked "Custodial Services." She laughed. "Ah, no. Lucy was a wonderful person, but she was extremely ambitious. Children were not on her radar in any capacity. She would never have even considered babysitting. And why would she? Her family was very wealthy, and the work certainly wouldn't have added to her university résumé." She smiled and knocked on the door. An "It's open" echoed, and Garrison turned the knob and stepped inside. Finley followed.

The door entered into a good-size office that had two other doors on the far side, one marked as a lavatory and the other as a supply closet. An older man, seventyish, sat behind the desk. He peered over his glasses at them.

"Mr. Brewer, this is Finley O'Sullivan, she's helping with the Lucy Cagle case. You may or may not know that it's been reopened. She wanted to ask some questions about Lucy. Do you have a few minutes?"

He nodded. "I do." To Finley, he said, "Have a seat." He gestured to the molded-plastic chairs in front of his desk.

"I have to get to my office," Garrison said. She smiled at Finley. "Is there anything else I can do to help?"

"Since you ask," Finley said, "if you have an in with Natalie Williams, I would like to speak with her as well."

"I'll see what I can do."

Garrison flashed a smile for Brewer and then left the office. Finley sat down in one of the chairs and placed her bag on the floor next to her feet.

"Thank you for taking the time to talk with me, Mr. Brewer." There had been no mention of this man and his connection to Lucy in the part of the official case file she had received from Houser. Likewise, there had been nothing on Cagle's case board about him. How was that possible, considering what Garrison had just told Finley?

"Call me Howard. Do you think you'll be able to find Lucy's killer this time?"

Finley opted not to take offense at his question. She wasn't with Metro, and she had not participated in the previous investigation. She wasn't even exactly participating in it this time. Not the way he likely thought anyway.

"I hope to find the truth about what happened to Lucy, yes."

His eyes narrowed. "You sound like a PI instead of a cop."

"I'll take that as a compliment," she said, evading his question.

"Maybe you shouldn't," he pointed out. "Others have tried."

She wondered if he meant Bauer. "You and Lucy were friends. Can you tell me what you remember about her?"

"She had a good heart. A loving soul. She wasn't full of herself, like most of these kids." He seemed to catch himself. "No offense to any of them." He took a breath and went on. "I watched Lucy grow up, and she was always good to everyone. Never unkind. Never got into trouble. They don't come along every day like that. Lucy was special."

Quite often when speaking of the dead—particularly those whose lives were stolen at such a young age—the ones left behind only remembered the best. Whether it was natural or by design, it was a point any good investigator kept in mind. But with Lucy those good memories appeared to be more consistent than usual. Perhaps she had been special.

Finley asked, "Did she talk to you about her life and things that were going on with her outside of school?"

He shrugged. "Not really, other than right after my wife passed. Mostly Lucy was just very kind to me." He stared at his gnarled-with-age hands. "I should have watched out for her better."

"How would you have done that?"

Surprise flared in his eyes. "I . . . I don't know. I suppose it's just wishful thinking."

"My goal, Howard," Finley urged, noting the regret in his expression as well as his voice, "is to find out who did this. Anything you can tell me might help toward that end and would be greatly appreciated."

He considered Finley for an extended moment. "There was a man she was talking to. A boyfriend, I guess. She was worried about getting too close to him."

"Because a relationship would interfere with her education?"

He shook his head. "Because she feared her parents wouldn't accept him."

Finley got it. Been there, done that. "He wasn't the kind of guy they saw their daughter ending up with." His description fit with the idea that Lucy had a relationship with Ian Johnson—as his friends had stated.

"He had money, she said, but he wasn't a good guy." Brewer made a pained face. "He was a good guy, but he came from a bad family. That's what she said."

"Did she tell you his name?" Additional confirmation would be helpful.

He shook his head. "I wish she had."

"Did you talk to the police about this thirteen years ago?" She chose not to say *after her murder*. The man appeared sincerely aggrieved by the memories.

He shook his head. "They never questioned me. It wasn't like I knew anything useful anyway."

Finley let him off the hook without pointing out that it was often what a person didn't say that mattered most. Instead, she passed her card across his desk. "Please call me if you think of anything else that might help us find the truth."

Brewer nodded, studied the card. "I don't think there's anything else, but if I'm wrong, I'll call you."

Finley thanked him and exited his office and then the building. She wound her way around the lovely campus to her Subaru. Based on what she had learned from Ian Johnson's friends and from Gwyneth Garrison, there was no denying the good guy from the bad family Brewer mentioned was Ian Johnson. If she found reason to push Brewer harder, she would. For now, she saw no reason to punish him for a mistake more people than not made during a criminal investigation. He hadn't believed he had anything relevant to contribute, so he hadn't come forward.

Finley had just backed out of her parking slot when her cell sounded off. The number looked vaguely familiar. She accepted the call. "O'Sullivan."

"This is Natalie Williams. You've been trying to reach me."

Wow. Gwyneth Garrison worked fast.

"Yes," Finley said. "When might you have some time to speak with me?"

"How about now?"

"Text me the address, and I'll be on my way."

Davidson County Clerk's Office
Second Avenue, Nashville, 1:20 p.m.

Natalie Williams was completely different from her very polished friend, Gwyneth Garrison. Never married. No kids. She wore a bulky green sweater with greenish trousers and white walking shoes. Her hair was tucked back into a braid that hung to the middle of her back. She was busy and made no bones about warning Finley that her time was limited. A vase brimming with fresh-cut pink flowers seemed utterly incongruent with the woman, but Finley supposed even the brashest person had a soft side.

The flowers also reminded her she had not ordered any for her neighbor. Damn it. Not enough time in the day . . . or room in her brain.

"Lucy was ambitious," Williams said as she picked through a stack of forms. "She intended to make a name for herself, no matter who she had to trample on to get it done."

Beyond the ambitious part, this was a different story from what Garrison and Brewer had stated. Finley watched the woman's face closely as she asked, "How do you mean?"

"I mean"—Williams paused in her work and stared at Finley—"she was using this guy—a way older guy—to get her research done. This was not a nice guy. Nor was he a guy who needed money. What do you suppose she was giving this guy for the information he passed along?"

Before Finley could stanch the reaction, blood was pounding in her ears. She could not be talking about Finley's father. "Do you know his name?"

Williams shook her head. "She wouldn't say. Just talked about him being hot and hard to resist—he was like in his twenties. But she had to stay focused. That was all she worried about."

Finley breathed easier. Not her father. Ian Johnson, probably. As for Williams's statement, there was some ring of similarity in terms of the ambition that Finley had already learned about, just without the selfish means and motive on Lucy's part.

"Was she afraid of this man?"

"She didn't act like it." Williams leaned forward and spoke quietly. "They would have these secret rendezvous at a car wash, of all places. He would get in her car and tell her stuff while all the noise was blocking their conversation."

Holy shit. The damned car wash. Finley checked off another confirmed lead.

"Did she say where this car wash was?"

"Not that I recall. Anyway, things kept getting hotter, and she was meeting him other times and places too."

"Do you know if she planned to meet him on the day she was murdered?"

She shrugged. "I didn't see her that day. I wish I had." Sadness fell over her face. "I should have told her to stop. I should have told someone what she was doing. But I was afraid. I . . . was even afraid to tell the police." She stared at Finley, her eyes urging understanding. "I was only seventeen, and I didn't want my life to be over because people found out I failed to tell anyone what she was doing. My parents even said it was best if I didn't allow myself to get dragged into the case since I didn't really know anything useful. It's not like I knew his name."

All the little missing pieces that could have made a difference were never revealed. Finley desperately wished she could make people understand how even the smallest truth could make a difference.

"Was there anyone else who was close to Lucy with whom she might have shared her feelings on her project?" Obviously, just because it wasn't in the case file didn't mean it didn't exist.

Williams hesitated, her brow furrowed in thought. "That creepy custodian. Bowser . . . no, Brewer. He was always talking to Lucy. He was like obsessed with her or something." She rolled her eyes. "I don't know how Lucy tolerated his slobbering attention. It was pathetic."

"Are you referring to Howard Brewer, the custodian Lucy wanted to help after he lost his wife?"

"That's the one. It was like she flipped some sort of switch on the old guy. He followed her like a sick puppy."

"Do you believe he represented some threat to Lucy?" Finley couldn't see it at this point, but she had only just met the man.

Williams cocked her head and frowned. "Probably not. He was mostly just creepy. It didn't help that Lucy encouraged him by being overly nice. She never learned her lesson about being too helpful. Too kind. People take advantage of you when you're that way. If you ask me, that's probably what got her killed."

And only moments ago she had been talking about how bad Lucy was for taking advantage of the unknown older guy. Finley suspected this abrupt change was her guilt speaking. "Did you tell the police about Lucy's relationship with Brewer after her murder?"

Williams went still. Her eyes rounded a bit. "Like I said, my parents thought it would be best not to say too much since I didn't really know anything."

It wasn't easy, but Finley kept her thoughts on the matter to herself. Though she'd already said no, repeating the question might garner a slightly different response now. "Did you mention the car wash or any of the other details to the police?"

"Wouldn't have mattered," she said with an adamant shake of her head. "I didn't really know anything."

Too bad.

"One more thing," Finley said then. "Were you ever aware of Lucy having a babysitting job?"

Williams laughed. "Are you serious?"

"I'll take that as a no."

Finley thanked Williams and passed a card, the same as she always did. Though she wasn't sure this woman would bother calling even if she did think of anything else. Even thirteen years later, she was still too busy trying to prove how much smarter she was than her dead friend.

Though Finley had more questions for the custodian, considering this woman's comments, right now her focus had shifted to their client. Her questions for him would not wait. The more she'd learned about Lucy's secret project, the more convinced she was that Ray Johnson knew a hell of a lot more than he was sharing.

He was about to learn that it wasn't nice to stretch her patience this way.

As she drove away from the courthouse and before she forgot again, Finley called a local floral shop and ordered flowers for Helen Roberts. Then she called Houser and had him check the case file for anything regarding staff members at the school. He'd already done so, he said, and found nothing. There certainly had been nothing in the parts that he had been permitted to share with her.

With that out of the way, she could focus on lowering the boom on Johnson. He had climbed his way to the top of her shit list—even knocking her father aside for a bit longer.

Then she would circle back to Bart O'Sullivan. He had not returned her call.

Considering her father's lunch with Downey and then his visit to Johnson's office and what she'd learned from Lucy Cagle's friends, there appeared to be a lot that hadn't ended up in the case file.

It was way past time all those little pieces were put together.

19

Finley didn't stop at the receptionist's desk. She ignored the woman—Sylvia—who rose from her desk and followed, all the while calling out to Finley.

Johnson's office door was closed, but Finley didn't stop there either. She opened the door and walked in.

The scene she walked in on was not one she'd expected. She instantly turned her back to give Johnson and his friend a chance to uncouple.

If the image hadn't done so already, the smell of sex made Finley want to gag.

"Sorry, Ray," the receptionist, who had also turned her back, said. "She wouldn't listen to me."

Finley had been accused of much worse. Right now, she just wished she could hold her breath long enough for the smell to dissipate.

"Ms. O'Sullivan," Ray said breathlessly. "To what do I owe the pleasure?"

The young woman who'd been sprawled across the man's desk rushed out of the room, frantically attempting to right her clothes. The receptionist followed, paused long enough to glare at Finley, then marched out the door, slamming it behind herself.

"You can turn around now," Johnson said. "Please have a seat." He indicated the chairs in front of his desk—the desk that had been decluttered, since most of what had been on top of it now lay on the floor.

Finley had no choice but to take a breath, barely resisted a gag as she stepped forward and settled into one of the chairs. She blanked the previous images from her brain. She suspected they would haunt her for a long time to come.

Johnson took his seat, and she was grateful since one shirttail still hung free of his hastily fastened trousers. She didn't need any reminders of what she had witnessed.

There were things you could not unsee no matter how hard you tried.

Finley kicked the thoughts out of her head and summoned the frustration and anger she'd felt before walking into his office. Whatever the hell game this guy was playing, she was not interested in continuing. At least not on his behalf.

"When you are a client of our firm," Finley began, sounding far calmer than she felt, "our primary condition is that you be truthful with us. We cannot adequately represent you until you tell us the truth. It's that simple."

He scrubbed at his beard-stubbled face. Finley winced inwardly at the idea of what was likely on his hands. Damn. Her gut clenched.

"You're going to have to be more specific, Ms. O'Sullivan. What is it you think I've been untruthful about?" He leaned back, propped his feet on his desk, then crossed his ankles.

"First, about your brother. Your father mentioned that you didn't get along with Ian. In fact," she went on, improvising a bit, "I actually got the impression he felt you may have had something to do with his disappearance." When he would have spoken, she held up a hand to stop him. "I don't like playing games, so why don't you tell me yourself about your relationship with your brother and what you believe happened to him."

He laughed, long and loud. Anger steamed through her, but Finley kept her mouth shut in hopes her tirade had prompted at least a sliver of truth.

When Johnson pulled himself together and laid his eyes on Finley's once more, he said, "Look, I hated my little brother in some ways. This is true. He was a nuisance. Pop petted him like he was a lapdog—fun to look at but worthless for anything else. It was frustrating since I did all the work and got less recognition. Even when the old man pretended to try and toughen Ian up, he went easy on him. So, yeah, I said a lot of crap and even gave him hell sometimes. Kid stuff."

Finley chose her words carefully. "At the time of his disappearance, he was twenty-three. You were thirty-two. That's hardly kid stuff age."

He smirked. "I get it. Pop told you about the bathtub incident. I was fourteen when I tried"—he made air quotes—"to drown him in the tub. Did he also tell you that he beat the shit out of me for that? I wasn't really going to kill the kid, just scare the hell out of him for messing with my stuff."

Finley had saved the biggest surprise for last. Her mind worked that way. "Did you set all this up with the handbag and the cigarette butts to prompt an opportunity to prove your innocence to your father? Is that what you've been doing all this time? Trying to prove something to him?"

He didn't laugh this time. "My father is dying. He's a bitter old man because he didn't do a good job with his youngest son. He let our mother make him soft, and then he left me to straighten out the mess they had made. Considering the pain meds the old man is on, you can't trust anything he says." He shrugged. "In the grand scheme of things, we both know fathers don't always tell the whole truth."

Finley bit her teeth together. As badly as she wanted to demand to know how he knew her father and why he would visit this office, she couldn't. She wouldn't give this bastard that much leverage. He would only use it against her. She needed to understand the dynamics first.

When she would have tossed another question at him, he held up both hands to stop her. "As far as this evidence goes, I have no idea how that happened. You can believe me when I say that if I had found it, I would have for sure put it some place that was not connected with me or my family. Saved myself all this trouble and that big fat retainer your boss commands."

He appeared sincere enough, kept eye contact during his entire monologue. But she still wasn't sure she believed him. There were people who lied with such ease that the usual tells didn't appear. She did not trust this guy one iota.

"Here's my problem with the evidence," Finley said, giving him nothing of how she felt about his insistence. "First, the handbag may very well have been tucked away unnoticed on that top shelf all that time, but the cigarette butts on the floor beneath the bottom shelf, that just doesn't jibe for me." She shook her head. "The cops will latch on to it if it helps solve their case, but that's a reach, and I can't see any DA, much less a jury, going for it. Secondly, it's just too pat that it was found in a warehouse that belonged to your family. A clean warehouse that had been emptied and obviously swept in recent months. I'm guessing you're smart enough that if you or a member of your close family were involved with a murder, you would clean up the mess. So you can see how this just doesn't work for me."

His lips quirked into a grin. "I'm glad you think I'm smart. I was beginning to wonder."

"Which is why I believe there's an underlying motive for the evidence being found where it was found."

The cocky humor in his expression vanished.

"Just like the car wash receipt left in her purse. It was from a car wash owned by your family. You might remember it—one of three you owned and the only one that was torn down mere days after her murder. Now that intrigues me. Tells me something is not quite what it seems."

His face hardened, magnifying his lean jaw and blunt nose and making his thin lips look even thinner. "Gimme a break. It was a damned public car wash. How the hell do I know who patronized it? The fact is, you should be happy instead of here busting my chops. I agreed to your test," he snapped.

Like that was supposed to impress her. She hadn't heard the news from Jack just yet, but she wasn't surprised at all that he had worked the Finnegan magic and gotten Johnson's agreement.

"I trust *you* enough," Johnson growled, pointing a finger at her, "that I went over there this morning and allowed a cheek swab. I have done everything you asked, and still you treat me like a criminal."

Cry me a river.

"Give me a reason not to be suspicious of the tearing down of that particular car wash," she argued. "In fact, how about one little, tiny reason I should trust or believe a single thing you say."

His feet dropped to the floor, and he leaned forward. "I had no idea what was in that damned purse. I'm not the one who found it, and I'm damned sure not the one who put it there. If I'm not the one who put it there, how the hell would I know what was inside it?"

"Tell me about the car wash," Finley said, ignoring his lecture.

"There was an inspection because we found cracks in the concrete." He leaned back once more but kept his feet planted on the floor as if he might have to launch himself out of his chair. "The structural engineer we contacted said the place had major issues. We opted to take it down rather than spend the money to correct the problems. It wasn't doing as well as the other two anyway. I had no control over the timing of when Lucy Cagle got herself murdered or when she visited a public car wash."

If he hoped to smooth things over with Finley, he had no concept of how to make that happen. Finley would have kept this next part from him, except he'd obviously already heard it from his ex or he would never have warned Finley that nothing she said could be trusted. So why not toss this one in the mix and see his reaction? "Your ex-wife says she knew Lucy. Hired her to babysit a few times."

Ray glared at Finley. "I told you—"

"I know what you told me," she cut him off. "Any idea why she is suddenly telling me a different story from the one she gave the police after Lucy's murder?"

His face closed like a book. "No fucking idea."

"In any event," Finley countered, "I'm sure you can see how this looks. Even a jury would have difficulty buying your story when there was a receipt in Lucy's purse for the car wash you tore down. The cameras at the car wash are long gone because *you* tore it down. The prosecutor could suggest that Lucy and Ian met there. That maybe he confided in her about all sorts of things. I'm sure some of the former employees are still around. They would be rounded up and questioned. And let's not forget that your ex claims Lucy was in your home—alone—on three or four occasions, where she had access to your private office." Finley turned her hands up. "Not exactly the best-case scenario."

"That bullshit my ex fed you did not happen," Ray argued, fury cutting through, no matter that he struggled to keep his face clear of emotion.

Finley restrained a satisfied smile. "But, as I said, you must see how this all looks to me. How it would look to a jury."

His expression abruptly changed. His brow furrowed and his eyes narrowed. "What are you talking about, *confided in her?*"

With all that she had said, this was the only part that caught his full attention?

"That's the thing, *Ray*. If your brother was meeting with Lucy in secret—at the car wash or wherever—was it because of their age difference or the differences in their standing in the community? Or was it because Lucy Cagle was working on this big exposé for her senior thesis that involved—among other things—missing children, human trafficking? Your family's business has been under scrutiny many times.

More than once there have been rumors of criminal activities related to the family business. This is where the jury won't have trouble seeing past the meager evidence the state presents and finding guilt anyway."

Red rose up his throat and spread across his face. The man was furious now.

"All I want," he said quietly, too quietly, "is for you to clear this up. Maybe find out what happened to my little brother so my pop can die in peace. All this other stuff you're talking about is irrelevant. Even if this whatever-the-hell-it-is ends up in court, no one can prove any of it. It's only innuendos. And I think you know that."

"I know you want it to look that way," Finley offered. "Do I believe you're innocent and telling me the whole truth? No way. But it isn't my job to prove your innocence, it's only my job to find the facts so that Jack can properly defend you."

Johnson clasped his hands and pressed them against the desk, where he'd had the woman's ass planted only minutes ago. He took a breath as if struggling for patience. "It's important to me that you recognize I'm telling you the truth."

Funny, Houser had said basically that same thing—but then he was a friend. This man was not.

"I'm not your attorney, and I'm not your priest," Finley countered. "You don't need me to believe anything."

"Maybe I just want it because I like you, Finley. You intrigue me. You're super smart and nice to look at. I have to tell you, you've given me some seriously hot dreams."

Finley smiled but inside she recoiled in disgust. "Now you're just trying to piss me off. Don't try too hard, Ray, I already don't trust you."

His lips thinned, and his gaze turned angry. "We done here, Ms. O'Sullivan?"

"We are." She stood. "I'm sure Jack has already told you that we'll need the name of that structural engineer and his report if you can produce it. He likes to be well armed."

Finley walked out of his office. She smiled at the receptionist, who only glowered at her. She didn't slow down until she had reached her Subaru. She backed out of the slot and eased onto Hillsboro Circle, then made her way to the intersection at Hillsboro Pike and stopped well away from Johnson's domain. She took her first deep breath since walking into that damned place.

She put in a call to Jack. While she waited for him to answer, she merged into traffic on Hillsboro Pike.

"I'm guessing you visited our client and it didn't go so well, since my phone is blowing up with a call from Ray at the same time you're calling."

"You would be guessing correctly," Finley acknowledged. She gave him a quick overview of the impromptu meeting sans the compromising position in which she found their client. No need to resurrect those images.

When she'd finished, Jack laughed. "Yeah, he gave me that story, and I'll bet the other two car washes had the same cracks but that was the one he wanted rid of."

Sounded like Jack wasn't playing Johnson's games anymore either. "Look, I know you owe the old man, but something is wrong with this situation. I'm not saying that Ray Johnson killed Lucy Cagle. I'm not even saying the missing brother did, but there's something here. Something ugly, and it's got Lucy Cagle written all over it."

"In your opinion, do the police have enough to bring charges?"

Finley didn't have to think about that one. "Not yet. At least not unless Houser has something he's not telling us about."

She trusted Houser . . . didn't she?

He had followed her father . . . seen him go to Johnson's office, and he'd warned her. Houser could have kept that to himself. Finley appreciated the heads-up. She desperately needed to get a handle on what her father was hiding, damn it. He should have called her back by now.

"Nudge him," Jack suggested, meaning Houser. "Work your charm on him. The guy likes you. He'll show his hand, if he's hiding one."

Where Jack got the idea she had some sort of charm with the male of the species befuddled her. It was so not true. Particularly when it came to cops, Houser included.

"Look"—it was time she gave up the part she'd been holding back—"we may have a problem with my father."

"What do you mean?"

Finley braked to a stop at a red traffic signal. "You already know Lucy was going to my father for research on missing children in the system."

"And he told you it was nothing," Jack reminded her, as if she could have forgotten.

The light changed, and Finley shifted her foot from the brake to the accelerator. She took a breath and then said the rest. "I think he might be leaving out parts. Yesterday Houser followed him, and he stopped at Johnson's office. *My father stopped at Johnson's office.* Johnson wasn't there, so he came right back out and left."

When Jack didn't immediately respond, Finley swallowed the rock lodged in her throat and asked, "Why would he go to Johnson if he was telling me the whole truth?"

"Okay, kid, listen to me. Sometimes we don't tell the things we worry will make us look a certain way, even if it is only a look and nothing more. Especially when it comes to the people close to us. We're terrified it will change their perception of us."

"He's hiding something, Jack." Fear twisted in her belly. "I just don't know how bad it is yet."

"Bart would not hurt anyone. He definitely wouldn't kill anyone," Jack reminded her.

"But there are plenty of bad things that don't include murder, Jack. We both know that."

Finley had done more than her share of bad things . . . she just hadn't killed anyone—at least not directly.

Who was she to judge her father?

No. That was wrong. She wasn't judging her father. She was fucking terrified for him.

A beep told her she had another call coming in.

Houser.

"Gotta go, Jack. I'll catch up with you later."

Finley didn't wait for him to respond. She switched to the incoming call.

"Hey." She held her breath, hoping he didn't have worse news to pass along. Particularly if it involved her father.

"He's agreed to meet with you."

Her heart bumped into a faster pace. She didn't have to ask who. She understood he meant Carson Dempsey. "When?"

"Three today, at his house. I know it's short notice, but this is his offer."

She glanced at the digital clock on the dash. She had fifteen minutes. Her foot instinctively pressed harder on the accelerator. "I'll be there."

"You have his address."

"Yes."

"See you there."

She ended the call. Did she have his address? Please. She knew everything there was to know about the man responsible for the murder of her husband.

20

Carson Dempsey did not live in the typical prestigious mansion. The pharmaceutical billionaire lived in an opulent twenty-five-thousand-square-foot house on a forty-acre palatially manicured estate valued by Zillow at just shy of twenty million.

Finley parked behind Houser's sedan on the cobblestone drive that circled an enormous three-tiered fountain with statues of maidens standing beneath the spray of water. Finley rolled her eyes at the ridiculous opulence.

Houser emerged from his car and met her at the steps that led up to the front entrance, which looked more like the facade of a high-end hotel than a house.

"His attorney is with him," Houser explained. "You can ask anything you like, as long as the answer does not incriminate Dempsey."

"Got it," she lied. She planned to ask him whatever the hell she wanted either way. It was up to him not to answer.

They climbed the stairs that led to a veranda with three sets of double iron doors. The center set opened, and a tall man dressed all in black stepped back, opening the door wider for them to enter. The holstered weapon strapped to his broad chest and shoulder suggested he was a member of Dempsey's private security.

"Detective, you will need to leave any firearm you carry with me," the big guy said.

"My firearm is locked in my vehicle." He removed his jacket, held up his hands and performed a turnaround for the guy.

The bodyguard nodded. "Straight ahead. They're waiting in the great room."

Finley and Houser walked side by side along the marble floor. Past the iron-railed double staircases with their matching marble treads that curved along and up each side of the enormous space to spill out onto the second-story landing. Beyond the dual staircases was the great room, with an extraordinary view of the back of the estate. A sparkling pool and endless stone pathways meandered through extravagantly land-scaped gardens. Serving as a backdrop to all that were the acres and acres of beautiful horse pastures with stately barns and treed mountains.

She wondered how much of all this the bastard would be able to hang on to by the time his criminal trials were over.

Nothing, she hoped.

Carson Dempsey sat in an upholstered chair that likely cost more than she made in a year with his back to the awe-inspiring view of his property. His high-dollar attorney, Bernard Wellsby—a man Finley knew well—sat in a matching chair next to him.

Both men stood as she and Houser approached. Finley was surprised but not the least bit impressed.

"Please," Dempsey said, "make yourself at home."

Impossible.

Finley said nothing. She sat on the sofa, facing that view and the man she despised with every ounce of her body and soul. She could not take her eyes off him. He didn't look away. Instead he stared right back at her, seemingly as curious as she was or perhaps hoping the pale-blue eyes and the fair hair that his son had inherited would remind her how she had taken that son from him. Finley felt no regret. She was only sorry she hadn't been able to prove his scumbag son had raped many, many other women. Wasn't her fault that he'd ended up with a jailhouse shiv in his gut only days after his incarceration.

Carson Dempsey Junior, a.k.a. Sonny, had been a piece of shit who should have gotten his far sooner than he had.

"Thank you for seeing us," Houser said as he joined Finley on the sofa.

"I have advised my client," Wellsby said to Finley, "not to entertain a visit from you or speak to you and certainly not to answer any of your questions. However, Mr. Dempsey is sympathetic to your efforts to find the truth regarding your husband's tragic death. With that in mind, he feels compelled to speak with you. Be advised that I will not allow his kindness to in any way jeopardize his own case."

When Finley said nothing, Houser stated, "We appreciate your concerns. I will defer to my associate," he indicated Finley, "going forward."

Wellsby said something else, but Finley was too focused on Dempsey to hear or to care.

"Why do you have another thug following me?" she asked.

"Carson," Wellsby said, "I implore you not to respond to such an outrageous—"

Dempsey held up his hand to cut him off; then he smiled. She wanted to throw up or maybe spring across that fancy-ass stone coffee table between them and rip that smile right off his condescending face.

"Why would I have someone following you, Ms. O'Sullivan? I know where you live and work. Who your friends and family are. I know who you sleep with. What else is there to know about such a pathetic life?"

Next to her, Houser stiffened.

Finley only smiled. "I get what you're saying, since I also know every single thing about you and your life. You live in this palace like a king, but you are nothing but a sad little crime boss whose wife left him and son was murdered for being a womanizing piece of shit."

Dempsey's smile fell.

Wellsby shot to his feet and sputtered and stuttered.

Houser put his hand on Finley's arm and squeezed. All the while her gaze remained locked with Dempsey's.

Like a conductor leading an orchestra, Dempsey held up his hand once more, and Wellsby shut up, though he did not resume his seat next to his client.

"Gentlemen," Dempsey said, "Ms. O'Sullivan and I need a moment."

"Carson," Wellsby roared, "you cannot do this." His glower shifted to Finley. "And, Ms. O'Sullivan, you know very well that if you speak to him alone—without counsel present—anything you hear is not admissible in court."

"I have no problem with that," Finley said. "Everything I have to say about Carson Dempsey and his activities related to the murder of my husband are already on record. I have no additions. Anything I hear today will not change that."

Wellsby looked to Houser. "You are witness to this inappropriate decision by both parties."

Houser looked to Finley. "Are you sure this is what you want to do?"

"Abso-fucking-lutely," she muttered, her gaze still fixed on Dempsey.

Houser stood. "I am a witness," he said with heavy reluctance.

The two exited the room.

Dempsey's smile returned. "After all this time, here we are."

Finley didn't smile. She said nothing. She'd already asked her question.

"Do you have any idea what it feels like to lose a child?"

Finley remained silent. She would give him nothing.

He chuckled. "Perhaps one of these days you will."

Fury pounded against her chest. She gritted her teeth to hold back the words she wanted to fling at him. It didn't require a great deal of imagination to know he had video surveillance throughout this place. She would be a fool not to assume so. She would give him nothing to use against her or with which to entertain himself.

"I have no one following you. I no longer have any reason to wish you ill. There is nothing worse you can do to me. Nothing that would drive the stake deeper into my heart."

"Then why is he following me? The MO is the same as the three who previously made the mistake of getting in my way." The memory of blood splattering on her face . . . blood smeared down the front of her shirt flashed through her brain. She blinked it away.

"Derrick Reed—your husband—made many enemies during his time in Nashville. As you know, he lied and did whatever else necessary to get the job done. In fact, he lied to you from the day he met you until the day he bled to death on the floor of that shithole where you live."

She steeled herself against the second blast of rage that fired through her bones. Her entire being longed to attack him, to tear out his evil eyes and bludgeon his head until his warped brain ceased to function and oozed out his ears like slime. But then she'd be the one spending the rest of her life in prison. She needed it to be him.

"Keep that image close," she said. "Maybe it'll comfort you through all those lonely nights in prison, because you're going to be there for the rest of your life."

"You know," he said with a laugh, "I could sense that he really didn't want to get close to you when I first mentioned it. He certainly didn't want to marry you, but he did everything I asked, just as I asked."

Derrick had done exactly that. If Dempsey hoped to hurt her somehow with this retelling, he was wasting his time. She had already suffered through all the doubts and the questions about her marriage and life with Derrick. She knew what he had done, and more importantly, she knew why. She had forgiven him for both.

"Thank you," she said with utmost sincerity. "I should have said this before, but thank you for sending him to me. He was an amazing man, and I loved him completely."

Fury flashed in Dempsey's eyes, but he quickly tamped it down. "Watch your step, Finley O'Sullivan. For me the game is lost, but it is far from over. You'll see."

Finley stood. "Thanks for seeing me. Maybe you won't have to spend the rest of your life in prison either. Maybe someone will do you the same favor they did your son."

Finley turned her back and walked out. His ranting followed her out of the room. A good attorney could probably use her as a future potential threat to his client and get him into an *upgraded* prison situation. Let him. Proving it would be the problem. Besides, Finley actually did not want the old bastard to die. She wanted him to live every long-ass day he had left behind bars.

Houser walked out of the bastard's palace beside her as Wellsby hurried back to his client.

"Do I want to know what you two talked about?"

At the bottom of the steps, she paused. "I told him if he was lucky, he would die in prison the same way his son did."

Houser flinched. "Jesus, Finley."

"But what I didn't tell him is that I hope that doesn't happen because I want him to live as long as possible in his prison cell. The longer the better."

Houser shook his head. "Did he admit knowing anything about who might be tailing you?"

"He says not, but he did make one comment that tells me he knows something." She put her arm through Houser's and ushered him toward their parked cars. "He said, 'For me'—meaning him—'the game is lost, but it is far from over.' He mentioned that Derrick had made more enemies than just him."

Houser scrubbed a hand over his jaw. "I don't like the sound of that."

She had expected Dempsey would try and find a way to make her second-guess herself. And he was right—Derrick had been an undercover agent, so of course he had made other enemies. But this thing—the guy following her—had Dempsey's MO written all over it.

"He said I'd see." She didn't really like it either. What was new?

"I should put a detail on you."

Finley shook her head. "You'll just scare him off. It's better if I can see him coming."

It was when you didn't see them coming that ruined your day.

"Get me a license plate number. Anything," Houser urged. His gaze searched hers. "I'm worried, Finley. We know the stuff that went down last time."

He was almost killed. Matt was almost killed.

She was almost killed.

"I'll be careful. I promise."

He nodded. "I'm counting on it." Ever the gentleman, he reached for her car door. He paused. "Look, I feel bad for telling you about your father's visit to Johnson's office."

"I would have been more upset if you hadn't told me," she admitted.

"So did you get a chance to talk to him?"

Regrettably she could only shake her head. "I'm still trying to catch up with him. It's looking more and more like he's avoiding me."

"Let me know what you find out. I'd like to clear this up, the sooner the better."

So would she. For now, she was glad he didn't push the issue or insist on speaking to her father himself. This was something she needed to do. As Houser said, the sooner the better.

Finley left the Dempsey palace and drove straight to one of her resources, Pete Owens, over on Penn Warren Drive in Brentwood. She had him check her Subaru for bugs, and even her phone, although it never left her possession. Dempsey's thugs had used tracking and listening devices to keep up with her movements before. She wasn't taking any chances this time.

When Pete was satisfied she was clean, she drove to her parents' house.

O'Sullivan Residence
Jackson Boulevard, Belle Meade, 4:10 p.m.

Her father opened the door and blinked. "Finley, what're you doing here?"

Before this case, he would have been glad to see her any time she dropped by.

"Can we talk?" She knew the Judge wouldn't be home yet, which was a good thing. Finley and her dad needed privacy for this one.

"Well, sure." He backed up, opened the door wider. "Come in."

She waited until he closed the door. "Why are you avoiding my and Detective Houser's calls?"

More rapid blinking. "I don't know what you mean?"

"I've called you twice today, and you haven't called me back. Detective Houser said he had called you, and you haven't called back. In fact, he tried to catch up with you yesterday. But you were leaving, so he followed you."

Her father's face fell. "He followed me?"

"You had lunch with Maureen Downey at the Five Points Diner, and then you drove to Johnson Development Group. I don't really care why you were lunching with Downey, but I need to know why you would try to see Ray Johnson."

His face flushed; his gaze couldn't find a place to land. "I . . . I don't know what to say. Why would this detective be following me? And . . . and I've been busy, or I would have called you back."

Finley closed her eyes a second to clear her head. She couldn't do that with her father looking at her as if she'd just slapped his face. She took a breath and forced her eyes open once more. He had never been too busy to return her calls before.

"Secrets can be dangerous, Dad. Do you comprehend that the secrets Derrick kept from me almost cost me my life? He was murdered because he was keeping secrets—working undercover for the DEA in a very dangerous assignment. Lucy Cagle was murdered. Secrets are protecting the identity of the person who killed her. Are you helping to keep those secrets?"

"I . . ." He shook his head. "Fin, you must know that if I was aware of anything at all that would help your case, I would tell you. I've already told you about my and Lucy's brief friendship." He shrugged and threw his hands up in exasperation. "I mean I guess that's what you would call it. We hardly knew each other, but she was a very sweet girl and—"

"Dad," Finley snapped. "Why did you go to Ray Johnson's office?"

His arms dropped to his sides. "He . . . he has made an offer on some property in Belle Meade, and we're . . . we're very concerned about his intentions. I was tasked with questioning him. He wasn't in his office." He shrugged again. "End of story."

Finley nodded, no matter that her heart had dropped to her feet. "Okay. Thanks. I have to get to the hospital to visit my neighbor."

She left. Couldn't stay a second longer without risking that she would say something she could regret. Before she allowed herself to go there, she had to think . . . to somehow figure this out.

Because her father was lying . . . *again.*

21

It was almost dark.

Finley didn't care. She needed to think. She couldn't go to the hospital just yet, and she damned sure couldn't go home and face Matt. How could she tell him what her father was doing? He had lied to her, straight faced. He never did that. In her entire life she had never known him to lie until this case. Ever.

She got out of the Subaru. The streetlamps had already come on. The moon was big and bright. Time was short before it would be completely dark. She walked straight to *his* space. The place where her parents had buried her husband. She'd been in a damned coma at the time. She hadn't come here until months later. She hadn't been able, physically or mentally, to do it.

With ease, despite the looming darkness, she found the sleek black granite marker her mother had picked out for Derrick. Her knees went weak, and she eased down onto the grass. She brushed away the leaves gathered at the base of the headstone. Probably she should bring flowers more often. It wasn't her thing. Her grandparents had died when she was little, and she vaguely remembered the Judge and her father taking flowers from time to time, but she didn't remember a particular routine. She supposed they still did.

Routines weren't Finley's forte.

She drew in a deep breath, glanced around the ever-darkening landscape dotted with headstones and mausoleums. "I went to see Dempsey today."

Her words made it sound as if she'd paid him a social call. The bastard's warning echoed in her ears.

"I can't decide if he's still planning some sort of revenge or if he's right and someone else is plotting a way to even the score. You pissed off a lot of people, Derrick." She trailed her fingers across his name engraved in the cold stone. "But you were just doing your job. It would have been nice if you could have told me. Not that it matters. Really. Those few weeks together were amazing, and I don't regret a second of our time together."

She drew in a shaky breath. "I won't ever forget you. No matter how much I love Matt, I will always, always have a place in my heart that is empty because you're gone."

Tears spilled down her cheeks, and she scrubbed them away. "Okay. I should go. It's getting dark. I just needed to see you after that meeting. I'll be back soon."

She pushed up, wiped off her knees and turned to head back to her car. She paused and considered that Lucy Cagle was buried here also. Along with a host of other well-known Nashvillians, like Donna Summer.

Finley was here. It wasn't completely dark yet. She might as well drop by. Where to start her search? She surveyed the vast grounds.

She squinted, peered toward one of the mausoleums. Was that another person in the cemetery? She hadn't seen another vehicle. Maybe she wasn't the only one who liked breaking rules by being here after dark. Well, almost after dark.

She scanned the property once more and decided Lucy would likely be in one of the family mausoleums.

Finley's parents had one. She started in that direction.

The other visitor lingered near one of the mausoleums. Male. Tall. Thankfully not wearing a hoodie or dark glasses. She surveyed the names on the mausoleums she passed. Some were square and squat, like a concrete bunker. Others were taller and brick, like an elegant tiny house designed for one, only some of those housed several family members. As she neared where the other visitor stood, she could see that he was standing by one of the larger, more elaborate mausoleums. The redbrick one with the black columns and iron doors.

Moving closer, she noted that the walls weren't brick at all but a red granite or some other smooth, solid stone.

The man turned around as if he'd sensed her presence, and they both stood for a long moment staring at each other in the waning light.

Howard Brewer . . . the *custodian.*

"Hi." She moistened her lips. "Finley O'Sullivan. We met today—"

"I remember." He swiped his hands against his trousers as if he was nervous. Now that she was closer, she could see that beneath his coat he still wore the uniform he'd had on at the school today.

"I apologize for the intrusion. My husband is buried here, so . . ." She tried to think what to say next, but nothing came to mind.

Another moment of silence and awkward eyeing of each other elapsed.

"I bring Lucy flowers sometimes," he said, breaking the ice. "My wife is buried here too. Not in a mausoleum, but we bought plots when I first started working at the school. When they were affordable."

Finley moved closer, noted the fresh flowers he'd placed at the iron door of the Cagle family mausoleum. "That's very kind of you to bring her flowers."

He nodded slowly. "She doesn't have anyone else. It's the least I can do."

He was right. No siblings. Her parents were gone. Who would bring Lucy flowers if he didn't? She had been gone a very long time. It was doubtful any of her school friends had time for her memory anymore. Lucy had brought food and gifts to this man when he had no one else. He no doubt felt at the very least he owed her flowers.

He looked around as if just noticing the looming darkness. "I should go."

"Do you mind if I walk with you?" Finley was not one to waste an opportunity.

"It's a free country."

They walked slowly. For a few steps, Finley kept quiet. "This man Lucy was seeing," she ventured, "did she ever mention meeting him at a car wash?"

"No, but I decided she must be going to one pretty often, 'cause her little car was always clean. I mean shiny clean. More so than usual. I teased her about it, and she got embarrassed. I felt bad about it, so I didn't bring it up again."

When they reached her Subaru, Finley paused. "Mr. Brewer— Howard—I spoke to a couple of Lucy's closest friends, and they seemed to think you were particularly close to her. Maybe you saw her as a daughter."

Finley decided it was best to temper the one friend's words with more palatable terms.

"You can't take everything those girls say for the gospel, Ms. O'Sullivan. They're good girls, but they've got that fierce kind of competitiveness. Lucy was always one step ahead of them, and so they aren't gonna look back and say the nicest things. You'd think it would pass with time, but for some it never does."

"Should I be concerned they're not telling me the whole truth?" The lamppost wasn't giving off nearly enough light for her to see his face and eyes as clearly as she would have liked. The last of the daylight was gone now.

"I wouldn't say they're lying, just maybe highlighting the negative about the old competition. You gotta understand, in life Lucy was always achieving a little higher, always doing the good and right thing. Then, when she was murdered, she became like a saint. A martyr. The whole city, maybe even the state, cried for Lucy. No mere human can live up to that. Those girls don't mean to be unkind, it's just that old human weakness called jealousy."

Finley supposed he had a point. "Do you think Lucy would have wanted to be remembered that way?"

"That's the thing about memories, the rememberer gets to do the deciding on what he or she remembers about the remembered, not the other way around."

Well put. "I'll keep that in mind."

They parted ways. Finley unlocked and climbed into her Subaru. She tried to watch where Brewer went, but he disappeared into the darkness. She started the engine and ensured that the locks engaged before calling Houser to give him an update on her father.

Even as she waited for him to answer, thoughts of what her father could be hiding twisted inside her. There had to be a reasonable explanation. Maybe the planning commission really had sent him to speak with Ray Johnson. It wasn't impossible, just one hell of a coincidence.

Finley did not like coincidences.

Not one little bit. And the coincidences in this case seemed to be mounting.

Houser's voice mail kicked in.

This is Detective Eric Houser of the Metro Nashville PD, leave me a message.

"Hey, it's O'Sullivan. Call me. We need . . ."

Headlights flashed in her eyes, startling her. She blinked. "We need to . . . talk." *Oh shit.*

She ended the call.

The headlights bored straight into her vehicle, coming closer and closer until the car was nose to nose with hers.

Was that Brewer? Why would he—?

The other vehicle nudged her. Finley jumped. Foot on the brake, she instinctively shifted into reverse.

The headlights switched to bright.

She squinted. Looked away.

Something slammed against her window. She jerked her head around and stared out the driver's side.

The dim lights of the dash glowed eerily against a face—black hoodie . . . sunglasses pressed to the glass. Her heart banged against her sternum.

Without looking away, she let off the brake and hit the accelerator.

The Subaru rocketed backward. The man stumbled back. She shifted into drive and rammed the accelerator simultaneously, cutting the steering wheel to miss the curb . . . and the man. She jetted away from the threat. Barreling forward, she dared a glance into her rearview mirror. He stood in the beam of his vehicle's headlights, the glow casting him in shadow. But it was him . . . she knew it was him.

Heart pounding hard enough to burst from her chest, she didn't slow down until she made the left on McCrary Avenue. Even then she kept a close watch on her rearview mirror. He would know she was headed home. To give herself an advantage, she made a right and decided to take a long, jagged route toward home.

Her cell vibrated against her lap. She jumped. Shrieked.

Damn it. She took a breath. She had dropped her phone into her lap. This time the call connected with her car. She stabbed at the screen on the dash, hit Accept.

Before she could say anything, Houser demanded, "Finley, are you okay?" He was practically shouting.

"I'm okay." She dragged in a shaky breath.

"What happened? You were leaving a message and you suddenly say *oh shit*, and then the call ended."

She hadn't realized the line was still open when the words formed in her mind or that she'd even said them out loud. Drawing in another, steadier deep breath, she struggled to control the shakes quaking through her body.

"The guy—black hoodie and sunglasses—followed me to the cemetery. I didn't notice him when I arrived, but when I was leaving it was dark and he came up to my car door. Beat against the glass and—"

"Where the hell are you now?"

"I'm . . . I'm on Poplar Creek Road. I didn't want to make it easy for him to follow me home, so I'm zigzagging my way there."

"Okay, I'm coming to you."

"No." She kept a close eye on the rearview mirror. "I'm going home, and I do not want to take this home to Matt."

Silence.

Damn it. She hadn't meant to say that out loud either.

"You should tell Matt. This guy could be following him too. He needs to be aware of the potential danger."

Damn it. Houser was right. "Okay, I'll tell him. I just don't want him to overreact."

"It sounds like this guy got more aggressive after your meeting with Dempsey."

There was no denying that was the case. "Yes."

"We have to take that as a sign that maybe he is following orders from Dempsey."

"The problem this time . . ." Finley's throat closed with the building anxiety. She would be a fool not to be a little bit afraid.

"Finley?"

She hated like hell to throw this into the mix. "The problem I have this time is that Dempsey has nothing to lose. He's screwed and he knows it. What's one more dead body?"

"You need security, Finley. Whether you want it or not."

"I can handle this. Look, I have to go. I just remembered I need to stop by the hospital and check on my neighbor before going home."

"Don't forget what I said," he reminded her. "Bring Matt up to speed. If you don't, I will."

"I'll do it. Now let me focus on driving."

Finley ended the call before he could say anything more.

She had never carried a gun in her life. Never felt the need.

But this was different.

Dempsey wanted the kind of revenge she suspected only her death would bring.

She had to consider her options . . . whether she liked them or not.

22

Finley was tired. She needed to go home and talk to Matt. But she couldn't ignore this obligation. She owed Helen Roberts. When she walked into the room, Finley felt some amount of relief at seeing the flowers she had ordered.

"Better late than never," she mumbled.

Helen Roberts was asleep. Finley walked to her bedside and stood for a long moment, hoping she would wake up. The minutes passed, and she didn't move or open her eyes. Finley glanced at the clock on the wall over and over as she waited for the woman to rouse. Matt was home. He'd sent her a text as she pulled into the hospital's parking lot. He had probably gone straight over to feed and walk the dog. Spot.

Finley mentally rolled her eyes. Who named a dog Spot when the dog had no spots whatsoever?

Knowing Matt, he would finish that task and then go back to the house and prepare dinner or order something to be delivered. He always took care of everything. She thought of the face that had pressed against her car window. She had to tell Matt everything. She had to take care of him the same way he had taken care of her a million times.

"I hope you like your flowers," Finley said aloud. Maybe talking to her would get her attention.

Roberts didn't move, not even her eyelids. She looked even paler than before, which hardly seemed possible. Finley hadn't really paid that much attention to the woman's features in the past. She was reasonably tall, maybe five eight. Thin but strong. Her face was lined, but she had high cheekbones and well-formed lips. Nice nose. Her hair was quite silky now since it had been combed out. She could only imagine how that detangling session went. The nurse who had volunteered for that task likely hadn't realized what she was getting into.

Her neighbor's hands were small with long, thin fingers. Nails were a mess. She needed a manicure. Like Finley had any room to talk. She couldn't remember when she'd last indulged in a mani-pedi. Mostly she clipped her nails short and left it at that. She didn't work with her hair the way she used to. These days she only blow-dried it and went on. Hair clips and ponytails were her friends.

In all this time, Matt and her father hadn't said a word about her decision not to bother with makeup or hairdos. Her father had told her plenty of times he was just grateful she had survived *that* night—the night her husband was murdered and she was brutalized nearly to death. Nothing about her was the same after that night. She didn't dress the same or walk the same or feel the same.

But she wasn't living in the past anymore; that was the upside. She had uncovered the truth, and those involved with what happened that night were either dead or awaiting trial.

She had moved on.

She and Matt were happy. Jack was back on good terms with her parents (not that her father had ever been upset with him). She apparently was going to run against Briggs for Davidson County DA, and even she and her mother could get along in the same room together these days.

Frankly, if not for this new follower, she wouldn't have thought much about Dempsey—at least not until his trial started.

It was all good, she told herself.

Then why did she feel as if something was off?

There was a piece missing in all this, and she couldn't put her finger on it. Whenever she was investigating a case, she was generally so absorbed with the players and the events she paid attention to little else.

Maybe it was this dipstick following her that had her out of sorts. Even the scumbags who had followed her around before had never approached her. Well, except for that awful night, and at the time she hadn't known who they were. None had come near her after that. She was the one who had approached them when she'd figured out who they were. But this time was different.

She had no idea who this guy was or really who had hired him. Dempsey did appear the most likely candidate, but she couldn't be sure.

If not Johnson or Dempsey . . . maybe someone else who wasn't happy with how Derrick had turned the pharmaceutical empire upside down.

And then there was the unsettling aspect of her father having a part in the Lucy Cagle case. That scared her a hell of a lot more than the guy in the hoodie.

Finley sighed as another wave of exhaustion washed over her.

Roberts remained asleep or pretended to be. Finley wasn't sure which.

"Well, I should get going. See you tomorrow." Finley gave her hand a pat. A bumpy spot drew her gaze to the place she had touched. A raised scar cut through the webbed space between the woman's thumb and pointer finger, extending toward her wrist. It wasn't so noticeable on the hand, but it was thick and hard in the webby area. Finley traced the mark, and the elderly woman flinched.

So maybe not asleep.

It was possible she simply didn't want to talk. Finley got it. She had been there before too. Funny how she so easily related to all the fucked-up people around her. Poor Matt. He so did not deserve all her baggage.

Finley said good night and left the room. She waved to the nurses at the station and headed for the elevator. She pressed the button and closed her eyes. She thought of how her father had lied to her again today.

Whatever he was hiding, it couldn't be that bad. Her father was a good man.

She trusted him.

Then act like it, Finley, and let this go for now.

When he was ready, he would tell her whatever part of the story he was leaving out.

O'Sullivan Residence
Shelby Avenue, Nashville, 7:35 p.m.

Finley stood at the door and listened a moment before going inside. Matt had his favorite soft rock playlist going. She loved that he was such a romantic. That he still parked on the street, no matter that he arrived home before her most evenings. Leaving the only spot in the driveway available for her was just one of the ways he proved what a gentleman he was. Really, a true gentleman in the fullest sense of the term.

She opened the door, thinking instantly that she needed to tell him to keep it locked under the circumstances. She closed and locked it. He wasn't in the living room, so she wandered into the kitchen. Lucky lifted his head and stared at her from his place curled up on a chair next to the table. Finley wiggled her fingers at him. Matt stood at the stove, stirring a pot. Judging by the smell, it was his famously amazing chili. Finley had never tasted chili as good as Matt's. That was another upside to the cooler weather of December. All manner of soups would be on the menu. Even more appetizing than the incredible scent of his culinary creation was the gentle sway of his body to the music.

The thought of him being hurt again because of her was more than she could bear.

"Smells good."

He turned around, smiled. "Why, thank you, Ms. O'Sullivan." He set the wooden spoon aside and moved toward her. Her heart quickened. His arms went around her, and he pulled her close, then kissed her cheek. "Glad you're home. I've already taken care of Spot."

Her arms went around his neck. "Thank you for being what makes me want to come home."

This time his kiss landed on her lips, and Finley melted into it.

When they both needed air, she drew back just enough to accommodate the need. "Before we get too carried away," Finley ventured, "there's something we need to talk about."

He studied her a moment. "Sounds ominous."

It is. Taking the coward's way out, she laughed and said, "Maybe we should eat first. Before it gets cold."

"Good idea."

They worked together to fill the bowls and put everything on a tray. He'd paired a great wine, sweet enough to challenge the spicy heat. With the tray on the coffee table, they settled on the sofa and dug in. The chili was amazing, as she had known it would be. When they were finished, she couldn't put the talk off any longer.

"I have a new follower."

He set his glass on the coffee table tray and turned to face her. "I have a feeling you're not talking about social media."

Her heart sank a little more at the mere thought of Matt being in danger. "No. A guy wearing a hoodie and dark glasses in a black, nondescript sedan. Like before, only different."

She hated, hated, hated bringing this to him. This was her battle—her demons.

Matt took her glass and placed it next to his. Then he took both her hands in his. "Tell me what happened."

She walked him through the details of her first sighting the day she visited Jerry Bauer's office downtown all the way through tonight's ordeal at the cemetery. Matt's tension visibly escalated with every word.

"I didn't want to drag you back into it." The excuse sounded even stupider when she said it out loud.

"Fin." He moistened his lips. "I'm already there. We're in this together. We are *together*. You can't separate what threatens you from what threatens me, they're the same."

She felt sick. "Johnson says it's not him and . . ." She took a deep breath. Matt would not like this at all. "I forced Houser to set up a meeting with Carson Dempsey. I went to his house today."

The disappointment in Matt's eyes ripped at her heart.

Before she lost her nerve completely, she hurried to say the rest. "He said it wasn't him. Of course. He hinted at the idea that it could be others who were affected by what Derrick did."

"First," Matt said, "I wouldn't trust anything Dempsey says. As for Derrick, he had a responsibility to complete his assignment. It wasn't easy for him, especially since his primary goal was to somehow protect you at the same time. But he got it done."

"It killed him," she said, her voice hollow. Even through the fear and the pain, she couldn't help being even prouder of Matt for still seeing Derrick's side of things after all he had been through in this.

"Yeah," Matt agreed. "Sadly, it did, but what we have to remember is that Derrick was a hero. He gave his life to stop a monster, and you, by helping him finish the part he couldn't, are a hero too."

She leaned into Matt's chest, fought the burn of tears. "I'm not a hero, Matt." He knew the things she had done to accomplish her goal. She had told him everything. None of it was heroic. It was desperate, dangerous and mostly on the edge of legal.

"Yes, you are, but the part that worries me is that you don't seem to recognize your mortality."

She looked up at him. "I know I'm not bulletproof. Tonight scared the hell out of me." She had thought she was braver than that. Or maybe it hadn't been as much about being scared for her own survival as for the loss of this new life she was building with Matt.

"Good. You should have been scared. No more going to the cemetery so close to dark. In fact, no going anywhere so isolated alone again, got it?"

She nodded. "You're right."

"Anytime you want to go visit Derrick's grave, you tell me, and we'll go together."

What other man would be so willing to visit the grave of the one before him?

Finley kissed him, then pressed her forehead to his. "Now tell me about your day." She never wanted their relationship to be all about her.

He stood, held out his hand. "Let's clean up in the kitchen while I tell you all about it; then I have a plan that will take your mind off the bad day you've had."

Finley grinned. "Sounds like a very good plan."

The cleanup was done in record time with lots of touching and stealing of kisses. Finally, they moved to the bedroom and made love, then showered together and made love again. When Matt had fallen asleep, Finley scooted out of the bed and went to the living room. She rounded up her laptop to do some research on Howard Brewer. A series of pings warning her of notifications had her scanning her social media feeds.

District Attorney Briggs says O'Sullivan Not Fit to Hold Public Office.

DA Hopeful O'Sullivan's Infamous Crash and Burn in the Courtroom.

The last one was accompanied by a video.

Finley closed all the tabs and forced her focus on searching for anything on the custodian.

Who was he? Where had he come from? What made him obsessed with Lucy Cagle?

Was he why Lucy was dead?

Then her thoughts drifted to her neighbor. Something about the scar on her hand nagged at Finley. It shouldn't. She'd never really looked at her neighbor that closely. Not at all the little details anyway. The woman was always working in her yard. She probably injured herself with pruning shears.

Unable to consider going back to bed at this point, Finley set her laptop aside, grabbed her cell and the keys she needed, and headed for the door.

Didn't matter that she wore a nightshirt. It was late, and the neighbors were in for the night. Most of the houses were dark. She locked her door and stepped off the porch in her bare feet. *Cold.* So maybe she should have taken the time to put on her shoes. Too late now.

The air was chilling as she scanned the block before hurrying across the street. She entered her neighbor's yard, closing the gate behind herself, and hustled up to the porch. It took a couple of tries before she got the key in the lock and gave it a twist. She reached inside and flipped on a light.

"Spot," she called. "Where are you?" She didn't want to startle the fur ball and end up being nipped on the ankle for it.

The dog lifted his head but didn't bother getting out of his bed. She pulled the door closed and walked over to him. "Hey there." She reached down and scratched him between the ears. To her surprise, he rolled onto his back as if hoping for the same attention to his belly.

Finley frowned. Spot was not a he. She leaned down and did a closer inspection as she scratched his belly. A girl for sure. Maybe she'd misunderstood.

Finley sighed. She straightened and moved through the living room. The house was sparsely furnished. No family photos—no pictures of any kind—hanging on the walls. No decor items placed around the room. There was a television, a single chair and a sofa. One table that sat between the sofa and the chair. She walked toward the hall. The house was larger than Finley's. Three bedrooms but still only one bath. One of the rooms was empty. How strange that Roberts just left it empty. No storage boxes, no nothing. The third had a bed and a dresser, but again, no photos or decor items at all.

In the entire house, there were no photos of anyone—not even of Roberts. Nothing related to a husband. Not even in her bedroom.

"You are one strange lady," Finley muttered. Maybe it was her religion. She did keep to herself most of the time.

Spot had climbed out of her bed and was following Finley from room to room. She hadn't checked the garage since Roberts was hospitalized. Maybe she should check it out. Not because Finley worried that something needed her attention but because she was nosy. She wanted to know more about her neighbor and her weird habits. Maybe there would be boxes stored in the garage that gave some insight into her story.

It was a distraction. Finley was sick of the case . . . sick of Carson Dempsey. She needed a distraction, and her neighbor was it.

At the back door, Finley grabbed the garage key from the wall. The garage was like Finley's, detached. When these old houses were built, no one had attached garages, apparently.

When she opened the door, the dog darted past her, nearly tripping her. "Spot!" Damn it. She rushed after the animal, the white fur making him—her—easy to follow in the dark.

Spot ran all the way to the garage walk-through door and started to scratch as if to get inside.

Finley was grateful the little shit didn't go any farther. "You trying to scare me to death, girl?" she demanded. She was fairly certain she had closed the gate, but she wasn't taking any chances.

With the dog under one arm, Finley used her free hand to unlock the door, then slid her palm over the wall until she found a switch. Light filled the space. A vintage Buick sat in the middle of the garage. Finley hadn't been out here before, but all looked to be good. There were lots of built-in shelves, but oddly they were all empty.

"No Christmas decorations," she commented. Nearly everyone kept that sort of thing in their garages. No boxes of stuff. She stared down at Spot. "Maybe she's like me and stopped doing Christmas and decided not to keep anything that reminded her of the past."

The garage actually looked like Roberts had just moved in.

Finley walked over to the Buick and peered through the window into the front seat. Spot scrambled out of her arms, and before Finley could stop her, she took off. Finley called for her, but it was too late: the dog was under the vehicle. Finley went on with her inspection of the car. Nothing in the front or back seats. She glanced around the space once more. Nothing here but the car.

Her gaze stalled on the ceiling. Were those skylights? A total of six lined the backside of the space. Not something she would have noticed from her side of the street. Who put skylights in their garage? Maybe the builder had expected to use it as a sort of greenhouse. All those empty shelves may have held plants at one time. Who knew?

Shaking her head, Finley walked to the door. "I am leaving, Spot. You'd better come on, or I will lock you up in this garage for the night."

As if to reiterate her frustration, exhaustion settled down on her like a load of bricks. Why the hell did she even walk over here?

"Spot!" she demanded. "Come!"

She was not crawling around on the floor to try and catch that dog. With no other choice, she swiped the switch, turning off the light. She waited a beat and then started out the door. As if the turning off of the light had been her cue, Spot barreled out the door and into the dark yard.

She should never have let that animal out of the house at this hour. She locked up the garage and stalked back to the house. To her surprise, the dog raced ahead of her and waited at the door.

Thank God.

Finley had enough problems without losing her neighbor's dog.

When she exited the yard—closing the gate—she almost stumbled back when she made out the shape of a man waiting in the darkness on the street.

"Fin."

For three beats Finley couldn't speak.

Not her follower.

Her father stood in the dark by Matt's car.

"What're you doing here?" It had to be ten thirty or eleven. She noticed his car then. He'd parked in front of Matt's. "Is everything okay?" Her heart pounded harder.

"I was going to your door, and then I saw you on the sidewalk."

She moved closer, folded her arms over her chest. Damn, it was cold. Her feet suddenly felt icy on the bottoms. "What's wrong?"

"I didn't feel comfortable the way we left things today."

"You want to come in?" This was seriously weird.

"No. No." He shook his head adamantly. "I had a meeting tonight, and on the way home I thought I should drop by and see you. Sorry it's so late. I didn't consider the time."

Okay, she could see that, but still, he usually called.

"I could make coffee," she offered again, hoping to get him inside.

"I really should get home. Your mother will be worried. But I . . . I had to make sure we were okay."

"We're fine, Dad." No, she wasn't going to pretend. She walked right up to him and looked him straight in the eye with the aid of the streetlamp. "Tell me why you really went to see Ray Johnson."

"I didn't actually know the Johnson family," he said, glancing at her bare feet. "But I saw on the news—back then—that his brother was missing. That sort of thing is always sad to see, but really, I thought little about it beyond that momentary consideration. Then, a few weeks later, Ray Johnson came to see me."

Finley forgot all about the cold. "What did he want?"

Her father drew in a big breath. "He said the police had been harassing him about some connection between his missing brother and the—he called her *the dead girl*." He closed his eyes and shook his head. "He wanted to know if I was the one who told the police such a ridiculous rumor. I told him no, and that was the end of it." He rubbed at his forehead. "But with all this business being reopened, I began to worry that he—Ray Johnson—might again think this had something to do with me. Particularly since he hired your firm. Honestly, I'm just worried that he's using you to punish me for something I didn't even do. I never said one thing about him or his family to the police."

Finley couldn't be sure if he was telling her the whole truth, but he sounded sincere. Or maybe she just wanted him to be telling the truth. Either way, she was too exhausted to start a battle tonight. "Dad, I'm not worried that you did anything wrong. I know you wouldn't. My only concern is that you might know something—without understanding the importance of it—that would help my investigation."

He nodded. "Oh, I see."

Did he? "Why did you have lunch with Maureen Downey?"

He chuckled, but the sound was far drier than usual. "You should know the answer to that one. She wanted to grill me about your potential run against Briggs." He went for another laugh that failed just as miserably. "I fear there will be a lot more reporters knocking on our doors."

Finley forced a smile. "Probably."

Her father reached for her, pulled her into a hug. "Don't you worry about me and that no-good Ray Johnson. If I knew anything that would help you find answers, I would tell you."

Finley hugged him back hard and then said good night. She watched him drive away. With every fiber of her being, she wanted to believe his words.

But he was still holding something back, and whatever it was . . . it involved Lucy Cagle.

23

After the Murder

Thirteen Years Ago

Friday, November 24

O'Sullivan Residence
Jackson Boulevard, Belle Meade, 11:30 a.m.

Bart checked the steaks. Grinned. Almost done.

Ruth would be home in half an hour. It was the day after Thanksgiving, but she'd had to go into the office for a few hours this morning. Bart grinned. By the time she returned, he would have a celebratory lunch prepared. Finley was inside working on the rolls. Ruth didn't know that he and Finley had been told she was getting a very special award. Her assistant had given Bart a heads-up. Ruth was the first woman to receive the Nashville Bar Association's esteemed Jack Norman, Sr. Award. It was a tremendous honor. Bart was so very proud of her. The award was the reason she had been called in to her office today. She would be told the news before it was released to the press.

He carefully turned the steaks. The baked potatoes were in the warming drawer. He'd prepared a nice salad. The wine was waiting in the dining room. Ruth liked all manner of reds. Bart not so much, but he could live with it. This was her special moment, and he wanted every aspect of it to be perfect.

Finley had told him time and again that he never considered himself and he always put Ruth first. But that was what a man did when he truly loved a woman. Love and respect—they were the foundations of a good marriage. It was true that Ruth was far more outspoken than him. She had outshined him in most everything in their lives, but Bart was okay with that. It wasn't necessary for him to be a star to be happy. He loved his life exactly as it was. No one was happier to bask in the light that was his wife's.

Ruth O'Sullivan was an amazing person and brilliant legal mind. She had been as an attorney, and she really shined as a judge.

Finley was just like her mother. She didn't want to admit it, but she was. She had that same brilliant mind. The same dogged determination. She would succeed in the legal field as well. He anticipated her climbing high, just as her mother had.

The work he did was important too. He helped many families, particularly children. He was proud of what he had accomplished as well.

"I hope one of those steaks is for me."

Bart whipped around.

He was there . . . standing in the yard as if he had been invited.

Bart glanced at the door leading to the kitchen. Finley was in the house. His heart swelled into his throat.

"What're you doing here?" he demanded, struggling to keep his voice low.

Ray Johnson held up his hands. "Let's just stay calm, Bart. No need to get excited."

Was the man insane?

"My wife will be here any minute. My daughter is in the house. Do not tell me not to get excited!" Outrage blasted through him. What the hell had he gotten himself into?

"My car is parked on the street, and," Johnson said, "I will make this quick."

Bart reminded himself to breathe.

"I just want to make sure that we don't have any problems," the bastard said, stepping closer, eyeing the steaks.

Damn! The steaks! Bart ushered him out of the way and removed the steaks from the grill. Hell, he was shaken. He couldn't even think straight.

"I hear a certain someone paid you a little visit."

Bart faced him, more furious than he had ever been in his entire life. "What are you talking about?"

Johnson laughed. "I think you know what I'm talking about, Bart. I know she came to your office. She had that PI checking up on you, just like he was checking up on me. She wants to find her daughter's killer." He scoffed. "She should have known all PIs are alike, for sale to the highest bidder. Bauer knew his career would be over if he screwed with the Johnsons."

"Are you talking about Lucy Cagle's mother?" Bart hoped his confusion was convincing. God, he had never hated anyone in his whole life the way he hated this man . . . this . . . this thug.

Louise had figured out the damned PI had sold out. What kind of man did such a thing? Scum like this one, that was who.

Johnson sneered. "Don't fucking jerk me around, Mr. Social Services. I want you to get a message to her for me."

Fury bolted through Bart. "I will not do anything for you, you son of a bitch!"

Johnson shrugged. "Well, in that case I might have to talk to the Judge." He smirked. "Or maybe I'll talk to that pretty young daughter of yours."

Bart pointed the meat fork he held at the bastard. "You leave my family alone. I want nothing to do with you or that . . . that woman. She has done nothing but cause me trouble, when all I did was help her daughter."

Please, please let me be convincing enough.

Johnson's eyes narrowed. "Do I look stupid to you?"

Bart blinked, tried to come up with a response that wouldn't get his family hurt.

"I have a message for her, and you are going to give it to her," Johnson warned. "So listen carefully."

Bart's head bobbed up and down of its own accord. "I'm listening."

"She took something that belongs to me. I'm going to give her until Monday to bring it back. If she doesn't, she'll end up tucked in right next to her dead daughter and husband. You got it?" Johnson demanded.

More frantic nodding. "I'll tell her. You have my word."

"Good. Now I don't have to hurt your family. You do this for me and keep quiet like a good boy and you will never hear from me again."

"All right." Bart swallowed, forced his lungs to draw in a breath.

"Good. So why don't you make that call now." He glanced at the phone extension lying on the table next to the grill. "I'll just hang around and make sure you relay the message properly."

Bart placed the fork on the table and picked up the phone. He hated that his hand shook so badly. Then he frowned. "I . . . I don't know her number."

This was true. He'd only ever spoken to Louise Cagle face to face.

Johnson smiled and reached into his shirt pocket for a piece of paper. "Not to worry. I have it right here."

As the man called off the digits, Bart entered them into the phone.

"Put it on speaker," Johnson demanded.

Bart tapped the button for the speaker just as Louise answered.

"Why are you calling me?" she demanded.

Bart licked his lips and forced his brain and mouth to work together. "Ray Johnson stopped by my house." His voice failed him, and he made a low keening sound. A glower from Johnson had him clearing his throat. "He . . . he wanted me to give you a message. He said you have something that belongs to him and you have until Monday to bring it back."

The click of her ending the call echoed in Bart's ear.

"She . . ." He stared at Johnson, the phone hanging from his hand. "She hung up."

Johnson smiled. "No problem. I think she got the message."

Bart found the wherewithal to tap the End button.

"Good job." Johnson gestured to the steaks. "You enjoy your celebratory lunch. I'm sure you're proud of your wife. She's doing great things."

He walked away.

Bart clutched at the table next to his grill to keep himself upright. Never in his life had he ever wished anyone harm. But he wished Ray Johnson would die a slow, agonizing death.

"Dad?" Finley appeared next to him. "You okay?"

Bart produced a smile. Nodded. "Steaks are ready." He grabbed for the tray.

"Mom's on her way. She just called to say she had a surprise for us." Finley laughed. "She has no idea we already know."

Bart feigned a laugh of his own and walked back into the house with his daughter.

Silently, he prayed for Louise Cagle. It took tremendous courage and strength to do what she had done. Despite that bastard Johnson's unexpected visit, Bart was thankful he had been able to play a small part.

As long as they both avoided Ray Johnson, they might just survive this.

24

Now

Friday, December 8

The Finnegan Firm
Tenth Avenue, Nashville, 8:30 a.m.

"Good morning," Finley said to Nita as she strolled into the lobby.

Nita glanced up from her work. "Good morning. You look chipper today. You must have had a nice evening."

"Very nice." Finley wouldn't go into details, but last night with Matt had been awesome. They'd had an encore this morning. The sweet way he had touched her almost made her forget about Briggs's new campaign to make her look bad. But she had a plan for that now.

Good sex could clear one's brain of useless static.

The worries about her father still lingered, but a scenario was coming together, and she felt confident she would get to the bottom of his involvement very soon.

"I like what you did with your hair," Nita said. "Looks very nice."

For the first time in ages, Finley had styled her hair, sort of. It hung around her shoulders instead of being twisted into a clip or ponytail.

She'd even worn one of her nicer suits. The soft caramel-colored one rather than a navy or black.

"Thanks."

She left her bag in her office, went to the tiny kitchen–break room and grabbed a coffee, then headed to Jack's office. He was just ending a call.

"Morning, kid." He removed his reading glasses. "You look rested this morning."

She smiled, settled into a chair in front of his desk. "How about you?" She sipped her coffee.

"I had a very nice evening. Miriam Grant and I went to dinner."

Finley set her mug aside to prevent sloshing coffee on the soft beige cashmere sweater she had chosen to go with the suit. "You had dinner with relationship material?"

She hated to sound so surprised, but Jack usually stuck with the ladies who weren't interested in long term, no offense to him. He had never shown interest in long term. Of course, she knew why now. He'd been in love with the Judge for most of his adult life. He'd only recently admitted this burden and, apparently, decided to move on. Good for him.

"Don't go making something from nothing," he warned as he reached for his own coffee. He glanced into the mug and frowned.

As if the mug had a button that summoned her, Nita appeared, poured him a refill. "She lost her husband a couple of years ago. Her daughters are married, one in Florida, the other in Wyoming."

Finley grinned at the idea that Nita had been listening to their conversation. The woman made it a point to stay informed. "She sounds perfect. No baggage lying around."

Jack looked from Nita to Finley. "Stow it, the both of you."

Finley and Nita shared a laugh. Nita wandered back to her desk, and Finley resumed enjoying her coffee.

"Did you hear back from that lab?" Finley asked.

"I sure did. Just before you arrived. Johnson's results are in."

"Now," she said, "we just have to make this official with Houser and we can get this part over with." Not that any test was going to convince her that Ray Johnson was guiltless in the murder of Lucy Cagle. He may not have murdered her, but he was involved on some level. Had information or simply had covered for his younger brother. And he had threatened her father. Finley had a problem with all of the above.

"Let's make the call," Jack said.

Finley tugged her phone from her jacket pocket and tapped Houser's name. She put the phone on speaker and placed it on Jack's desk.

"You okay this morning?"

Jack frowned.

Finley flinched. "Hey, Jack is here with me, and I have you on speaker."

Houser cleared his throat. "What's up? You two have something for me? Like DNA results?"

"Let's go over the rules first," Jack said.

"We'll meet at the lab," Finley said. "You provide the test results you have from the cigarette butts to the technician, and he does the comparison. If our client, as he insists, is not a match, you have to clear him from your list—at least as far as the evidence you have now is concerned."

"If he is a match," Houser pressed.

"Then we may or may not have a problem," Jack said. "But the man was willing, so I'm guessing he knows how this is going to go down."

No question. Only a fool would agree to a test like this without being certain.

"Keep in mind," Finley reminded them, "that there is a strong possibility the butts were planted by someone who wanted to frame our client or prove he was there when Lucy was—in a building he owned."

"Got it," Houser grumbled.

The guy wanted so badly to get the Johnson family. Finley hoped he could. But, sadly, she felt confident it would not be with this meager evidence.

"So, do we have a deal?" Jack asked.

"Deal," Houser said. "Let's do this. What's the address?"

Finley gave him the location and ended the call. To Jack, she said, "I should get going."

"Hold on there, kid. You're not getting away that easy. Why would Houser want to know if you were okay this morning? Did something happen last night? Something you're not sharing with me?"

Why fight the inevitable? "The guy following me. Black hoodie, dark glasses, black sedan. Last night he came all the way up to my car, banged on my window."

"Where did this happen?" Outrage had already started its climb across Jack's face.

"I stopped by the cemetery to visit Derrick's grave on the way home last night. It got dark on me, and when I was leaving, he nosed up to my car and—"

"First of all," her boss cut in, "you don't go anywhere isolated like that alone. Particularly at night. You hear me? Not until we know who this guy is and who he's working for."

"Houser already read me this riot act. Matt did the same."

"You better listen to one of us," Jack warned in his sternest voice. "Think of your folks and Matt. You can't do this to them."

She nodded. "Got it." Pushing to her feet, she put her hand over her heart. "You have my word."

"I want to hear all the words," he countered. "I know you too well, Finley O'Sullivan."

"I will not go to isolated places alone." She mentally crossed her fingers. *If I can help it.*

"Go. Do this thing, and let me know how it turns out."

And then she was going to find the custodian and figure out the little truths he was keeping to himself.

Discreet Results
Hill Avenue, Nashville, 9:30 a.m.

Finley and Houser waited in a small office that belonged to the owner of the lab.

Dr. Randy Gainer, the owner, and Finley had been friends since her undergraduate years at Vandy. He'd been premed. She'd helped him out with organic chemistry. She had aced chemistry in high school. These days he was her go-to guy for anything related to private lab work. She could trust him, and he would stop whatever else he was doing to help her out. Everyone needed a Randy Gainer.

"Did you tell Matt?" Houser asked after he'd scrolled his inbox on his phone for five or so minutes.

She'd wondered when he would get to that. "I did. We're good."

"What about Jack?"

"I couldn't exactly not tell him after the way you kicked off this morning's call."

Houser flashed her a smile. "I may have done that on purpose."

"I figured."

"I just want you to stay safe, Finley."

She searched his face for as long as he held eye contact with her. He was a good guy. He knew her history better than anyone besides Matt and Jack. He'd given as much to protect her as anybody except Derrick.

She was lucky to have a friend like him. Being her friend was rarely easy. She could be pushy, among other annoying things.

"You're a good friend, Houser," she said, meaning it.

He laughed. "I think that's the nicest thing any lawyer has ever said to me."

How could she not laugh at that?

The door opened, and Randy walked in. Finley sat up straighter. She sure as hell hoped Johnson had known what he was doing. She didn't really care if he ended up in prison—he probably belonged there—but it would be a little difficult for Jack to explain how it happened if a complaint was filed by the family. After all, this little deal had been her idea. Putting one's client in jeopardy—even just a little bit—was frowned upon.

That was the thing about Jack and Finley. They sometimes played fast and loose, but they always got the job done the right way.

Randy sat down behind his desk. "These donors are *not* a match."

Finley hated that she felt the tiniest bit relieved. She so wanted the bastard to have to fight harder to get away with what she felt confident was some connection to Lucy's murder.

Houser looked a little deflated as well.

"But," Randy said, in true Randy fashion. He liked the buildup. "They are related. If you'd like me to determine how they are related. I can do that." He turned to Houser. "For a small fee."

"Randy," Finley said, shooting him a pointed look.

He rolled his eyes. "Whatever. I should have the results later this afternoon. We're a little shorthanded today."

Finley stood. "Thanks, Randy, I owe you one."

"Just remember that when you boot Briggs out of office. I could use some of those lucrative government contracts."

"If it happens, I will have you at the top of my list," Finley assured him.

"Thanks, Dr. Gainer," Houser said. "Appreciate the assist."

He gave Houser a nod.

Once they were outside, Houser glanced around the narrow parking area. Their cars sat side by side. "You think it's the missing brother?"

"It's looking that way," she admitted. This had cleared Ray Johnson with the police for now, but Finley had her doubts as to the authenticity, or at the least the nature, of how this evidence came to light. She suspected Houser had the same issues, but she kept the notion to herself. For now, the only choice was to focus on other potential persons of interest. At the top of her list was the custodian. "You're sure there was nothing in the official case file about a staff member at Lucy's school?"

"Like I told you, they all checked out. Some of them are no longer there. Retired. Died. But all who were there at the time of the murder checked out."

"What about a custodian named Howard Brewer? There was nothing about him?"

"There was nothing on anyone who was employed by the school. Why do you keep going back to this?"

She wanted to say because it was more comfortable than bringing up her father.

Instead, she said, "Brewer lost his wife the December before Lucy's murder. She and some of the other students decided since he didn't have any family left to help him out, they would take him meals. They even took him presents on Christmas. As time went on, he and Lucy remained friends. I interviewed him yesterday, and it was very obvious, he was fond of her. Maybe more so than one would expect. Then, completely by chance, I ran into him at the cemetery last night."

But was the meeting really by chance on her part? She had known Lucy was buried there. Had she decided to visit Derrick in hopes Brewer might feel inclined to visit Lucy after their talk? Looking back, the idea seemed a stretch . . . but he had made an appearance at the cemetery.

She shook off the thought. "He was putting flowers at her mausoleum. He said he felt compelled to do that since she had no one left to bring her flowers. I suppose the same way he had no one that long-ago Christmas."

"You think he knows something?"

She grimaced, then, reluctantly, nodded. "I do. He was very protective of her. She talked to him about an older guy she was seeing. She even revealed that she was torn about the relationship. He mentioned that he noticed how clean her car was all the time, which ties in to our car wash theory. By the way, Johnson says he was forced to tear down the car wash after a structural engineer said there were serious issues."

Houser grunted. "Yeah, right. What else have you got on the custodian? I'm really curious why he didn't tell any of this to the detectives doing the investigating thirteen years ago."

"He insists that he didn't believe he knew anything that mattered at the time, but who knows? He seems to be clean. No criminal record. No other family around. Excellent record at the school. I was planning to go to see him again."

"We could go together," Houser suggested.

"We could ride together, although that might be seen as a conflict of interest."

He grinned. "Right. Okay, I'll meet you at the school."

Finley doubted his insistence on tagging along was only about talking to Brewer, but she opted not to push the issue. Like Matt and Jack, he was worried about her. She could tolerate a bodyguard for a little while. So he followed her to Harpeth Hall. They parked and walked in together.

"I made a call on the way over here," he said as the entrance doors closed behind them. "I've got someone running a deep background search on Brewer."

"Probably a waste of time," she said as they paused at the administration office. "You know this school turned over every rock in the man's past before hiring him."

Houser shrugged. "Never hurts to have a second look."

"Never hurts," Finley agreed.

The lady at the desk was the same one who had been there yesterday. "Good morning, Ms. O'Sullivan. You're back so soon?"

"Good morning. This is Detective Houser." Houser gave the lady a nod. "We wanted to speak with Mr. Brewer again. He was very helpful yesterday, and anything else he can offer regarding Lucy Cagle will be greatly appreciated. I believe Detective Houser's case will benefit from talking to him."

Finley did not want to get the man in trouble if he was innocent, and she had a feeling he was innocent of anything related to Lucy's murder.

"I'm sorry, he's not in today. He wasn't feeling well, and Lord knows the man has enough sick leave and vacation time to take the next ten years off. He never misses a day. I'm guessing he's really under the weather if he's staying home. He's just so reliable."

"Thank you," Finley said. "We'll catch him another time."

He'd seemed fine to Finley last night. Maybe there was something he had to do today. Something that Finley's questioning had prompted. Only one way to find out.

They left the building. The sun was brighter than usual and damned warm for a December morning, making her wish she had reconsidered the sweater.

"Where to now?" Houser asked.

"I say we drop by his house." Finley sent him a look. "Are you trying to hang around me to protect me or for some other male-ego-driven odyssey?"

He laughed. "No, actually I'm just trying to be eco friendly. If we're going to the same place, we might as well go together."

"Nice try, but with my neighbor in the hospital and not knowing when Jack might need me, it's better to stick with two vehicles."

Houser gestured to the cars. "Lead the way."

Brewer Residence
Cherokee Lane, Nashville, 10:30 a.m.

The house was a smaller ranch style. Brick with a carport. On a large lot. Most of the houses along the block looked the same. A few were multilevel, but most were like this one. Fairly compact on one floor.

"Doesn't look like anyone's home," Houser said as he emerged from his car.

Finley closed the door of her Subaru. Though the carport was empty, there was a detached garage. "His car could be in the garage."

Houser shook his head. "I'm betting not. The guy is a lifelong fixer. There're no other buildings. No shed. He has to have a shop around here somewhere."

She could see that scenario. "You figure he uses the garage for a workshop."

"You got it."

While Houser walked around the yard, Finley went to the door. She stood on the small stoop of a porch and opened the screen door to knock on the wood door behind it. Since no dogs came rushing toward her and none barked, she assumed they were safe from the possibility of being bitten.

Finley knocked again. There was no window in the door. No sound coming from the other side. She knocked a couple more times; then she did the sneaky-peeky thing. Any window not covered with shutters or blinds was fair game as far as Finley was concerned.

"Where are you, Mr. Brewer?" she mumbled.

Typical eighties-style furnishings inside. Tidy. Clean. The shrubs around the house were all neatly trimmed. The lawn was well kept. Probably fertilized and seeded for the winter. The man was meticulous with his maintenance. Never missed a day of work. If he was so meticulous with all that he did, wouldn't he have been more careful than he'd let on about keeping up with Lucy?

Finley felt certain he knew more than he'd shared.

When she and Houser made their way back to their parked cars, she said, "Maybe he went to the doctor." It wasn't impossible, though he had looked fine last night.

"Guess so." Houser jerked his head toward the garage. "There was a window. It's a workshop."

"Good call," she said. She hitched a thumb toward the house. "I'll leave him a note."

She tore a page from her notepad and scribbled a quick message asking Brewer to call her. Some older folks didn't check their voice mails regularly. She left her number just in case he'd lost her card. Once she'd tucked it in the wood door and ensured the screen door closed, she headed back to her car.

"Have you spoken to your father again?"

Finley hesitated but then decided she could use Houser's help, which meant she couldn't keep this from him. "I did. He's still not telling me everything, but he explained his hesitation a little better." She gave him a recap of her father's late-night visit. Then added, "Although he didn't say as much, I got the feeling Johnson may have been threatening him. Maybe he still is. The idea has me wondering if Johnson chose Jack's firm for that reason. Or that maybe my working there was a part of it."

Houser thought about all she'd said for a bit before reacting. "We certainly can't rule out the idea. To tell the truth, I can see how Johnson may have been grasping at straws thirteen years ago. Trying to figure out if anyone could connect him or his family to Lucy's murder." His eyebrows went up. "By the way, I reinterviewed the two friends of Ian's, and both claimed to have no idea if Ian was involved with Lucy or anyone else. Maybe they just didn't want to rat him out to a cop, or maybe Johnson had them spoon-feed that info to you alone."

The big question was why.

"What about the ex-wife?" Finley asked.

"Funny that you asked," Houser said. "She called me back. Was happy to chat. She claims she has never met you. She has no idea why you would"—he made air quotes—"talk shit about her."

Her frustration edging up, she shook her head. "He's using me or trying to set me up." No way to deny the idea. "Maybe because he believes my father knows something or, as you say, that he ratted him out."

"I don't like it," Houser said with a lingering survey of the street, as if he feared the hoodie guy or some other scumbag might be watching.

"Agreed." She glanced around too—for exactly that reason. The very notion that Johnson was using her somehow to get to her father infuriated her. "I should check in with Jack and then give the good news to Johnson."

Houser shrugged. "Tell him I may still have questions."

Finley smiled. "I will. See you later, Houser."

"You look nice today," he said before she could open her car door. "You should always wear your hair down."

She laughed. "Thanks, but that is probably not going to happen."

He grinned. "You look exactly like a prominent district attorney."

Finley laughed again as she climbed into her car.

He waited while she backed out first. She waved and drove away.

Finley had a hunch about where that custodian might be. Since Johnson's office was on her way, she would stop by and talk to him first.

Or maybe she'd let him sweat a little longer.

She grinned. She liked that option way more.

25

Bart tried to concentrate on his work, but he couldn't. He hadn't been able to all week. Not since he'd heard the news that Finley was working with Ray Johnson. She wasn't convinced that he was telling her everything, and that was the part that terrified him most. He knew his daughter. She would not stop trying to find the truth.

His chest tightened, felt as if an elephant was seated there. He got up from his desk and walked to the window. He stared out across the lawn he had so carefully cultivated over the decades. Ruth had always been in charge of most things. The house, the finances, their social lives. But she had left him alone when it came to the automobiles they drove and the grounds around their home. He kept up with all the maintenance and was able to plant and mulch and add little ponds and enclaves with seating areas in the landscape to his heart's desire.

Their entire marriage had been that way. Other than the yard and his work, Bart had nothing that was completely his. Finley had always seemed to gravitate toward him a bit more than she did her mother, but that was likely only because he was available more than Ruth.

His relationships with clients in his work were his own, and he had cherished those. Lucy Cagle's appearance in his professional life had also been a cherished relationship. By then Finley was so busy with college that she barely had time for him. But Lucy was eager to hear whatever he had to say on the subject of the children and families he helped in his work. She had adored his stories.

Perhaps he had been selfish to keep their time a secret from Ruth, even from Lucy's own mother. But he hadn't meant any harm, and in the end, he was certain that nothing he did had caused harm.

But the things he knew almost certainly had prevented justice according to the law, and for that Finley and Ruth would never forgive him.

Still, any way he looked at it, he had done what he had to do.

There was no question. No question at all.

If he could go back in time, he would do the same thing all over again, for there simply had been no other choice.

If the whole truth ever came out, he hoped that the people he cared about would eventually understand.

His cell phone vibrated against his desk. He turned to the intrusion. Since no image accompanied the number, he moved closer to see who was calling. The number was local but not one he recognized.

He took a breath and prayed he would not regret answering.

"Hello."

"I need your help."

The voice . . . it sounded vaguely familiar. He swallowed the worry welling up in his throat. "Who is this?"

"For God's sake, you know who it is."

It couldn't be. That was impossible . . . it had been—

"I need your help," she repeated.

No. No. No. This couldn't be. "I don't know who you are, and I don't know how you got this number, but I'm hanging up now."

"You haven't changed your number in all this time."

The breath left his lungs.

"You promised to help me if I ever needed it. I need it now. *Right* now."

He nodded, sucked in a gulp of air and attempted to gather his wits about him. "All right." He swallowed again. Fought the urge to vomit. "Tell me where you are, and I'll come right away."

26

Finley had known Houser would take I-65 when they left Brewer's house, so she had deliberately chosen Hillsboro Pike. When she was confident Houser hadn't doubled back and followed her, she had put through a call to Maureen Downey.

Downey was meeting her at the Cagle house. One way or another, Finley intended to know what her father was hiding. Since he had so far refused to share whatever uncomfortable secret he harbored, Finley opted to move on to the next most likely source—Maureen Downey. No one had been closer to Louise Cagle. Their daughters had been best friends. And Finley's father had met with Downey at least once this week. Made sense that Downey could potentially know the answer.

On some level Finley wondered if knowing would assuage the worry and dread tearing at her insides. She told herself repeatedly that it couldn't possibly be so terrible.

Only one way to find out.

Finley entered the code and waited for the gate to open; then she rolled forward. She glanced around. Spotted what she hoped was Downey's car. She checked her rearview mirror and ensured the gate had closed. They should have the place to themselves. No code. No entrance. At least not via a vehicle.

After parking near the house, she climbed out and scanned the yard again. Matt and Houser had made her nervous.

No, that was wrong. The damned guy in the hoodie following her around had made her nervous.

Was it a good thing that she hadn't seen him this morning? Maybe.

But she wasn't counting on him being gone for good. Not yet anyway.

Still, here she was, in a mostly isolated area. But it was broad daylight. And Downey was supposed to be around here somewhere.

Since she wasn't in her car or anywhere that Finley could readily see, she moved on to the porch. The front door was partially open. Nerves jangling as the cold abruptly invaded her, Finley hesitated. She took a deep breath, held it and listened intently. No sound.

Just do it. Go in and see if she is in there.

Moving quietly, her gaze roving from left to right, Finley stepped through the door and into the entry hall.

No Downey.

Her heart thumped harder. Where the hell was she?

When she reached the door to the first parlor, Finley spotted her. Relief made her knees weak. Downey stood in the middle of the room staring at the painting of Lucy and her family hanging over the fireplace.

"Thanks for coming," Finley said, announcing her presence.

Downey turned around slowly. She dabbed at her eyes. "Sorry. I was lost in thought."

Finley decided not to ask about her having a second key. Didn't actually matter, in the grand scheme of things. They had far more pressing issues to discuss.

"There was a key hidden under a certain rock in a flower bed out back," she explained as if reading Finley's mind. A vague smile moved across her lips. "I'd forgotten about it until I arrived and couldn't get in." She shook her head. "Funny how you remember the oddest little details out of the blue."

Finley offered a sad smile. "The little things can sneak up on you sometimes."

Downey looked around the room as if seeing it for the first time. Finley watched the sadness play across her face. The thing was, Finley had only called the woman maybe ten minutes ago. How had she gotten here so fast with time to wander around?

"You were already here when I called," Finley suggested.

Downey dabbed at her eyes again. "I was. I can't really explain why. I suppose because I was feeling nostalgic. The second weekend of December, Louise always held a big holiday party here." The smile was back, a little brighter this time. "The house was filled with soft music, and the festive spirit abounded. No one decorated the way Louise did. The place, inside and out, was like a Christmas village. Just beautiful." She looked away a moment. "I miss those times. I miss her."

Her sincerity—regret, nostalgia, whatever—was real. Few people could fake that level of emotion. The rawness of the moment sharpened Finley's own feelings of regret for things lost. She pushed the response aside and focused on the reason they were here. There was another little detail Finley wanted to clear up before hitting Downey with the hard questions.

"There's something I want you to see."

Downey blinked. "All right."

"I assume you know about Louise's home office," Finley said as she moved out of the room and toward the rear of the house.

"Oh sure. That little building was an old smokehouse," Maureen said as they crossed the kitchen and exited through the french doors into the backyard. "Louise had it renovated for her home office."

The air had a bite to it this morning. Winter was coming. Finley wished she had worn a coat over her jacket.

She paused at the set of french doors installed in the former smoke-house, picked out the proper key from the ring and unlocked the door. Inside, she instantly recognized there was something different . . . a throw pillow that had been on the small sofa lay front-side down as if someone had been sitting there and gotten up, knocking the pillow over in the process. A few leaves were scattered on the floor.

"Have you been in here?" Finley asked.

Maureen shook her head, her eyebrows furrowing in confusion. "The hidden key was only for the house. You have the keys to every-thing else."

Finley moved beyond the fireplace that split the space in half and shielded the case board from view.

The case board was empty . . . blank. All the notes, the newspaper articles, the images . . . were gone.

Frustrated, Finley moved around the space, checked in drawers and on bookshelves. Any and everything related to Lucy's murder was gone.

She faced the woman who stood near the fireplace watching curi-ously. "The last time I was here, just yesterday, this board was covered with notes and photos and newspaper articles about Lucy's case. A time-line had been made that started one week before Lucy died. You told me Louise hadn't created anything like that—that she had no notes on her current work in progress or on Lucy's case."

Downey shook her head. "It wasn't here before." She glanced around. "I came here after it was obvious Louise was gone." She frowned, shook her head again. "Then several more times after it was obvious she wasn't coming back." She stared directly at Finley then. "I am telling you there was nothing on that board. Nothing. I mean . . ." She blinked rapidly, looking around once more. "I . . . I've been here a few times over the years, but I never came into this office. Why would I? There was nothing out of place during my previous visit. When Louise was working on a project, she sometimes slept in her office downtown.

She kept everything related to her project there—in the city. She rarely brought work home."

A strange sensation burned in Finley's veins, banishing the cold. Then who the hell . . . ? "Who else has a key besides you and the caretaker?"

"No one. What's going on, Finley?"

Finley should have asked this before, but until now it hadn't seemed relevant. "Who did you hire to take care of the maintenance?"

Confusion deepened on the older woman's face. "A very trustworthy and highly recommended gentleman. Howard Brewer. He's a custodian at Harpeth Hall. He called me about the job before I even really began looking. I'd mentioned it to one of the ladies at the school, and I suppose she told him." She frowned. "Why do you ask?"

Finley wanted to kick herself. Of course it was Brewer. Giving the man the benefit of the doubt, she crossed the room and checked the lock for signs of forced entry. No marks or cracks. Nothing to indicate the lock had been tinkered with or the door forced open.

"What're you looking for?" Maureen asked, her impatience showing.

"Like I said"—Finley surveyed the space again—"it was all here just yesterday. Now it's gone. If you didn't take it, then Brewer must have."

Either that or Louise Cagle had come back.

Finley dismissed the idea. It had been thirteen years. The woman was likely dead. Deep inside, that conclusion didn't sit well or right. If Louise was still alive . . . add that to her father keeping things from her . . . then Finley had a bad, bad feeling about where all this was headed.

Could her father know that Louise was alive?

Finley went stone still. Or where she was?

"No." Downey made a face that suggested the idea was ludicrous. "I can't see Howard doing anything of the sort. He thought the world of Lucy and of Louise."

Finley's own frustration started to simmer once more. She needed to get this done, and then she intended to hunt down her father. This time, she wasn't letting him go until she had whatever the hell he was holding back.

She held up a hand for Downey to stop with the monologue about what a great person Brewer was. Finley had no reason at this point to doubt the man's character. "He's a great guy. I'm with you on that one. What I need to understand is why you had lunch with my father on Wednesday."

Downey blinked, obviously startled by the subject change. Her face blanked. "I . . . I wanted to interview him regarding your run for DA, but he refused to answer my questions."

Finley rolled her eyes. She would love for that to be the actual reason, but it wasn't. She knew it wasn't. Why the hell couldn't anyone just tell the damned truth when it mattered? "I know my father was helping Lucy with her senior thesis. I know Ray Johnson threatened my father because he was afraid Lucy may have told him something." She looked Downey dead in the eye. "Whoever you and my father believe you're protecting by lying, trust me, you're not helping. If Johnson had anything to do with Lucy's death, he is going to get away with it because you two are cowards."

Downey straightened, allowed her own frustration and no small amount of anger to show. "I am not a coward, and neither is your father. You"—she pointed a finger at Finley—"have no idea what you're talking about."

"Then, by all means, enlighten me." The frustration that had been simmering boiled over into anger.

Downey drew back as if she realized she had talked herself into a corner.

Finley threw up her hands. "I'm all ears. Explain to me why the two of you want the bad guy to get away with murder. Who cares that Lucy was murdered and her death killed her father and maybe her mother? Why bother with justice?"

"Justice has already been served," Downey snapped. Then her lips pressed together tightly as if she hadn't meant to allow the words to escape. Her eyes widened in horror at her own gaffe.

"What the hell does that mean?" Finley demanded. All the little bits of truth that she'd uncovered . . . all the little pieces of the story suddenly came together. "Oh my God." She tried to shake the thought away, but it was there to stay. "Louise disappeared. Ian disappeared. Louise learned the truth and took justice into her own hands."

Downey's eyes told Finley she'd hit the nail on the head before she opened her mouth. "Louise, whether she's dead or alive, deserves peace."

"I couldn't agree more." Finley took a breath, forced herself to calm the hell down. "But, whatever the story is, you need to start from the beginning and tell me the whole truth."

"This is what I'll tell you," Downey fired back. "Louise was the bravest, most courageous woman I have ever known." Her voice cracked as pain gained momentum on the anger. "Do you know how many times she was almost killed trying to get a story? The woman was shot— twice, no less. Once she was almost stabbed. She literally grabbed the blade of the knife in her hand and forced it away from her chest. And even when everything—*everything*—was taken from her, she still fought for justice. So do not," Downey warned, "drag her name through the mud to save that piece-of-shit client of yours. If you dare, I swear to God I will ruin you and your whole damned family."

Finley laughed a dry sound. Shook her head. "Fine. I get it. Louise Cagle—wherever she is and whatever she did—is your hero. Just tell me what my father had to do with all this."

Downey took a breath and appeared to tamp down her emotions to a more manageable level. "Lucy had told Bart certain things about the man she was using as a source of information. After . . . Bart couldn't be sure of who did what, but he was fairly certain that the person responsible for Lucy's murder was one of the Johnson brothers. His conclusion was confirmed when Ray came to him and warned that if he opened his mouth about what he knew or thought he knew, he would kill you and Ruth." Downey closed her eyes a moment, dragged in a ragged breath. "Your father and I have lived with this for all these years, but there was nothing we could do because we had no evidence. But—" Her gaze zeroed in on Finley's, fierce and determined. "But we were able to live with it because we knew that Louise got what she wanted. She got peace."

"How?" Finley demanded. "Where is she?" What the hell had these people been thinking? What the hell had her father done?

Downey laughed, the sound sad and weary but somehow ironic at the same time. "I truly have no idea. I've kept her home ready for her return, just in case. But I honestly have no idea if she's dead or alive. No one has ever heard from her since she disappeared."

Finley spotted not one tell. If Downey was lying about that, the woman really was a master. The need to see her father suddenly hit Finley with hurricane force. "Thank you for telling me the truth. Make sure you and your daughter watch out for each other until this is over."

Downey squared her shoulders. "What're you going to do?"

"What I always do."

Downey didn't ask what that meant. If she knew Finley at all, she would understand.

The two of them locked up the house and headed to their parked cars. Finley waited for Downey to drive away first. When her car had disappeared in the distance, Finley considered her next step. She felt torn between tracking down Brewer and showing up at her father's door. She had a hell of a lot of questions for them both.

Pondering the best option, she turned her Subaru around and headed for the gate. After entering the code, it swung open. Finley rolled through and waited until it automatically closed behind her; then she pulled out onto Murfreesboro Road. She made the decision to find her father first. It was possible Brewer would call her once he'd found her note. If he was the one who made that timeline or took those notes, she would figure it out later. For now, she needed to verify with her father all that Downey had said.

The idea that Ray Johnson was still waiting for the DNA results nudged her. She rolled her eyes at the thought. Had no time and certainly no desire to talk to the man just now. Instead she called Jack and asked him to take care of it while she went in search of her father. Jack was happy to do so, and he reminded her to be careful. No doubt he'd heard in her voice that she had more on her agenda than just *catching up* with her father.

As Finley reached Hillsboro Road, a black sedan popped up in her rearview mirror.

Son of a bitch.

Her fingers tightened on her steering wheel as her fury and frustration ramped up once more. She told herself there was a good amount of traffic. Didn't have to be him. Still, sweat popped out on her skin in anticipation of a confrontation.

She focused forward, glancing into the rearview mirror from time to time. As she drove past Franklin High School, the sedan eased closer and closer. The dark glasses and the black hoodie came into view.

Shit.

It was him.

She focused forward. Considered the best route to take. Going to her father's house with this guy on her tail was out of the question.

Call Houser?

Maybe. Not yet.

An intersection was coming up. Mack Hatcher Memorial Parkway.

Finley steeled herself, focused on the traffic. She had the green light. As she neared the intersection, it shifted to yellow. She floored the accelerator. The Subaru rocketed forward.

The light changed to red.

Finley didn't stop.

The black sedan sped up.

A brown car whizzed around the black sedan and then slammed on its brakes, forcing the bastard to stop for the light or plow into him or her.

Finley barreled forward, putting as much distance as possible between her and that intersection. Whoever the driver in the brown vehicle, she appreciated his or her indecision about running the light.

An incoming call yanked her attention to the dash, where her cell had connected to the car. Local number. She tapped Accept.

"O'Sullivan." Her fingers tightened on the wheel as she navigated the next right turn.

"Ms. O'Sullivan, this is Laurie Gifford. I'm a nurse at the hospital. You're the only contact listed for Helen Roberts."

Finley made another unnecessary turn and braced for bad news. "Is she okay?" Surely the woman hadn't died. She'd looked okay last night.

"Well, that's the problem. We don't know. She removed her IVs and left without telling anyone. Security started a search of the hospital but didn't find her. A review of the security camera footage showed that she left through the main exit. We have no idea where she is, but it's imperative that we find her as soon as possible. She is very ill and should not have left the hospital."

What the hell? Had the woman lost her mind?

"I'll go to her house now," Finley said. "Maybe she went home. She mentioned wanting to get home."

"Please let us know, Ms. O'Sullivan. She still needs care."

Finley assured the woman she would and ended the call. She pressed forward, moving from lane to lane between cars. Then she made several turns, continuing to zigzag her way toward Shelby Avenue in hopes of ensuring the guy in the hoodie didn't catch up with her.

Surely Roberts wasn't that worried about her dog.

Whatever the woman had been thinking, Finley had no choice but to put off confronting her father and tracking down Brewer for the moment.

Jesus. What next?

Roberts Residence
Shelby Avenue, Nashville, 1:20 p.m.

Finley parked on the street. She glanced at her house out of habit, then emerged from her Subaru. A car was parked in Roberts's drive. It sat back from the detached garage the way a visitor would.

A frown tugged at Finley's face. Had someone picked Roberts up and brought her home? A taxi? Uber? If she'd paid someone to drive her home, why were they still here?

Not once in the nearly two years that Finley had lived on this street had she seen a vehicle—other than Roberts's personal one—go into or come out of her driveway. And she hadn't seen that old Buick come and go more than once or twice.

As Finley walked toward the house, she took a big breath and focused on calming down. The appearance of her damned follower had set her nerves on edge. Speaking of which, she glanced toward one end of her street and then the other. No sign of a dark sedan. The tense band of muscles around her skull and neck relaxed a little. Between that creep show and the story Downey had told her, Finley was way beyond rattled.

As if that hadn't been enough, then came the call from the hospital, and with the case rushing toward a crescendo, this was just too much. Still, her neighbor was ill and likely not thinking clearly. She didn't need Finley bursting in all pissed off. She took a breath and ordered herself to calm.

Finley studied the car in her neighbor's driveway as she grew closer. Dark, almost black. *Charcoal.*

Like her father's.

Finley froze midstep.

But why would her father's car be here? She glanced back at her house. Had Matt asked him to stop by and check on the dog for some reason?

Surely not. The idea made no sense.

She started forward once more. The Lexus insignia confirmed the model was the same as her father's. No denying the possibility any longer. Then again, her father wasn't the only one who drove a charcoal Lexus. She paused at the passenger side window and cupped her hands around her eyes to peer inside.

The cup phone gadget she'd gotten him for his cell phone Christmas before last was in the console. The slim briefcase he carried lay on the passenger seat.

Her heart dropped into the vicinity of her feet.

Disbelief rushed through her. Why would her father be here?

The abrupt grind of an overhead door opening drew her attention to the detached garage. On instinct, Finley hunkered down far enough for the Lexus to conceal her presence. She watched through the windows as the old Buick sputtered and then lurched out of the garage, coming to a hard stop in front of the Lexus.

Feeling as if she were watching a movie, Finley stared at the scene. The driver's side door opened, and a gray head rose above the roof of the vehicle. The man straightened to his full height and closed the door.

Dad.

Finley's jaw dropped. No matter that she knew the Lexus was his . . . to see him . . . here . . . was wrong somehow.

"This is not a very good idea," he said, looking toward the open garage.

Finley blinked, shifted her gaze to the garage, beyond the open overhead door.

Her neighbor, dressed in the jeans and mustard-colored sweatshirt she'd been wearing when Finley found her facedown in her yard, stood there as barefoot as the day she was born.

What the hell were they doing? And where, for the love of God, were her shoes?

Roberts said something Finley didn't catch, and her father hurried into the garage, and the door promptly started to lower. He hadn't turned around. Hadn't noticed Finley. Neither had Roberts. Of course they wouldn't. She was well hidden.

What. In. The. Hell?

The door closed fully.

Finley straightened and walked closer, her movements feeling oddly jerky. Her heart pounded harder with each step. This was wrong on so many levels. She paused at the side walk-through door. She had gone in that way only once. There was a key. All she had to do was go to the house and get it. But what would she say when she confronted her father?

Reminding herself to breathe, Finley took a moment to consider the question. This was her father—a man she loved, respected . . . this could not be as bad as it looked. Then there was her neighbor, a woman who had saved Finley's life on perhaps more than one occasion.

But they were both lying about . . . so damned many things!

As if rising from a fog, Finley suddenly became aware of the dog barking inside the house. She glanced that way. Had she heard the arrival of a vehicle? Or the garage door opening? Maybe she wanted out or fed . . .

Ignoring the barking dog, Finley crossed the yard and got the key from beneath the concrete turtle in the flower bed by the front porch. She and Matt had decided to use the hiding place so that whoever arrived home first would have access to the key.

Bracing for Spot's attempts to escape, Finley unlocked the back door but only opened it far enough to reach inside and get the garage key. The little fur ball stuck her head out, but Finley scooted her back inside with her foot. Once she had the door closed again, she hurried back to the garage. Breathless and hands shaking, she pressed her ear there and listened. No sound on the other side. What were they doing in there? There were no boxes or any damned thing else in the building.

The bigger question was why move the car?

Was something hidden under the car? Something her neighbor needed badly enough to run away from the hospital without proper authorization? Ridiculous. There had to be some other reason. But why would she call Finley's father to bring her home? Had she made him believe she had been released just to get a ride?

How did she even know Finley's father?

Why wouldn't she call Finley? Or an Uber?

Because Finley would not have allowed her to leave. She would have talked her out of it. And if she'd left her purse at the hospital, she probably had no money for a taxi of any sort.

But still, how had she gotten the number for Finley's father? Maybe from back in September when she rescued Finley from the would-be assassin? Had her neighbor and her father met during all the insanity that night?

Finley had no idea.

The man—assassin . . . the memory of that night flashed like a scene from a movie through Finley's brain. Helen Roberts had stopped the bastard with nothing more than a garden shovel. Finley would never have expected the elderly woman to be so strong . . . so savvy at recognizing danger.

Finley thought of the scar in the webbing between the thumb and pointer finger of her right hand. Had she . . . ?

The scenario that sifted through her startled Finley . . . made her breath catch. No . . . way. Then she thought of her neighbor's eyes . . . of the shape of her nose . . . and the image took form.

"Son of a bitch."

Shock making her movements stilted, Finley unlocked the door and eased it open. Whatever the hell was going on, she was about to raise absolute hell with her father and . . . this . . . *woman*.

The garage was empty.

Finley blinked twice to ensure her eyes weren't betraying her. A big metal door in the floor beneath where the Buick had been parked stood open. A railing of sorts stuck up from the opening. Sunshine from the half-dozen skylights showered down on the scene, making the space feel too bright . . . too stark.

Forcing away the idea that she was about to step into Pandora's box, she moved closer. Storm shelter? Her brow furrowed with confusion. She'd seen the advertisements for putting them in a garage. Vaguely remembered considering one for the garage at her condo back in the day—before she'd stopped caring if she lived or died.

Focus.

Finley took a big, ragged breath. Her father and . . . *she* must have gone down there.

This was beyond wrong. This was crazy. Over the edge. Finley's head was still swimming at the scenario her mind had pieced together.

She inched closer to the center of the garage. Her heart bumping harder and harder against her sternum. When she reached the opening, there were steps. The railing followed those steps downward. Somewhere below, she heard voices—the deep rumble of her father's voice, then the weaker, frail sound of her neighbor's. Both had a hell of a lot of explaining to do. And if Finley found what she feared she would . . . she shook herself. Christ, she didn't even want to think about that.

Holding her breath to ensure she didn't miss a sound, she eased down the first step. Moving as quietly as possible, she crept down another step and then another. The thundering in her chest had turned into an ache that swelled and swelled, pressing against her insides . . . making her feel the need to run back up and pretend none of this was happening.

When she reached the bottom, she was in a small space one would expect in a storm shelter such as this one. The lighting was very dim. Benches lined the sidewalls. But there was more . . .

A door waited directly in front of her. It stood partially open. The voices she'd heard were coming from beyond that door. With effort, she swallowed back the lump pressing upward into her throat and took the six steps across the cramped space to the door. Steeling herself once more, she reached out, gripped the knob and pulled it more fully open.

A not-so-pleasant odor met her. Musty. Like an old basement or space that stayed shut up too much.

Keep going.

What lay beyond the door was yet another smaller room or hallway. Still dimly lit. From where Finley stood, the hallway went forward about four feet and right maybe a dozen feet, then opened into a larger, well-lit room. She could see the light and the opening from where she stood in a sort of numb status. She should keep going, but her feet refused to move. This . . . *this* was like an episode from *Stranger Things*, and Finley felt as if she were watching from some other place. If she kept going, there would be no plausible deniability. If she turned around now, she could simply walk away wondering what the hell *this* was and never look back.

Except, beyond the denial and the shock, she already knew exactly what *this* was.

The voices were louder now. Her father was arguing about something the woman had done. Finley couldn't see them yet, but she could hear their voices quite well.

Forcing one foot in front of the other until she reached the larger space, Finley stood still and assessed the situation. The two stood before what could only be described as a cell made for holding an animal. No, too large for that. It was big enough for a human . . . a *prisoner*.

Holy hell.

A rock settled in Finley's gut, and her knees nearly buckled. What looked like lengths of iron—rebar, she decided—had been installed vertically and horizontally to create the front of a cage. The other three sides were concrete as far as she could see. This place extended well beyond the length of the garage.

Finley closed her eyes tightly for a moment. This couldn't be. Couldn't be. Then she opened them and looked once more. The area where her father and *she* stood was maybe six feet by twelve. The space beyond the bars looked larger, maybe twice that size, but she couldn't see it very well because the two of them stood in the way arguing.

Finley spotted the corner of what might be a bed or cot.

Oh. My. God.

"It's too late to change it now," *she* said, her voice so very weak. "What's done is done. It's not like you didn't fully grasp my intentions."

"I didn't think . . . ," Bart O'Sullivan stammered. "My God, what have we done?"

Finley inched closer still. Her father shifted away from where he'd been standing just far enough for Finley to see something—no, *someone*—beyond the bars.

The reality was far harder to accept—even when she saw it with her own eyes—than the idea that had formed in her head.

A blast of outrage throttled through Finley, and before she could stop herself, she'd stepped fully into the room. "What the hell is going on down here?"

The two wheeled around to face her.

Her father's face froze in a mask of horror. Her neighbor simply looked pale and weak, desperate. Her long gray hair hung around her shoulders in thick strings. All the things that Finley felt certain she should have noticed before suddenly drilled into her brain. The color of her eyes . . . the tilt of her nose and shape of her jaw.

Louise Cagle.

"Finley, you shouldn't be here."

This from her father. Finley snapped to attention, almost laughed. "I shouldn't be here? What are *you* doing here?" She pushed past him. Stared at the prisoner.

The person . . . male. Blond hair. Blue eyes. He stood in the middle of the cell and stared at her without fear or any other discernible emotion.

Jesus Christ . . . it really was him . . . *Ian Johnson.*

Finley moved closer to the bars that held him prisoner. How in the hell had this woman . . . her damned neighbor, managed this?

"You explain it," Cagle said. "I need to sit down."

Still assimilating what to say next, Finley glanced back at the woman. She made her way to a bench that lined the wall opposite the cell. Above the bench were doors to what appeared to be built-in cabinets.

Finley pointed a finger at her. "You . . . you should still be in the hospital. They called me. You have to go back."

This, of course, seemed utterly irrelevant considering the situation she'd walked into, but the words had burst out of Finley all the same.

Louise Cagle just turned her head, hair falling over her face like a veil to shield her from view.

Finley wanted to yell at someone. She wanted to demand answers. Her emotions wouldn't land in one place. She waffled from furious to worried to . . . she didn't know what. She stared at the prisoner again, assessed his overall condition. Confusion tugged at her brow. He wasn't as thin as she would have expected, and his skin wasn't nearly as pale as it should have been if he'd been held prisoner all these years. He wore a reasonably new-looking flannel shirt and jeans. Name-brand sneakers.

Wait . . . wait. This wasn't right. She turned to her father, and the fury kicked in again. "Talk. Now," she ordered.

He scrubbed a hand over his face. "First, you should know"—he gestured to her neighbor—"this is not who you think she is."

Finley waited, her eyes shooting daggers at him. She knew what he was going to say, but she wanted to hear the words from his mouth. Wanted him to have to admit whatever the hell it was he knew and however the hell he was involved.

"This is Louise Cagle."

"I figured that part out," she snapped. Her head swiveled toward the woman on the bench. "It would've helped if I'd known—I don't know, say, four days ago."

Again, her words seemed vastly unimportant, all things considered, and yet she'd said them. This was so far over the top she wasn't sure there was any seeing past it . . . no excusing it . . . and damned sure no making it right.

A new wave of fury swept through Finley, shifting her attention back to her father. "I have lived across the street from this woman for nearly two years. You have been to my house hundreds of times. You couldn't tell me this?"

"He didn't know." This from Cagle.

Finley stared at her. Cagle's sad face from all those news interviews after her daughter's murder transposed itself over this older woman's. It was her . . . no question.

Lucy's mother.

Finley's attention pivoted back to her father. "But you saw her at least once in her yard when you came to visit me," she argued, addressing her father.

"Did you recognize me?" Cagle demanded, glaring at Finley until she met her gaze.

Finley blinked. "No but—"

"He was never close enough to see me very well," she said. "Time changes everyone." She allowed strands of gray hair to slip through her fingers. "I doubt even Maureen would recognize me now, and we were best friends. It's been thirteen years. The longest of my life."

"What I want to know," Finley demanded, looking to her neighbor, "is how you managed to kidnap this man?" Finley's attention then swung to her father. "And what the hell you had to do with it."

"You don't know the whole story," Ian Johnson said.

Finley stared at the man beyond the bars. She vacillated between feeling sympathy for him and outrage at herself for feeling anything at all—particularly for the man most likely responsible for the murder of Lucy Cagle. "Then explain it to me."

"No," her father announced. "This whole mess is my fault."

Finley's heart ached with equal measures worry and frustration. Did he not understand that this was not fixable? She couldn't protect him from what was coming because of *this*. Couldn't make it right.

"Then *you* explain it to me," she said, her voice nearly failing her. He nodded. "Very well."

27

After the Murder

Thirteen Years Ago

Thursday, December 7

Cagle Residence
Murfreesboro Road, Franklin, 5:30 p.m.

Bart watched as the car turned into the driveway, paused so that the driver could enter the code and then, once the gates were open, drove on through. He didn't recognize the vehicle, but he did know the driver even if he couldn't see her in the darkness.

It was Maureen Downey, Louise's friend and editor. No one else would have access.

Taking a deep breath, Bart quickly pulled away from the side of the road and followed the path the car had taken before the gates could close, locking him out. He didn't turn on his headlights and only rolled through the open gates far enough for them to close. Then he powered down his window and waited.

He heard her car door slam. Waited until he heard the front door of the house open and then close as well. Once he was confident she had gone inside, he rolled forward, past where she'd left her car and closer to the detached garage. There were no exterior lights on to reveal his presence.

Bart climbed out of his car and made his way to the nearest window. He peered inside. The lights inside had been off, but Maureen had started to turn them on one by one as she moved through the house.

What was she doing here?

Did she know where Louise was? Did she know what the two of them had done?

Dear God, if Johnson found out, their lives would be in danger. He needed to warn Maureen . . . but what if she knew nothing . . . what if she was here just checking on things? For all he knew, she could believe that Louise had gone on a much-needed getaway.

Something cold and hard pressed into the back of his skull. He tensed.

"Who are you, and what the hell are you doing here?"

Bart instinctively lifted his hands. "Maureen? Maureen Downey?"

"Who the hell are you?"

"Bart O'Sullivan. Judge Ruth O'Sullivan's husband."

A hand clutched at his arm and spun him around. The hard thing she'd been holding was not a gun—a flashlight, which now blinded him.

"Where is Louise?" she demanded.

"I . . . I . . ." He used a hand to shield his eyes. "I have no idea. I thought you might know."

"All I know is that she came to her office on the twenty-third, Thanksgiving—I suspect because she knew I wouldn't be there. She took some of her things and left me a note. I haven't heard from her since, and I'm really worried."

She lowered the beam of light to the ground.

"What did the note say?"

Maureen looked away. "She said I shouldn't look for her. She couldn't be in this life anymore."

"Oh my God." Bart shook his head, felt sick. What had he done?

"I know what you did," Maureen hissed. She flashed the light in his face again. "She told me you had been meeting with Lucy and that she was going to talk to you. What did you tell her? What did she say?" She shivered, hugged herself. Her thin coat wasn't doing its job very well.

Bart took a breath. "Why don't we go inside, and I'll tell you all that I can?"

"All right." She lowered the flashlight once more. "But just so you know, I am trained in self-defense, and I do not have a problem kicking your ass if you try anything." She lifted her chin. "In fact, I'll do worse. I'll tell your wife."

Dear God, would he ever survive this?

Maureen insisted he go first. Bart made his way around the corner of the house and through the front door. The warmth spread through him instantly. He'd been sitting in his car for hours with the engine turned off. He'd hoped to find Louise sneaking into her house for supplies or clothes. Something. He'd been watching her house every chance he got.

Maureen closed the door and leaned against it. "Tell me everything you told Louise. Start with how you were involved with Lucy."

Bart sank onto the bench that sat against the wall. He was too tired to hide the truth. Too exhausted from worry to navigate the lies.

"First, we need to set some parameters."

She raised her eyebrows at him.

"I will not put my family in danger just to satisfy your curiosity." She rolled her eyes. "Fine."

"You can never tell anyone—no matter how badly you want to," he began, "what I'm about to share with you."

If Ray Johnson learned he had uttered a single word . . . he banished the thought and focused on doing what he hoped was the right thing.

God knows he'd done everything wrong so far.

"Why would I do that?" she snapped. "My friend's daughter was murdered. Now she's missing. If you know what's happened, we need to go to the police."

"Because," Bart snapped right back, "if you tell another living soul, my daughter will be murdered—my wife too. And, I suspect, then he would come after your family."

Maureen drew back slightly, as if he'd slapped her. "Who the hell are you talking about?"

"Do I have your word or not?"

She exhaled noisily. "Fine. I give you my word."

Bart desperately wished that he could tell her a story that would give her some sort of relief . . . some sort of happy ending. But there was no happy ending in any of this. "I was helping Lucy with her senior thesis," he said, so damned tired. So sick at what had happened to that poor girl. "I'm sure Louise told you this much."

Maureen shrugged. She wasn't going to make this easy.

"Lucy didn't want to go to medical school. She wanted to be like her mother." He smiled sadly. "She wanted to do the biggest story possible to impress her. She found her mother's notes on her own secret project and decided to go at the subject from the perspective of those involved in doing the human trafficking."

Maureen's eyes narrowed. "How did Louise take all this?"

He sighed. "She didn't want to believe she had missed her daughter's true feelings about med school, but when I explained how Lucy adored her and wanted to be like her, she came to terms with the idea. I think."

Maureen made a motion with her hand for him to continue.

"I had no idea how far Lucy was going with her research until the day before she was murdered. She mentioned she'd met a young man who was helping her from that gritty perspective. I don't think she meant to say as much, but she did."

"You're saying she was talking to someone involved in the trafficking?"

He nodded. "I didn't know that for sure until after . . ." He drew in a heavy breath. "Anyway, I warned her she needed to discuss this with her mother and that she needed to be more careful. This was far too dangerous. She promised she wouldn't see him again and she would talk to her mother." He paused to collect himself. This was the worst travesty of all. His terrible, terrible mistake. "Sadly, I believed her."

"You have a teenage daughter—they lie," Maureen ranted. "You should have known this."

"I was busy at work and . . ." He shook his head. "I suppose I just wanted to believe her. It was easier. She'd made me promise never to tell a soul, and believing her gave me the easiest out."

Maureen only glared at him now.

Didn't matter. She couldn't possibly make him feel worse than he already did.

"I couldn't get the idea that she was taking far too many risks out of my mind, so I called her. It was the day she . . . died. She didn't answer or return my calls. I suppose she didn't want to hear my warnings anymore. I left her several voice mail messages. I had done some research into the family. I'd deduced—based on the things she had told me—what she was investigating, and none of it was good. She was playing with fire, and I was terrified for her."

He closed his eyes and thought of that bastard Ray Johnson, who had come to his home and warned him what would happen if he opened his mouth. How did men like that get away with their evil deeds? No one in the family had ever been arrested. Maybe the evidence wasn't there, but the innuendos were. Still, no one had ever been able to stop them.

The one thing Bart knew for a certainty was that Raymond Johnson Junior, a.k.a. Ray, had a younger brother named Ian, to whom Bart suspected Lucy was talking. He was likely her source, and he was somehow involved in what happened to her. Bart was sure of it. Why else would he have been hidden away only days after her murder?

God, he didn't even want to think about the rest.

Bart should have gone to Louise as soon as he recognized Lucy was skating too close to danger. He should have gone to her father . . . someone. But he had not, and now she was dead. What if he could have stopped her murder?

The question gutted him. He could scarcely bear to even consider the possibility.

"What exactly did you tell Louise about this family?"

"I told her what I just told you." He considered the rest. He'd broken laws . . . Ruth would never forgive him. Worse, Finley wouldn't understand. "You see," he went on, "I was so certain of what I believed—particularly after the younger son disappeared—that I started to follow the older brother. I took vacation days from my work and tailed him like I knew what I was doing. Finally, and I'm sure by the grace of God, I discovered where the missing brother was. He was in a warehouse—an old closed-down warehouse—that his brother visited each day about the same time. I foolishly thought all I had to do was prove it—whatever it was."

"So you broke in to the warehouse," Maureen suggested.

Bart nodded. "After I saw the brother take food there a third time, I waited until a couple of hours after he left, and I went inside. Based on his routine until that point, he wouldn't be coming back before the next day. Getting in wasn't that difficult. I had seen where he hid the key. Apparently, he worried about forgetting it or keeping it with him." Who knew what the bastard had been thinking.

"Anyway, when I got inside the warehouse it was empty. The younger brother heard me come in, I think, because he started to demand why I had come back. Obviously, he thought I was his brother. He kept asking why I didn't just kill him and put him out of his misery. He wailed . . ." The agonizing cries echoed in Bart's brain.

He closed his eyes, remembered just standing there and listening. The man had cried and pleaded. He wanted to die.

"What did you do?" Maureen demanded, clearly horrified.

Bart opened his eyes. "Nothing. To do anything would have been to sacrifice my wife and daughter. The bastard—the older brother—had found my voice mails on Lucy's phone. He warned that if I told anyone what I knew, he would kill my family. He bragged about all the things he and his father did without ever getting caught and if I didn't believe him, I should just check it out. And I did. He was right. There were endless crimes the family was thought to be responsible for, but no one could ever touch them."

"I want the names," Maureen demanded, moving toward him. "I swear to God, I will kill you myself if you don't tell me."

Bart stared up at her. "Then you'll have to kill me, because I cannot tell you, and even if I was willing to take the risk, it would not bring Lucy back. And it would in all likelihood get you and your own family killed as well as mine."

She shook her head. "They can't be that untouchable."

"They are. Trust me. I'm married to a judge."

"But you told Louise everything."

"She swore never to connect how she learned the information to me and my family. She would tell the older brother—in the event she was caught—that she had found Lucy's notes and had been following him. I could see how he would believe her story." Bart released a beleaguered breath. "The truth is, I would have told her anyway. She had a right to know, and I couldn't bear to keep it from her any longer."

"You didn't consider you might need to protect her?"

"She didn't want my protection. She said she had nothing left to lose and that I should worry about protecting my own."

Maureen's lips trembled and a tear slid down her cheek. "Did she go to the warehouse?"

He nodded. "I followed her there. She didn't like it, but I did. I wanted to help her." His head wagged side to side. "To protect her. Like I could have. She was beyond feeling anything but pure rage by that point."

He would never forget Louise wielding those giant bolt cutters. She'd cut the lock away while he kept watch. Once the door to the janitor's closet was open, the man Lucy had been seeing was just sitting there. He was shackled, wrists and ankles. But he made no attempt to protect himself or to escape. He'd looked young and so very sad.

"What happened then?" Maureen demanded.

"He didn't try to run. He went willingly with her."

Maureen's jaw dropped. "She took him with her."

"She loaded him into the back of a small cargo van she had rented and told me to go. She said I should forget everything I had seen. I tried to reason with her, but she was so far beyond reason. There was no reaching her."

"We should call the police," Maureen said. "If we go to the police together, it might not be too late to fix this."

Bart thought about the suggestion, but then he said, "No. She did what she had to do, and we need to leave her be."

"You can't be serious? Obviously, she was out of her mind."

"Possibly," he admitted. "But I'm going to say to you exactly what she said to me."

Her face was set in stone, her body braced for battle. "I'm listening."

"If the murdered girl had been your daughter and the heart attack victim your spouse, what would you do?"

The tears came in a flood now, flowing down Maureen's cheeks in rivers. "What are we going to do?"

"We're going to honor her wishes and get on with our lives as if we know nothing."

Maureen inhaled a shaky breath, then nodded. "Okay. Okay."

Room by room, they wandered through the house that had once been a home to a loving family. They turned off the lights and then exited through the front door, locking it behind themselves. And then they left.

Maybe they were wrong not to call the police, to just walk away and tell no one, but Bart couldn't find the rationale to do otherwise.

Sometimes you just had to do what you had to do.

28

Now

Finley had patiently heard her father out. She'd listened to his explanation of why and how he'd ended up in this situation, but now she was calling Houser. Reaching for her cell, she said as much.

"You cannot call Detective Houser," her father argued. "You can't. You just . . . can't."

Finley started to argue but hesitated. There was one other thing, she decided, that needed to be clarified first. She tucked her cell back into her pocket and fixed her attention on the man on the other side of the bars. "Are you ill or injured?"

"Of course he isn't injured," Cagle grumbled. "Are you blind?"

Finley ignored the irritating remark.

He—Ian Johnson—shook his head. "No."

Finley drew in a breath. "Can you confirm your identity?"

"Give me a break," Cagle griped. "You expect him to whip out his driver's license? Who else would he be?"

Finley ignored this too. The man . . . his skin was almost tanned. His hair looked neatly trimmed. He was clean shaven. If he had been down here all this time, wouldn't he be pale and maybe disheveled? Ian Johnson would be what? Thirty-six now. If he'd been locked away for thirteen years, he should look thin and frail.

But he didn't. He looked healthy and fit, even a little muscular.

"What have you been feeding him?" This whole thing was off the rails. Finley still felt stunned.

"Not much since you sent me off to the hospital," her neighbor said, with more snark than a woman in such ill health should be able to muster.

Jesus Christ. "Are you hungry?" Finley asked the man.

He shook his head. "There was enough until yesterday. But . . ." He moved closer to the bars. "You need to understand—"

"Think," Bart warned, speaking to the man behind the bars, "before you—"

"Dad," Finley cautioned, "do not dig that hole you're in any deeper." She wanted to shake him. Her father, of all people, had to know just how bad this situation was—for all of them.

Ian grabbed the bars with both hands and leaned closer.

Finley resisted the impulse to step back.

"This is not his fault," Ian urged.

"Unlock that door," she ordered, looking to Cagle. "Let him out."

"In the cabinet," Cagle said wearily, her strength obviously waning. "The key is in the cabinet."

Finley crossed to the wall of cabinets and started opening doors. There was bottled water and all manner of snacks. Vitamins. Ready-to-eat meals. Toilet paper. This was insane. Finley glanced back to the cell. Sure enough, there was a toilet and a sink. Even a narrow shower.

She picked up the key and glared at her neighbor. "How on earth did you do all this?"

"The storm shelter was in the garage when I bought the house. I had the rest added." She dragged in a rattling breath. "There are plenty of contractors who will do unpermitted work for the right price. I knew them all from past research. It was easy to hire them under an alias. All that mattered was the money."

Shaking her head, Finley turned back to the cabinet. She grabbed a bottle of water and a bag of chips, walked back to the cell, passed them through the bars, then unlocked the door and opened it. Ian eyed her speculatively as he stepped past her and settled on the same bench with Cagle. He placed the chips and water Finley had given him on the bench next to himself as if they were the furthest things from his mind.

"You okay?" he asked her.

Finley was startled by the genuine concern in his voice. How was that possible?

"I'll probably live," Cagle muttered, meeting his gaze briefly.

Finley turned on her father then. He'd explained how he came to be a part of this and the final decision he and Downey had made. Still, the whole situation was unbelievable. How would she explain this to her mother? To Matt? She put a hand over her mouth, felt sick. How would she protect her father?

When he reached for her, she drew back. "What the hell were you thinking?"

"Good God, you are one overbearing child," Cagle growled. "He only did what I told him. He allowed his emotions to override his good sense. Something I believe you're familiar with."

Finley glared at her before turning back to her father.

"If I had gone to Louise in the beginning," her father said, "like I should have, Lucy might be alive today."

Cagle looked away, swiped at her eyes before squaring her shoulders and facing them once more. Her eyes were red rimmed, and her lips trembled. Evidently she did still have a heart. Shocking, considering what the woman had done. Finley refused to feel sympathy for her father or for her neighbor at this point.

That was Finley's anger talking . . . deep down, part of her understood. Like Cagle said, Finley had acted on emotion plenty of times.

"When I heard the news that Lucy had been murdered," her father went on, "I was so stunned. I rushed to the car wash to find Ian. I thought if he was there that perhaps I was wrong. But Ian wasn't there. It was his brother, Ray. He was already working on having the place torn down. Ray realized I knew something. He'd listened to the voice mails I'd left on Lucy's phone, and with me showing up . . . he put it all together."

"Johnson had her phone," Finley guessed. Son of a bitch! There was only one way he had gotten the victim's phone. Rather than say as much, she kept her mouth shut and allowed her father to go on.

He nodded. "He warned if I said a word, he would kill you." He looked to Finley, tears brimming in his eyes. "And your mother. I didn't know what to do. So, I did exactly what he said. *Nothing.*"

"Until I made him," Cagle interjected. "I had gotten close to the truth in my own investigation, but I couldn't be sure until I discovered through the private investigator I hired that Bart had been talking to Lucy. He gave me Bart's name in hopes that he would help me, since the bastard had already sold out to Johnson and wouldn't tell me the real story himself." She moistened her dry, cracked lips, closed her weary eyes for a moment. "It's always about money and power. Always."

Finley's chest constricted despite her efforts not to feel sympathy for the woman. She grabbed another bottle of water and thrust it at Cagle. "Drink this now, before you expire."

What the hell was she going to do with these people?

She had to call Houser. She reached for her phone once more.

"Don't do it," her father said, his voice sounding as weary as Cagle looked. "Not until we can figure out how to handle this. We can't just . . ." He shook his head, moved to join the others on the bench as if his legs would no longer support him.

"Houser will know what to do," Finley argued.

"He can't help you," Ian warned, his gaze steady on Finley.

She gestured to the cell. "I can't just pretend I didn't see any of this. You've been here for thirteen years!"

He shrugged. "Mostly."

Mostly? What the hell did that mean?

As if she'd asked the question aloud, Cagle said, "I kept him in the safe room at the house where my family lived at first. Until the work here was done."

"You lied to me," Finley accused, suddenly aware of the many conversations she'd had with this woman.

"I lied to a lot of people," Cagle admitted, her tone growing more listless. "Including myself."

The three of them—her father, Cagle, and Ian Johnson—all stared at the floor for a long moment.

Finley paced the length of the room, turned and retraced her steps. Finally, she drew in a big breath and braced herself for the hard questions. "Ian." When he met her gaze, Finley asked, "Did Cagle bring you here against your will? Hold you against your will?" If he'd killed Lucy or was involved somehow with her death—well, even killers had rights until a jury of their peers decided otherwise. God damn it.

"She found me. I begged her to kill me, but she wouldn't. She said that would be too easy. But to answer your questions, I came here willingly, and I've stayed willingly. It was better than I deserved." His eyes brightened. "Then things changed."

"Changed how?" Finley demanded of the three, sitting in silence as if what they'd already said was sufficient.

Ian looked to Cagle. She looked away.

"A year ago," Ian said, "she got sick."

"*She* meaning Louise Cagle—a.k.a. Helen Roberts?" Finley wanted no misunderstandings in this twisted tale.

He nodded. "She came down to bring my dinner one night and just collapsed."

"It was my first heart attack," Cagle said, lifting her gaze to Finley's. "I'd had what I thought was one before. But this time I was very ill in addition to the heart issue. A bad case of the flu or covid, who knows? I was out of it for days. When I finally came around, I figured he would be long gone. But he was sitting next to my bed."

Finley tried to hang on to her frustration, but it had started to slip away. "You had the key with you when you collapsed."

Cagle nodded. "Turns out I was delirious for days and he took care of me the entire time. He's probably the only reason I survived." Her gaze turned distant, remembering. "When I was back on my feet, I asked him why he stayed. He just said—"

"She needed someone to take care of her," Ian explained, "and it was my fault that she had no one. For the first time since . . ." He clasped and then unclasped his hands. "I had a reason to want to go on."

His words pushed against a soft place deep inside Finley. "What do you mean?"

"Lucy loved her mom so much." A ghost of a smile lifted his lips. "She talked about her all the time. Taking care of her mother was like doing something good for Lucy. Like making up in some small way for what I did. I've been helping her out around here ever since."

Finley kicked aside those softer emotions. She needed the whole story from this man. And then she damned well intended to call Houser. "Are you admitting that you killed Lucy Cagle? Be advised," she warned, "you are entitled to legal representation. Anything you say can be used against you."

He blinked. Shook his head. "It doesn't matter. I was there . . . I helped . . ."

"It does matter," Finley argued. "You have a right to legal representation."

"I don't want a lawyer. I want to finish this." He stood. "Now that you're here"—he looked from Finley to her dad and back—"you can take care of Louise while I do what I should have done thirteen years ago."

"Don't let him go," Cagle cried, reaching out as if she could stop him in her weakened condition.

Finley stepped in the man's path, though she wasn't entirely certain it was the right move or that she would be able to stop him from whatever he had in mind. "What is it you have to do?" Adrenaline roared through her, tightened her fingers into fists at her sides. Part of her wanted to put him back in that cell just to ensure he didn't disappear, but the rational side of her brain warned that there was a hell of a lot she still didn't know.

Ian stared at Finley with enough fury to make her a little worried that she didn't have a weapon.

Her father was suddenly at her side. "Talk to her," he urged the other man. "My daughter is the smartest person you will ever meet. She can help."

As upset and frustrated as she was, Finley wanted to hug him.

Still, Ian said nothing.

"I planted Lucy's purse at the warehouse," Cagle said from where she still sat on the bench. "Ian had hidden it that weekend . . . after what happened. He'd been devastated and wanted to hold on to the only part of her he had left. Once he told me where it was hidden, I retrieved it."

"You?" Finley demanded. "Why? What made you decide to make a move after all this time?"

"I didn't know he had her purse before." Cagle stared at the water bottle she grasped with both hands. "Two months ago, I got sick again."

"I was afraid she wasn't going to make it that time," Ian said. "It was bad, really bad, but she wouldn't let me call for help. I realized I couldn't . . ." He looked away, his words trailing off.

This story just got more bizarre by the moment. When Finley would have prompted one or the other to go on, Cagle said, "He didn't want me to die without knowing the truth."

Finley turned to Ian. Maybe now she would get the real story. "What truth?"

"I didn't kill Lucy," he said, his eyes—his face—reflecting the torment he suffered, "but I was there. When the old man found out what I'd been doing, he promised they were only going to scare her off. And then as long as I stayed away from her that would be the end of it, but that's not what happened, and I couldn't stop it."

"He hadn't told me that part," Cagle said. "He felt her death was his fault, and he wanted to pay the price. He knew if he gave me the whole story, I would probably get myself killed trying to take them down."

If Finley's head hadn't been spinning, it sure as hell was now. "Who is *they*?" she asked Ian. She wasn't about to put the names in his mouth.

Ian said nothing, just stared at the floor.

"We devised a plan to make it right." Cagle went on with her story as if Finley hadn't said a word. "To bring the whole truth out." Fury tightened her frail features. "But somehow he figured it out and changed things."

"Who?" Finley repeated. "I need names."

"I knew you were the best. That's why I hired you."

Her attention swung to the door.

Ray Johnson.

"Nice story. I was almost brought to tears." He stood in the doorway, hands in his pockets like a kid trying to hide the candy he'd stolen. He scanned the room, made a surprised face. "Damn, bro, you're looking good for a guy who was supposed to die more than a dozen years ago."

The guttural sound that burst from Ian's throat had Finley shifting toward him, but he pushed past her, planting himself squarely between her and his brother.

"You're going to pay for what you did," he roared, going nose to nose with the other man. His hands fisted at his sides, ready for battle.

"Is that so?" Ray tossed back, staring at his brother as if he were a bug, a nuisance.

Ian grabbed him by the throat with both hands. Ray's eyes bulged. Finley snatched for her phone. "I'm calling Detective Houser."

"Not a good idea," Ray choked out as he shoved a gun in his younger brother's face. "Back the fuck off," he snarled.

Ian didn't budge, his fingers still locked tight around the bastard's throat. "I've waited a long time to do this."

The weapon swung in Finley's direction. "You want her to go first?" Ray squeaked out. Then he shifted the barrel toward Cagle. "Or maybe her? I know how you love watching."

Ian spit in his face before shoving him away.

"Finley doesn't know anything," Bart insisted, suddenly next to Finley and edging his body slightly in front of her. "Like you, she stumbled upon us down here. You let her call the detective, and Louise and I will confess to everything."

Ray laughed. "Yeah, right. I'm no fool, Bart my boy. I've been watching you since the case was reopened. I knew when that purse turned up that Cagle hadn't avenged her sweet little daughter's murder the way I had hoped she would." He scoffed. "I mean, why the hell bother stealing my brother from me if she wasn't going to make him pay? It would have been so easy if you had taken care of the problem for me." He shook his head at Cagle. "But I guess you just didn't have the guts."

"Cagle admitted to planting the evidence," Finley offered, in hopes of confusing Ray and buying time.

"That's all well and good," Ray tossed back at her, "but the trouble is, as long as my little brother is alive, there's a risk to me, and I just can't let that go. That's why I hired you, Finley. I figured if Ian was still alive that Cagle and your daddy had something to do with keeping him that way." He laughed. "The minute your daddy found out you were working for me, he got all antsy. All I had to do was wait and watch. Now, here we are."

"Nothing found in that warehouse," Finley assured him, "connects to you, Ray. Don't make it about you now."

"Course it doesn't," he tossed back. "I hadn't touched that little purse." He made a "well you know how it is" face as he shook his head. "But I had touched that phone, and it was there too—haven't figured that one out yet. I guess someone was trying to set me up—like my little brother." He shot a glare at Ian. "Good thing I did a thorough walk-through before the closing on that warehouse. Imagine my surprise when I discovered it." He laughed. "I took the phone and left a little something else."

"The cigarette butts," Finley said. This was why Ray hadn't been worried about the DNA pointing to him. "This was your way of steering the police toward someone else, but you were the one who killed her." She'd known this guy was a piece of shit right from the beginning. Admittedly her timing in confirming as much left something to be desired, since he was armed and she was not.

"I was always the one who had to do the dirty work." Johnson glared at Ian, then Cagle. "You could have saved me a lot of trouble if you'd just killed the little bastard the way you should have. After all, he was the reason your little girl got herself murdered."

Ian charged his brother.

Cagle cried out in distress.

The weapon discharged, the sound echoing like a bomb exploding. Finley pushed her father into the nearest corner. Shoved her phone at him. "Call Houser."

Grunting and snarling, the brothers struggled wildly for domination.

Heart thundering in her chest . . . blood roaring in her ears, Finley glanced around. There was nothing she could use for a weapon.

"Screw it." She hurtled into the fray.

She slammed into Ray's shoulder, sending him off balance. The move knocked the wind out of her, almost sent her tumbling over. She managed to catch herself. Ray hit the floor, Ian on top of him. The gun flew free . . . hit the floor and spun away. Finley dove for it.

Weapon in hand, she scrambled to her feet and rushed toward the tangle of brothers. Ray was on top now. Adrenaline firing red hot in her veins, Finley drew her leg back and kicked him in the side with every ounce of strength she possessed. The bastard howled and jerked with pain but didn't let go of his brother's throat.

Finley pressed the barrel of the weapon against Ray's skull. "Let him go, and put your hands on your head," she ordered. To her father she said, "Get the key from the cell door."

Bart hurried to the cell.

Ray had stopped moving but still had Ian pinned down. "Do it," Finley repeated. "Or I will pull this trigger."

"I don't believe you," Ray said, panting from the battle.

"It wouldn't be the first time I've had blood and brain tissue splattered on my face," she warned.

Still hesitating long enough to make Finley want to damn well pull the trigger, he finally released his brother, clambered up onto his knees and propped his hands on his head. Ian got to his feet next. The two glared at each other warily, both poised for a second round.

"Over there," Finley ordered the younger brother, nodding toward the bench.

"Get up." Finley used the weapon to direct Ray's attention to the cell. "Get inside."

"No way," Ray sneered.

Finley aimed at his head once more. "Suit yourself."

"You won't shoot me," he argued again.

"Give me the gun," Cagle demanded, suddenly next to Finley, her face twisted in fury. "I'll do it."

Finley angled her a warning look before nudging Ray again. "I'd get moving if I were you."

"Okay, okay." He pushed to his feet and shuffled into the cell. She turned to her father. "Lock it."

He shoved the door closed and locked it. Cagle moved to the bars and stood there staring at the man who had murdered her daughter.

"Houser is on his way," Finley's father announced as he passed Finley's phone back to her, his shoulders sagging with exhaustion.

Finley let go a breath. Drew in another, but she couldn't seem to get enough into her lungs. "Thanks." She tucked the phone into her back pocket. Her legs felt rubbery, and her heart pounded hard enough to burst from her chest.

Her father collapsed onto the bench. Cagle joined him there. The poor woman looked ready to fall over. Finley turned to join the two, but her phone vibrated with an incoming call. While Ray ranted through the bars at his brother, Finley stepped away to check her cell.

Randy. Her favorite lab guy.

She moved farther from the fray and answered. He was likely calling about the DNA comparison. Ray hadn't smoked those cigarettes, but someone related to him had. Finley hoped it wasn't Ian. She needed good news on this one for a change. "Hey, Randy. You have something for me."

"I do," her friend confirmed. "The genetic material tested from the cigarette butts was not from a brother of your client."

She watched the two men glaring at each other through the bars. A smile slid across her face. "I'm listening."

"It was from your client's father."

Now that was the best news Finley had gotten all week. "Thanks, Randy. I'll pick up those results later."

She ended the call and put her phone away. Took her first deep breath since she'd found her father's car in her neighbor's driveway. She surveyed the bizarre scene. This, Finley had a feeling, was going to take some time to fully sort.

She settled on the bench next to her father and the woman who had been carrying this awful burden for thirteen long years.

If they were lucky, it was almost over.

5:45 p.m.

Ray Johnson had given his statement, which was basically all lies. Jack had rushed over to mediate the questioning. Finley didn't relax until the bastard was placed under arrest and removed from the premises. She really had to talk to Jack about his choices in clients.

After Ray had left, Houser questioned Ian. The younger Johnson provided details about the family operation going back two decades. These operations included everything from drugs to human trafficking. When the latter had begun, Ian had known he had to get out. Sadly, that was about the time Lucy sought him out for research purposes, setting the two of them on a collision course toward tragedy. Ian had broken down as he explained in detail how Lucy's life ended.

Now they sat at the kitchen table with Cagle as she prepared to tell her story. Houser had read her rights to her, but she refused representation. Finley had ignored this and stayed put. Jack too.

The Judge had arrived. She and Finley's father were on the front porch, waiting for his turn to give an official statement. Matt was with them. Finley was glad he was here. Her father would need someone to serve as a buffer. The Judge wouldn't be so understanding or forgiving of his secrets. Finley was still damned pissed herself, but a part of her could see how he had reached those painful decisions.

"I started watching Ray Johnson several weeks after my daughter's murder," Cagle explained to Houser.

Finley still couldn't get right with the idea that Helen Roberts was Louise Cagle, a.k.a. Louise Scott. As it turned out, Roberts was her mother's maiden name. Helen was her middle name. When she'd decided to go dark, she'd known she needed a new name and place to hide herself away with her prisoner.

Damn. Twelve years was a hell of a long time to keep a guy in a basement. The past year he had lived in the house with Cagle, a good deal of that time taking care of her. Right across the street. Finley was still stunned by the idea.

Cagle had admitted that she hadn't been able to bring herself to abuse or neglect him—not even in the beginning. She'd followed the usual prison protocols for violent criminals. The skylights had been installed in the garage to give him an hour or two in the sunlight each day. He'd been able to roam the garage under her supervision. When she'd learned the whole truth—that it was Ray who'd actually murdered Lucy—she had wanted to see that he got what he deserved. Eventually she'd been well enough, and she and Ian had started to plan. When their plan had seemed to be going awry, Ian wanted to go after Ray on his own—the way he should have long ago, he'd insisted. Cagle had locked him up again—only this time to protect him.

"I hired a private detective, and he discovered the connection between Lucy and Bart O'Sullivan," Cagle was saying to Houser. She glanced at Finley as she continued. "Lucy had been working on a special project for her senior thesis. She'd gone to Bart for research information. My investigator learned that when Lucy would leave the social services office, she would go to a car wash and meet with Ian Johnson."

Finley frowned, then blanked her face. This was not exactly the way the story went, based on what her father had said. Finley opted to keep her mouth shut and see where Cagle was going.

"By the time he reported this news to me, Ian was missing." Cagle took a sip of water. "That's when I knew I had to follow Ray to determine if he was hiding his brother. I suspected he was, in an effort to protect the family."

Finley understood what the woman was doing then. Cagle was protecting Finley's father. She bit her lips together to prevent herself objecting. He was her father—no matter what her legal training told her.

"What were your intentions?" Houser asked. "Why did you want to find him?"

"Don't answer that question," Jack said to Cagle. "Your motive at the time is irrelevant. You were overwrought with grief. Detective Houser is surely aware of this."

Finley bit back a grin. *Go, Jack, go.*

Houser dipped his head in acknowledgment of Jack's comment, but Cagle shook her head. "It doesn't matter, but thank you, Jack." She settled her gaze on the detective. "I intended to find him and force him to admit what he had done by whatever means necessary. Then I planned to call the police and turn him over."

Finley doubted this had ever been her plan, but it was a good story. One with which a jury would sympathize.

Houser nodded. "When did you find him?"

"On November twenty-second. Ray had him stashed away in a warehouse on Trinity Lane. He was locked in a small storeroom or janitor's closet. I waited for the right opportunity, broke in, cut the lock, and Ian came willingly with me. I took him to my home on Murfreesboro Road and locked him in the safe room. I bought this house, on Shelby Avenue, and started the necessary work to move him here. I became Helen Roberts, and my sole reason for living was to see that Ian never had a minute of freedom for the rest of his life."

"You changed your mind about calling the detective in charge of your daughter's case," Houser pointed out.

"I think we can," Jack said, "conclude as much from her statement without further explanation."

"I knew what Metro would do," Cagle said to Houser, ignoring Jack's help. "He would go to prison. Have visitors. Get letters from family and fans. He would be able to interact with the other inmates. Take college courses. Go to the gym." She shook her head. "I couldn't let that happen. He took Lucy's life. I didn't want him to have a life either. I wanted him to live so he could think about what he'd done for the rest of his days, but I did not want him to have a life. And I wanted him to have to look at me every day of his life and remember what he'd taken from me."

Houser glanced at his notepad. "Why did you call Bart O'Sullivan to pick you up from the hospital? Had the two of you communicated about Ian Johnson previously?"

Finley steeled herself for what she feared would implicate her father. She told herself that whatever parts he was responsible for, he was obliged to own. Knowing this, she held her breath and waited.

"His daughter is her neighbor," Jack reminded Houser.

Cagle nodded. "I had only met Bart once back when the private investigator told me about his interactions with Lucy. I asked him about my daughter. His kind words about how much she had admired me and wanted to be like me helped me get through the worse time in my life. I still had his cell phone number in my notes from the investigator. When I realized my new neighbor was his daughter and she seemed to keep getting herself into trouble, I put his number in my cell in case I ever had to call him for her. I felt I owed him as much since he had been so kind to my daughter."

Emotion rose so sharply inside Finley that she had to fight tears. Even if Cagle's words weren't the whole truth, they hit their mark.

Finley needed to talk to her dad, and then she had one more thing she had to do before this was done and while Houser was still occupied. She withdrew her phone from her pocket, looked at the blank screen as if she'd received some sort of notification, then leaned toward Jack and whispered, "I have to go. I'll be back in a bit."

He was focused on Houser's questioning, so he only nodded.

Finley slipped out of the kitchen and exited the house. Seated on the porch swing, her father stared up at her, his face pale with worry.

Matt walked over and hugged her. "You look exhausted."

She kissed his cheek. "I am." She looked to her parents. "Houser will be with you shortly. There won't be much to cover. Louise has been very thorough." To her father, she said, "She told Houser how you had helped Lucy with the research on her senior thesis. She also related how thankful she was that you relayed all that Lucy said about how much she adored her mother and wanted to be like her. Louise said your words were what got her through the worst days of her life."

Ruth blinked, her perfect comportment a little shaky. "I'm unclear about her having called him to pick her up at the hospital."

"That appears to have been my fault," Finley said. "She witnessed all the stuff happening in my life. By then she had recognized who my father was and felt compelled to be able to call him if I needed help. He had helped her daughter, and she wanted to do the same. She had his number in her notes from the PI who worked on Lucy's case. Dad has had the same number for like a quarter century."

The relief on her father's face was palpable. Her mother's as well.

"Don't worry," Finley said. "Dad is still the same old good guy he's always been."

Ruth squared her shoulders. "I never thought otherwise."

Finley turned to Matt and spoke quietly. "I have to do something before this is finished. Can you take care of them until I get back?"

This man she loved so much looked her straight in the eyes. "I think Jack and Ruth have this under control. I'm going with you."

He knew her too well.

Johnson Residence
Wilson Pike, Brentwood, 7:15 p.m.

The nurse let them in. Matt waited in the main room downstairs while Finley was escorted to the old man's bedroom.

"He hasn't been doing so well today," the nurse said. "The doctor said he's taken a turn for the worse and it wouldn't be long now, so be brief."

"Of course."

The nurse left her at the door and went on her way.

Finley knocked, then opened the door. "Mr. Johnson, it's Finley O'Sullivan from the Finnegan Firm."

"Come in," he said, his voice low, weary.

She walked closer to the bed. The only light in the room was the one at his bedside. This time there was an oxygen line running to his nose, helping him breathe.

"Do you have news for me?"

Finley smiled. "I do. I found your son Ian. He's alive."

"I want to see him." He tried to sit up but failed. "Where has he been?" He put a frail hand against his chest as if his heart needed help to steady its rhythm. "How did you find him?"

"I'll make sure Detective Houser fills you in and that he knows you would like to see Ian. Hopefully he can arrange a meeting for you in a few days."

"In a few days?" he demanded. His legs moved restlessly, as if he wanted to get up but couldn't make his limbs execute the necessary actions. "Why can't he come here now? Who knows if I'll still be breathing a few hours from now?"

Finley refused to feel one iota of sympathy. "You can't see him now because he's being charged in connection with the murder of Lucy Cagle." This was not true, but it would hopefully prompt what she'd come here for.

The old man stared at the ceiling; his thin lips formed a hard line as if he were contemplating how he should respond to this news.

"That's why he's been in hiding all this time," Finley lied, the second one rolling off her tongue as smoothly as the first.

Johnson moved his head side to side, his stringy hair scrubbing against his yellowed pillowcase. "He didn't kill her. He didn't have the guts. I ordered him to, but he couldn't do it."

Tension moved through Finley. She had known this was the answer he would likely give, which was the primary reason she was here. There was one little loose thread she needed tied into a neat little knot. "Why did you want Lucy dead?"

A heavy breath rattled from his frail chest. "Lucy made him weak," he said listlessly. "When she'd wrapped him around her little finger, he told her things he shouldn't have. He was young and foolish."

"Like the fact that one of your businesses was a cover for human trafficking, specializing in children?" This was just one of the many operations Ian had listed off for Houser. Drugs. Prostitution. Human trafficking. All those crimes the family had been suspected of for far too long.

The old man laughed, a dry, wretched sound. He scratched at his head. "Who told you such nonsense?"

"Ian did. He said Ray made a deal to traffic children in the Nashville area and you sanctioned it. When Ian learned what was going on, he wanted out." All true. He wanted to be with Lucy. Finley's chest tightened with the regret she felt for Lucy and Ian and the anger at this old bastard that throttled through her.

Johnson cut her a look. "I sanctioned nothing of the sort. I wasn't even aware of how this deal had happened. Ray was trapped into that deal. He had no idea what would really happen. And together we put a stop to it."

Possibly there was some degree of truth in the statement. Maybe the "do anything for money" Johnsons had standards and human trafficking of children was the line in the sand. Although they apparently had no issues with trafficking adults.

"But that didn't stop Lucy. She had the goods on both your sons," Finley suggested.

"The little bitch was just like her mother. She trapped Ian with her lies."

"You ordered him to deal with it, but he couldn't do the job, so you did. You killed Lucy Cagle."

He stared at the ceiling. "I did. My sons didn't touch her. You can call the detective, and I'll give my statement."

How easy was that? Finley rolled her eyes. Ian had already told the whole story about that night. Finley needed—wanted—the old man's confirmation of those events. She had known how this would play out if she didn't intervene in exactly this way.

"Funny thing," Finley went on, ignoring his request, "you see, when the evidence—Lucy's purse—was found, there were also a couple of cigarette butts. Kool menthol. DNA showed you were the one who had smoked those cigarettes."

He glared at Finley and laughed a rusty, deathly sound. "So what. I've already told you I did it. There's your evidence."

This was precisely the route she had anticipated the old man would go to protect his sons. He was dying; what did he care about a murder charge? The problem was, his statement would go directly against Ian's. Whatever else happened from all this, Finley intended to see that Ray Johnson did not get away with what he had done.

"You're right," Finley agreed. "But I felt it was important that I explained how Ray had planted the cigarette butts with the intention of ensuring that you were fingered as Lucy's killer. He expected you to be dead by then, of course."

"Well, there you go." The old man's angry, clipped tone warned he was not pleased with this news. "Stop wasting my time. Talk to that detective, and get my son over here."

"I'll do that," Finley promised. "There's just one other issue." One last little push. "Ray also said you ordered him to kill Ian to protect the family. That's why Ian has been gone all this time. He was in hiding from his brother."

Using all his strength, the old man actually managed to push himself up onto his elbows so he could properly glare at Finley, his gaze pure evil. "What the hell are you talking about?"

Finley almost had him. "Look, Mr. Johnson, you're dying. If you agree to all Ray has said, then this shit show dies with you. Ian will likely be charged as an accessory to murder, since he lured Lucy to her death, but Ray will be okay. He'll still be able to run the business and keep the family legacy going. It's an easy decision."

"You," he roared, as best a dying man could, "work for me, and I want you to listen: I did not tell anyone to kill my son." His face had gone beet red, and his chest heaved with the breath raging in and out of his feeble body.

"I can tell Ian what you've said," she assured him, "but I don't know that he will believe it. Ray had him pretty convinced of what you wanted."

Something changed in the old man's eyes. "Call that detective. I want to make my own statement. Ray was the one who killed Lucy Cagle."

"Mr. Johnson," Finley countered, fingers mentally crossed, "are you certain that's what you want to do? As I said, this is all going to shake down in a way that protects Ray. Anything you do—"

"Call him. Now." He collapsed back onto his pillow. "I told Ray to take care of it, and he did. He forced Ian to take him to Lucy that night. He waited, hunkered down in the back seat, until she got in the car; then he killed her, even though Ian tried to stop him." His mouth tightened with new anger. He shook his head. "He stole all this time from me with Ian. Now it's his turn to have his life stolen. I should have killed that bastard myself when he was born. He was an evil little shit even then."

Finley could barely hold herself back from grabbing her phone and calling Houser. She had him . . . she had that bastard Ray Johnson. "But

Ray said he had an alibi for that night. He and his wife had dinner and drinks."

"He lied. Mark my word," the old man said, "his ex will confirm he was lying."

All tied up in a perfect little inescapable knot. Now Finley had all she needed.

Finley called Houser and waited with the old man until he and Jack arrived. Finley's father and the Judge had taken Louise Cagle back to the hospital and were going home. Finley was more than ready to do the same.

29

8:10 p.m.

Matt put his arm around Finley's shoulders as they walked to her Subaru. "You never cease to amaze me, Fin. You're going to make one hell of a district attorney."

She laughed. "We'll see about that. Briggs isn't going down without a fight."

"Make your decision official, and we'll squash him like the bug he is."

At the car, Finley turned to face him. "Thank you for being my best friend all these years. For becoming my partner in life. I really don't deserve you."

His arms went around her, and he kissed her. "I am the one who doesn't deserve you."

"Probably." She laughed. "But not in the same way I don't deserve you."

They laughed together as they climbed into the car. Matt slid behind the wheel and adjusted the seat. Finley was too damned exhausted to drive.

Finley closed her eyes and savored the idea that this case was done. It was Jack's show from here. She supposed it was time she started to focus on this race for the DA's office. She needed a campaign team and about a million other things.

The next few months should be interesting.

For a couple of minutes, she allowed herself to relax. She felt good. Exhausted but good.

And she needed to sleep for days.

"Fin, brace yourself. We've got a tail, and he's determined to nose up to our rear bumper."

Finley straightened to attention. She twisted around in her seat. Squinted against the bright headlights. Fear had her heart leaping. "I'm calling 911."

Matt was in the car. She wasn't taking any chances.

Why could she not have one fucking moment of peace?

Pulse racing, she made the call. The dispatcher answered.

The car rammed into them. Finley propelled forward until the seat belt locked. Her cell flew out of her hand.

Matt focused on driving. He accelerated, rocketing forward.

Heart racing, she scrambled to find her phone. Clutched it and raised up to get a handle on where they were as she explained to the dispatcher what was happening. "Are we on Concord?" she asked Matt.

Matt divided his attention between the highway and the rearview mirror, pushing the Subaru for all it was worth. "We are. Heading into the curve next to the I-65 off-ramp."

Finley twisted around to look behind them, the bright lights of the other vehicle blinding her. She provided their location. The other car was bearing down on them again. Fury burst inside her. Whoever this son of a bitch was . . .

He rammed them again.

The car skidded and bumped off the road.

Air rushing out of her lungs, Finley grabbed on to the dash. Her phone flew away again. A gasp wrenched from her throat.

The dispatcher's voice called out in the air.

They hit the fence that ran alongside the road, tore through it and came to a bumping, grinding halt.

"Get down," Finley yelled at Matt, her hands instinctively reaching for him.

If the bastard had a gun, they were sitting ducks.

Seat belts came off. They hunkered down.

Fear pounding in her brain, Finley reached across Matt and shut off the interior lights. She opened her door and scooted out, staying low.

"Follow me," she whispered. She had to keep him safe . . . had to.

Matt snaked across the console and slid out of the car. They sat on the ground, the Subaru blocking them from view of the highway and the bastard who was likely parked up there and maybe heading their way.

Somewhere in the car was the sound of the 911 dispatcher's voice.

Please, please just let her send help.

Finley turned around, got on her knees with the intention of peeking beyond the window to see if the guy was coming.

Matt pulled her back. "Stay down. You need to let someone else play the part of the hero for a change."

Before she could argue, he crawled past her, headed for the rear end of the Subaru. Finley held her breath as he peeked around the end.

A gunshot echoed in the air.

She jumped.

Matt drew back. "He's coming this way."

Her brain scrambling for a workable move, she considered the distance to the tree line. Thirty or forty yards. Not good. She surveyed the streetlights and the moon that were spilling way too much light to make a run for the trees a reasonable risk even if they weren't so damned far away.

"We have to try," Matt murmured, following her gaze.

Desperate, she nodded. They scrambled onto all fours in preparation for launching into a run.

"We go on three," Matt whispered.

Finley nodded.

"One . . . two . . ." Matt darted forward.

Before Finley could make her body move after his premature launch, another shot blasted in the air.

Matt jerked with the impact.

Finley's heart wrenched. She had to stop this bastard.

She shot into action. Rather than run toward the woods, she scrambled around the end of the car and rushed toward the shooter.

He leveled his aim on her.

Finley braced but kept going. Rage driving her. She had had enough.

A car whizzed past her, cutting between her and the shooter and causing her to stumble back onto the ground.

The shooter swung his aim toward the car, but it was too late. The car plowed him down.

Finley leaped to her feet and ran in the direction where Matt had fallen.

He was down. Her heart lunged into her throat. Then he moved. Relief rushed through her.

She dropped to the ground next to him. "Are you hit?"

"He got me in the thigh, but I'm okay."

Finley tried to see in the darkness. She could see the blood but not how much. What if he'd hit an artery? "How badly are you bleeding?"

The sound of sirens in the distance had another surge of relief flooding through her.

"Help me up."

Finley pushed up and helped him to his feet. They started the slow walk-hobble toward the road. Her entire body shook with the receding adrenaline. *Please let him be okay.*

A figure stood over the downed shooter. Finley couldn't tell who it was. Male, she thought. She tensed. Hoped to hell it was friend and not foe. She was so fucking over having thugs messing with her life. Anger burned through her, giving her the strength to push on. She had to get help for Matt.

Four police cruisers pulled to the side of the road behind the car the shooter had been driving.

An ambulance skidded to a stop behind the last of the cruisers.

Thank God. She wanted to weep with relief.

The man who'd run down the shooter hurried in their direction. Finley's pulse skittered with a jolt of shock as his face came into clearer view. "What the hell is he doing here?"

"You know this guy?" Matt asked with a grunt of pain.

Finley made a sound that should have been a laugh but didn't quite make the cut. "I sure do."

Howard Brewer.

The overwhelming sense of gratitude almost made her knees give way.

"You two okay?" Brewer asked.

Then she noticed the car he'd been driving. It was the brown one that had cut off the damned hoodie-guy follower the last time he'd been tailing her. Had Brewer been watching her? How could he have known? Didn't matter right now.

"Matt's hit." *Please, please let him be okay.*

"I thought he got one of you before I could reach him," Brewer said. "That's why I called an ambulance."

Suddenly cops were all around them. Two paramedics rushed through the array of cops and vehicles and took care of Matt.

Finley somehow managed to stay upright during the next few minutes, which were a blur of activity. She got in a hug and a kiss before the paramedics whisked Matt away to the hospital. They had the blood loss under control, and he was stable, but it was essential to get him to the hospital quickly since the bullet would need to be removed.

The shooter was not dead, but he was injured. Another ambulance had arrived to take care of him. An officer accompanied him to ensure he didn't attempt an escape.

Finley and Brewer stayed behind to give their statements.

Brewer claimed to have just been driving along when he spotted the trouble and tried to help. He lost control of his car and ended up hitting the shooter.

Finley knew the man was lying through his teeth, but she was so grateful to him she didn't care what kind of story he gave. She was just glad he'd shown up.

They were both permitted to go. Since all the vehicles involved were being towed for further investigation, one of the officers offered to give them a ride. Brewer was going home, and Finley needed to get to the hospital.

As the cruiser rushed through the cold December night, she turned to the custodian. "Thank you. I'm certain you saved our lives."

He glanced at her, his face unreadable. "I didn't want to make the same mistake twice." Then he stared at his clasped hands. "Not long before Lucy died, I thought I spotted someone following her. I told her about it and that she needed to be careful, but I guess she didn't listen. I've always regretted that I didn't do something more. Keep an eye on her for a while. Call her mother. Something. But I didn't. And then it was too late. After the funeral I talked to Louise, told her what I knew, and she insisted that I'd done all I could . . . but I never stopped feeling like it wasn't enough."

He fell silent for a few moments.

"I wasn't going to let that happen again." He lifted his gaze to Finley's. "I saw that guy at the cemetery. I've been watching you ever since."

Finley reached across the seat and squeezed his hand. "I owe you." She thought of how he'd run the guy down. "I like your style, Mr. Brewer." She grinned. "You'd make a good private detective."

"You know"—his face turned somber—"I spent a lot of time trying to figure out what happened to Lucy. I even found some of her mother's notes and started my own timeline—like the cops on TV—over at the homeplace."

So he was the one who created the case board. "In Louise's home office?"

He hummed a confirmation. "When I found out you were going over there, I was worried Ms. Downey would fire me for touching Louise's things, so I took it down." He looked a little sheepish. "I guess you'd already seen it."

"I did. It was great work, by the way."

He sighed. "I wanted to help in some way, but I never could figure it all out."

"Only because you didn't have enough facts," Finley allowed. "You did your best, and that's what matters."

He nodded. "Sometimes I guess that's all we can do."

"And then we have to move on," she said, the words echoing deep inside her.

It was time to move on. She couldn't keep looking back. Not even a little bit. She'd started the process of moving forward a few months ago. Allowing herself to get past that awful night and to put all the hurt that came with it behind her.

But it was time she did more.

Hope swelled in her chest. Time to move out of the house formerly known as the murder house. To enjoy her life with Matt. Time to fully own the fact that she wanted to be Davidson County's next district attorney.

Time to do more. To make change, as Houser and Jack had suggested.

Feeling more determined than ever, she relaxed into the seat as best as one could in the back of a police cruiser. She glanced at the man beside her and felt immensely grateful for the people like him who made this damned world worth fighting for.

She liked this new level of moving on.

Vanderbilt Medical Center
Medical Center Drive, Nashville, 11:00 p.m.

Finley poked her head into Louise Cagle's room. The bed was adjusted into a moderately elevated position, and she was watching the news.

"You up for a visit?" Finley asked.

Louise glanced at her. "As long as you're not a cop or a lawyer."

Finley grinned. "No cops here. Only me and my guy, Matt, and we don't have on our attorney hats."

"In that case, come on in."

One of the nurses had helped Louise comb her hair and style it up out of the way in a bun. She was back on the needed IVs. The other machines had been reconnected, showing a respectable blood pressure and good steady heartbeat.

Finley pressed her back against the door to hold it out of the way as Matt rolled the wheelchair he had been sequestered to into the room.

"Allowing me to walk would be a lot easier," he grumbled for the fifth time.

"You heard the nurse," Finley reminded him. "You have to stay in the chair until you're wheeled out of here. It's the rules."

They moved closer to the bed, and Finley took the chair next to it. Cagle looked surprised to see Matt in a wheelchair.

"What happened to you?"

Finley explained about the follower she had and how Mr. Brewer had come to their rescue. Just before Matt had been released to go home, Houser had called to check in on his condition. He'd told Finley that the hoodie guy—one Lonnie Eckert, with a whole host of prior convictions, including stalking—had refused to talk without a deal. Although it was possible the Johnsons had hired him, Finley was fairly certain it was Dempsey or someone related to his fall. Houser had set up a meeting with Dempsey and his attorney for first thing in the morning. Hopefully by then Eckert would give Houser something.

"My God," Cagle said, "I can't believe that business with your husband's murder is still going on."

"Hopefully it will be over soon," Matt said. "Dempsey is going to prison."

Would it really be over even then? Finley pushed away the thought. This was the first time she and Cagle had a moment without Houser or some other cop around, and there were things Finley needed to say.

Besides, no more looking back.

"Thanks," she said to Cagle, "for covering for my father."

"Your father did nothing wrong," Cagle said. "He only wanted to protect his family. He didn't deserve trouble with the police. I'm sure he has punished himself enough over the years."

"I think he has," Finley agreed, feeling another gush of relief as well as sadness. Lucy Cagle was gone forever, and no matter that those responsible for her death had finally been exposed, Louise was still alone.

Cagle smiled forlornly. "Lucy was an amazing young lady, and she was unstoppable. Nothing he could have said would have diverted her from her chosen course. I've come to terms with that."

Finley nodded. "The same applies to you."

"But I'm her mother. It was my job to protect her."

"You did," Finley argued. "But you couldn't change who she was or what she wanted to do with her life."

Finley had had to come to terms with something very similar with the death of her husband. She couldn't have saved him . . . and as much as he had loved her and wanted to be with her, he'd had a job to do. In life, sacrifice was inevitable.

"I'm the one who should be thanking you," Cagle said. "You saved my life and made sure Ian and I both survived our own stupidity."

Finley waved her off. "Just doing my job." She made a face. "But I do have one question."

Cagle shrugged. "I might have an answer."

Finley grinned. This woman. She was like no one Finley had ever met. "What about Brewer? Why didn't you tell the police what he knew about Lucy? He said he talked to you after the funeral."

"The information he gave me helped to confirm what I eventually figured out. Having the police drag the poor man through questioning when he was innocent—like your father—was unnecessary. So I never gave his name to anyone."

"I made a call to the governor," Matt spoke up. "It's our understanding there will be no charges filed against you since Ian Johnson refuses to say that you forced him to stay, but if DA Briggs decides otherwise, the governor is prepared to pardon any convictions levied against you."

Cagle blinked rapidly against the new shine in her eyes. "I appreciate that, Matt, but I know what I've done, and I am prepared to face the consequences. Ian paid a terrible price for my grief. What I did to him was wrong. I've had a good long while to come to terms with that. It's time I owned my wrongdoing."

"The way I hear it," Matt argued, "you likely saved his life. His brother would have killed him."

"This is true," Finley agreed.

"Still," Cagle countered, "I was wrong."

"Get over it," Finley interjected. "Take whatever you can get and move on. Sell the house on Shelby Avenue, and move back to the home you shared with your family. Your friend has made sure it was kept ready for you."

Houser had also told Finley that it was likely Ian Johnson would be cleared of any charges related to Lucy's death, considering his father's statement. It wasn't as if Ian had purposely withheld information or obstructed justice, since he had been indisposed. Ray had been charged with first-degree murder, among an array of other crimes, like tampering with evidence. The old man wasn't being charged at this time, but Houser felt numerous investigations would be launched into the family business. By then the old bastard would be dead anyway.

May he rot in hell.

"In fact"—Finley leaned forward to make sure both Cagle and Matt heard her—"I'm planning to move into this amazing house that's just sitting empty."

Matt's attention swung to her. "What?"

"If you're agreeable, I mean. You have a great house. We shouldn't just leave it sitting there empty. I planned to sell the condo over on Woodmont anyway."

Matt smiled. "I'm good with that."

"Well then," Cagle said, "I'll need the name of your real estate agent. If you're selling, I guess I'll do the same."

Smart lady. Finley smiled. "And don't worry, until you're out of here, Matt and I will take care of your dog."

"By the way," Matt said, "we've been wondering why you named your dog Spot?"

"Good question," Finley agreed. She would love to hear that answer as well.

Cagle shook her head. "It's a bit silly, but I was just so desolate after losing Lucy and Scott. There was a spot inside me that felt like a bottomless pit, and I was certain nothing was ever going to fill it. When that dog, a stray, showed up in my yard all scraggly and half starved, I took her in. Somehow she managed to fill that empty spot just a little. So I called her Spot."

Finley had a spot like that, and Matt—she glanced at him—had helped her fill it to overflowing.

That stray cat they had named Lucky wasn't the only lucky one.

30

Saturday, December 23

Quinn Residence
Nevada Avenue, Nashville, 12:10 p.m.

Christmas music streamed from Finley's iPad.

She leaned back as far as she dared while standing on a ladder and studying the soaring twelve-foot tree. She needed a few more silver ornaments and it would be perfect.

This was what happened when she put off the decorating until the last minute. She should have taken Matt up on his offer to help. Finley had really wanted to do this part herself. There were still several hours before dinner. She could do it. She climbed down and went to one of the many boxes stacked on the floor. She dug through the perfectly packed Christmas decor. Matt had some awesome holiday decorations.

Even Nita would be impressed.

Matt had driven over to the Shelby Avenue house to give the key to the Realtor. The former murder house was going on the market on Monday. The Cagle house across the street was set for a reno before it went on the market. A new beginning for all involved.

Better days were ahead!

Finley and Matt had driven out to the Murfreesboro Road house and taken a casserole to Louise yesterday. She was doing great. A crew had come in and cleaned the place. Maureen Downey had stocked the fridge and the pantry. She would be staying with Louise through the holidays. Finley smiled. The way the case had turned out felt right. She wished more stories ended that way.

Matt's parents, as well as Finley's, and Jack were coming to dinner here tonight. Finley paused and glanced around the spacious room. At her and Matt's house. Technically it was his, but they had decided this was the perfect place for them, so now it was theirs. She was so, so happy. Happier than she had ever expected to be again. Everything was as perfect as life would allow.

On Monday, she had even officially announced her run for Davidson County DA. It felt exactly like the right thing to do. The Cagle case had solidified that idea for her. Knowing that Lucy's killer was finally being brought to justice and that Ian now had his life back was empowering. Ray and Ian's father had died in his sleep two days after seeing his younger son again. He'd gotten what he wanted and also gotten his in the end. Louise's struggle to find all the missing pieces of her daughter's case had further confirmed that Finley needed to do more to help victims. No one should have to feel alone in the search for justice.

Finley walked to the expansive front windows. The house was one of those übermodern ones. The main living areas and the owner's suite were on the third level, which was actually the street level on one side. On the other, it looked out over the view of the city below. The view was incredible. At night, it was nothing short of breathtaking.

Moving here was the very best decision. She turned back to the Christmas tree. She planned to make lots of happy memories here with Matt. This was a clean start for their new life, and she couldn't wait to see where their journey took them.

She walked back to the pile of boxes and selected more silver ornaments. As she climbed the ladder once more, she spotted Matt's car pulling back into the drive. Speaking of cars, her Subaru had been totaled, so she'd bought a new one.

The front door opened, setting off the chime of the security system. "I'm back."

Matt's voice echoed through the space, making her smile. Warming her.

"In here!" Finley placed another ornament on a branch.

"I brought lunch."

The spicy scent wafted through the air. Finley's appetite stirred. "Smells great."

The smell and the bag told her he'd stopped at their favorite Asian restaurant. That was another thing about this neighborhood: all sorts of restaurants and shops were nearby. She loved that their favorite eateries were so close. Particularly since it seemed they only had time for home-cooked meals on the rarest occasions.

"The tree looks great." He winked. "You're a natural at this decorating thing."

"Yeah right."

Finley added the last of the other silver ornaments while Matt set up lunch on the island. By the time he'd poured the wine, she had joined him. She hated that he was still limping. Damn it. This was the second time he'd been physically injured because of her. She hoped it was the last time.

Finley accepted a glass. "Thank you." She gazed out the windows. The multidirectional views were another perk. All of Nashville was right there. She turned to Matt. "I really like it here."

He took her hand and pulled her closer. "When I built this house, I kept thinking how you would like this or that about the place." He laughed softly. "It might sound a little crazy, but I think I built it as much for you as I did for me."

She hugged him. "I'm glad you did. Now sit. You need to give that leg a rest."

He slid onto a stool. "Hey, I saw Jack at the restaurant, he was grabbing lunch."

"I didn't think he liked Asian food." Finley frowned trying to recall a single time when he'd eaten cuisine even remotely Asian.

"I don't know, but he did say he was bringing a guest tonight."

"Really?" Finley was shocked and at the same time curious. This was certainly an interesting bit of news. "I had no idea he was dating anyone right now."

Matt grinned. "Guess who it is."

She rolled her eyes. "I can't. I'm not even going to try."

"Louise." Matt took her glass and refilled it.

"As in Cagle? Seriously?" Finley's mouth dropped open, then closed in a grin.

"The one and only."

"He said they had a thing way back when." She smiled. "Maybe Jack will finally settle down."

"That would be like the end of a legend or an era," Matt pointed out.

They laughed. It really would be. God, it felt good to laugh and just enjoy the small things. How long had it been since she'd felt that way?

She dismissed the idea. Didn't matter. No looking back. The Dempsey trial would be starting next month, and he was so screwed. Although her last follower, Lonnie Eckert, hadn't given a statement on Dempsey. He'd died in his jail cell before his plea deal came through. Hung himself, apparently . . . except Finley was certain that wasn't what happened. Houser had been all over Dempsey and his attorney with questions and warnings. Didn't matter. Finley knew who had sent Eckert, and that bastard was going down.

"Eat before it gets cold," Matt urged.

Finley pushed away the distracting thoughts and slid onto a stool. "It all looks so good. I'm suddenly starving."

"I picked up all our favorites. With the decorating and preparing dinner for what? Eight? I figured we would need the fuel."

"Good idea." She passed him chopsticks and reached for the second set herself, pulled them free of the slim paper packaging. These disposable ones were always too pointy and rough, but she wasn't about to go searching for the nice bamboo ones she knew Matt had around here somewhere.

The doorbell rang.

Matt started to get up. "Stay!" Finley held up a hand. "I'll get it. It's probably the flowers for tonight."

She admired the view once more as she crossed the great room. She actually enjoyed flower shopping in person, but she'd had too much to do to go out today. And this close to Christmas, traffic would be murder. Besides, who could resist delivery when it was available.

Singing along with Mariah Carey, she walked into the entry hall and opened the door.

The business end of a handgun stared her in the face.

Her heart crashed against her rib cage, then plummeted to her feet. *Not flowers.*

Carson Dempsey moved across the threshold, forcing her to back up a step.

"You," he kicked the door shut, "are a fucking cat with nine goddamned lives."

Finley didn't move a muscle. Didn't breathe. "I thought you were the florist." Her heart rushed back into her chest and fluttered like the wings of a trapped bird.

Please don't let Matt get up. Please don't let him hear any of this over the music.

Dempsey waved his free hand. "I finally realized if I was going to get this done, I had to do it myself. You just can't hire good help anymore."

"I get it," she said. Rage roared to life in her veins. Pulsed in her muscles. "Every time I think this is over, you pop into my life again."

She was so over this back and forth.

"Fin, who is it?" Matt called.

"The flowers," she shouted, her gaze never leaving the bastard in front of her. "I'll just be a minute."

Dempsey smiled. "Isn't that sweet? Do you really think you can protect him now?" He adjusted his grip on the weapon. "In case you haven't figured it out, I'm about to kill you. Finally."

Something dark and all consuming expanded inside her.

Enough!

"Then fucking do it, you piece of shit." Her fingers tightened on the cheap-ass chopsticks.

"With pleasure."

Determination exploding in her chest, Finley threw up her right hand, sidestepped, simultaneously bringing down the chopsticks like a dagger, aiming for the bastard's neck.

The gun went off.

Blood squirted across her face.

She blinked, the blast echoing in her ears.

The gun clattered on the floor.

Dempsey grabbed at his throat.

Blood spewed between his fingers as he clawed at the wound and the chopsticks planted deep in his artery.

He crumpled to the floor as the final chorus . . . *all I want for Christmas is you, baby* . . . filled the air.

"Fin!"

Matt was suddenly holding her against himself, but she couldn't take her eyes off the man flopping around on the floor like a fish out of water.

"Fin. Oh my God, Fin." Matt's fingers gripped her chin. "Are you all right, baby? Look at me."

But she couldn't. She had to watch this son of a bitch die. Had to make sure he took his last breath.

When Dempsey had gone utterly still, she collapsed against Matt. Relief flooded her being, and she couldn't hold back the tears—not if her life had depended upon it.

"Please tell me you're okay," he murmured frantically.

He's dead.

"I'm okay now."

The nightmare is over.

Cagle Residence
Murfreesboro Road, Franklin, 9:30 p.m.

Finley watched Louise Cagle play "It's Beginning to Look a Lot Like Christmas" on the baby grand while Matt's parents, Maureen Downey, Jack, and the Judge sang the lyrics. Finley's father chimed in from time to time, but mostly he watched his wife and friends and smiled. Finley hadn't considered until that moment how difficult this terrible secret must have been for him to keep all these years.

The past couple of weeks had been a transformative time for all of them in some way or another. Cagle had been to the salon and gotten her hair done. She looked very much like her old self now. The gray was gone, replaced by a good color job to bring back the blonde of her younger days. Though she was still too thin, her skin had a healthier glow. The surgery and her new medication had her on the right track. She smiled as her fingers flew across the keys, and that smile gave Finley great pleasure. Jack watched the woman's every move as if he couldn't resist.

Finley suddenly wondered what life would be like with Jack no longer playing the field. Time would tell, she supposed.

Matt's folks were thrilled that he and Finley had moved into his house—though not so much about Dempsey's appearance. But that was over now. Finley expelled thoughts of him and all that he represented. He was dead, and she was glad.

She had killed him. After, while she'd answered Houser's questions and watched the cops do what they do at a crime scene, her mind had seemed to float above the whole spectacle. She had killed a man. His death was by no means the first she had witnessed . . . but it was the first time she had been solely and entirely responsible.

But once the shock had worn off and the cocktail of emotions that followed had subsided, she wanted to run and scream and . . . celebrate. It was over . . . the son of a bitch was dead.

Now she could really live again.

Her smile reappeared and her heart felt full as Matt walked back into the room, two new bottles of wine in hand. He placed them on the coffee table tray and joined Finley where she stood by the fireplace, watching the show.

"It was nice of Louise and Maureen to pull this off after we had to cancel."

Finley leaned against him. The image of Dempsey lying dead on the floor flashed in her mind once more despite her best efforts. She kicked it out. Refused to allow him to intrude in her life ever again.

"It was," she agreed. "And I appreciate Houser moving things along for us today rather than keeping us tied up for hours."

Their house had been crawling with crime scene investigators and cops who had managed to get the job done in record time. After tomorrow's second walk-through, they would be able to call in a cleaning service and then return home. Tonight, though, they had reservations at the Four Seasons. After the day they'd had, they both deserved a special night out. Why not go the distance?

"Houser is a good man, for sure," Matt agreed. He kissed her temple. "I believe your quick thinking today will bode well with the voters."

Finley had to laugh. "How do you figure that?" She'd killed a man with a pair of chopsticks—the cheap kind, at that—just inside the door of their home. Briggs would have a field day with this news.

Not that she actually cared. She would do it again in a heartbeat. Whatever it took to end the nightmare that was Carson Dempsey.

"Well," Matt mused, "with violent crime on the rise in most larger cities, you just showed the folks of Davidson County that you aren't going to stand by and let the criminals have their way."

She laughed again. Couldn't help herself. "I suppose you're right about that." She half expected to be disqualified for taking a man's life—even if it was self-defense. Politics was a strange animal.

When the song ended, Finley and Matt clapped and hooted their approval. Jack, Louise, and Maureen hurried out of the room. Finley watched the three scurry away and wondered what they were up to. As soon as she and Matt had arrived, Maureen and Louise had announced they were banding together to serve as Finley's campaign management team. Louise pointed out that based on the ads Briggs was running, Finley needed serious help. Maureen had agreed, though her work would be more behind the scenes since the paper had to remain neutral on politics. Basically good but slightly overwhelming news. Finley had hoped to put off the big decisions until after the holidays. No such luck with those two—three, counting Jack—putting their heads together.

"That's not suspicious at all," she whispered to Matt about the threesome's exit.

"I learned a long time ago," he said sagely, "that with Jack, you have to expect the unexpected. To have women following him is no surprise either."

Another laugh burst out of Finley. She couldn't remember when she had laughed so much. Matt's words were absolutely true.

Speaking of unexpected, Finley was happy for Ian Johnson. He'd dropped by the office yesterday and asked that Jack help him with developing a plan for the family money. Obviously, the Johnson

Development Group assets were frozen until the criminal cases were done. But, like the PI, Jerry Bauer, had said, the old man was smarter than anyone knew. He'd set up a personal account in Ian's name the year he was born and had been stashing money there ever since. Ian wanted to use that money to start a victim's advocacy organization. In particular he wanted to focus on young people and kids. It was an amazing idea, and Finley was very proud of him. He deserved the opportunity for a happy and purposeful life.

Matt's folks, the Judge, and Finley's father joined them near the fireplace. "Just so you know," the Judge said, drawing Finley's attention from her pleasant thoughts, "you and Matt are up next."

Finley scoffed. "I think you've forgotten how awful my singing voice is, Mom."

The Judge blinked; then a smile spread across her face.

Finley frowned, then realized why the Judge was smiling, and she smiled too. She had just called the Judge *Mom*. She couldn't remember the last time she'd done that. Things, Finley mused, they were changing.

"It's coming back to me now," her mother said, still smiling despite remembering that her only child could not carry a tune in a bucket.

Bart laughed. "We always knew you had other skills, sweetie."

Matt turned up his glass as if to say he had nothing in this. Finley didn't blame him.

"Matt has quite a nice baritone," his mother, Eleanor, pointed out.

"Takes after his father," Martin, Matt's father, agreed.

Matt cleared his throat. "You two aren't exactly unbiased."

A bell rang. Finley jumped in spite of herself. The sneaky threesome returned to the parlor. Louise set the silver bell she'd used to get their attention on the nearest table and called out, "Listen up, everyone."

Matt leaned closer to Finley and whispered in her ear. "Saved by the bell."

Finley pressed her fingers to her lips to prevent laughing out loud at his gratitude for not having to sing.

"Here we go," Jack announced. He carried a tray filled with champagne flutes and a bottle of bubbly as well as a bottle of water. "Come on, now. Everyone gather around."

He placed the tray on the coffee table, scooting the other one aside. Maureen grabbed the champagne and popped the cork. Bubbles flowed from the bottle as she quickly started to fill the flutes.

Apparently one of the three had an announcement. She looked to Matt, and he shrugged. The Judge and Finley's father did the same. Finley supposed she'd just have to wait it out.

Louise and Jack passed around the dainty flutes. He grabbed the last one and filled it with water just as Louise raised hers for a toast.

"To Finley. May . . ." Her voice cracked, and she had to take a moment. "May the future bring her all that she so well deserves and," she tacked on, "allow all of us along for the journey."

Hear-hears floated around the room.

Finley gave a nod and then drank deeply of the sweet bubbly.

She was so ready for what came next.

But it was this moment—these people—that really mattered. She intended to relish every step of their journey together.

ACKNOWLEDGMENTS

I love using actual places in my stories. Before I begin each one, I peruse real estate websites for the perfect homes for my characters. I generally only use the street name and not a house number. Sometimes I will add the perfect home to a street, as I did Finley's murder house. I select locations for their work, schools, and dining spots. Sometimes I change the names, but I prefer to keep the setting as authentic as possible. However, I never want to cast doubt or negativity on any real place. If anything that one of my characters says seems to do so, please know that it was not intended. Nashville is one of my very favorite places!

ABOUT THE AUTHOR

Photo © 2019 Jenni M Photography LLC

Debra Webb is the *USA Today* bestselling author of more than 170 novels. She is the recipient of the prestigious Romantic Times Career Achievement Award for Romantic Suspense as well as numerous Reviewers' Choice Awards. In 2012, Webb was honored as the first recipient of the esteemed L. A. Banks Warrior Woman Award for her courage, strength, and grace in the face of adversity. Webb was also awarded the distinguished Centennial Award for having published her hundredth novel. She has more than four million books in print in many languages and countries.

Webb's love of storytelling goes back to her childhood, when her mother bought her an old typewriter at a tag sale. Born in Alabama, Webb grew up on a farm. She spent every available hour exploring the world around her and creating her stories. Visit her at www.debrawebb.com.